SOME GUY FROM **SADISTO!**

CHUCK AUSTEN
WITH CLYDE ALLISON

CLYDE ALLISON

Was a pseudonym of the nearly unknown William Henley Knoles, an incredibly talented, very funny, highly influential satirical writer who was mind-blowingly active in the sixties. He wrote as many as 50,000 words a week—most of them in 'men's erotica.' From 1965 to 1968 he wrote an astonishing 20 books in the *0008* series—ridiculous, hilarious, violent, sexually graphic spy spoofs about the top agent for the spy/murder organization *SADISTO*.

His most famous of these *0008* books was, and still is, **Nautipuss**, with that iconic Robert

Bonifils cover of the sexy 'Captain Demo' in her submarine (although Allison's character was neither blonde, nor white).

Allison/Knoles longed for, and eventually gained opportunities to write similar, more mainstream (sexless) versions of his satirical adventures, but sadly died never having achieved his dream of fame outside the adult men's market. Childless and unmarried, his works fell into obscurity with his death.

CHUCK AUSTEN

Has long been a fan of Allison's/Knoles' writing, and believed that the germ of the satirical SADISTO books was too brilliant to let die with him. The originals were only about 40,000 words each, and not 'stories' so much as imaginatively executed, literate, smart, brilliantly satirical, stream of consciousness craziness, and Chuck saw that with some time, editing and expansion they could be structured and refined into actual novels.

He began by taking the basic 'plot and many scenes' of the fourth book from the original series, *Go-Go Sadisto*, adjusted the sex to be a more integral part of the story while making it steamier, more adventurous, funnier, and reimagined it as a nearly 109,000 word opening novel in an ongoing series. He wanted to keep the concept true to Knoles' wholly original, utterly unique satirical approach while making the stories more—well—stories.

He intends to rework and expand all the books in the original series as a continuous tale, and is already building out the next three.

Nautipuss, (renamed *Nautilust)* will be the third book in this new series.

ISBN: 979-8-9887142-1-7

PROLOGUE

"YOU WANT ME," I said, still not believing the request, "to tell you how I met your grandmother?"

The kids nodded their heads, rapidly, all smiles, and enthusiasm. I knew if I gave them their request, those smiles wouldn't last. I'd be lucky if they ever again spoke to me.

"For posterity," my oldest daughter said. "Quinn is into these genealogy sites, now, and it was his idea." Quinn, on her left, was her son. My grandson.

I looked at my wife of sixty plus years in absolute shock. "And you *want* me to do this?"

She grinned that adorable, skewed grin I could never refuse, and shrugged.

"The truth?" I asked.

She shrugged, and grinned again.

I looked at my collected family, gathered for what I assumed would be my last milestone birthday, all eager eyes, and ears.

"It isn't like we met in a charming New York City loft as friends, you know," I said. "Or hung out in some trendy bar until we eventually realized we were perfect for each other, and banged out four kids."

"What we know," Carver, my youngest son said, "is that you met when you were both working for the government, but the other day we all realized you'd never told us the whole story."

"So, let's have it," Jelena, Penny's middle girl said. "Spill, Pops."

I took one last look at my beloved wife, who still only grinned, and I sighed. With creaky age I leaned forward, and saw most of them lean forward as well. Sasha set down her phone on the coffee table to record me.

"I'll leave out the dirty parts," I said, to a room full of chuckles.

"Leave out *nothing!*" Quinn said. "This is for posterity. Family history. Get on with it."

I paused, considered, then shrugged myself.

"Okay, you asked for it," I said. "Keep in mind, this was back before Political Correctness was even a term. When we defined ourselves in all ways as 'us' versus 'them.' Whatever 'us' was, and whatever 'them' might be. Because we were right, and they were wrong. Period. The world was a different place. That's just how it used to be. Simple. We learned to be who we eventually became as your parents and grandparents, and kept learning as time went on, but back then…"

I stared for a long while at a lot of confused looks on a lot of faces.

"Enough preamble," Jelena said, as if I'd been describing the mating habits of salamanders.

"Fine. So, your mom and I met when I was a spy-slash-government assassin, and she was a hooker hired to entertain me, sexually."

Everyone laughed, and stopped when I didn't. Slowly the smiles all dripped away like snow off a wood-burning stove, all except for Pyotr's. He was always a little slower on the uptake, God love him.

"What?" Pyotr said. "He's joking. Right, Pops?"

"Yeah," I said sarcastically, "it's like a Candid Camera skit."

"A what?"

"A Candid Camera… an episode of Punk'd."

Pyotr smiled, and got it. None of the younger kids did.

"You'll have to update your references for everyone," my wife suggested, helpfully.

"I guess I will," I agreed.

"And you should start back a little further, dear," my wife said, helpfully. "To when you killed Madame Phu in Singapodia."

"Oh, right," I agreed. "Probably the best place to begin."

Sasha snatched up, and turned off the phone, putting it away in her purse as if she'd suddenly noticed she'd left her favorite vibrator buzzing away on the sofa.

"Kids?" She said. "Get out of here."

"What?" Tina began to argue. She was always arguing. Future lawyer, that one. "Why?"

Sasha just turned and gave her, and the others 'that look.'

Being good kids who knew well enough when to fear their parents, they obeyed instantly.

Room cleared of impressionable underage minds, Sasha returned to listening.

"Continue," she said.

"See," I said, continuing, "I worked for a government agency during the height of the Cold War that basically eliminated our worst enemies. I was becoming rather famous for it, actually, though I had no idea at the time. To my fellow spies, and your mother, I was Trevor Hawke, *Agent 8*, but to our foes, I thought I was just *Some Guy From Sadisto...*"

CHAPTER 1

"SHE WAS SHOT," I began, "as she stepped from her shower," the news stories would say the following day. No mention, though, of the fact that she'd been humming an old Singapodian folk song, a song of seduction, when she stepped daintily and drippingly from behind those glass doors, still wearing her silver strap high heels...

No mention of the fact that she'd smiled at me, sexily, while humming, as the water slipped down her lovely, golden body, or that she'd purred to me, with just a trace of Asian-French fusion accent, "I really shouldn't be granting you an exclusive interview while I am nude in my boudoir, Meestair Hawke, but you Ameri-can journalists are so... persuasive."

"We are," I admitted.

That's what I'd told her; that I was a newspaperman. And of course, I'd had the forged credentials to verify my story. But I didn't have to be persuasive. She'd eyed me like a piece of flavorful seasoned meat the moment she'd laid eyes on me at her inaguration party, had stepped fluidly and unbidden out of her sheer evening gown the moment we were alone.

Being a fairly young man, I'd become instantly erect. Something she'd appreciated with a lingering glance of her golden eyes, and warming grin.

She'd invited me to join her in the shower as she stepped in still wearing those silver heels, but the last thing I wanted was damp gunpowder. She took my refusal as nervous

American prudishness, and left the doors open as continued invitation while she soaped and sponged the smoothness of her lean body—her long legs, sculpted ass, small, but firm breasts, smiling and eyeing me with her half-lidded, lit-from-within, golden flecked eyes the entire time.

"Yeah, we don't need all the sexual detail, pops," Jelena said.

"Sssh!" Pyotr hissed, and smiled. "I think we do!"

I continued.

"And now, Meestair Hawke," she'd purred, stepping toward me, ignoring the nearby towel, stroking an erect nipple with one, dainty finger, while raking the fingertips of her other hand through her glistening netherhair, "I invite you to join me in my bed, only thees time I weel not take 'no' for an answer, as I show you how persuasive we French-accented, Singapodian Comm-oo-nists can be..."

She'd begun to walk slowly toward me, strikingly, purposefully, seductively, nakedly, high-heel-edly...

I shuddered. Once again, I was going to have to bed a foreign seductress. How would my future wife feel about my seemingly endless, amorous misadventures? Would she ever truly understand that frequent illicit sex was something I was required to do for the sake of The Free World? No. It was hard to imagine.

Madame Phu reached for my fly, and I cursed my young man's libido, and above-average girth. There was no hiding my fully aroused sexual interest, and she purred sounds of Singapodian delight as she fondled its thickening length through thin fabric, slowly lowering the zipper that would allow it to spring forth like the happy puppy it was, knowing she would pet, scratch, and stroke it affectionately. At least until she killed it... and me.

"Come," she said once I was a freed man, not meaning it the way you're thinking—not yet, anyway—taking hold of it like a handle, and pulling me toward her luxurious, opulent bed. "Satisfy me, and I weel speak of all my many Comm-oo-nist secrets."

Well, I thought. That's what I'm here for.

She reached the edge of the bed, turned back to face me with a smile, still tightly gripping the solidity of my shaft. She sat her shower-moist, bare ass back on the bed, and in a very unladylike way, spread her legs. She continued to pull me—

forward and, down—until I was forced to put away my notebook, and place my hands to either side of her so I could brace myself on the bed and avoid falling over. She teased the head of my cock just inside her very wet folds, moving it up and down firmly, but gently. It was a fabulous sensation, and her expression showed that she had been expecting my positive response.

"Moof forward, jost a leetle," she said, quietly.

I did, and my smaller head was enfolded within snug layers of softness and warmth.

She cooed, and mmmm'd, released me, leaning back on her elbows, staring at my face with appreciative intensity.

"The look on a man's face when he first feels me around him," she whispered, "is my favorite moment of the love-making."

"And this is my favorite," I said, shoving fully into her moist grip, watching her eyes widen in surprise, and erotic upheaval.

She reached out and grabbed my shoulders, her face flush with ardor, her lips parted in a shocked 'O' of ecstasy, her wide eyes gazing deeply into mine.

"Oh, yes," she said, "Oh, absolutely, yes."

Her hot, pliant lips attacked mine, our tongues leaping—one into the other's mouths. She lay back on the bed as I continued to move—slowly now—in and out, the intensity of our kisses growing.

I broke my lips from the suction of hers, and asked, "What Communist secrets did you wish to reveal, my beautiful Madame Phu?"

But instead of answering, she pulled a Type 56 Chinese assault rifle from under her pillow, and placed its barrel against my head.

"I don't know, Trevor Hawke, SADISTO agent 8," she snarled. "What secrets did *you* wish to reveal *to me?*"

She laughed, then, at my change of expression, and I admit to being a little surprised, though not enough to stop moving in and out of her.

She had known all along! Known that I was an agent of *Security Administration Division of the Institute for Special Tactical Operations*, or SADISTO for short! I had thought my cover foolproof. I was wearing false glasses! They always worked for Clark Kent! But apparently, I'd become a better-known agent than I realized. Gathering myself, I began to withdraw, but Madame Phu reached around, clasped my ass, and yanked. I can't tell you how often that happens. Just when I think I'm out, they pull me back in.

She tapped my forehead with the 56. "Finish first," she insisted.

Staring at the gun in her hand, I slowly resumed moving my hips, and saw her will to fight getting lost in the sensation, expressions of deep pleasure inadvertently fading on and off her beautiful Communist features. Then she reached down with her free hand, and began stimulating herself in rhythm with my movement, and for a brief instant, her eyes closed.

In that instant I pulled my own weapon—not that one, the gun—and aimed it at *her* head. She looked mildly surprised, but kept stimulating, as I continued thrusting.

"Really does not change anything, does it," Phu said.

"No, I suppose not," I agreed.

"It doz make zis... somewhat..." she said, "... sexier."

"Somewhat," I admitted, still moving in and out of her.

Suddenly she gripped me with her thighs, twisted, shoved, and in an instant, I was on my back, her on top, gun barrels still at one another's heads. Now I was immobilized, and she was moving on me.

"Still doesn't change much," I said.

"But now I can move in way that please me," she said, and laughed.

"What's so funny?" I asked.

"You want to keel me," she said, a little out of breath. "and yet you stare at ze bubbling of my breasts."

"Bobbling," I corrected.

"English is strange language," she said, hips still grinding. "Whatever. You move happily inside my puss-puss. Stare at movements of my naked tit-tits. Soon the distractions will become too much and I will disarm you."

I cursed inwardly. She was probably right. My inability to control my innate male weakness for visual stimuli was going to get me killed. Probably as I came. Which might not be a bad way to go. But I didn't want to cum and go. Not yet.

I assessed the situation.

We were focused on one another. Both armed. Both moving rhythmically. Both had one free hand. Hers on my chest for balance as she moved with pressure against my abdomen to continue stimulating her clit.

My free hand was doing nothing, and I needed to put it to better use.

I licked my fingers, and quickly pinched her right nipple. Twisting, kneading, pulling, massaging, after a moment I gripped the entire breast tightly, and squeezed. I saw her eyes roll up, that I'd regained my opportunity.

Twist, pull, thrust, and in less than a moment we had rolled to the floor with me on top once again. Guns still at each other's heads.

Phu again laughed in my face.

"Still you fuck in and out of me," she said. "But faster. Mmm. Better. You love the danger, and my puss-puss—mmm—and it will keel you."

She twisted, rolled, jerked, and swung, and once again she was on top, her gun at my temple, my gun at hers. She ground her hips faster, and harder.

"Same way you love my cock," I said, laughing at her, and driving said instrument deeper with each vigorous thrust, while she stared deeply into my eyes, moaning, deliciously, "*and...* how I use it. *It...* will be the death of *you*, Madame Phu, and I will enjoy watching you enjoy it to the very end."

"Is good cock," she admitted, momentarily serious. "Nnnnh... I geev you zis." She ground her hips much faster along with my thrusts. "Eet fuck puss-puss good. So good. But is cock of freedom. I could nevair *love* cock of freedom. Like very much, but nevair love."

She twisted, and spun, and flopped, but I adjusted so we landed again on her back, with me on top. I was momentarily distracted by the wild bouncing of her tits, she saw her advantage, twisted, spun and flopped again, and regained the upper hand. As she sat atop me, hips now driving madly, she gave an extra bounce to those tumescent titties.

"I tol you... zees boobies... would be zee end of you," she laughed, gasped for breath, and ground—ground, gasped, and laughed—her expression and flushed color showing she was nearing climax. Though still laughing.

"Soon I weel cum," she said, and pressed the machine gun barrel more firmly against my temple, "and you weel go."

I pounded my hips into hers, harder, and faster, until she was bouncing up in the air with each thrust.

"Yes, agent Hawke! Yes!" she screamed. *"Fuck me! Fuck my puss-puss harder with your Freedom loving American cock! Fill my cunt with your Conservative American idealistic sperm!"*

As she reached new heights in so many ways I shoved her upward with one last drive, her eyes closing, her face flooded red with intense passion, and yanked myself free. As she launched into the air I rolled to one side, and aimed, firing at her as I stumbled backwards, stupidly tangling up in my own drawers.

She rolled away from me, discharging her 56 without aiming, bullets ripping through her bed canopy, and ceiling, dislodging the chandelier. I shuffled my snarled feet insanely, my butt barely escaping the falling fixture's blast radius of glass shards, cable, sparks and wire as it exploded on the floor behind me.

I shuffled, fired, shuffled, fired.

"Damn you, Hawke!" she yelled. *"I was close! Typical American tactic! Always pulling out before zee job is done!"*

Rising up from behind her bed, Madame Phu took more careful aim just as I tumbled to cover behind a sofa. Bullets shredded fabric, wood, stuffing, loose change caught between seat cushions—everything blasting apart, splintered shrapnel flying everywhere, into everything... including by butt.

"AAH!" I said, in a very un-agent-like way.

"HA!" She laughed. *"I hope that got you in your smug, 'pulls out too-soon' Freedom Loving, American Ass!"*

I shucked the pants off my ankles, tossed them aside, ignored the splinters, and dropped to the floor to look under what remained of the sofa. On the other side of the room I could see Madame Phu's similarly naked butt crouching near the bed. I took careful aim, and watched her left cheek indent, and wobble furiously, creating a feminine scream almost identical in tone and pitch to mine. Abruptly the naked lower body disappeared as she—what?

"You will never stop our evil, Manchurian plot, Agent 8!" she cried, triumphantly. *"You will die having never even discovered its existence! I leave you as dissatisfied as you leave me!"*

I poked my head up to see her charging across the room, firing too much in my direction to feel good about. I rolled aside, aimed, fired, and saw a look of surprise spread across her face, the 56 falling from her loosening fingertips as she toppled forward onto the lush, luxuriant lime-green shag carpet before me.

She rolled onto her back, and looked up at me in shock. Slowly she began to laugh, choking it off in a bloody gurgle, red rivulets flowing from the corners of her mouth.

"Kiss me," she said, her voice soft, and feminine, more bubbling red fluid flowing from between her lips, "before... I die."

"Ew," I said, grimacing. "I'd really rather not."

"Zen... just... hold me..."

"Mmm..." I said, scowling and shaking my head.

"I get ... no... satisfaction... even... in... ze end..."

Dead.

As she said: *before* I could learn what her evil, Manchurian plot was. But she was wrong in that I *had* 'discovered' its existence.

I stood to stare down at her magnificent, naked body for a brief, sad, reflective moment, then sighed with relief, wallowing in the glorious sensation that I'd survived. Survived, and won. Somehow, weirdly, still erect. Or maybe not so weirdly. That's more a question for psychiatrists.

I was scanning the room for my pants when then the door erupted inward followed by too many guards to count, weapons firing. I returned fire, dropping the first two. That gave me enough time to grab the chandelier wiring, race to the window, and dive through the paned glass.

Excellent escape plan, but I was three stories up, naked from the waist down, and still—surprisingly—erect.

The wiring caught somewhere above me, flipped me over, and I wound up hanging and swinging outside the third floor, at least until something ripped loose and I fell, caught, flipped, hung, and swung all over again just beside the second-floor balcony. I repeated that a third time, just for fun, but this time I halted, bobbing alongside a woman in a ninja mask.

She was nude except for gloves, tabi boots, and fundoshi, bearing a pair of samurai swords strapped to her back. She was climbing a rope up to the floor I had just vacated.

She stared at me with understandable surprise, her wide eyes the only part of her face visible behind the mask. They darted frantically up and down, assessing me, stopping for a lengthy moment on my lengthy moment—shockingly still stiff and pointed more or less directly at her. Her eyes finally rose, and settled on mine, and I swore I could read in them a profound sense of, "what the fuck?"

Before I could even blink, she pulled one of her swords, sliced my wires, and watched me fall. Our eyes stayed continually locked to one another until I hit the koi pond far below.

I was under its surface for only a few seconds, but by the time I sat up, ninja girl was gone, her rope swaying emptily beside the chandelier wiring. Higher up, men were running out onto Madame Phu's balcony, aiming a variety of weaponry at me.

I leapt to my feet, sloshed quickly out of the two-foot pond, across the fake, grassy shore, as bullets rained down all around, doing in a lot of innocent koi, but fortunately missing me. I scampered toward the ornamental gate, intending to climb, or open it—anything but what I actually did which was fall through it. I rolled onto the street outside, covered by broken and splintered pieces of red painted wood.

"You idiot! What did you do?" Měi Nǚ—my Chinese driver—said. Then bullets began hitting her car. "Never mind! Get in!"

She threw open the door of the compact, Singapodian sedan parked across the street, and frantically waved me in beside her. Bullets were pinging around us, seemingly from everywhere, and I guess I was moving a little too slowly for her tastes.

"*Will you MOVE!*" She snapped.

I stood, raced across the street, my erection bobbing around frantically, painfully, and leapt into the vehicle, slamming the door behind me. Staring wide-eyed at my dick, Měi floored it, lurching into the narrow, crowded lanes, knocking over cyclists, forcing shoppers to dive for safety. Which was more or less how she always drove. Maybe a little worse because she was clearly distracted by my pantslessness.

"Does that mean," she said, looking at my still erect penis with distaste, "that you... you know... sexed with her and... em... extracted the necessary information?" she asked.

"No, it does not," I replied.

"So why is your Yīnjīng all..." she demanded, waving her hand vaguely in its general direction, "*like that?*"

"I was in the middle of…" I said, searching for the right word, "interrogating her."

"I've never heard of *that* being used as an interrogation tool!"

"It *can* be," I said, not all that confidently.

Měi stared at it, scowling in a way that confused me.

"Eyes on the road," I said, as a woman with groceries crashed across the hood, the roof, the trunk, landing somewhere behind us.

Měi glanced back at her, then forward to the road, but quickly turned her full attention back to my erection.

"Why is it sticking up like that?" she asked.

I looked at her with surprise.

"What do you mean? This is what happens when a man is…" I stopped and just stared. "How do you not know?"

"I've never seen a man's… um… thing before."

She brought her eyes up to mine, and we locked gazes. She kind of smiled, and shrugged. Then a bullet smashed through—first the rear window, then the front, flying right between us. We both ducked, but her attention came instantly back to my erection.

"Are we going to die?" she asked.

"*Not if you pay more attention to the road,*" I snarled, "*and less to my dick!*"

"*I was just supposed to drive you places,*" she yelled, "*not get shot at!*"

"*This wasn't exactly part of **my** plan, either!*"

Another bullet ripped by her face, flipping up strands of short, black hair.

"*Oh, God, I'm going to die a virgin,*" she cried.

"*Not if you DRIVE!*" I yelled.

"*I'm not an Indy driver!*" she snapped, then looked almost desperately at my cock. Or was it hungrily? Both? "What does it feel like?"

"What does *what* feel like?"

"Is it hot?" Měi asked, tentatively reaching for my erection. "Can I touch it?"

"*Are you kidding?*" I said, stunned. "*No, you can't touch it! Focus! **Drive!**"*

"*I won't hurt it,*" she said, scrunching her face at me as if I were an annoying brother who wouldn't let her play with his toys. "*I just want to see what it feels like!*"

More bullets ripped through the rear window, shattering more glass, and making us both flinch. I turned to see several motorcyclists chasing us in, around, through the debris and bodies we were leaving behind. Some of their bullets tore deeply into the fabric of our seats.

"Another time," I said, turning around and aiming my gun out what was left of the back window. *"When you're not busy with far more important things!"*

She glanced again at the road, once over her shoulder, but quickly returned her eyes to my penis—now closer to her since I'd shifted position to shoot bad people. She was clearly mesmerized. After too many seconds of staring, she reached out and took hold of it.

"What are you doing?" I asked, annoyed that she'd spoiled my shot.

"I'm not going to die without ever touching one!" she yelled.

I tried to ignore her, and fired blindly, but effectively, at our pursuers. One motorcyclist was aiming back at me, shooting right into my face, I ducked, the shot nicked my ear. One of my shots found his leg, he fell from his bike, flipped into the air, and landed in an oversized fish tank. The water roiled madly. I hoped because whatever was in there was eating him.

Meanwhile, Měi was holding me tightly, stroking absently, her attention thankfully returned to the crowded street ahead. Though she still ran over a couple kissing, and their dog.

"It's so soft, and smooth, and warm," she said, stroking and squeezing, "and firm. Why does it get so hard, and—*oh, my God, touching it is making me horny! Why is it making me horny?"*

"How should I know?"

I pushed her hand away but it snapped back onto my solidified flesh like it was magnetized. I tried to ignore her clasp as I returned to killing, wounding or at least distracting our attackers.

I fired and missed first one cyclist, then another, too damn distracted myself as Měi slipped her fingertips along my shaft, pulling along its entirety, first up, then down.

"Mmm," I said, involuntarily.

Měi perked up.

"You like that?" She asked. "That feels good?"

I heard a bicyclist scream and collide with the driver's side front fender, and rebound into a spice booth. I turned to see his tumbling body sending up clouds of colorful dust. Red, blue, turquoise, pink, and green. It was kind of magical, actually. Finally, Měi returned her attention to where she was driving. Most of it, anyway.

"Oh, my gosh, the more I hold it, the more my face is getting hot," she said, smiling. She looked at the street. Then at my dick. Then at the street. She made a decision. "Get under me!"

"I'm sorry, what?" I asked. I'd almost completely forgotten about our pursuers. Fortunately, they reminded me they were still interested in us with more bullets and shattered glass.

Měi didn't repeat what she'd said. She'd already let go of the steering to open the front of her jeans.

"You're the agent," she said, still gripping my stiffness tightly, using a free hand that shouldn't have been free to quick-wiggle her tiny butt so she could shove pants and panties down along her smooth thighs, all the way to mid-calf. "You drive better than me."

"*Who's going to shoot back at them?*" I asked.

"It's not like you were hitting anyone, anyway," she said with an irritated sneer, bunching her jeans and underthings down far enough that she could easily spread her legs. "This will be better," she said, unclear on what exactly she was referring to, and plunged the 'shouldn't-have-been-free' hand into the fuzz covered space where her legs met.

I don't know whether it was intended or not, but as the fingers and palm of that hand worked furiously in and around her fine, delicate pubic hairs—massaging, kneading, fingering deeply—her other hand continued to slide all around my staff in wonderfully erotic ways.

"Whoa," was all I could manage to say.

"Oh, my God," she said, smiling up at me, "It gets me hot knowing that you like how that feels."

"We're both going to die," I said, as more machinegun fire ripped through the cabin. "That won't feel good for either of us."

"*And yet, I can't stop,*" she said, with a little laugh. "*My body won't let me!*"

She yanked on my dick, and jerked on it uncomfortably until I finally slid under her. She maneuvered around awkwardly, only running over one innocent Singapodian in the process, and positioned her bare ass over my lap.

I had taken the wheel, and was now the only one actually looking at the road.

Or trying to. I swear I was.

Which was good, because as she pleasured herself—and sort of me—more bullets zinged through the cab, into seats, past my ears, and her excited foot depressed the gas pedal further and further until our speed became ridiculous.

"I can't aim it!" Měi said.

"The car?" I asked, confused.

"No, your thing! Put it inside me!"

She finally released my shaft, and at long last retook the steering wheel, eyes back on the road. Well, if it made her focus on her driving.

I gripped myself and felt around between her legs with my tip as the car swerved, jerked, bounced, and moved her moistened target in all directions but the right one. After what seemed like minutes of maneuvering, my tip felt warmth and wetness, and I just shoved.

"OH, MY GOD!" Měi cried. *"OOOOOH, MYGOD!"* she cried. *"THAT FEELS AMAZING!"*

"Thank you."

Seeing she'd lost focus again I snatched the wheel and jerked the car this way and that, desperate to avoid things, and people, and failing—dodging around vending stands, bullets, street-sellers, bullets, customers, men, women, children, food, vegetables, bullets, and animals both living and dead. At one point I took out a churro stand, wondering how those had migrated to Singapodia.

"They have churros in Singapodia?" I asked.

"I love churros," Měi said, lost in the magic of my dick, and her own fingers. "Mmmm…"

A motorcycle pulled up alongside me, aimed his weapon at my face, then paused a moment to stare at Měi, whose head was back, eyes closed, naked from the waist down, doing what she was doing. It gave me the moment I needed to raise my own weapon and drill him through one eye. His bike veered away, he immediately fell off, slamming into a vat of hot cooking oil that had been frying something that smelled really delicious, but was now frying him.

As I tried to navigate a tricky section of the curved road, a second motorbike pulled alongside Měi, preparing to aim at one or both of us. I knew I couldn't fire anything but wildly if I was going to get us safely around that curve.

"Lift your shirt, Měi," I said. *"Pinch your nipples."*

"OH!" she said. "GOOD IDEA!"

Eyes still closed, she hoisted shirt and bra revealing two pretty, petite, puffins, which she immediately began squeezing, and groping. She moaned, and squirmed in my lap, and her passionate self-play had the effect on the motorcycle killer I'd hoped for. Attention distracted he didn't see the bend in the road ahead, plowed straight into a dress shop, taking out three customers, several mannequins, and the cash register. Singapodian money flew everywhere.

Perfect!

Well, not for the customers and the shop owner. But for me… definitely!

There were two more machine-gun firing cyclists behind us, and the law of averages said they wouldn't all be distracted by my and Měi's antics, so I had to get us out of there. We finished rounding the curve and a pretty little park appeared alongside us, sloping in an upward incline away from the sidewalk to plateau around a historical building of some kind.

I jerked the wheel, skidded across the street, between diving pedestrians, over the sidewalk and rumbled up the slope. At the top, I crashed through a metal fence overgrown with some beautifully tended rose bushes—Osiria, I believe, based on the velvety colors, and delightfully heavy scent. The fallen fence formed a kind of ramp, and we launched into the air, soared a good fifty feet or more, until we crashed down onto the grounds of some incredibly wealthy Singapodian's mansion.

"Holy shit," Měi practically sang, *"what a rush! Was that an orgasm? Did I orgasm?"*

Luck being on someone's side, not necessarily mine—the mansion's owner appeared to be in the middle of an extremely elegant garden party. I couldn't help noticing we were crashing through a much better class of people as tuxedos, evening gowns, and expensive jewelry dove in all directions to avoid us, or bounce over us when they couldn't.

Unfortunately for Měi and myself, the motorcycles were well equipped to stay on our asses. At least until one of them plowed into a guest wearing a white tuxedo jacket and bowtie, sending him, his drink, and the bike's rider sailing over a nearby table loaded with some truly delicious looking cakes, canapés, and cocktails.

My stomach growled. I sighed. Never spy hungry.

Our car also collided with a man—some old waiter who got lodged on our windshield where he glared in at us and screamed—as if we had done it on purpose. Seeming oblivious to his pain and peril, Měi briefly let go of me to rip her shirt and bra the rest of the way off. She tossed them out the window, then quickly did the same with her pants and panties. Now fully nude, she re-gripped herself much more aggressively, wiggled her ass vigorously to circulate my erection inside her. Her moans grew louder, far less inhibited, her fingering and bouncing in my lap more rapid and enthusiastic.

"Can you move it around?" she asked.

"I really can't," I said. *"Still trying to escape, and all."*

Even so, the car was racing, our pulses were racing, andour bodies were nearing climax.

"Zhè tài lìng rén xīngfènle!" Měi yelled, her hands doing their best to arouse every square inch of her nakedness, rubbing one erogenous zone after another, and lots of only borderline erogenous zones.

We bashed aside a few more guests, clearing a path that led up wide, marble stairs to an elegant set of paned, glass doors, which we—of course—blasted through. I pulled Měi sideways and covered her to keep her from being shredded by the impact which ripped away most of the car's roof.

"WOW!" she said, impressed. *"That was INTENSE!"*

When we sat up, and retook the wheel, I saw we were still followed by the finalist in the motorcycle chase who missed us so consistently he seemed to be intentionally shooting the civilians.

Somehow—bullet-riddled, pieces falling off, car top partially shorn away—the sedan continued running.

And thankfully we'd lost the angry old waiter.

Now inside the mansion I drove the only direction available in an attempt to run over the fewest guests possible. That was toward the wide, main staircase leading to a second-floor landing. As we rumbled up the elegant steps, Měi's sexual moaning took on a funny vibrato.

"OoOoOoOoOoOoOoOhHhGoOoOoOdD…"

Partygoers threw themselves over the railing, the preferred alternative to being crushed under our wheels. Sadly for them, most were killed anyway by the machine-gunning biker who couldn't seem to hit us no matter how hard he tried.

At the top of the stairs there was no way to turn quickly or sharply enough to avoid what was coming next, so I let go of the wheel, reached around and crossed my forearms and hands over Měi's face and bare body for her protection. She promptly began licking them.

We hit the windowed wall, exploded through, sailing out into the space above the back yard, as the rest of the car top got ripped away by the impact. The little coupe arced through the air, outward, and downward toward the lighted, Grecian swimming pool three floors below.

Měi and I—unsecured by safety belts, lifted out of our seats—she nude save for her shoes, me bare below the waist, her hand still gripping herself, me tightly inside her as we drifted outward with inertia. We seemed almost to hover momentarily in airborne doggy-style before all the gathered, elegantly dressed guests, just before the car impacted the water.

"*Kuángxīīīīīīīī!*" Měi shrieked, finally feeling the gravity of the situation. Giving in to the inevitable I knew exactly how she felt.

Seconds later we hit the pool just in front of the rapidly sinking scrap heap we'd been driving.

We both stood, spent, gasping, glad to be alive for so many reasons. Měi stood, reaching out to again take hold of my— at long last—deflating equipment. We looked around at the startled guests. I nodded, shyly, smiled, and waved.

A neatly dressed older couple moved from somewhere back in the crowd to the pool's edge, staring at us in shock, and horror. I recognized them immediately as the Chinese ambassador to Singapodia, and his wife. I groaned, inwardly. Could this mission go any further off the rails?

"Hello, daddy," Měi said, smiling and waving at the ambassador.

I shoved her hand away from her grip on me, and she reluctantly let go. After a moment under the ambassador's intense glare she very slowly reached back up, and took hold of me again.

CHAPTER 2

I DIDN'T REALIZE I was staring at the pretty blonde—or more accurately her oversized tits—until she busted me for it. Her intense, turquoise eyes shot my way, inner eyebrows dropping like machetes between them.

I couldn't help it. There were so many things about her that were glaringly out of place. First, she was a white woman in Singapodia. Second, she was filthy, wore a threadbare, deep, V-neck shirt, jeans and shoes so worn they barely qualified as clothes, while the suited man sitting across the food court table from her wore a tie that cost enough to buy her an entirely new wardrobe. But her obvious beauty beneath the dirt and grime, her natural, long blonde hair in a country filled with ebony-tressed women, along with her magically massive mammaries had, unsurprisingly, drawn my libido—I mean my attention.

Without interrupting her conversation with the suited man, she shot a pair of middle fingers up at me, which made me laugh.

Still glaring, she slowly smiled against her own will, as her hands went back to the tabletop, and formed a "goal post". The well-tailored man 'kicked' a paper football between her upraised thumbs. On the table between them was a pile of money. A huge pile of money. American. The football sailed over that pile, and hit the center of the girl's lovely chest, wedging itself between her breasts. As I stood there envying that football, her shoulders and expression melted away like the smile off a snowman in a fireplace.

I scowled, wondering what *that* was all about, shook my head in confusion without realizing it, bumped into someone, adjusted course, and continued my way through the crowded airport—with a little help from a few poking gun barrels.

See, I was being escorted by Singapodian guards. I was being sent back to DC to meet with my boss, The General, for a debrief and probable dressing down—something I wasn't looking forward to—so I was easily distracted.

But what the hell had I just seen? I mean besides one of prettiest girls with the most amazing rack, ever? I turned to look back, and the girl—head still down—was now standing. The man with the expensive tie was also standing, reaching for her upper arm. She reacted fairly violently, jerking away from him, and glanced my way.

The fear in her eyes forced me to move involuntarily in her direction… protectively, as a man will often do when he sees a beautiful woman he knows nothing about threatened, yet feels certain she's the one being wronged. Mostly because she's beautiful. But a well-placed rifle butt to a kidney put a stop to that nonsense.

Through the pain I watched as she reacted with horror and concern to my suffering, as *Expensive Tie Man* walked around the table toward her. I nodded his way, she turned to see him approach, and quickly moved with him, keeping the table between them. After a few circles, and a thought or two that I should brave more kidney shots, and run to her defense, she finally stopped, let him take her by the arm, and gave up, accompanying him as he walked her away toward… what?

I was still obsessing about the unusual scene while being escorted aboard my flight, mostly to avoid thinking about the embarrassment of having been forever banned from Singapodia, China, and anything else related to the Chinese ambassador, his wife, and *especially* their daughter Měi Nǚ. I was a trained spy, and I'd made a botch of this job. Perhaps I was getting old. I was already twenty-eight. Ancient by SADISTO standards.

Fortunately, I hadn't been connected to the murder of Madame Phu, mostly because all the witnesses were dead, so in a way I was lucky to be getting out of the country alive. Humiliated, definitely, but alive.

As I settled at gunpoint into my first-class accommodations I continued obsessing about the blonde, all other unpleasant, partially failed mission thoughts easily derailed by memories of those intense, turquoise-blue eyes. But after several dozen slightly altered replays in the theater of my mind, the highlights of which had me breaking free of the guards, killing them in unnecessarily painful ways, rescuing the blonde and then having highly satisfying sex with her after first getting her a nice, long bath... even that obsession got old.

I opened *Your Happy Flight* Magazine as a way to stop thinking entirely, and skimmed the opening paragraph of an article about the average American couple averagely having three-point-two average children. But I couldn't focus. The 60's style hyper-colorization of the accompanying photo showed everyone with blue eyes veering toward the turquoise, the mother eerily resembling the pretty airport blonde, and I couldn't help picturing myself as the happy husband.

Maybe I did need to retire. The years were taking their toll. Too many missions, too many bad memories, too much meaningless sex, and now I was making mistakes. Most agents didn't live to be as old as me. I was practically a seasoned veteran within our organization. In my early years I would have fucked Madame Phu willingly, murdered her heartlessly, and escaped un-discover... ed... ly.

I'd thought I'd retire last year, but instead...

No. Definitely don't think about that.

I closed the glossy pages and jammed them back into the seat pocket in front of me, obviously in need of still more distracting thoughts of surprising beauty beneath dirty blonde skin and hair, radiantly intense turquoise eyes, the silliness of paper footballs, and the delightful, mouth-watering appeal of my face being trapped between happy hills of succulent breast flesh, our lower halves grinding lustily together in that perfect puzzle-fit design of man/woman parts necessary to make turquoise-eyed babies. Three point two, to be exact.

With nothing else on my mind—not The General's inevitable anger, not Měi Nǚ pleading with her father to let me stay, not my bullshit reasons for *not* retiring—I fell immediately asleep.

8   8   8

As always, she was incredibly beautiful, her honey-gold hair tumbling in lustrous waves over her shoulders, her eyes like glowing blue jewels, her body lush and youthful and entirely feminine.

And—as always—she was completely nude beneath a white silk robe that was so sheer it was barely more than a thought.

She took another step toward me, her breasts swaying with the movement, her ripe, luscious lips parting in a smile.

"Darling," I heard her whisper, "my darling, does it really matter so much?"

"It matters," I heard myself snarl.

"But darling," she murmured, her hands sliding over the partially open front of her misty robe, untying, loosening, "darling," she repeated, more lustily, "this is our wedding night—the night I make you a present of—this..."

She parted the white silk, and let the robe drift away from her magnificent body.

Completely naked now other than fur covered heels, she stood smiling at me confidently, proud of her full, heavy breasts, proud of the breathtaking narrowness of waist, proud of the flaring womanly curve of her hips, ass, and legs.

She was so lovely it hurt; her body so beautiful—its movements so fluid—it was like a living flame of purest desire. So lovely, so beautiful, so...

... treacherous.

"My body is all yours, Trevor darling," she whispered, fingers finding the tips of her inflating nipple. "Yours to touch, to caress, to kiss..."

As always, sweat poured down my face, and exuded from the palms of my hands. As always, my hands were trembling so I had to use both of them to steady the .45 Colt automatic I had pointed at her middle, pointed at a spot just below the dimpled delight of her navel.

"Darling," she crooned, taking another step toward me, out of a Singapodian, glass shower, fur lined high heels clicking on the tile, "darling, you aren't really going to shoot your love, your desire, your bride... in the stomach—just because I let slip the fact that I'm a dedicated agent of the Communist conspiracy?"

As always, I felt my entire body clench with those words; tighten in on itself with searing pain.

"What about our dream?" she asked. "Our dream of a home in Upper Westchester... the groomed lawns, the perfect yard, the three-point-two children..."

And—as always—my answer was to squeeze the trigger...

The gun bellowed deafeningly and the heavy slug smashed into her with the force of a giant's fist. She doubled up, reeling backward to crumple to the bathroom floor in a naked, tangled heap of limbs and hair—blood spurting from the round, raw hole in her middle.

"How—how could you?" she gasped.

I snarled. "I just aimed and pulled the trigger."

"I—I'm dying..." she moaned.

"Good!" I laughed.

"Dying in *agony*..."

"Even better!" I snarled.

"Won't you—won't you kiss me goodbye?" she asked weakly.

"No!"

"Hold me then... as I die..."

"Never," I snarled—and, after spitting in her lovely face, I turned and walked away...

"Mr. Hawke!"

I ignored her.

"Mr. Hawke, wake up!"

I woke up instantly. Where was I? Oh, right. Sitting in the first-class section of the jet from Hong Kong to L.A. I must have dozed off. The stewardess was looking at me with genuine concern. She was a very pretty woman, seemed kind, and I briefly wondered how she felt about Westchester, and children.

"Are you all right, Mr. Hawke?" she wanted to know. "You were moaning in your sleep, so loudly—something awful."

I smiled at her. "I'm all right. I just, uh—just had a bad dream."

The stewardess still looked worried. "You transferred from the Beijing plane, didn't you, Mr. Hawke?"

"Singapodia," I corrected her.

"Right. Sorry. Don't think I'm being intrusive, Mr. Hawke, but, well, maybe you should—you know—get a medical exam. You look as if you'd been... I don't know... run over. By a truck. Multiple trucks. You're breathing heavily. Sweating. You seem sick. Really sick. Scary sick. People around you are getting nervous, and asking to be moved. You know how they have all kinds of strange diseases that come out of the Far East because people there have sex with monkeys."

I looked around at the concerned faces staring at me, took out a handkerchief and daubed my face. The cloth came away wet. I gathered myself, gave the stewardess a polite smile, and saw the creeped out look on her face that said 'getting naked with you and joyously making three point two children is the farthest thing from my mind.'

"I'm fine, thank you," I said. "I'm just—tired. I've been under a lot of strain, and I... don't worry. I wasn't in the Far East long enough to catch any diseases. I'm always very careful when I'm in non-American countries. Everyone knows that's where all the most horrible diseases originate."

The stewardess looked doubtful, and I turned away. She took the hint and moved down the aisle, but those around me continued to stare. Mostly to avoid their gaze, I kept my attention out the window, and watched the green country flow by thousands of feet below. I checked my watch. We'd be arriving in D.C. in about an hour. My eyelids felt heavy from lack of sleep, but I forced myself to stay awake. If I dozed off again, *the Dream* might return...

The mere thought made me break out again in a cold sweat.

I hated and feared it—*the Dream*. The dream that was not entirely a dream but mostly a suppressed memory I couldn't shake. The details changed, but the core of it remained the same. I'd talked to the doctors about it the last time I'd had my compulsory checkup. The psychiatrist had been very polite, very kind, very useless.

"I take it," he'd said at last, after I'd told him about *the Dream*, "I take it that this dream has a basis in reality—that you did, in fact, shoot your bride in the stomach on your wedding night?"

"I did," I'd admitted. "What else could I do? She was a dedicated agent of the Communist conspiracy, and I'd found her…"

He waited. I waited.

"Yes?" The psychiatrist had asked. "You mean there's more to the story than what's in the dream?"

"Much more," I'd said. "The dream is really a kind of metaphor…"

"They usually are."

"… and a man in my position…" I'd trailed off, again.

"A man in your position…?" the psychiatrist had mused. "Just what *is* your position, Mr. Hawke?"

"Are you cleared for Ultra Secret?" I'd asked.

The psychiatrist had nodded.

"Give me the Ultra Secret password."

The psychiatrist did so.

"Okay," I said, "then I can tell you what my duties are. But first—you know what a double-0 number means in the British secret service?"

"Well—yes. It means a man has been cleared to kill in the national interest. Or his own interest. Or both, I guess. Or if he just feels like it. Or if he's had a bad day. For any reason at all, I suppose, really."

"Well," I said, "I work under Old Glory, not the Union Jack—but organization-wise, the parallel is somewhat there. I don't have a double-0 number, though—just a single-digit…"

The psychiatrist had gasped. "Which means…?"

I'd nodded.

He'd turned pale. "Good grief, man—no wonder you have nightmares. No wonder the distressing events of your wedding night keep coming back to you in metaphorical dreams. So… just how many men, women and children have you murd—I mean—have you eliminated in the national interest? Or for other reasons?"

I'd shaken my head. "That's classified information, doc. *Above* Ultra Secret. All I want to know is; how can I stop dreaming about—what I keep dreaming about?"

The psychiatrist had pursed his lips. "In my educated opinion—you can't. Not while you continue to pursue the profession you're now pursuing. Stop doing it. Look inside, find your true bliss—make yourself a life that gives you joy, then come back. Then I can help. "

So that was that.

If you can't find your true bliss—in my case; family, home, happiness, love—then you have to learn to live with the pain. As I'd learned to live with *the Dream*.

The airline hostess was again leaning toward me across the empty seat.

"Yes?" I asked curtly.

"Was there something you wanted, Mr. Hawke? Your lips were moving. I thought perhaps you were calling me."

"No," I said, "I wasn't calling you. I was just—thinking out loud, I guess."

The hostess nodded dubiously. "Better fasten your safety belt, Mr. Hawke. We're expecting a little turbulence during the remainder of the flight."

"Right," I grunted, and began fumbling with my restraint as the hostess moved again down the center of the plane.

Damn. I must be really close to cracking up. I talked to myself all the time—all secret agents do, to help kill the awful loneliness they endure. But I didn't usually do it around other people. A bad sign. I needed a rest, a long rest. Especially after a job like the one I'd just blown...

My eyes strayed to the newspaper on my lap, to the banner headline that shouted MADAME PHU, INDO-CHINESE COMMUNIST, SLAIN IN SINGAPODIA...

I shuddered. I could still see, all too clearly, the look of crumpled terror splashed over her lovely, Communist face as it lay dead at my feet. Which reminded me, I never did get back my pants.

"Wasn't that dreadful?"

I spun my head around. The airline hostess had lowered herself into the seat next to me, and was fastening her seat belt. Suspicious? Possibly. She had to sit somewhere if the plane hit turbulence—I knew that—but why had she chosen the vacant seat next to *me*? There were other vacant seats on the plane.

"Wasn't *what* dreadful?" I asked my natural spy caution bordering on paranoia barely held in check.

"That political assassination in Singapodia," said the hostess, nodding at the paper on my lap. "Funny," she went on, "how many women—good-looking women—are big shots in Far Eastern politics these days, considering how downtrodden most women in those countries are. Almost as if they're acting out some kind of bizarre, male sex fantasy for men who dream of bedding powerful, exotic women as a way of showing that *they* still have the power over *them*. Madame Chiang Kai-Shek, Madame Nu, Nehru's daughter, Milton Caniff's The Dragon Lady—and what's her name—that lady Prime Minister in Ceylon—Bandersnatch or something—and of course... Madame_Phu."

"The *late* Madame Phu," I corrected.

"Right," she said, so sadly. "So sad. Who do you suppose killed her?"

"What makes you think *I'd* know anything about it?" I asked, keeping my voice casual.

"No reason. You seem nice, so I was just making conversation."

I studied her face intently. I couldn't read it. *Was* she just making conversation? Or was there something more behind those focused, blue eyes? Not as entrancing as the turquoise eyes of the homeless blonde with the huge tits in the airport— or maybe it was the *tits* that were entrancing? Food for thought.

"And—you know—seeing as how you've just come from the Far East," the hostess continued, "I thought you might be interested in the murder. Murder is fascinating, isn't it? And a great conversation starter," she stared a moment longer, then pointed at the paper. "I see Peking has issued a statement blaming her killing on the C.I.A."

I said nothing. Just stared. Waiting.

"But then it says further down," she continued, "that our State Department put out a *different* statement blaming her killing on the Chinese Communists. Can't both be true, now, can they?"

Did she know something? Did she suspect me of something? I looked again at the paper, trying to believe she really was only curious because of the newspaper, not because of anything to do with me.

Good old State. In point of fact, their statement was closer to the truth. Because the Chinese Commies had wanted Madame Phu out of the way. As—apparently—did the Japanese. Or did the Chinese have ninja? I thought of the masked woman climbing the wall outside Phu's mansion. If I'd been fifteen minutes slower in shooting Phu, someone else would have undoubtedly saved me the trouble, whatever ninja country she was from.

"Poor Madame Phu," sighed the airline hostess. "Why would anyone be so evil as to shoot a poor woman in her own shower?"

"To serve as a warning to other Communists, I suppose," I said, searching her eyes for a subtextual response. A giveaway. A tell.

The airline hostess looked momentarily surprised, then nodded, sadly. "I suppose so. Nasty business, politics. What do you do, Mr. Hawke?"

A very pointed question. One I was spared having to answer because the plane was abruptly rocked by turbulence, followed quickly by a loud DING, and a blinking "Fasten Seat Belts" sign. People were thrown around in the aisles, desperate to reach seats, as the hostess told everyone to sit down, and buckle in. Her authoritative voice made me want to yank up her skirt and fuck her from behind while she commanded passengers.

The entire aircraft was bouncing, jostling, thrown around like a child's toy in a dryer. I shot a wary glance at my young companion as she held a woman's hand, guiding her into the seat across the aisle. *Jane*, or so the little nametag on her blouse proclaimed her to be. A pert, young, pretty girl, with a lovely pair of bouncing breasts poorly concealed behind cheap, company-issue fabric. Exactly the kind of pert, young, pretty girl you would *expect* to find in an airline hostess's uniform. The perfect, unsuspected Communist plant. The kind that gave you thoughts...

Thoughts of joyously making three point two children.

Why had she asked so many questions...? Coincidence?

Perhaps. But in my business, one learns to be suspicious of coincidence. And pretty girls. Both together was a flashing warning sign in neon letters ten feet high.

She glanced my way, caught me staring at her flailing tits, and grinned, confidently, and appreciatively.

Eventually the plane's bouncing subsided, and not long afterward so did the bouncing of her breasts. The flashing "Fasten Seat Belts" warning sign went dark, and several of those around us stood up to clog the aisles. As I moved to join them, the stewardess—without looking—placed a hand firmly on my thigh, to keep me down in my seat. I glanced over at her to see what she wanted, but she never looked my way, simply continued to study the other passengers as they stood, replaced bags, pillows and blankets overhead, and under seats, moving toward restrooms, mumbling.

I took a sheet of paper from my notebook and scribbled on it: *Jane, airline hostess aboard Flight #222, may be a dedicated agent of the Communist conspiracy. If I am dead when you read this, please investigate. Also, feed my dog. – Hawke, 8*

I folded the sheet over, wrote *Deliver to F.B.I.* on it, *No Postage Necessary,* and slipped it between the pages of the in-flight magazine in the seat pocket before me.

If Miss Jane was a Commie agent—it was crucial, of course, that she be exposed. If she was innocent, well, the worst that could happen would be that the investigation would cost her a job, maybe a livelihood, possibly most of her friends. Compliments of J. Edgar Hoover. But she'd still be alive.

Probably.

Finally, 'Jane'—if that was her real name—looked my way, and smiled, pleasantly.

"You're very handsome, Mr. Hawke," the hostess said to me, with the warmth of a woman who wants to touch you naked, "and sexy. Yet you seem so sad, and damaged. I like that in a man."

I studied her intently for a moment, not knowing which way was up.

"Have you ever been in the Mile-High Club?" she asked.

"In a plane, hang-glider, parachute, or rocket?" I asked.

Her eyes widened, slightly, and her mouth formed a small 'o' of surprise.

"Meet me in the rear, left toilet in five minutes," she said, unbuckling her seat belt, standing quickly. I watched the curves of her small, rounded behind move away toward the rear of the plane, until she suddenly spun and returned, leaning down close to my face. I smelled lavender. "The door will be unlocked, and I will already be naked."

She moved with speed and efficiency down the aisle, unobtrusively unbuttoning the cuffs of her long sleeves.

As my head swam with concerns, questions, and contingencies, my smaller head swam with blood. I was already inflating at a rather surprising rate, had to shift in my seat, and tug at my pants front to avoid being 'strangled' by my own boxers. Four minutes later, somewhat adjusted, and mostly concealed, I took the in-flight magazine from the pocket in front of me, stood, and followed her directions down the aisle using the pages as a screen for what I couldn't entirely hide. I reached the restroom door and pushed it open. A fat old woman was sitting there with her granny-panties around her ankles, clearly straining. She looked up at me, and screamed!

"Sorry!" I shouted. *"So sorry! But really! You should have latched the door!"*

I slammed the door between me and her screams.

The door behind me flew open, a pretty young hand reached around my throat, yanked me inside, and closed us both in.

"The left one was occupied, obviously," Jane said, already removing my shirt. She was—as promised—almost entirely naked. She still wore the stewardess cap, kerchief, and heels, but everything else was deliciously bare. "Sorry I couldn't warn you. Get naked. I don't have a lot of time."

Her breasts were lovely, small, and distractingly jiggly as she worked to help me undress—much nicer revealed than behind that ugly company blouse, and bra. Her body was smoothly curved, softly rounded, and what little I could take in within the confines of that tiny room only made me want to see more.

I helped her with the undressing of me, and we attacked each other like starving wolves. Hands groping, tongues fighting, mouths clamping tightly. Her flesh was soft, pliant, hot, and it was an intense thrill to press the firmness of my hands, my chest, my everything into her. The feel of Jane's young body was a luxuriantly intense sensation inadequately described with words.

She gripped my ass cheeks, and turned us slightly sideways so she could get one leg up on the toilet seat, then spread the other out and around me with a giggle, pushing a knee against the door to give me room. I lifted it, shoving quickly, and deeply into her hot wetness. Her mouth abruptly let go of mine to gasp, to breathe, to moan, to encourage, then returned to my mouth for more of what we both wanted.

She pushed her hips hard into me, moving with erotic friction against my stomach as I stirred around inside her.

She cupped my bare butt, and pulled hard, to keep my body in constant contact with her grinding pussy, as I did the same—lightly digging my nails into the lower part of her pretty little ass—she again let go of my mouth to breathe, and purr happy, guttural sounds.

"UuuuuuhmyGoooooood..." she said. "I'm-al-rea-dy-close..."

She reached down to help stimulate the cumming finale, as I raked my fingers up her butt cheeks and felt the beginning of uncontrolled quivers and movements that told me she was no longer close, but there.

And that's when the door flew open, and the gun was in my face.

"OW!" Jane screamed, as the door slammed her knee, "OCCUPIED, DUMBASS!"

Eyes closed, she hadn't seen the gunman, as he was single-mindedly focused on me, so when Jane tried to slam the door closed, she nearly broke his arm. That knocked the gun out of his hand, and sent it bouncing around inside the restroom. When Jane finally opened her eyes, the gun was now lost, and she didn't understand the danger. She kept slamming the door angrily on the attacker's arm, telling him to "GET! OUT! GET! OUT! GET! OUT!"

Contrary to her order he stayed and fought, as I reached out, grabbed his collar, and yanked his upper body inside, slamming a fist into his face. Repeatedly. He, in turn, defended himself by returning the favor to *my* face. The situation was rapidly devolving, and I could only imagine what the passengers outside thought they were witnessing.

"*What are you doing?*" Jane demanded to know. "*Just push him out, and close the door!*"

I looked her way, blood already streaming from my nose, and attempted to explain as he pounded the side of my head. That's when I noticed the reflection of the gun on the closed toilet seat in the mirror behind her. Behind me?

Reflections confuse me.

Instead of returning my attackers punches, I reached back toward the gun, fingers straining as both he, and Jane's loins held me tightly in place. I felt like I was going to black out with the next impact, but instead I remained semi-alert as he punched me closer to the gun.

My hand strained, clasped, gripped. I turned instantly, and blew a hole in my attackers Singapodian face.

His body went instantly limp, but remained trapped in the door Jane had slammed on him.

She looked at me aghast, eyes bouncing back and forth from one of mine to the other, to the dead gunman, to the gun, then back to one or more of my eyes. Flecks of blood had spattered on her horrified young cheeks, nose, and forehead.

"You could have just pushed him out," Jane said, her voice a frightened whisper.

"This was more satisfying," I said, grinning.

"Where did that gun come from?" she again whispered.

"Oh, you know," I said, pleasantly. "The person in here ahead of you takes their pants down and everything in their pockets just falls out."

"Keys, maybe," Jane said, fear oozing from every syllable, "a pack of gum. Weaponry, not so much."

Still holding the now lifeless gunman by the collar, I pushed him out the door to collapse in the aisle, sticking my head out to cluck my tongue, and shake my head.

"Really, sir," I said. "Wait your turn."

I slammed the door, making absolutely sure to latch it, this time, and went back to fucking Jane.

8   8   8

The plane was now nearly empty other than a few stragglers moving quickly toward the exit. 'Jane' stood beside me near the open plane door, holding my hand, staring as deeply into my eyes as I stared into hers.

"Can I call you?" I asked.

She hesitated, and I knew instantly that her answer would be 'no.'

"You shot a man in the face," she whispered, quietly horrified. "You got blood on me. Then you joked about it. And then you had more sex with me. That part I liked, but the other parts…"

"I'm sorry," I said.

"And then making me help you throw the body out an open door somewhere over Pennsylvania…"

"Thank you," I said.

"Does this happen to you a lot?"

"Yeah. Pretty much." I shrugged. "It's my job."

"A job you'd keep doing while we dated?"

"Well," I said. "I have to pay the bills. But if things worked out, eventually I would give all that up for…"

She studied my eyes for a few moments more, her thumb gently stroking the back of my hand.

"I took this job," she said, "so I could basically have a lot of fun and meaningless sex with exciting passengers in exotic locations around the world." She stared silently for a moment, and her thumb stopped rubbing. "But you're too exciting for me."

And with that, she kissed my cheek, let go of my hand, and walked out of my life.

8   8   8

I strode silently through the terminal, head down, trying to dismiss all thoughts of Miss Jane Smith from my mind—if indeed that was her real name. It was beginning to disturb me how many things I was trying not to think about.

I reached the pick-up area without accomplishing that mission, and raised a dejected hand to hail a cab. A white, unmarked van pulled to a stop before me, its side-panel door sliding open like a shot.

I reached for my gun.

"Compliments of The General," the driver said, and I recognized him from the SADISTO Motor Pool. Scottie.

I nodded polite thanks.

"Scottie," I said, released my pistol grip, and climbed aboard, taking the seat beside him. The door slid back fast, and sealed behind me on its own.

"It's McCoy," Scottie said.

"Oh," I said. "McCoy. Thanks for making a special trip."

"I was in the area," Scottie said, nodding toward the back. "Hadda pick up some new recruits."

I turned and looked over my shoulder at the people I hadn't noticed before. Eight, or so. Most of them were dirty, nervous, scowling, their clothes ill-fitting and as filthy as their occupants were, though one man was well dressed, wearing an expensive suit, holding a briefcase, and one woman wore a blazer, conservative heels, and business skirt. Both refused to look my way, and seemed quite uncomfortable among the others.

"These can't be agents," I said quietly to Scottie.

"Oh, hell, no!" he laughed. "They're recruits for Gran, and *The Place*. Which is where I'm taking you, after a job well done, apparently. Or… not so much 'well done,' I guess, as 'somewhat successfully completed.'" He chuckled. "Sort of."

I stared silently at him. He stared silently at me.

"You're alive!" he said, trying to end on a high note.

I nodded, turned back again, and stared at the bedraggled group behind me; the angry, suspicious, fearful faces—men and women—and noted that under the dirt, the fear, the darkness, they were all very attractive. Probably. Which made sense if they were recruits who were ultimately headed for *The Place*. Because if there was one thing an agent could always get at *The Place* it was pleasure—any kind of pleasure he or she craved—and meaningless sex with cleaned-up beautiful people down on their luck and willing to do anything for cash is a fairly universal pleasure.

The General was kind of straitlaced about some things—politics, for instance—but when it came to his agents' relaxation after a difficult mission, the sky was the limit.

"My boys, and girls," I'd heard him say many a time, "face death and torture on their missions. When they come back alive, they deserve to relax, to have fun, to enjoy that life. Whatever my boys or girls ask for, they get."

Like most of my young, newly recruited fellow agents, I'd—just for fun—put his promise to the test. Once, checking in after the completion of a successful if bloody mission, I'd jokingly asked for a pipe of opium. It had been delivered to my room within fifteen minutes; carried by a naked, voluptuous Chinese Nationalist opium addict.

Another time I'd kiddingly demanded the services of a girl who was willing to—well—willing to do something so depraved that even the wicked Emperor Caligula had fainted when a girl did it to him. Naturally I'd assumed no such girl could be found.

I was wrong.

Within six hours a girl skilled in—well, skilled in an art it would be best not to discuss—was delivered to my room. To find her, The General's agents had ransacked every brothel in *Port Said* and Panama.

And I, like Caligula, had fainted with pleasure.

Yes, staying at *The Place* could be fun. But since my meeting with the psychiatrist, my idea of fun had changed. I was becoming numb to fleeting, physical pleasures. I wondered if, at *The Place* that offered everything, I could order up—perhaps—a loving wife, a happy home, and three point two perfect children.

I shook my head.

No. Enough with the funk.

Tonight, I am in the mood for fun...

"You and me both, buddy," said the van's driver, turning his head and grinning. "Just what kind of fun did you have in mind?"

I swore. Silently. I must have been talking to myself out loud. Again!

I went rigid. All except my right hand, which slid silently toward my left armpit, where my silencer-fitted Beretta was nestled, my fingers closing over the butt of the automatic.

One couldn't be too careful, I thought. Had I said something I shouldn't out loud? Was he really just a guy from the Motor Pool? Perhaps. Or perhaps he was actually an enemy agent.

"What did I just say?" I asked the driver.

"You mumbled, shook your head, and said; enough with the funk, you were in the mood for fun. And, buddy, if you want fun, *The Place* is the place!"

"I see," I said, sliding my hand away from my gun.

That was one of the worst things about being a spy; it made you overly suspicious. There's an old joke in intelligence circles, to the effect of; the ideal agent is a schizophrenic with paranoid tendencies. There's too much truth in the joke for any real agent to laugh at it. A man, or woman, needs to be a bit schizoid if he or she is to successfully lead two or more lives. And you have to be a bit paranoid, a bit inclined to suspect everybody you meet—like Jane, and Scottie—if you hope to survive more than a few missions.

The best motto for a spy is: *Trust no man—trust no woman—trust no pets.* I'd learned the truth of that motto the hard way. Learned it from a girl with honey-gold hair, a girl I'd loved completely, trusted utterly, only to learn, on my wedding night, that she was an enemy agent. And expected me to become an enemy agent alongside her. Oh Laura... Laura,

I mused; why did you force me to shoot you in the stomach? Why—

I shoved the cruel memory from my mind. It had been long ago. Far in the past, in another country, and the lovely witch was now dust, in her unmarked grave.

Think of something else, I told myself. Think of the naked girl waiting for you at *The Place*; with any luck she'll be in your bed, and you'll be in her, within minutes. Loving. Enjoying. Experiencing. Forgetting. I looked again at the people behind me.

One woman picked her nose, testing the mucus viscosity between her fingers. I winced, and turned away.

"Don't you worry," Scottie said, reading my thoughts. "They'll be cleaned up, trained, and ready to go in no time. You'll see. Us guys in the Motor Pool get to help train 'em, if you know what I mean."

I knew what he meant. The people behind me had been recruited as potential sexual companions, so Scottie and the men and women of the Motor Pool would act as their 'trainers,' offering themselves up as Guinea pigs for the ultimate benefit of we agents. But he was wrong. None of them would be ready for our libidinous needs by tonight, or tomorrow night, or even for the next month of nights. Longer, if the recruits washed out for either being sexually unsatisfying, or simply deciding they had no interest in becoming paid, government prostitutes. They would then be offered other jobs, support positions at SADISTO, janitorial, maybe. Gift shop. If they failed at those… well…

I took one last look at the group, most of them averted their gaze, or never looked my way in the first place.

Except for one.

I locked eyes with her—a woman in the darkness of the very back who continued staring right at me, right into me, intense, unblinking. Her hair was stringy, likely blonde, though I couldn't be sure in the dim light, and her eyes a light color so only her pupils were really visible, making her focused stare more otherworldly, more off-putting. She looked at me with an intensity that unnerved me, and as an experienced SADISTO agent, I am not easily unnerved. I'm the one who does the unnerving. I turned away from her mind-drilling gaze, and looked out the window at the passing city.

That unblinking stare made me uncomfortable, but I shook it off. Our paths would likely never cross again. It would take weeks for these people to be trained, and the few that didn't wash out would be gone before I returned from another mission. I quickly put them all out of my mind—especially the creepy woman in the back.

I began, instead, to think beyond the present moment. I'd have to report to the General, of course, but not until morning, according to the last orders I'd received. For now, I needed to get through the night, without thoughts of 'Jane'... without thoughts of Madame Phu, or Měi, or the Chinese ambassador, without... *the dream.*

I wondered what kind of woman I'd find waiting for me at *The Place.*

I wondered if I'd lose myself in her, or just dismiss her, and mope alone.

For a moment I imagined Airline Hostess 'Jane' smiling at me from our home in Upper Westchester, standing on a groomed lawn, in a perfect yard, affectionately cuddling our three-point-two children... with blood on their cheeks.

Mope, it is.

CHAPTER 3

IT WAS LIKE COMING home, I mused as a neon sign of a green palm tree came into view, and underneath '*Blue Hills. THE hotel*'. We drove in and up the drive lined with neatly rounded bushes of bougainvillea.

As Scottie dropped my bags in front, I pushed my way through the revolving door that fronted *The Place*. That's not its real name, of course; that actually is *Blue Hills*, or *The Hotel*, and from the outside it looks like a small, rundown dump—the kind of place retired couples without much money would hole up in to die so their families wouldn't have to deal with the corpses.

Few strangers stop at *The Place*; for one thing, there's a permanent NO VACANCY sign on the lawn; for another, a large, unfriendly-looking Doberman is always on duty, at the end of a long leash, just outside the front door. Actually, one of six Dobermans, each working four-hour shifts.

The Place is not, of course, a hotel at all in the strictest sense. It's a combination home away from home for agents of my outfit stopping in Washington, and medical facility-slash-sanitarium for those recovering from minor blunt instrument, knife, gun, small explosives wounds, or ego damage from spy-on-spy taunting, or cyber-bullying.

It's no dump, either. Inside it's as modern as any hotel in the world, one wing, at least; the other wing is as modern as any hospital in the world.

I always enjoy staying at *The Place*. Not only because, when an agent checked in, it meant that he or she had completed a mission successfully, or with partial success. If he or she checked into the hospital wing, or—as in my case—simply had not died but also hadn't cleanly killed a target, and quietly escaped, then it was—obviously—only a partial success. But—full level of success or not—Pierre, the chef, prepared meals for you that would rate five stars from Michelin; Pedro, the bartender, would mix you the driest martini known to science; Frieda the masseuse would unknot any cramped muscle; Junka the podiatrist could remove a bunion like it was butter—stopping at *The Place* was a reward for a job well done, and the nearest thing to a home life, a family life, that an agent such as myself seemed allowed to enjoy.

Inside, the air was cool and air-conditioned, unbelievably refreshing after the muggy heat of Washington in August.

Granny Hands saw me and hobbled up to kiss me on the cheek. "Velcome back, Trevor, velcome back!" she exclaimed. "It sure doez zese old eyes of mine good to zee you again. I had a funny premonition you veren't going to come back from zis last mission of yours."

I chuckled and chucked her under the chin. Good old, white-haired Granny. Though her premonitions were usually on the ghoulish side, her heart was solid gold.

Granny ran *The Place* like a combination fraternity housemother-slash-madam, both of which she'd been during her long and checkered career. Heaven—and The General—alone knew how old she was, though she'd been young enough during World War II that, as an OSS agent, she'd parachuted a dozen times into occupied France to fuck some Nazi or other for information, and then murder him.

Reportedly she'd been a star—a deadly agent who'd accounted for over two hundred high-ranking Nazis. I didn't doubt it. Even the most brutal Nazi wouldn't have suspected a sweet little thing like she must have been. Not, at least, until she sprang at him like a tiger and slashed his throat with her til-then-concealed, razor-sharp emory boards.

Those days were long past for Granny, though. Advancing age, and a machine-pistol burst that shot off an arm and a leg while she was stirring up trouble in Algeria in 1957, had forced her retirement from active duty: a little old lady with an eye patch, a wooden leg, and a steel hook in place of her left hand was just too conspicuous to seduce anyone for information. Even the loneliest of Nazis.

I knew that The General had tried many times to get her fitted with some proper artificial limbs, but she'd refused. She *liked* having a peg leg and a steel hook, the tip of which was sharp enough to kill, maim, pick teeth, and easily remove irritating warts.

Now Granny contented herself with acting as a sort of hook-handed den mother, a job she enjoyed, and did splendidly.

"I won't detain you," she told me. "I'm sure you're eager to relax with a cool shower and a warm girl. Did you have a preference for the night ahead?"

I sighed.

"Not really," I said. "I think I'll be alone tonight."

"Trevor, Trevor," she said compassionately. "You don't vant to be alone vis your dark thoughts. You vant to suppress them, *repress* them, pretend they never happened, and vhat better vay to do that than on top of someone hot and villing vith no emotional connection to you? That's vhat a real man vants."

I smiled at her. She was right. She was always right. I thought of Jane, and nearly asked for a double. But instead, I remembered the girl from the airport who'd flipped me off. I hadn't been able to stop thinking about those turquoise eyes... those oversized tits...

"Short," I said. "Blonde. Strong-willed. Large tits..."

"Vith you, zhat goes vissout saying," Granny grinned.

"Not always," I said, thinking of Jane's petite little breasts. "I also want turquoise eyes,"

Granny's own brown eyes widened.

"Oooh," she said. "*Very* specific. *Very* rare. Testing Granny's acquisition skills?"

"Not intending to," I said. "Just asking for what I honestly need tonight. And my dog. If you would be so kind."

"Uv course. Zen you vill have *Suite Forty-two*," Granny nodded, "challenge accepted, Trevor."

"*Forty-two?*" I asked. "I thought Gus Devlin would have grabbed that by now."

Granny frowned. "Oh dear, hadn't you heard? Gus took the long jump a couple days ago. In Albania."

I swore. I'd been fond of Gus.

"Was he alone?" I asked.

"No," sighed Granny. "Tina vas vis him. She took ze long jump too."

I swore again. I'd been even fonder of Tina. We'd shared many a mission and talked often of retiring to Westchester—though not with each other. The sex was good, but we didn't see eye-to-eye about raising children. Or how to squeeze a tube of toothpaste.

"Did they take the jump easily or hard?" I asked.

"Relatively easily," Granny told me. "I understand ze enemy tossed zem alive into vats of acid, after raping and torturing Tina unt skinning, and emasculating Gus. You must admit, for captured agents, zhat's a relatively easy death."

I nodded. "Thank heaven for that," I said, remembering the horrible ways in which some of my fellow agents had been killed. Or, for that matter, the horrible ways in which I'd killed some of the enemy agents luckless enough to fall into *my* hands.

Spying was, in a lot of ways, really a grownups game of 'tag, you're it.'

CHAPTER 4

I FELT A BIT DEPRESSED as I took the elevator up to *Suite Forty-two.*

Gus, Tina, the unexpectedly painful loss of them, coupled with the different loss of Jane, the stewardess I'd sort of loved briefly on the plane was all catching up to me. Add in the emotionally meaningless sex with yet another woman I'd had to kill, the emotionally meaningless sex I was about to have with a complete stranger I'd chosen only for looks, and this life was becoming harder to handle than I'd ever expected. When you're young, and wildly hormonal, a job like this would seem to be 'The Dream.' As opposed to the other kind of *'The Dream.'* No one ever warns you about the bad kind of dreams.

I remembered starting as a fresh-faced agent in my late teens, feeling a zest for the job like nothing I'd ever experienced—certain this life would never get old. I mean, what could possibly be better than having lots of sex of *any* kind and killing lots of people? Bad people, I mean. It was all so much fun right up until you had to kill people you liked. Or have sex with people you didn't. So over the years the job had somehow—surprisingly, shockingly—gotten old. Even, dare I say it, a little unpleasant. I noticed my hands shaking, and held them to my stomach to stop the trembling.

I exited the stairwell, and found a bellman pushing a cart to my door.

"For Suite 42?" I asked.

"Yes, indeed," he said, a little too happily for my present mood. "And you must be the famous Agent 8. There may be seven agents ahead of you, but you're number one in our book!"

"I am," I said, surprised. "Why?"

"Because you tip!" the bellman said, pleasantly.

"No one else tips?" I asked, surprised.

The bellman looked like he wanted to spit, and I was glad my food was covered.

"Most agents assume it's all a part of their compensation," he sniffed. "Which... fine. But *you* still add a little extra, and so do we, in return!"

He lifted the lid, and showed me what was under it. Grilled sole, mashed potatoes, veal, steak and fries—three of my favorite meals under one cover. My mood began to lighten.

He lifted a second lid to reveal cold roast beef with gravy, and potato salad, as a third, smaller silver dome hid scrambled eggs and sausage. They really had gone the extra mile for me.

I tipped him, generously, and told him I'd take the cart the rest of the way myself. Which I did, salivating the entire length of the hall.

8   8   8

My depression vanished completely as soon as I opened the door to Suite Forty-two, and my spirits—among other things—began to rise. At the same time, I felt my heart double its tempo, sensed a prickling in my scalp, a pounding in my head, a dryness in my throat, a throbbing in my groin.

She was *that* kind of a girl.

My kind of girl. *Exactly* what I'd asked for.

She was young, somewhat petite, blonde, fully packed and well-rounded where she should be fully packed and well rounded. She was already nude and lying on my bed, petting my dog. Her heavy breasts hung firmly to one side, as she leaned up on an elbow to smile at me—a sultry, sensual smile.

Ignited by bright, turquoise eyes.

Granny, you precious scamp.

As the delicate aromas of my meals began to fill the room the girl sat up with a movement that caused her round, ripe young breasts to swing and bobble enticingly, lowered her bare feet off the bed and rose to stand, which elicited even more entrancing swinging, and bobbling.

"Hello, handsome." she whispered throatily, as my dog dropped to the floor, and nuzzled my hand.

"And hello to you, too," I said, almost as throatily. To the girl. Not the dog. "You must be special. He doesn't just take to anyone."

"Oh, I'm *very* special..." she paused, and studied my face. "Agent 8, is it?"

"You can call me Trevor."

"Trevor," she said, smiling again. A ten-thousand-volt smile that made my already growing erection pound with potent prospect. "I like that name. *So much*..."

She began to walk slowly toward me, her hips swaying in counter tempo to the swaying of her full, firm breasts. I grinned and stared right at the swinging scarlet bullseyes more or less at the center of those most magnificent mammaries.

"Fantastic," I said. "Possibly the most beautiful pair of breasts I've ever seen."

"I'm glad you like them," she said. "Because they like you, and your sweet dog. But is that all you like? Are you exclusively a tit and dog man?"

She sauntered and swayed my way, reaching out quickly to open my fly, free my pulsing cock, and take it firmly in hand. I scratched my dog's head, and told him to go lie down. Papa was about to get busy.

Keeping those intense, beautiful eyes locked to mine, the girl leaned over until one breast was pressing fleshily against the tip of my extended manhood, deeply dimpling her lush pectoral pleasure dome. She moved my dick around slowly, gently, sliding it along the heavy weight of her fleshy chest, teasing its tip against the end of her erect nipple.

"Not exclusively," I moaned. "Especially not with you. I've never seen a more perfect woman ..."

She smiled ever more brightly, until abruptly that smile faltered.

"You look..." she said, her head tilting to one side as she examined me, "kind of familiar."

"I have that sort of face," I said, as my eyes slid over her nude, young body, and my dick's head slid smoothly back and forth against that lovely, encouraging breast.

This girl was worth studying, caressing, taking time with, and then some. Young, but not too young, I thought, somewhere in her mid-twenties. Not for the first time I wondered where Granny, and the General, found these girls they supplied to agents for our relaxation.

I knew that some, at least, were amateurs, girls from good families who—for patriotic reasons—jumped at the chance to put out for tired, secret agents like me. Similar to the *Victory Girls* in World War II.

I'm too young to have seen active service back then, but I'd heard plenty of tales about the *Victory Girls*. Back in those stirring days, young women felt it was their patriotic duty to give their luscious, young bodies to any soldier or sailor who looked like he could use some love. And what soldier or sailor couldn't?

Since those soldiers and sailors were going off to battle and perhaps death, the girls of that era figured that the least they, the girls, could do was make their fighting men happy while they were still alive to *be* happy.

The mainspring of the *Victory Girl's* motivation was always the romantic menace of imminent death, a motivation the GIs of that era well understood and played upon: the most often used line in those days being; *'Honey, I'm going to be shipped out tomorrow, and there's a better than even chance I'll never come back, so why not let me undress you and take you in the back seat of this jeep...'*

So few men in government service today face death in action, but among those few, those proud, are, of course, we brave, we secret agents.

And that's why otherwise prim, proper and moral young girls will often fight like tigers for the honor of relieving a secret agent of his sexual tensions. Secret agents have inherited the mantle of death-drenched glamour that was once the exclusive property of dashing RAF fighter pilots or PT boat captains.

And rightly so. Because secret agents *do* face death— horrible death—day in and day out, week in and week out; often the *least* horrible death being raped, skinned, castrated and tossed into a vat of acid. What other government employees can make that statement? Certainly not Postmen. I don't think.

And I could tell from the gleam of hero worship in the light eyes of this full-bodied young blonde I was now taking into my arms that she was intoxicated by the realization that I was a real, live secret agent. This wasn't one of those dirty, unwashed girls they had to spend months cleaning up, teaching and training so she could fake adoration. This was the real deal.

"What's your name?" I asked, knowing she'd give a false one.

"Juliet," she whispered. "And you're... 8?"

"I told you, Juliet," I smiled. "Call me Trevor."

"Such a nice name."

She pushed against me, my stomach nearly buried in lush, creamy breast flesh. She lifted her head, and looked up at my face, stars shining in her turquoise gems.

"Trevor," she whispered, "you're very handsome. I didn't expect that." Her head turned away, and she rested it warmly against my chest.

"Where are you from?" I asked, stroking her bare shoulder, her bare back, her bare backside.

"It's not important," she said, the tone of her voice changing to... sadness? Shame?

"It's important to me," I said.

Neither of us said anything for a good long while, until she sighed, and her tone changed to one of almost anger.

"I was somewhere else," she said, leaning back and smiling up at me. Then her voice changed back again to its pleasant purr. "And now I'm here."

I studied the soft, lovely face. Her bright, turquoise eyes were luminous, and reminded me of something I desperately wanted to remember.

"Why are you here?" I asked.

"You have to ask?" she nearly laughed, squeezing my dick with one hand, and my butt cheeks through my trousers with the other, pulling me against her pelvis.

"No," I said, laughing. "I mean, *besides* that. Are you a volunteer? Here to give aid and comfort to..."

"Volunteer works," she said, interrupting. "I was offered money, so I *volunteered*."

I pushed her gently back from me and stared, incredulous.

"You're being paid?" I asked.

"Sure," she said. "But that doesn't mean I can't enjoy it. That we *both* can't enjoy it." She pulled my cock, and rubbed, firmly. "Mmm. I will *definitely* enjoy this."

I don't know why it mattered to me. I suppose it was—yet again—the beginning, fleeting thoughts of love, happiness, and children having been dashed by her easy willingness to capitalize on her sexuality—with me—with anybody. But the more intently I stared at her, and the more she massaged my hardened attraction to her, the less I cared.

"Trevor," she murmured, her big, turquoise eyes shining like beacons, a charming, sarcastic flicker turning up the corner of her lips "Trevor... are you... dangerous?"

"I can be," I told her.

She sighed with a kind of rapture.

"I knew it. I knew that you would be much too dangerous for me."

"In what way?" I asked.

"The kind of work you do. Risking your life all the time, day after day, week after week." She paused, and her thumb rubbed the dimple in the tip of my penis. "Hurting people."

"Oh, yeah?" I asked. "Why would that make me too dangerous for you?"

"Trevor," she murmured, avoiding the question, "You're handsome, and exciting, and you make me... a little nervous. A little afraid. And very wet." She studied me for a long moment. "Would you ever... hurt *me*?"

"Never," I said.

"No?" She smiled, but seemed a little disappointed. "Okay."

"Unless you wanted me to," I said.

"No," she said. "But a little fear can be fun."

Her stroking fingers were making me tingle with anticipation, and I began to unbutton my shirt. Juliet stopped me.

"Let me," she cooed.

And with that, she took to the work I had begun.

"If you feel it's in your job description," I said.

"It's my patriotic duty," she said, ignoring my hostility.

And I stood, rocking a little with desire, as she undressed me. Slowly. Lovingly. Patriotically. Unless you, too, have been undressed slowly, lovingly and patriotically by a naked, petite, blonde goddess, you couldn't possibly appreciate just how fine, how intense an experience it can be.

She made quite a production out of removing my clothes. Her hands drifted over my body like hungry white doves, unbuttoning, unzipping, unclothing. That took quite a while; Juliet really made a production out of stripping me; I didn't urge her to hurry, though. Why should I? She seemed to be having fun—and I certainly was.

Each time she bared a fresh square inch of my flesh she stopped to caress it lovingly with her fluttering white hands, to nuzzle me with her smooth warm cheeks, to press her ripe, soft red lips against it. And since, at six two, I have a lot of square inches of flesh, it all took a bit of time. The best kind of time.

Eventually she had me completely naked, fully exposed, slowly lowering herself to her knees in front of me, kissing, licking, stroking as she went.

I stood, insane with ecstasy, stood while Juliet's hands seemed to leave trails of glowing sparks across the flesh of my stomach, legs, penis, balls, ass; her lips scorched my skin; her touches darting flames of pure delight.

Lower and lower she moved, past my navel, through my tangled hairs—lower, and lower.

Her eager hands were sliding instruments of rapture, her searching lips a promise and a fulfillment.

Lower. And lower.

She squeezed my bare behind lovingly with her delicate, warm hands, I flexed, thrust myself forward, waiting for her to caress me again.

And when she did it was like flame. No more delicate, dove-like touches. It was tugging, teasing, gripping fire...

"Kiss me," I urged, stroking her golden head encouragingly. "Kiss my cock."

And so she kissed my cock. Licked it. Enveloped it. Wantonly, shamelessly, lingeringly...

Her ripe lips were resilient rapture around my flesh, her moving touch along its underside, and down, a teasing, tormenting fuel to my raging fire of desire.

Oh yes, I thought, oh yes oh yes oh yes oh yes...

And she kept kissing, licking, sucking, caressing while the pressure in my emotional boilers doubled and cubed with each passing second. All too soon I'd be past the point of no return...

Her face was flushed with excitement, with passion as she looked up at me, mouth full, and happy; her breathing now ragged and irregular. I pulled her off of me, up to me, bending my lips to mash against the lushness of hers, feeling the fullness of her breasts, those outflung ramparts of lust, press in to cushion and spread out softly against my bare chest, and belly.

Her mouth tormented me with the temptations of the serpent that dreamed up original sin, her hands were searching my back and ass cheeks with scoring fingernails, her naked body was churning suggestively, insistently against mine.

She was eager for me, ready for me, asking for me...

I was kind of eager myself.

I lifted her until her legs were wrapped around me, her hot wetness rubbing slickly against the underside of my firmness. Juliet groaned softly, her lithe body twisting as if in pain from the contact, hips moving rapidly up and down to slide her moist fissure against me.

"Come inside me," she pleaded.

"Not yet," I said, and she groaned with mock displeasure.

I carried her to the bed, laying her back on the soft spread where she fell away from me, her face flush with passion, and desire. Her lovely breasts bounced and bobbled, and she smiled appreciatively as I watched them with desirous eyes. Instantly she was reaching for me, and I let her pull my hands down to cup those full breasts, which she guided to massage, fondle, thrill.

Soft breasts, youthful breasts, warm, eager breasts; breasts that quivered like coiled springs; breasts that shivered and swayed with her writhing, squirming form, joyfully, jubilantly, ecstatically...

I brushed the tips of my fingers across those breasts, washboarding her already erect nipples until they became throbbing scarlet fingers of passion-distended funflesh.

I bent and began kissing them, kissing the warm sweetness of those pulsing nipples, the glossy delight of the creamy curves of her breasts. I bathed my face in the honey-sweet valley between those breasts, inhaled the perfumed fragrance of her flesh, gloried in the softness and warmth and aliveness of her vibrant body.

Again and again I kissed her, and her sigh of pleasure became a hiss, a shout, a shriek, a cry… her breasts, obviously, were unusually sensitive to stimulation. I wondered how responsive the rest of her was. Well, that was easy enough to find out…

I began to kiss her elsewhere; to kiss the swan-like whiteness of her throat, the downy softness of her cheeks; to kiss the upturn of her nose, the gentle sweep of her chin, the hollows of her eyes, the soft lobes of her ears, which I nibbled for good measure, making her chuckle, and moan with pleasure.

I kissed her neck, her gleaming shoulders, the sleek expanses of her arms. I kissed, again, the rotund splendor of her domed chest cushions, then moved down to kiss the supple flesh of her waist. I kissed the smooth flare of her hips, the milky perfection of her full, youthful legs, and the soft, brown-blonde down where her thighs met, pressing out my tongue to flick, and tease her pink.

I reluctantly raised my head and rolled her over to caress and stroke and kiss the back of her, to let my hands and lips and tongue glide over the sweeping curve of her spine, hips, and then around and around her quivering hemispheres of heaven.

Again, I turned her over and played more games with her breasts. Somehow, I couldn't seem to get enough of those throbbing hillocks, those great rounded slopes of untamed female flesh, pulsing mountains that demanded to be climbed by a man's hands, lips, mouth, tongue…

"Please stop playing around," she said, "and get to fucking me. I want your cock inside me. Now."

And so, the preliminaries ended and the end game began—

I tore my attention from those mounds of jiggling desire and drifted quickly down across her ribs, her belly, the indent of her navel, the gentle swell of her stomach, and finally through the delicately wild trail of hairs surrounding my ultimate goal.

As my mouth surrounded her lower lips, she responded instantly, ecstatically.

"OH!" she said, her voice a trill of surprised delight, "or you could do that. That works."

My mouth, and tongue swirled firmly, yet softly, her hands gripped my head, tugged my hair, and I knew her eyes were closed.

"Oooh, that feels so good..." she said, and then made simply pleasant sounds. I dipped my fingers into her wetness, and spread them to increase the moans, and non-words, and she began to move, uncontrolled.

It seemed almost incredible that a girl as slightly built as Juliet could manage the movement she did, could have the strength to seize my head with her thighs, and literally shake it the way a terrier shakes a bone.

I made no effort to match her for the moment but let myself relax—as much as I could relax—to ride out the storm of thrashing flesh, one hand fingering deep, as the other hand clasped tightly to the firm lusciousness of her squirming ass, my lips and tongue softly servicing her swollen lower lips, fissure, and clit.

"Ooooh, God, yeeees..." she said.

Eventually—her hands tightly yanking at my head and hair—she stopped her deliciously uncontrolled movements and just pulsed, vibrated, shook, her voice moaning out a high-pitched song of jubilant joy until she finally powered down, and released—released herself, released me. In return I released my mouth from her with a loving kiss, moved above her, and finally entered her... slowly at first, gently in... then gently out... then around, repeating the motion with ever-increasing power and speed, gradually driving myself harder and harder into the soft tightness of her.

Juliet began to shriek rhythmically with pleasure, her head back, eyes closed, a sound that blended pleasingly with the other sounds of love, the quiet thumping of the mattress, the slapping impact of our bodies, the rasping of our breathing, the cries of pleasure from me...

And still I worked; still I used my energies to continue the mad flight to the heights.

"Faster, Trevor!" she screamed, "faster—harder—*fuck me harder, Trevor! Fuck me HARDER!"*

She screamed at the top of her voice, screamed with insane delight and her soft arms wrapped themselves around me, tightly enfolding as her fingernails raked my back and she sank her teeth into my shoulder—and still I continued, as the room, the universe, seemed to dissolve, to become a rippling, pulsing beat of scorching, searing, blinding, dazzling rapture.

"Cum, Tevor! CUM INSIDE YOUR JULIET!"

My whole body seemed suddenly to contract, to convulse with a shattering, mind-annihilating purity of passion as a thousand fusion bombs ignited in my skull—until I had done as she asked, and I collapsed into her grateful embrace.

Both sweating, breathing, gasping, she held me, stroked her fingers delicately through my hair, petting me sweetly, and purring my name.

"Trevor, Trevor, oh, my God, Trevor," she said. "That was so good. SO good."

And I wanted to believe her. Wanted to believe I'd taken her places she'd never been. Wanted her to hold me and pet me this way forever and ever and ever until the maid came in to clean the sheets.

"No one's ever done that for me, before," she said, an apparently emotional blending of joy, and regret mixing in her words. I thought I heard her sob, quietly. "Thank you."

I raised my head to face her, and she held it down,

"Don't look at me," she said, with genuine concern in her voice. "Not yet."

I lie there and let her hold me, her hand leaving me only briefly to—I believe—wipe away tears.

"Juliet?" I asked between breaths. "How do you feel about... Westchester?"

"Oh," she said, seeming evasive, chuckling a bit, "I don't know. I prefer more tropical locations."

Well, I thought, reality dimming the glow of hope, and amazing sex, *nobody's perfect.*

I sighed with disappointment, lifted myself onto one arm to stare at her, stare deeply into her, into those mesmerizing, turquoise eyes.

She *had* been crying. I wanted to ask why.

"Don't ask why," she said. "Please."

Gently, slowly, I kissed her soft lips, warmly, wetly, wondrously, those lips melting over mine, her tongue flowing tenderly between, her hands embracing me, holding me close against her softness.

Round two was already beginning.

"Oh... my... goodness..." she said, feeling my return, chuckling, and reaching down to guide it home. "Hello, little fellow. Is this what you're looking for?"

"He says, 'yes'," I said.

Round two was nice, and took quite a while. No more tears. Just lovely, happy, and fun.

Round three was a short round, but also fun, and mutually satisfying. We spent a bit of time after that playing with the dog, and even took him for a walk around the darkened neighborhood without getting dressed, stopping frequently to let him sniff, and for us to kiss and fondle one another's private parts.

Round four was a novelty. Giggly, and sweaty, back in bed with various desserts, toys, and candies. She laughed so much at one point that she snorted like an angry pig, and we laughed even more until...

Rounds five through seven I don't recall too well. Possibly because after round two Juliet and I ordered a magnum of champagne and got slightly trashed. Or... maybe extremely trashed.

Okay, we got obliterated. Wow. So obliterated. I hope I didn't do something stupid like reveal classified information, or propose marriage.

So—if I can't remember any of that—how did I know that Juliet and I made love seven separate and distinct times? Because Granny Hands congratulated me on my stamina the next morning. See, each and every room has a suite of cameras recording every minute of every agent's words, and actions, and Granny... well, she likes to watch.

It's for the agent's own protection, of course. And convenience. What I mean is, no secret agent dares to get drunk—gloriously, foolishly, falling down drunk—under ordinary circumstances: he might let slip vital information.

Only within the safe confines of *The Place* could an agent really relax and get completely plowed, secure in the knowledge that, if he started to babble about anything in the Secret, Top Secret, Ultra Secret, or Cosmic Alien Autopsy Secret category, a monitor would press a button, activate a small siren, and armed guards would arrive to take him—or her—and his—or her—companion away to Decommissioning to be sobered, memory scrubbed, or killed if the damage was severe enough.

Being discreet and taciturn by nature, I have never yet had the siren blown for me; but it's comforting to know that a monitor—usually Granny—is always on guard when I'm getting drunk with a girl at *The Place*, which is the only place I do get drunk with a girl.

Doesn't it bother us agents, having a monitor ogle us while we make love to some strumpet, or stud?

At first, a little. But an agent soon gets used to it. An agent—an active, working, secret agent—very quickly gets accustomed to the fact that his private life is subject to government inspection at any time, either by direct TV monitor, monthly lie-detector tests, IRS tax auditor, forensic proctologist, or direct observation through two-way mirrors. Now and then it's simply someone with a notepad sitting in a chair beside the bed.

After a while it no more worries an agent to know that his most intimate contact with a naked girl is being observed and listened to than—well—than it bothers a stripper to have one extra potbellied man in the audience when she unhooks her bra.

The monitoring also serves to double-check the people who do the servicing, whether for fun or profit. No boy, or girl is admitted to *The Place* without being cleared for at least Secret, of course; and lie-detector tests are administered to all sexual partners both when they arrive and when they leave.

Nevertheless, a few snoopers do slip through the net, bedmates who ask a few too many questions of the agents they're here to oblige.

Such people—there were three in 1963, one so far in 1966—are always greeted by Granny Hands on their way out the next morning. In each case Granny insists that the sex-partners in question stay for breakfast, a breakfast she cooks with her own, dear, wrinkled hand and hook. The breakfast always consists of scrambled eggs sprinkled with cheese, sour cream, salsa, and botulism toxin, Type E.

A couple of hours later the sex-partners in question die, in horrible agony, of food poisoning, and weirdly, with faces that look younger, and wrinkle-free...

CHAPTER 5

WHEN I AWOKE THE next morning Juliet had gone; only a warm spot on the mattress alongside me, and an aching tiredness in my muscles and prick assured me she hadn't been a dream. Thankfully, I'd had no dreams. Though I don't suppose I'd really slept enough to.

Juliet was amazing. I looked forward to more time alone with her, at least until I was sent out on another dangerous mission, and likely to never see her again. The girls at *The Place* had a limited shelf-life. For the first time in my many years staying there, that thought left me... emotional. Probably. Being a man in the sixties, when it comes to whatever emotions I was feeling, I never knew if I was actually having them, or not—while doing my best to not.

I rose, showered, shaved, dressed, straightened my tie, slid my silencer-fitted gun into my shoulder holster and departed for my morning appointment with The General at—*The Office.*

The Office is about a twenty-minute drive from *The Place*; it's situated in the rolling wooded hills of Maryland and it houses—so many things. All the administrative, executive and training staff of the organization, for one thing. Giant computers and extensive files; rifle ranges, flamethrower practice areas, parachute jump training towers, vehicle ejection seat test range, a MacDonald's; it is, in short, the heart and brain and nerve center of our organization.

From the outside it looks harmless enough; like a big country estate, or a country club that's been taken over by the government. It should; it *is* a country club—or a *former* country club—taken over by the government; the old OSS back in 1942, to be exact. It had been government property ever since.

The OSS added quite a few novel features, including huge "swimming" pools where underwater breathing—and destroying—apparatus could be tested; rifle ranges; a gigantic bombproof cellar; several alien autopsy rooms; secret space program offices; The Time Funnel; cryptid interrogation rooms; along with the living quarters of Elvis, Einstein, John F. Kennedy, Saint Germain, and Abraham Lincoln.

When The General took it over back in **CENSORED**, he began building on a lavish scale—underground.

Today, glancing at the rambling brick buildings situated on deep green lawns, few people would guess that beneath the innocent-looking country club are some forty miles of office space, labs, and corridors, along with tunneled access by way of high-speed electrostatic rail systems to Areas 50 through 62, Dulce Base, Pine Gap, Porton, Wright Patterson, and even Kapustin Yar before that was sealed off. In fact, only one-fortieth of *The Office* is above ground; the more secret parts are deep, *deep* below the earth.

I paid off my cab at the gate and started toward the main entrance. I had to show my forgery-proof ID card five times, and give different passwords eight times. Finally, I reached Central Visitor Control, and Suzi, a cold-eyed blonde, glanced at my ID card, then at her *Orders of the Day* and finally back up at me.

"Come around the desk and drop your trousers," she said, matter-of-factly, pulling a pair of rubber gloves from a drawer and snapping them on.

"With pleasure," I said, and did.

"Boxers, too," she added, focusing on the area about to be revealed, adjusting her gloves to fit.

Done.

Suzi turned her head side-to-side, studying my flaccid subordinate agent, then doctor-like reached out and lifted, turning 'him' this way and that to look at all sides. It inflated instantly. Her eyes widened a bit in surprise.

"Thank you," she said, "for not making me ask." She pulled a ruler from the still open drawer.

"Circumsized, correct length, correct thickness, apparently natural, and unaltered surgically, slight discoloration under the left-side crown—"

Still holding me, she looked at the orders, then pulled up an image on her computer screen beside them. The image was a close-up of what she was holding.

"It's a match," she said, letting go of me, and turning to fish in the drawer again. Her gloved hand removed a squeeze bottle which she used to fill her palms with dollops of clear goo. She rubbed her hands together vigorously, then reached out, and again took hold—firmer this time—sliding her grip up and down, pulling me in various delightful directions.

"Umm..." I said, curiosity tingeing my voice. "What's this all about?"

"We had a rash of surgically altered doubles of our agents slip past security, recently. Secrets were stolen, people killed," Suzi explained mechanically.

Hmm. Apparently "forgery proof" was more a concept than a reality.

"But some things can't be surgically altered as easily as a face," Suzi continued. Her eyes were on mine, her hand still tugging and sliding on my *some thing*. "Consequently, this is the best, and easiest way to test an agent's—um—authenticity. So, if you could ejaculate to prove that this is *not* an artificial construct, that would save us all a good deal of time."

"I—what?"

"E-jack-you-late," she said, as if explaining to a child. "See if this helps," she moved her legs apart, and lifted her skirt with her free hand to reveal an absence of underwear, and a delicate patch of blonde fur, which she immediately began to run a finger through.

"Doesn't hurt," I admitted.

She reached up to unbutton her blouse; it was fastened by small magnetic stays that popped open instantly revealing her small, firm, pointed breasts. No bra. Apparently, Suzi dressed for ease of access.

"Please don't get any on my clothes," she warned.

"Of course," I said. "Am I allowed to touch?"

She grinned, though she tried to hide it.

"Anything to move things along," she said, pressing her chest forward.

Fabric pulled aside, her small, tantalizing titties pointed sharply up at me, areolas forming mini mounded slopes like tiny, pink, Hershey's kisses. I smiled and began to run my index fingers around those nipples, sliding across them to feel their firmness bend, then spring back upon release. She, in turn, tugged and stroked me faster.

"Mmm," she said, involuntarily, her mouth falling open, her cheeks flushing. "This isn't supposed to be a seduction, Agent 8, please get on with it."

"Two birds, one stone?" I asked.

"I don't have the time," she whispered, though clearly, she wished she did.

She nodded her head toward other waiting agents at the counter, with several more in line behind.

"Yeah," said the next male agent, annoyed, "she has to get to me!"

"Right," I said, and stopped holding back.

Suzi's bare chest was instantly covered as I spurted all over her delicious breasts and enticing nipples, making her gasp, then groan with her own, unexpected pleasure, climaxing right after me.

Two birds…

She brought herself to a satisfying finish for all, and within seconds, was back to business, pulling tissues from a nearby box, wiping clean her stomach, breasts, still erect nipples, removing the gloves, and tossing all into a nearby receptacle, pink cheeks the only telltale indication of what had just occurred.

Refastening her blouse, she said to me curtly: "Go right down. Due to these unexpected agent-double incursions The General won't be able to see you today. He wants you to spend the day in training, then getting weapons updates from Department X, and will let you know when he's ready for your debrief. *Next!*"

I nodded, closed up my pants, adjusted my tie, and stepped toward my office as Suzi's voice repeated her opening command to the next agent, "Come around the desk and drop your trousers."

He did. Happily.

8 8 8

I put in an intensive hour at my desk memorizing reports, papers, newly devised codes and cryptographic devices, studying original pictures of UFOs that had not yet been airbrushed out, then an hour doing nothing but pushups, then an hour climbing ropes, first with both hands, then using just one hand, while also studying a cram course in one of the twelve languages I speak with reasonable fluency, then an hour of advanced chemistry boning up on new poisons, gasses, truth serums, libido enhancers, etc., an hour of nude judo, karate, sabot and tango, an hour of instruction on new electronic snooping devices, an hour of practice picking locks and opening safes without combinations, an hour of **CENSORED**, an hour of boxing and wrestling, an hour of dirty knife fighting, an hour of swimming nude under water while dirty knife fighting, and so on.

Exhausting.

Yet stimulating, fun, and satisfying! There's no such thing as an over-trained agent. It made me really look forward to another sleepless night of laughing, drinking and fucking with Juliet.

But now I was thrilled to catch up on the latest devices, gimmicks and methods dreamed up by the backroom boys— the Research and Development Department; *Department X!*

I loved the place. It was staffed with a cheerful, fun-loving group of scientists, the Department X Men—which also included women, but... you know—an odd assortment of characters that did nothing but dream up imaginative, clever ways to kill people—or at least make them very sick and need to lie down.

They developed, designed, and created such tried and true devices as pencils that fired a bullet, erasers that fired a bullet, and even a bullet that fired a bullet. There were cat toys that exploded and burst into balls of white phosphorous flame, cigarette lighters that were actually tiny hand grenades, specially formulated, brightly colored plastic explosives that could be molded into colorful shapes, and sizes with a Play-Doh machine that—besides being highly deadly, was hours of wholesome fun. These gadgets were mere routine for the Department X Men, who preferred to dabble with more esoteric concepts, and devices, such as unique body enhancements; like claws that retract into your arm, and skin that turns into metal, as well as more apparently 'mundane' devices like a rifle that killed—not with bullets but with rays of light.

"A handheld rifle that kills with light instead of bullets?" I'd gasped to the head of Department X Men, who was actually a woman, a kindly, old, former Cal-Tech professor. "But, that's impossible—the craziest kind of bad children's television science fiction!"

The ex-professor had laughed at me. "Nonsense, 8. The laser can generate coherent light beams so powerful and concentrated that you can bounce them off the moon, which—of course—the moon Nazis hate, hahaha, and was successfully developed early in 1963. And, if you read the New York Times, you know that the U.S. Army accepted delivery of an experimental laser rifle by February of 1964." She winked. "Of course, we put ours together much earlier."

"Fantastic!" I cried.

"Just hard work," sighed the ex-professor, who I call 'Professor Ex.' Leader of the Department X Men, which includes women—like her, "And common knowledge to our enemies, thanks to the *Times* and *The Post*. I sometimes wonder why our enemies bother to maintain intelligence organizations. It'd be simpler and cheaper for them to simply subscribe to US magazines and newspapers."

Professor Ex also showed me how they were experimenting with more conventional, but still kind of incredible, rifles. Like a Colt AR-15 made of a lightweight aluminum alloy, with a fiberglass stock—a rifle that fires bursts of 223 Remington boat-tail slugs. An odd-looking little weapon, with a straight stock and a pistol grip reminiscent of a Tommy gun. I found it easy to hold and aim even when firing full automatic, once I got used to the straight stock. It kind of tickled.

"This gun more or less tears a human target apart," Ex said, giddily. "The slugs have blown heads right off of bodies, and one man hit in the back had his heart blown out his front. It was really something to see."

She ran a loving hand over the weapon, and you could tell from her smile that she was remembering the moment in explicit detail.

"High velocity," she whispered in a faraway voice, "rifling in the barrel that's much more gradual than most rifles so the bullet isn't spinning as fast in flight, giving it a lower threshold of stability."

"Ah," I said. "So, when the bullet hits something, like flesh, it instantly tumbles end over end."

"We call it keyholing," she said. "Makes quite a mess out of a human target." She looked at me with bright, excited eyes. "Want to see?"

"Yes, please!"

She showed me some color movies of human targets being hit by tumbling bullets. It was messy all right. I felt bad for whoever had to clean it up. Even messier were the results achieved by what the instructor called hydraulic expansion bullets.

"What are they?" I asked. "Something top secret?"

"Hardly," said the professor. "Fucking *Times*. Do you know how a regular hollow-head dum-dum rifle bullet is constructed?"

"Sure," I said. "They drill a small hole lengthways through the bullet, from the nose almost to the base of the slug. Then they cover the front with a pointed tip of thin metal, to improve the bullets aerodynamic qualities in flight. When the bullet hits flesh, it expands."

"Right," she said. "But not as much as it *could* expand, theoretically. Know why? Because, in all the years they've been making hollow head dum-dums, nobody stopped to think that the hollow "tunnel" in the bullet was full of air, and air is compressible. Water, on the other hand, is not. Some of the bright boys at *Remington* realized this, and tried filling a tunneled bullet with water. It made a fantastic difference, as you can imagine."

"No," I said, "I can't imagine. Tell me."

"Well, the moment the bullet starts drilling through flesh the water in the "tunnel", being incompressible, expands the sides of the bullet, violently. A hydraulic dum-dum enters a human body like a pencil and exits flat as a saucer. As you can see for yourself in this high-definition movie."

And what an exciting movie it was! In widescreen Technicolor format!

"Say," I gasped, "can you doctor up the slugs in my silencer-fitted gun so they'll expand that way?"

"Sure," said Professor Ex, chuckling. "Want to do maximum damage with minimum output, eh? Heh, heh. We here at Ordnance love a man who appreciates efficiency."

"Violent efficiency, especially," I said, cheerfully.

"I'll have a year's supply of exploding bullets ready for you by the end of the week," she said. "But right now, let me show you this dart firing rifle that the Army has been experimenting with."

"Dart firing?" I asked, barely able to conceal my disgust.

She nodded. "Don't be so quick to judge."

"I wasn't judging," I sort of whined.

"I could hear it in your voice," she sneered. "These are plenty lethal. The Army calls them flechettes; flechette being a French word for 'little arrow.' They're tiny two-inch-long steel darts, or needles, about the thickness of a pencil lead, with tiny fins on the rear end."

"Oh yeah?" I said scornfully. "A rifle firing two-inch-long steel darts no thicker than a pencil lead? Do little girls use them to tease little boys in class?"

"Um… no," the Ex said. "Not unless they want a criminal record, or to work in our children's division. The Marines have been experimenting with the gun for some time, as has the Army, at Aberdeen Proving Grounds. They can pack up to thirty-two flechettes into a single cartridge, kind of like elongated shotgun pellets."

"What's the point?" I asked. "I mean, what's the advantage of firing thirty-two darts instead of one bullet?"

"Really," said Ex. "To a man as violence prone as you, I should have thought it was obvious. When you fire thirty-two missiles at a man you don't have to aim with pin-point accuracy—you just have to point the gun in his general direction, and spray."

"The entire idea behind machineguns," I said. "Yeah, but a bullet can… I mean really, can a single dart kill?"

"To put it mildly," said the professor. "You see, the flechettes are also at the lower fringe of stability; when they hit flesh they also tumble end over end. Here, don't take my word for it. Read this article by Hanson Baldwin, clipped from the Sunday, March 15, 1964 issue of the *New York Times*."

I did so. She was right. There was such a gun. And each of the flechettes it fired was appallingly deadly. Hanson Baldwin, the *New York Times* military expert, quoted an Army medic who'd been asked what kind of medical problem a wound inflicted by a tumbling flechette would cause. The medic had said that any man hit by a flechette would never be of concern for the medical corps, only for gravediggers. And then they laughed.

"Wow!" I gasped. "That really is one for the violence prone! Can I have one?"

"I'm afraid not," said Ex. "Orders from The General. No flechette guns are to be issued to agents until at least one other nation has publicly admitted to having one. You can see why. If an agent were sent off to a neutral country like, for example, Switzerland, and used a flechette gun on his target, the Swiss would quite naturally suspect that the target had been bagged by a U.S. agent."

"I suppose," I said sullenly. "But I sure would like to have a gun like that. Got any color movies showing human beings getting shot by flechettes?"

"Not yet," said the Ordnance instructor, "one of the flechettes ricocheted and killed the cameraman. We suffered the loss of one great, and very expensive camera. But why don't we step down to the target range, and you can fire the gun yourself!"

"Hot damn!" I said, as excited as a kid being offered a new toy even better than an explosive Play Doh machine!

And down we went to the target range where I had the good fortune to try the flechette gun on a number of targets, both static and moving.

"You're right," I said an hour later, wiping a fleck of blood off my boot, "this gun really does fragment its target. I haven't had so much fun since I blew up those crippled orphans in Romania. Got any more really deadly new weapons I can try?"

She had. But since the weapons I then had the good fortune to use on static or moving targets have not, as yet, been reported in detail by newspapers or magazines, I cannot disclose them here.

Suffice to say that one was a pocket CENSORED, another a diabolical device using string and paper clips to CENSORED and then focus CENSORED beams on its target, which was instantly vaporized. We got that from the CENSORED of Sirius One. Best of all I liked the rapid firing CENSORED which completely CENSORED anything within half a

CENSORED! And turned the air purple! But precisely because they were new and secret weapons, they unfortunately couldn't be issued to agents, or even discussed outside a SCIF, or a bathroom at Mar-A-Lago. Agents, and their weapons, are too likely to be captured by allies, enemies, or other.

Nevertheless, I didn't regret the time I spent in Ordnance, Chemical Warfare, or Deadly Vehicles—especially the new, heavily armored, air-droppable ATV—or any of the other departments whose refresher courses I took. I especially enjoyed catching up on the latest collectibles in the Alien UFO gift shop. As opposed to the *Nazi* Alien UFO gift shop, which is just plain creepy. I don't shop there.

A lot of useful gadgets, tchotchkes, toys, and gimmicks, as well as killing, murdering, torturing, oral hygiene, and self-defense equipment, and the techniques to use them had been developed during the eleven years I'd been constantly in the field, and I was glad, very glad, to have a chance to bring myself up to date. And practice-kill things.

And even more glad to spend my evenings, nights, and mornings with the turquoise-eyed Juliet. She was lovely, funny, charming, warm, a delightful conversationalist, and sexually amazing. She lifted me out of my 'aging superagent' malaise, and made me feel like the perfect man. If she hadn't been a paid companion who was *supposed* to make me feel that way, I could have easily drifted into thoughts of evenings by a fire in Westchester, children's softball games, dance recitals, PTA meetings, barbecues with neighbors, and beautiful spring nights on our patio, looking at the moon, and cuddling under the stars with my dick inside her.

Yet every morning I would awaken to nothing more than a warm spot on her side of the bed, a reminder that she was paid by the hour, and my hours were up.

Sigh.

Thus passed the first business week of my return to headquarters.

I naturally expected that the rest of it would be a continuation of the first; instead, I was summoned to The General's office where a new, rather voluptuous assignment would be more or less forced upon me...

"Granny," I said, spotting her on my way to the car. "Is there any way I can have a morning with Juliet? I suppose it's technically overtime to have her there until I awaken, but..."

"It is not overtime," Granny said. "You want her zere, she should be zere vhen you avaken. Vhy izn't she?"

"Oh," I said, surprised. "I don't know, I just assumed …"

"I vill sprechen mit her," Gran said, her eye twitching with irritation. "She has no reason not to stay until you dizmiss her."

"It's okay," I said. "No need to get her in trouble."

Grumbling, Gran stalked away, and I worried that Juliet might be upset about my 'tattling' on her.

But—then—why *was* she leaving in the mornings if she didn't have to?

CHAPTER 6

CENTRAL VISITOR CONTROL was busy today, and Suzi was otherwise occupied with someone else when I arrived, so I wound up with Ruth. You never want Ruth pulling on your schvantz for any length of time, especially if you want, or need, to orgasm. Her grip is like an iron glove strapped to a paint can shaker. You're lucky to keep your skin when she's done. She also does nothing to help the cause, as Suzi would. She simply jerks disinterestedly, usually working on files and forms or having conversations with the other receptionists as she does, then gets frustrated with you for taking so long. Eventually I forcibly removed her from my bruised and tortured member to finish up myself. Into a cup.

Approved, she pointed me toward the elevator as if I hadn't been there a thousand times, then called up the next man—who immediately offered to let the man behind him go first.

§   §   §

Inside the elevator I pushed button 15. Down the box dropped. Past Personnel Department, Floor 2, past Ordnance, Floor 3, past Unarmed combat, Judo, Karate, Sabot, and Tango, Floor 4, past Biological and Chemical Warfare, Floor 5, past Conspiracy Theory Dissemination, Floor 6, past Language Instruction, Floor 7, past **CENSORED-**

CENSORED-CENSORED-CENSORED-CENSORED-CENSORED, past Post-Murder, Bad Punning, floor 14, until finally the elevator hissed to a stop fifteen stories below ground.

The doors slid open and I strolled through them into a large waiting area where The General's assistant, Miss Punnymany, was on a step ladder pinning up urgent reports too high for anyone to read.

"Agent 8," she said, without looking at me. "I thought I recognized your distinctively squeaky shoes."

"You recognize me by my shoes?"

"I'd know a heel anywhere," she said, and even though I couldn't see it, I could hear the smile in her voice.

"You're angry because my shoes didn't run away with you to the Mediterranean," I said.

"That's not my sole reason," she said, continuing to pin memos.

"Sorry, but I had to walk," I explained. "The General shoehorned me into another mission."

"Your tongue is always laced with lame excuses," she said.

"You must have had a good run on the beach without me," I said. "You're Buster Brown."

"My Busts are pale!" she said, turning to me with a smile and lifting her sweater to show the deep tan-line around her lovely, braless, pink breasts, and pinker nipples. "Hand crafted in Italy. My hide has indeed been tanned—shoe-leather brown—but as you can see these pristine peaks are still covered with virgin snow, unseen, and unexplored by even the most well-heeled man." She turned away and lifted her skirt, revealing a defiant lack of panties, and a bikini bottom coloration that would have put an Oreo cookie to shame, mere inches from my mouth. "As unexplored as my back country. So hold your insole-lent tongue."

"I feel like I'm stepping up to receive a special travel award," I said.

"Two Golden Globes, no waiting," she said, pushing them toward my face.

I stepped forward, and kissed those magnificent brown-and-cream hemispheres with all the passion I could muster.

"Mmm," she said, shifting her hips. "Allow me to turn the other cheek,"

I repeated the kiss on her other, glorious crescent moon, taking hold of her hips, extending my tongue, intending to go deep when a buzzer on her desk behind me went off.

"Send in 8," said the General's voice.

"You always get behind in your work," Punnymany said, dropping her skirt between me and the rapture of her rump.

"I prefer it when you butt out," I said, opening the General's door.

"You're too much of a bum for my bum," she said, returning to her memo posting for the far-sighted. "Though a good agent should always check in with hindquarters."

She winked at me, and with that, I gave up. There was no beating Punnymany's wordplay. But if I could, I felt certain a pleasant home in Westchester awaited us. If only The General would stop interfering with our attempts to really get to know one another.

Closing the door, I found myself in the comfortable, if rather untidy study that housed The General, a robust, confident man whose silver hair, tanned skin, general's cap, sunglasses, bathrobe and slippers make him look rather like a blend of what's his name; that Spartacus actor, Hugh Hefner, and Douglas MacArthur.

He rose to his feet as I entered, put aside his briar pipe and shook my hand.

"Glad to see you back, 8. I had a nasty premonition you weren't going to return from that last mission. Glad I was wrong. Have a seat. Tell me about it."

I winced. Were he and Granny sharing the same psychic reader? Why had they thought I wouldn't survive? I shrugged it off, and described my mission, in complete detail.

"Have a drink, he said. "Mix me one, too. You know where the concealed bar is."

I nodded, unconcealed the concealed bar and mixed us a couple of drinks—bourbon on the rocks for me, grain alcohol and distilled water for The General.

"I'm glad to see you've been relaxing so completely with that little blonde you've been banging in suite 42, 8," he said.

"You mean you're glad to *hear*," I corrected him. "Or *read*. Your use of the word 'see' implies that you have personally been observing me during the past week, which of course is not the case." I felt rather pleased to be able to thus criticize The General's sloppy grammatical form the way he was always criticizing mine. I should have known better.

"I said *see* and I meant **SEE**," The General snapped. "Thanks to one of the largest and finest closed-circuit television systems in The Free World, I am able to peep on—I mean observe—just about everything that goes on here at hindquarters! I mean headquarters!"

"Everything?" I asked, wondering.

"Everything," he said, firmly. "Even what you've been doing in the men's room on twelve. Really, 8. Can't you do that when you're at home?"

I lowered my head, and studied my drink.

"I especially enjoy checking in on the new proofing procedures for agents at Central Visitor Control," The General said.

"As do we all, sir," I said. "Except, perhaps, when Ruth is on duty."

"Yes, so I've seen," The General mused. "She mistakes vigor and speed for efficiency. We both know those are not the same."

"Less can be more," I said.

"Agreed. Here; have a look at this new monitoring system..." he said, smiling proudly. "I know you'll enjoy this as much as me.

He pressed a button on his desk and the huge map of the world covering one wall slid aside.

I gasped. Behind the huge map was a glass wall, and behind the glass wall were half a dozen gorgeous, naked female secret agents taking showers.

"Niiiiice," I agreed, then gasped. "Wait. General. I didn't know that your office adjoined the women's shower on the fourth fl—no—wait—that's impossible! This office is on the *fifteenth* floor! How—why—what...?"

The General chuckled, and in response simply pushed another button on his desk. Instantly the women's shower room vanished, to be replaced by an overhead view of the main gym, where two nude male agents were fencing with bowie knives, sparks flashing from their weapons as they practiced feints and thrusts before a crowd of other, nude agents, men and women.

The General pressed the button again. Suddenly water was on the other side of the glass wall, so real it was like looking into a huge, ocean-themed fish tank. Through the water swam a lush-bodied, naked, black female agent, Scuba tank on her back, straps tight around a pair of freely floating funbags, holding a dummy underwater demolition charge in her hands.

"Agent 42," mused the General, and I noted the coincidence with my suite number, as if someone were trying to communicate a clue of some kind about life, the universe—possibly everything. "Practicing underwater mass homicide. Shows good 'form', doesn't she?" He chuckled at his pun.

"*Use a pun—go to jail!*" Punnymany yelled from the outer office. "*People who pun badly should bend over and take it innuendo! Et tu equivoce! Et TUUUU!*"

"Enough of that," The General sniffed, dismissively, turning off the office intercom, "it was a perfectly good pun."

He punched the TV button again on his desk. Now we were watching the main target range. An agent was waiting in the pit with a rifle at the ready. Suddenly a naked man with a machine gun was released and he sped across the range firing a spray of bullets wildly in the direction of a nude female agent, who scarcely moved. The agent raised her rifle, squeezed off a shot, a light beam exploded from the barrel, and the target erupted into uncountable red and white fragments, each partially cooked.

Damn! I *really* wanted one of those!

The General punched the button on his desk once more. Now a class attending a lesson in nude-safe cracking was on the other side of the glass wall. Then a class in nude Bulgarian dialects. Then another view of the women's showers, a close shot that revealed Sasakawea from Ladies Spy Apparel bobbling her soap-smeared breasts. Then the glass wall went black and the huge map slid back into place.

"Incredible!" I cried. "It really did look like a window! I just saw it with my own eyes, yet I find it impossible to believe that a television screen can be so large, or have such sharp definition—and natural color!"

The General chuckled. "That's because you've only seen commercial television. The size and definition of a TV image is actually only limited by the amount of money you care to spend. This cost the US taxpayers almost twenty million dollars. Worth every penny, though, especially because they weren't my pennies. Enables me to peep on—I mean keep track of—everything I need to peep on—I mean keep track of.

Now, as I was saying before we got off on this pointless Chekov's Gun, TV tangent, you've been doing well, 8, very well."

"Thank you, sir," I said, knowing what was coming.

Always lead with praise, was the General's motto knowing what he really wanted to do was get to the criticism part.

So, I sat back and waited for his critique. He lazily puffed pipe smoke for a while, until:

"So... I read your report. You were quietly, and carefully slipping out of the building, having silently, and masterfully slaughtered your target, Madame Phu, when you spied an enemy agent climbing in? Is that right?"

I nodded. "Yes sir. If I'm not mistaken, it was Hata Mari, a cold-blooded but beautiful young Eurasian girl who's reputedly Japan's top, um, disposal expert in Southeast Asia. Evidently, she, too, had been assigned the job of liquidating Madame Phu. Odd, isn't it, that both we and an enemy-turned-ally should come to the same ruthless, tactical decision at the same time..."

The General gave me an icy stare. "Are you suggesting, 8, that we and the Japanese should temporarily join forces to liquidate the Communists?"

"Am I what?" I said heatedly. *"NO! Of course not!"*

"Good!" snapped The General. "Those idiots in War Games up on Floor **CENSORED** actually came up with that suggestion, believe it or not. They 've decided a coalition is in order similar to that which existed during World War II, when, as you may recall, the U.S. and Russia became allies in order to defeat Hitler. Their specific recommendation was that we should team up with Japan to crush Soviet Russia and their troublesome allies, like Singapodia and Albania, the result being that the non-Soviet Russia—having gratefully thrown off the horrible yoke of Communism—would become our devoted friend and help us crush *our* troublesome allies—like France. I turned the idea down cold, of course."

"Glad to hear it," I said, not at all following what he was saying. France?

The General stood, and I saw that his robe was—awkwardly—open in the front, and he was nude underneath. He puffed on his briar pipe, strolled over to glare at the huge map of the world that covered the TV screen, and one entire wall of his study. The map was dotted with pins marked *Us, Them,* and *Other.*

"Look at all those red pins," snarled the General, "each one representing a Red agent. And to oppose them, you know how few agents we have?"

"Ummm... two... hundred... thousand?" I guessed.

The General whirled, skewered me with a cold stare. "How do you happen to know that *exact* classified figure?" he grated.

"I don't know, I heard it somewhere," I told him. "Articles in *Time* or *the Post,* I think."

"**CENSORED!**" snarled The General, almost white with rage. But within a moment he had regained his self-control, and went on talking calmly, if emotionally.

"Yes, 8, all over the world we are pitted against ruthless agents of the Communist conspiracy—men, women and children who live by the cruel, un-Christian creed that the end justifies the means."

"Such an evil creed," I agreed.

"Evil creed? It's more than evil, it's diabolical. Utterly opposed to such Western concepts as *Do unto others as you would have them do unto you, love thy neighbor, support mental health, yield the right of way, if it's brown, flush it down,* and so on." He thrust his bony index finger toward me. "Never forget, 8, that to crush those diabolical men, women and children who live by the creed of *the end justifies the means,* we of The Free World must use any and every means at our disposal! For which we are totally justified!"

"Hear, hear," I said. "Uh, shall we drink to that, sir?"

"Fine idea," said The General.

We each slammed one.

"Tell me, 8," The General said, his voice deceptively casual, "if you were close enough to this enemy agent, Hata Mari, to identify her, WHY THE HELL DIDN'T YOU SHOOT HER?"

Ah. We'd reached the criticism part.

"Well," I said, not wanting to explain my—literally—being caught with my pants down, "you know, for the simple reason that, um, well, just last week, you told me not to complicate my missions with a lot of unnecessary, tangential killings."

The General frowned. "When I said that, I had in mind the regrettable incident of the *Crippled Orphans Institute*, in Romania."

I got a little heated when he said that.

"Look, General," I said, "as I told you when it happened, the only time my target wasn't surrounded by heavily armed guards was when he paid a propaganda visit to that *Crippled Orphans Institute*. I had to get him then, or not at all. *So, I got him then.* And since I had no possible way of knowing which part of the *Crippled Orphans Institute* he'd be in when the explosive charges went off, I had no choice but to blow up the entire complex. I didn't like having to exterminate two thousand crippled orphan children, but really—what was the alternative? The ends... well they justified... I mean, necessitated... I mean... you know, as you've said repeatedly, even just moments ago, General, we must use any and every means to crush those whose philosophy is that... uh... the end... justifies... the means."

The General hung his head. "You're right, 8. I deserved that rebuke. Forgive me for criticizing you. I sometimes need you to remind me of my own, most firmly held belief; that what we do..."

"We do for the greater good," I finished. "It's a phrase tattooed on my heart. I repeat it like a mantra when things are at their toughest."

"And Singapodia was tough," The General said. "The important thing is that you succeeded in permanently neutralizing Madame Phu. Did she die hard?"

I nodded. "Real hard." I neglected to mention that I had also been hard. "She wanted to be held as she died, and I refused."

The General rubbed his hands together gleefully. "Good. That should teach those damned Commies that evil doesn't pay."

"Diabolical-ly-ness... doesn't pay, you mean," I said, unsure.

"Indeed," he said. "Probably why they sent an agent to kill you on the plane. They knew you'd done it, but couldn't prove it, and knew we'd raise hell if they killed you on their soil."

"Yes, true," I said, then realized. "Are you saying you wouldn't raise hell if I'd been killed on the plane?"

He ignored my question, and walked over to a long table on which a number of chessboards had been puzzle-pieced together in the shape of another map of the world. The area nearest me, I noticed, was Southeast Asia. On it was a red knight, labeled *Bad*, a white knight, labeled *Good*, and between them, a black queen labeled *Madame Phu, Communist*. The General reached down, picked up the black queen, broke it in his hand, and tossed the fragments into the wastepaper basket. Then he moved the white knight back to SADISTO headquarters.

Awww... I was a white knight.

"Now that the female head of the Communist forces in Singapodia has been eliminated," he murmured, "the stage can be set for a clear-cut confrontation between Good and Evil."

"Yes sir," I said. I glanced down the long table; it was crowded with chessboard markings, each with chessmen and women set up to represent a problem, each carved meticulously to look like the friend or enemy they represented. Not for the first time, I saw how The General managed to keep track of all the concerns and difficulties he and his trusted agents were attempting to stop—primarily by being weirdly obsessive.

I indicated the chessboard from which he'd just removed the Madame Phu sculpted black queen. A remote Island not far from Singapodia that had a little dinosaur on it, with a naked toy girl riding its back, and a red knight.

"Isn't that the island of Jícama?" I asked. "My friend Glenn Strangeways, and his sometime partner, sometime lover Trueblood have a field office there. I spoke to him not long ago. Do they know about this red knight, and its pawns?"

He shook his head. "Strangeways and Trueblue have disappeared."

"Really?" I said. "What happened to them? Should I go down, and see? And deal with this red knight myself while I'm there?"

"I've already assigned new agents for those jobs. Gus and Tina left several days ago for Jícama."

"Gus and Tina?" I asked. "That's funny. I just heard they'd been liquidated in *Albania*. Guess I heard wrong."

The General looked surprised, then snapped his fingers. "No, you're right, 8. I did send them to Albania. Sometimes I lose track of the massive number of concerns and difficulties I and my trusted agents are attempting to thwart throughout the Free World. Though not often, of course. Not often."

He reached down and knocked over the Gus and Tina pieces into tiny vats of acid, where they quickly melted into colorful goo, sliding everything off the board into a box marked "recycle." He was nothing, if not environmentally conscious. At least with the Free World pieces.

"You've accidentally put a little dinosaur on the board there, too, General. You want me to..."

I reached for it, and he slapped my hand.

"That belongs there," he said, sharply. No further explanation was offered, the clear implication being not to ask.

The General looked at the pool of colorful goo in the bin.

"I should never have let them go together," he said quietly.

"What's wrong with sending them together," I asked. "They're excellent agents who work well as a team. Or, 'worked,' past-tense, I guess I should say."

"Too well! They were a couple!" The general glowered at me. "In *love,*' apparently." He said the word 'love' as if it were a small rodent that had repeatedly shit in his shoe. "It's never a good idea to send a couple *in love* out on a mission together. If they're not sneaking off someplace to fuck, then they're doing their best to keep the other from getting hurt. Injured. Raped or tortured." He shuddered. "Love. Empathy. Concern. These are—as you well know—terrible traits for an agent to have wandering around loose inside his brain. A good agent cannot be concerned about someone else's suffering. Especially a 'loved' one."

"You don't have to worry about that with me, General," I said, chuckling, and feeling glad I'd stopped short of anything more than a few questions about Westchester with Juliet. "I don't fall in love."

"Your best asset!" The General said, pressing the button on his desk. "Punnymany? Has the new cadet arrived?"

"It's not yet 6:30, sir," Punnymany replied. "She'll be here... hands down."

"Dammit! I expect my cadet agents to be early and enthusiastic! You know that!"

"She'll be here, Punnymany assured. "She loves to cook, and always wakes up ... *on thyme.*"

"I don't get it!" The General snapped. "Is that one of those spelling puns? You know I hate those! Stop doing that!"

He stabbed the button and disconnected.

"You're bringing in a new cadet agent?" I gasped. "Why?"

"You'll see," The General said, mischief in his eyes.

"Oh, sir, no," I said, unable to contain my discomfort, "please tell me you're not expecting me to…"

"I am!" he snapped! "Your agency needs you!"

I groaned, sat slowly back in my seat, and sulked. I knew it. He was going to assign me a cadet agent to mentor. He must be really angry about the assignment with Madame Phu, my offending the Chinese ambassador, and not killing Hata Mari.

I sat there hoping this new cadet agent was at least hot, willing, and liked Westchester.

CHAPTER 7

"OH—*HELL*," I SAID, standing, unable to be hopeful for any kind of bright side.

I'd been through this too many times before, with starry-eyed young newbies who gush endlessly about the gloriousness of the agency, its celebrated history, its legendary missions, and 'what an honor it is to meet you, Agent 8, you're an icon, and so much more handsome and virile in person, blah, blah, blah.' Meanwhile nearly getting me killed on some training mission. If it was a woman, at least there was hope that she might give me those compliments while naked, slathered in baby oil, and sliding around on top of me.

"Do you mind if I pour myself another drink?" I asked.

The General shook his head and I poured myself second bourbon on the rocks—or was it a third?—overfilling the glass.

"Interesting, most interesting," murmured the General, watching me with hooded eyes. "A custom that originated with the ancient Greeks. Didn't think you went in for pagan superstitions, 8."

"I'm sorry, went in for what?" I asked.

"I'm referring to how you're blessing this mentoring mission with the custom of pouring a little of one's drink on the ground, as a libation to the unknown god."

"I wasn't pouring some of my drink on the ground as a libation to anything, sir," I said. "I just slopped some on the carpet by accident. I—uh—I have a slight nervous tremor in my hands.”

The General frowned. “Put down your drink, 8, and hold out those hands.”

I gulped down my Michter’s—sloshed, not poured—put the glass on the table and held out my hands.

“Hold them steady,” snapped the General, “don’t flutter and wave them around like that.”

“I’m not fluttering or waving them, sir,” I said a little too whiny for my tastes. “I’m holding them as steadily as I can.”

The General frowned. “If that’s true, 8, you’re in bad shape. You look like a pianist trying to play the minute waltz before a bomb goes off while holding in your pee.”

“I am in rather bad shape, General,” I admitted. “Madame Phu was rough, then the assassin on the airplane, then the Gus and Tina news got to me, as well, I suppose. Now Strangeways and Trueblue. People dying, or vanishing without a word. I really don’t have the time or the energy for new cadets, sir. They’re always such a pain. In fact, I’d like to have a serious talk with you about something.”

“Then act seriously, 8,” growled the General. “Don’t keep winking at me.”

“I’m not winking,” I protested with a wink, “at least not voluntarily. I’ve developed a nervous tic in my left eye. Also, my hands tremble almost uncontrollably, as you’ve noticed. And I repeat myself. Also, I repeat myself. Also, I’ve rather fallen into the habit of talking aloud while thinking, or sleeping. I don’t sleep so good, either. Because I’m talking. In my sleep.” I took a deep breath. “And sometimes I repeat myself. I also have these recurring dreams, and… the fact of the matter is, General, I’m on the verge of a nervous breakdown. Sir, can I please have a short vacation?”

“Rephrase that last sentence properly, 8,” snarled the General.

“Yes sir. Sorry, sir. May I have a short vacation, sir?” The General was such a stickler for grammatical niceties.

He frowned at me. “If I thought you were malingering, 8...”

“I’m not, sir,” I assured him. “I’m really, and truly on the verge of a nervous breakdown. I’m—well—I’m practically unfit for duty, sir.”

"Practically," snarled the General. "This isn't just some lame excuse to get out of cadet-agent mentoring duty?"

"Sir," I said, trying to sound as wounded as I needed to.

"Hmm..." The General said, turning to pace. "Vacations, vacations. Next thing I know my agents will be demanding 8-hour days, a five-day work-week, scheduled lunch hours, and double time for working on Sundays. Do I not give you prostitutes? Drugs? Alcohol?"

I wiped my lips, and said nothing.

"Didn't you see a psychiatrist once?" he asked. "Cleared for Top Secret."

"And you'd think one visit would be enough!" I said. "But I seem to need time off more than ever."

"Didn't you just get *back* from a vacation, 8?" The General continued, unabated. "In December, I think it was."

"Well, yes sir," I said. "December of *1959*. I haven't had a day off in seven years, sir; and, sir—all this lying, killing, and illicit sex—the strain is beginning to tell on me."

The General sighed. "I had another important lying, murder and illicit sex assignment lined up for you, 8, but, well, I guess I can assign it to 9. And as to this new cadet... I figured you'd be perfect for her, but... all right; I'll give you a little vacation."

"Thank you, sir," I said, emotion all but overwhelming me, "thank you!"

A vacation! Two whole weeks off! I could go to Bermuda, or Palm Springs, or Las Vegas, or Tahiti with Punnymany! Or maybe just go off into the mountains to fish and hunt. Or—

"Yes, 8," continued the General, "I'm sending you to the Jícama islands!"

"The Jícama islands," I repeated, already floating calmly on a sea of relaxation. I could see the blue waters, the warm beaches, the topless Punnymany...

"Wait..." I said, as it dawned.

"Yes, we have that little weirdness going on down there with Strangeways and Trueblue," The General explained, "Gus, and Tina, and the agents I had planned to send to deal with that have been killed."

"Yes sir, I was here... when I told you."

"Damned horny agent and his mistress just took off—apparently thinking they could skip out on SADISTO. Ha! As if," he said, and chuckled to himself, puffing his pipe.

"Strangeways?" I said. "And Trueblue? That doesn't sound like them."

"You know them?" The General asked.

"Am I repeating myself, again, or…? I feel like I just told you…"

"Answer the question!"

"Yes, sir. Glenn Strangeways and I indoctrinated together. We double-teamed Trueblue one night in Modesto after a wedding. Or maybe during. Glenn's wedding, I think. You really think they've tried to skip out on SADISTO?"

"Yes. And we need you to button it up."

"So… this *isn't* a vacation…" I said, the relaxation already fading, the tremor revving itself back up.

"Essentially!" the General snarled. "Easy job! Tropical island! Sunny skies! Find them in bed together, two shots, done! A nice, quiet little hit, no danger, no illicit sex required. For a skilled assassin like you, it'll be a real vacation."

I begged to differ. Internally, anyway. On the outside, I begged for nothing.

"Sir…" I started to say, intending to mention that I'd be murdering a good friend. Two good friends. One good friend, and a girl I'd enjoyed having sex with.

"Don't 'sir' me," snarled the General, "You said you were on the verge of a nervous breakdown, not a physical one. Best cure for jittery nerves is a *job*, 8. Distracts the mind."

I nodded, pouted, and slouched my way toward his office door. At least I wouldn't have to play Big Brother to one of our cadet agents in training.

"Where are you going?" he snarled.

"I thought…" I said, groping for understanding. "Didn't you just dismiss me to go to Jícama? To kill Strangeways, and Trueblue?"

"I did nothing of the sort. Let those two think they've escaped for a while. The rest of your week will be spent acting as Big Brother to one of our cadet agents in training, and *then* you will take *her* with you to Jícama as lead agent on her first training mission."

"What? Aw, no, General, I told you I don't have the time or interest, or mental wherewithal to—my hands, my nervous tic—"

He silenced me with the quick wave of a scolding finger, then used that finger to press a button on his desk.

"It's 6:30. I assume she's here by now?" He said, tersely.

"She is timewise," Punnymany's voice replied. "Was here five minutes ago. Slept on a clock so she could be... *on* time."

"Stop that, and send her in, Punnymany," he said, releasing the button. "I think you'll be delighted to mentor this one, 8."

A door opened and a voluptuous girl with a blonde ponytail dressed simply in agency-colored shorts, tennis shoes, and T-shirt emblazoned with a large FUCK ME logo, and "Ask Granny How" in small text underneath walked in, speaking to Punnymany, behind her.

"She's beautiful, she's rich, and she's got *huge...*" the blonde said, appearing to search for her next word, then cupping her hands before her expansive tits, "tracts of land..."

"It's a beautiful place," Punnymany said from the outer office. "Hilly. Thanks for pointing those out to me."

The blonde waved, dismissively, and laughed. "You win. I thought I could get you with old *Monty Python*, but you hit back with *Four Weddings*? Genius. *There's no beating you, Punnymany!*"

The woman strode confidently forward, halting in front of the General's desk and saluting smartly, winking at me with a turquoise eye. I sucked wind.

"Cadet agent Juliet Jones reporting, sir," she said, stone-faced. Then she turned her bright and lively eyes my way, smiling with that charming, sarcastic flicker at the corner of her lips.

"Juliet..." I said, my face expressing at least as much shock as my voice. "You're the new cadet agent?"

"I am! Does that surprise you?"

"Well, yeah," I admitted. "And ... Punnymany? You know her?"

She giggled. "Well, only since about 2:30 this morning, until we left at 5. But I'd say we both know her pretty well. Intimately, in fact. Several times."

I gulped.

I might have to review the tape from 2:30 to 5 last night.

"At ease, cadet agent Jones," The General said, turning to me. "8? Cadet agent Jones. Who—being still in training—has not yet been assigned a number. Jones, I believe you've... eh... *met* agent Trevor Hawke, better known as Agent 8."

"Met?" she said, chuckling. "Oh, General. We've *fucked*," she laughed harder. "A *lot.*"

"Yes," the General said. "I've seen a good deal of the video. Quite a bit of stamina you've both got there. Seven times that first night, I think Gran said? So, you already know how to..." the General began to chuckle, *"Parallel park* together."

"Never use a pun without a license!" Punnymany yelled. "Or someone better at it will PUNish you!"

"Close that door, will you, cadet agent Jones?" The General said. "I can't take any more of that."

Smiling happily, she bounced across the room and did.

"Sooo... you remember cadet agent Jones, Agent 8?" The General asked. "Weren't too drunk to lose her from your memory?"

"Yes," I admitted. "I mean, no. But we're not close, or anything. Or in love. Nothing like that. Just... you know... fuck-buddies."

"Trevor..." Jones said, hurt spreading out from those magnificent eyes, across her face, down her neck, and throughout her entire body. "That's not what you said at 3:45 last ..."

"Of course not!" I interrupted, realizing that I had plainly forgotten too much due to excessive alcohol consumption. "I was... already training you! On how to deceive an enemy!"

She slumped, wounded, and I felt the waves of pain flow out of her, and invade my own body.

"Of course," The General said. "Of course. No love between agents is permitted. Can't have any more Gus and Tina episodes."

Cadet Agent Jones looked at the General, and realization slowly soaked into her. Her mouth formed a small 'o' of understanding, her eyes widened, and she turned back to me with a quick wink.

"Gotcha," she said, waggling a finger at me. "No falling in love with another agent," she said, her voice loaded with sexy teacher-like admonishment, "no matter how great her tits are."

I looked cadet agent Jones up and down, from the tip of her blonde, ponytailed head, over her beautiful face with those transfixing turquoise eyes, and charming, sarcastic smile, down her long, smooth neck, lingering on her magnificent forty inch bust, twenty-six-inch waist, thirty-eight-inch hips and long, *long* legs. How did she actually look sexier in a *The Place* Call-Me-Girl's exercise uniform than she did totally nude, lying on my bed? Under me? Flushed and moaning. Tits jiggling with each of my animal thrusts. Screaming my name in unbridled...

I had to steady myself on the desk.

"8?" The General said. "Are you unwell?"

I didn't answer. I could think of nothing but being on her, being in her, being pressed against the luscious all of her. Yes. Luscious was the only word that came to mind, and I hoped I wasn't saying it out loud.

"Luscious *is* your nickname for me," Jones said, still smiling at me, then stage-whispered, "but really. Is now the appropriate time to bring it up, Trevor?"

"Woof," I said.

Jones chuckled with appreciation.

"8!" The General snapped, and I came back into the room from wherever my head had taken me—somewhere beyond the outer fringes of space doing exciting things with Jones' weightless, nude body. "Get hold of yourself. This may be the 60's, where you can sexually harass a co-worker and it's considered charming, but it's still a government workplace, and your boss's office."

I glanced down at the bottle of baby oil on his desk. He saw where my eyes went, reacted slightly, snagged the bottle, and shoved it into a robe pocket.

"Cadet agent Jones," he continued, turning to Juliet. "From now on you will take orders directly from 8, who will be your Big Brother for the next week."

"'Big Brother,' eh?" she said, still grinning. "Incest is best."

"Woof," I repeated.

Jones again chuckled with even more appreciation.

"*8! Jones!*" The General snapped, anger spreading out from him like a red mist into every corner of the room. He placed his fists on his hips, and his robe fell open in the front, revealing an aging erection.

Juliet gasped, then laughed quietly. The General quickly belted himself back inside his terrycloth.

"Was that for me?" Jones asked, flirtatiously.

"Perhaps," the General said, quietly. "Later."

I bristled.

"After a week of training together," The General continued, double-knotting his belt, "you will join 8 on his mission to the Jícama islands."

"The Jícama islands!" gasped cadet agent Jones. "How perfectly romantic! I—I mean, exciting! How, perfectly unromantically *exciting*."

"I'm sorry, but she will not," I said.

Cadet agent Jones flinched.

The General frowned at me as a thick silence hung out in the room, impatiently.

"Wait outside a moment, cadet agent Jones," he said, still looking at me.

She moved quietly toward the door, glancing back over her shoulder once to scowl at me with confusion before exiting. The General stared at me with old-man fury.

"Are you having difficulty with this assignment, 8?"

"You bet your ass I am!" I snapped. "It's a—it's an insult to ask me to act as Big Brother to anyone. I'm a single-digit, top agent! But especially to a… to a girl like *that*."

"A girl like what?" The General asked, fists going again to his hips, and even belted, his erection popped forth. Which was—to say the least—distracting.

"Like… Jones," I said. "Like a… what she is. A… a paid consort. A honey girl! A hooker! A prostitute!"

"Do you not sleep with women when we ask you to?" he demanded. "And pay you to do it? Madame Phu being only the most recent example?"

"Well, that's different," I said, looking at the ceiling. The floor. Anywhere but the General's wrinkled stiffy.

"Is it?" he asked. "Is it *really*? So, when you slept with the head of the *Sockson Corporation* before throwing her out a window…"

"There was no *throwing*," I said, defiantly. "And I didn't *sleep* with her, we were both awake at the time. I was ramming her from behind against the plate glass of her office when she tried to kill me with a sword, so I ducked, and thrust at the same time. The glass shattered, and… well… there was no sleeping."

"I read the report," he admonished. "So, you didn't 'sleep', but you fucked her. To death, basically. As you fucked her on that circus trapeze to gain vital, Free World information. As you also fucked her on the roof of her corporate headquarters while you both dangled from a helicopter simultaneously trying to get hold of that decrypted Translation of the Voynich Diaries. *For which you were paid.*"

"There's more to agenting than just hanging from dangerous places while having sex," I insisted. "Jones could—in fact most definitely *did*—provide a man with one or more entertaining evenings in bed, but she is much too young, sweet, and innocent to make a good agent. An agent for *this* organization, at least. It is called SADISTO. The *Security and Administration Division of the Institute for Special Tactical Operations.* You didn't work out an acronym that spelled *WARM AND FUZZY*, which would suit her more."

The General pursed his lips. "8? Do you have feelings for cadet agent Jones?"

"Whuh! Huh! Wah!" I said. I think. I'm not sure.

"I admit," the General said, eyes slitted, "it would be highly unusual after only one week of continuous sex. But stranger things have happened. Like Tiny Tim becoming famous. I will never understand that at all."

"Me neither," I said. "And I likewise assure you, I do not have feelings for Jones."

"Because, for the life of me," The General snarled, "you seem very concerned about her welfare."

"I... am... NOT!" I said.

"Concern. Empathy," the General said derisively. He studied me intently, and, again, I began to tremble. "8? Are you... in love with cadet agent Jones?"

"SIR! NO! SIR! Come on! You know me better than that! I just happen to think that a beautiful young woman like that; smart, witty, charming, highly intelligent, easily social, with such mesmerizingly beautiful eyes, and luscious, oversized tits, would make the worst kind of secret agent imaginable, and should remain a simple, basic, bed-partner for me. For someone. For whoever. Not just me. More as an overall asset for *The Place*, really, but who I get dibs on whenever I'm in town."

"8?" the General asked, sounding as if he didn't believe a word slopping out of my mouth. "What is the prime... no... the *sole* purpose of agents working for this organization, and for which they are licensed?"

"Um," I said. "Murder?"

"Right. But before any of our agents can carry out their assigned duty, what must they do?"

"Lots of things, really," I said, again searching the room, and scratching my head. "Are we talking warm weather, or cold, or… I don't know specifically. What?"

"Get within striking distance of their victim!" snapped The General. *"Weather unimportant!* Which is where good-looking agents like you, and especially *smart* good-looking agents like cadet agent Jones come in handy."

"I don't follow you, General," I said.

"Which is why I left out the 'smart' descriptor for you," The General sighed. "Are you being intentionally dense?"

"I think you know me better than that."

"Take a look at yourself in the mirror, 8."

"What mirror?" I asked, looking around. I found three other strategically placed bottles of baby oil, but no mirror.

The General punched a button on his desk and a section of one wall slid back revealing a full-length mirror. I walked over and looked in at myself.

"Describe what you see," The General said.

"Well," I said, striving for objectivity, "I see a stunning young man in his late twenties, tall, lean, but muscular, suntanned, darkly handsome, with fashionable Cary Grant hair, and a come-hither smile. Wearing a stylish, deep blue business suit."

"Correct," said the General. "A look which easily gets you close to female targets. But, 8—successful though you are in your chosen profession—hasn't it ever struck you that you have other—well—built-in *disadvantages*?"

"No," I said. "Never. Like what?"

"Like you *look* like a secret agent," said the General.

"How is that a disadvantage?" I said, again scratching my head. I really should consider a medicated shampoo.

The General muttered something under his breath. *"Like your victims can see you coming,"* he snapped. "Especially male victims. Let me give you an example. Suppose, just for the sake of argument, our organization decides to liquidate a certain South American general."

"Does this south American general like baseball?" I asked.

"Possibly. Who would have the best chance of getting close—really—close to such a target? You—or a smart, charming, beautiful, voluptuous twenty-something woman like cadet agent Jones?"

I frowned. "Well—I also like baseball, but… if I'm being honest, cadet agent Jones, I suppose. Unless the South American General was gay, in which case…"

"HE ISN'T! Not in *my* hypothetical! So even though you may be, let's say, ten times more efficient and deadly than cadet agent Jones—"

"Twenty," I said. "Easy."

"—okay, whatever. Cadet agent Jones has *twenty* times as much chance to get close—really close—to such a target. So, in actual practice, you and cadet agent Jones would be equally effective lethal weapons."

"Logic tells me you're right, General. But—but surely… I mean, if an agent, a *killing* agent's effectiveness is measured by his or her ability to get close to his or her chosen victim, why… if that was how an agent's effectiveness was measured," my enthusiasm increased as I realized I had him! "Well, then little children would make the ideal killing agents!"

The General smiled. "Have you ever read that short story by Saki," he asked, "in which a Balkan prince—or somebody like that—is assassinated by a small child handing him an explosive Easter egg—or something like that?"

"No," I said. "Nothing like that."

"A pity," mused The General, his hands straying over the array of buttons on his desk. The huge map-wall slid back a moment later. And on the immense screen flashed the image of a first-grade classroom. Or what looked like a first-grade classroom. I smiled at the charming, cherubic little faces.

The teacher, a white haired but lethal-looking old lady was saying, "Now children, who can tell me the best places to stab a man with an ice pick?"

I gasped!

"I know, I know!" squealed the excited little boys and girls, jumping up and down and waving their tiny hands in the air.

"General!" I said in a voice that was surprisingly high-pitched, even for me.

The General started, punched a button on his desk. Instantly the huge screen went black and the wall map slid back into place.

"General," I went on, eye blinking, hands shaking, "surely those—those innocent little children weren't being taught *murder methods?* I can barely work, **now!** That would disturb me into nonfunctioning immobility! I mean, even though I truly believe that we of The Free World must use any and all methods against those who—"

"No, no!" said The General, looking at my twitchy eye, and shaking hands, interrupting me, apparently realizing he'd gone too far. "Those weren't *really* young children, they were, ah, midgets and dwarves. Yes, that's it—midgets and dwarves! Little people! Pygmies, even! Agents of diminutive stature who can *pass* as children. But are not *actual* children. Ho, ho, ho."

"Oh," I said, "well, I'm really glad to hear that. I felt my mind going there, for a second."

The General stared at me, unblinking, nervously shifting from foot-to-foot.

"You really do need a vacation," The General said.

"What have I been saying?" I snapped. "So, anyway, that brings us back to cadet agent Jones. If you really insist that I act as Big Brother to her for the rest of the week, and take her with me to Jícama, well, I'll accept that assignment. But I want to register my protest in advance. Also, it is my strong belief that cadet agent Jones doesn't have the makings of a killer."

"Why are you arguing so hard against her?" The General asked, confused. "You said you're not in love with her, and *you* suggested her for the job."

"I what?"

"You arrived at my door," The General said, "in the middle of the night… woke me from a… um… a sound sleep… I was sleeping… and you insisted I make Jones an agent."

"I would have done no such thing," I said.

"And yet you did," The General said, more confused. "Woke me from a—as I said—a sound sleep, stood there naked in my doorway, insisting she would make a fantastic agent."

"Was I drunk?"

"Yes, but what difference does that make?"

"Well," I said dismissively, "I can't be held responsible for the things I say when I'm drunk."

"But you specifically told me," The General sputtered, now irritated as well as confused, "you said, 'General! Even though I'm drunk, you can absolutely hold me responsible for what I'm saying!' and then you nodded a lot."

"And that was good enough for you?" I asked, incredulous.

"No," the General said, "actually it wasn't. Which is why I asked you to sign this note."

He took a note from his desk and showed it to me. In a nearly incoherent scrawl, it read:

> General! Even though I am drunk, you can absolutely hold me responsible for what I am saying! Juliet Jones wood make a fantassic agent, ideeelly sooted to lickidate South Americann generales who are not gay, or wom...

And then it sort of trailed off the page. There was an attempt at a signature, which was only recognizable to me because I've written such drunken notes before.

"Why would I recommend her to become an agent?" I asked—myself, mostly.

The General shrugged. "You, of all people, are best qualified to spot agent material. But I'm listening if you don't really think she can cut the program. Because beyond today, if she doesn't measure up, I'll flunk her. Your decision."

"And by flunk her, you mean..."

"Yes, I do mean..." he said.

I gasped.

"She's had just enough training to let her go," he said, "but beyond this..."

The General turned away, side-eyeing me, and said nothing more as he pressed a button on his desk. Cadet agent Jones, trotted back into the room and saluted. She caught me staring at the settling wobble of her breasts.

She grabbed one and squeezed it in my direction. In a high, squeaky voice she said, playfully, "Kiss me, Trevor. I love it when you lick my..."

"Cadet agent Jones," The General interrupted, and she dropped the tit, straightening into attention for him. "8 has consented to accept you fully as his mentee, and be your Big Brother for the next two weeks."

"Awesome!" cried cadet agent Jones, clapping her lovely little hands together. "Thank you, thank you, thank you, Trev… I mean *Agent 8!* And you too, General! Thanks so much. I won't disappoint either of you!"

The General's mouth quirked into a bitter smile. "Before you get *too* thankful, cadet agent Jones, I should make some hard facts clear to you. Up until now you have had only a couple days of basic training in espionage and murder techniques."

"You have?" I asked.

"I have," said cadet agent Jones, smiling, and saluting again.

How many nights in a row had I been drunk? I wondered.

"Four, I believe," The General said.

"I said that out loud?" I asked.

"Yes," Juliet said, "Why are you shaking? And winking at me?"

"You, you, you…" I tried.

"I was going to Basic Training," Juliet said, trying to be helpful. "And it's gone super well."

"And as I'm sure I don't have to tell you," The General said, "it was a tough, grueling course."

"Phew, was it," agreed cadet agent Jones. "The first day we had fifty students at the start of the course, but only five of us made it to the end. Me and four men."

"*I* and four men," snapped The General. "Next to blind obedience and ruthlessness, I demand grammatical precision from my agents. Now, cadet agent Jones, those forty-five men and women who flunked out of basic training, do you know what happened to them?"

"I believe so," said cadet agent Jones. "They were given a fifty-dollar bonus, a hand-shake, made to sign a statement that they'd never disclose what they learned in basic spy training, and then they were sent home."

"That's what you were *told*," said the General. "Because, in basic training, you mostly do a lot of calisthenics. Excellent video, that, by the way. And the men who failed learned nothing that was Secret, Top Secret, Ultra Secret, or Cosmic Alien Autopsy Secret. Once that basic training course was finished, however, cadet agents are given Ultra Secret training and have access to Cosmic Alien Autopsy Secret documents, videos, and collectibles. In other words, cadet agent Jones, from this point on, if you flunk out you don't get sent home," He leaned in over his desk, peering intently into her eyes. "Understand my meaning, cadet agent Jones?"

"No," she gasped. "Are you saying...?"

"I *am* saying," The General said, a cruel smile twisting his lined old face.

"No, I... I don't believe you," said cadet agent Jones. "You—you're just trying to scare me. Right? Aren't you?"

In unison, the General and I shook our heads. I sadly, the General grinningly.

The General pressed a button on his desk and the huge wall map slid back once again revealing the massive television screen.

"This," said The General, pressing yet another button on his desk, "is a taped film of an event that took place earlier today."

The huge TV screen lit up, again with such sharp definition that it once more seemed as though we were merely watching through a glass wall. On it, The General was rolling around naked on the floor, laughing hysterically as a nude woman wearing a garter belt and high heels poured a large pan of chocolate pudding all over him.

He quickly jumped forward and pressed another button. "Wrong video," he said, sheepishly. "That was from... a... uh... cooking class, that I attended yesterday. They had asked for volunteers."

And, again, we were watching through a glass wall. Watching, this time, an exquisitely muscled naked young male leaning against a stone wall puffing nervously on a cigarette.

"That's Cadet agent Smith," said Juliet. "He was in the class just ahead of me. Wow. He looks good naked. Wish I'd known."

"He flunked his advanced training this morning. Observe as he smokes his last cigarette."

"His... *last* cigarette?" said cadet agent Jones. "You mean he... he quit smoking this morning?"

"You might say that," said The General, his voice tinged with irony.

On the screen the nude young man The General had identified as former cadet agent Smith took a final puff, and flicked his cigarette aside. Someone off screen tossed him a gun, which he snagged expertly, chambering a round as he moved away from the wall. The camera followed. Presently he crouched behind a crumbled jumble of rubble amid some fake ruins, in an area designed to look like a bombed-out city street.

A burst of rifle fire followed, Smith shooting over the stone pile as the incoming fusillade of bullets slowly broke it apart. Recognizing that he had no time left, he sprang to his feet, raced for better cover, firing in the direction of the attack. He didn't last long. Red and white fragments of Cadet agent Smith exploded in all directions. It was—rather messy.

Jones flinched, visibly.

The General pressed a button and the screen went dark. Cadet agent Jones turned back to us, and went white.

"Marvelous what those new exploding bullets can do, isn't it?" he said. "And those little flechette things? Wow. Quite impressive."

I nodded. "And the micro-grenades, and Play-Doh C4. Very nicely modeled little unicorn pony that got tossed in at the end, there."

"Clarkson's work," said the General. "Agent 11. Quite a talent, that one. You should see her garden gnomes. Fiendish, yet adorable."

"You—you—you—" Cadet agent Jones had now turned a peculiar shade of green. "I—I—I—you—you—you—" she stammered.

"*Speak up, cadet agent Jones,*" snapped the General. "*Don't stammer and mumble!*"

"You've got to be kidding me!" gasped cadet agent Jones. "That was trick photography or something. You didn't really have that man blown to bits by exploding rifle bullets, flechettes, and exploding unicorns just because he flunked out of this program!" She paused and we all sat in the silence. "Did you?"

In unison, stone-faced, the General and I nodded.

"This is a rough, tough organization cadet agent Jones," the General said. "There's a reason it's called SADISTO, and not *WARM AND FUZZY!* From now on if you flunk, or if your Big Brother 8 here turns in an unfavorable report, you'll be assigned to the rifle range. As a target. Still want to stick with us? This is your last chance to back out. And I should warn you—now that he's sober, 8 here doesn't think you're cold-blooded enough to make the cut. He is, in fact, wanting to flunk you right now, before you can be killed for it, and I'm inclined to think he has a point. Still want to join us, cadet agent Jones?"

She glared at me, snake venom clouding her eyes, and took a deep breath. Her eyes darted back and forth from mine, to The General's, to mine again. Finally, she fixed me with an intense, bone-shriveling glare, straightened her shoulders and pushed out her expansive chest.

"Yes, sir," she said dramatically.

"Congratulations," said The General, shaking her hand. "Now, the first Ultra Secret disclosure I've made to you is the name of the organization to which you now belong, body and soul. *SADISTO*."

"Wow," she said, her eyes widening.

"She didn't know?" I asked with some surprise.

The General shook his head. "She and the other consorts knew only that they were being trained as *Fuckers for The Free World*. They even get these T-shirts with that slogan printed on them as a part of their orientation goodie-bags."

"Incredible," she said, "All this time I was trying to figure out if you might be the head of the FBI or the CIA or the CIC or Naval Intelligence or Army Intelligence or Air Force Intelligence or the Secret Service or the NSA—"

"Yes, yes," said the General, stopping the slop of alphabet soup, "I'm not."

"Or maybe the outfit they call the Wrecking Crew."

"No. They do similar work, but have no connection with us."

"Then for a while, I thought this was the Crushing Machine..."

"Nope. Also close, but not them."

"But, wow!" gasped cadet agent Jones. "This is—this is the *Security Administration Division of the Institute for Special Tactical Operations?*"

"Right-oh," said the General, smiling proudly. "You are as of this moment a partially-fledged member of SADISTO—an organization which, if I say so myself, ranks up there with, or above such offices as MI6. SMERSH. SPECTRE. SKRUNCH. GABA. SMARMY..."

"Yes, yes," agent Jones said, waving a delighted hand to stop the outpour of alphabet soup. "Me, little me—a partially-fledged member of the premiere killing organization, and highest paid of government agencies, SADISTO! And... we also get full medical and dental?”

“Of course!” The General and I said in unison.

“Oh, my God,” Juliet said, her eyes tearing up. “Oh, my GOD, I am *SO* happy!”

“Speaking of happy,” said The General, glancing at his wristwatch, “I almost forgot today is the day I play golf with **CENSORED.** Important political bonding time with the leader of The Free World. I’d best be off. You two may use my office for the rest of the day.” He winked. “Don’t get oil on everything.”

I nodded, cadet agent Jones saluted, The General grabbed his golf bag, and stepped into the elevator. Once the doors had closed, Juliet turned and smiled at me adoringly.

“So, what do you want me to do first, Trevor?” she asked.

“What else?” I said. “Strip.”

CHAPTER 8

"STRIP? RIGHT HERE?" Cadet agent Jones asked, giggling. "I thought he was kidding with that 'don't get oil on everything' comment. You want me to get naked right here. In the actual General's actual office?"

"I do. Yes," I said. "This is your first training session."

She cocked her head, her sarcastic smile curling up, and raised an eyebrow. "Getting naked is training?"

"Absolutely," I said.

She stepped back and looked around the office, taking in the plaques, the trophies, the small collectibles, the plastic trolls with wild hair, and the multiple bottles of baby oil. I watched with anticipation as she moved slowly around the room, studying, lightly touching, absorbing.

Finally, she stopped and turned to look at me directly, scowling slightly, as if assessing my sincerity. After a moment or two, she softened, and smiled.

Eyes never leaving mine, she slowly lifted her shirt in front until her chest chubbies slipped free of the thin fabric. FUCK ME logo bunched atop their smooth sensuousness, she leaned forward onto the General's desk, and mashed them down on his desktop blotter. Still focused on me, she reached back to slider the shorts off her ass, exposing its magnificent curves, and the inviting space between I so adored.

"Then train me, Trevor, right here, on the General's desk," she whispered, "Shove that thick cock of yours deep into my ignorant pussy, and teach it what it needs most to know."

My brain melted more than a little. What was left of it was already planning to takie her up on that request, and almost against my will, I even bent down to kiss each of her lusciously smooth hemispheres. But instead of following the kisses with something firmer, I pulled her shorts back up over those rounded orbs of delight, and lifted her off the desk to face me.

"In good time," I said. "You see, cadet agent Jones, I am now your Big Brother, which is an immense responsibility. It negates our previous agent-slash-girl-who-sleeps-with-agents relationship as it is now my obligation to guide, train, and instruct you in the ways of SADISTO. Of being an *agent* of SADISTO. And one of the first things you need to learn is how to remove your clothes... seductively."

"Um..." Jones said, playfully, "... okay. But I don't mind stripping and just getting right to it, you know. In fact, I'm a little horny."

"You're a lot horny," I said. "But humor me."

She looked at me as if I was the stupidest thing on the face of the earth.

"All right," she sighed. "If you insist."

"I do."

She gripped the top of her short-shorts, began moving them down again, slowly, seductively, taking a sultry step toward me, smiling with that charming, sarcastic flicker at the corner of her lips.

"Agent 8," she said, "teach me the proper way to grip the boss's desk to best get drilled from behind."

"No, no, no," I said. "I mean, yes. But no. This is more than just you and me making love in fun, forbidden places."

She stopped undressing, and scowled. "It is?"

"It is," I said. "It's about having sex with someone you don't know, in all kinds of possibly unpleasant places. Please continue... seductively."

"As if you're someone else?"

"Someone you don't know," I said, "and maybe don't like, but have to *pretend* to like."

"I have to pretend I don't like you, but act as if I do like you, which is different from *actually* liking you... how?"

"It's... um... different in that you're pretending... that you... in that you... because you don't like me, but need to act as if... it's a performance thing. Method acting. That's it. I need to see you method acting... but not see you acting, because that would give you away."

"This is so weird," she said, cocking an eyebrow.

"This is *training*," I said. "You have to do things you've never done before, and act as if you're comfortable with it.

"Trevor," she said, as if speaking to a small child. Which I am *not!* "I **have** done this before! I was waiting naked in a stranger's room to let him have whatever kind of crazy sex he wanted to have with me on my first night here, and when you walked in pushing a tray of food, I acted as if you were the most amazing thing I'd ever seen,"

"Wait," I said, my mind muddling. "Wasn't I?"

"No," she said, the corner of her mouth turning up. "You were cute, but for all I know you wanted to beat me to death with chains, and rape my corpse."

"Eew," I said.

"And I approached you seductively, and without fear."

"Hadn't thought about it like that," I admitted.

"And then you took the time to make **me** cum, and caress **me**, and talk to **me** like a person, make me laugh, and have fun, and even walk around the neighborhood naked, and it wasn't until **then** that I started to like you."

"But... I thought you liked me right from the beginning."

She grinned that charming grin, again.

"Because I already know how to do what you're asking me to do," she said, her eyes shimmering with knowing confidence.

She lifted her shirt in front revealing her smooth, silken belly, her lovely dimple of a navel. She smoothed a hand across it, slid it upward, under the hem of the cloth, pushing the fabric slowly until her luscious lobes again fell free, bounding joyfully, delectably, delightfully into view.

She released the shirt, licked her forefingers and rubbed them over her nipples, sliding the fingertips around, and around, down, then off, so that the pink buds popped suddenly out at me, nipples and areolas firmly erect.

"Boop," she said.

Next, leaving the shirt bunched atop her massive mounds, she slowly finished sliding her shorts down over her thighs, revealing the delicate fur of blonde between her legs.

"Oh—goodness me—did I forget my panties?" she said, turning slowly, bending provocatively, to best display the golden tan that covered her bare behind. "And look at that. Nothing back there, either. Not even a tan-line. How did *that* happen? Was I sunning outdoors, again, completely nude? Naughty me."

I felt the front of my pants tighten.

"Goodness," she said, genuine joy in her voice, or genuinely acting genuine joy—I was no longer sure which. She whirled her hips, and amazing ass around in very slow circles. "It does appear I am undressing seductively enough to make you *very* hard."

She turned away, and hopped backward toward me, extending her ass, pressing those fantastically fleshy fundomes firmly on either side of my elongating erection, swirling her hips in a rhythmic circle that had a spectacular effect on my hormones and cardiovascular health.

"Oh," I said.

"Oh," she mimicked, looking back at me over her shoulder, feigning surprise with wide eyes, and rounded mouth like a Gil Elvgren painting gone very bad. "Is that a gun in your pocket, Agent 8, or are you just glad to see me?"

"Yes," I said.

"Well, why don't you pull out your... big *gun*... and show it to me?" she said.

I quickly opened my fly, shoved my pants and boxers down, and let agent 8 and a quarter spring forth to rest in the warm groove of her ass.

"Goodness, how ready you are," she said, with a tantalizing butt-wiggle and a smile.

Juliet abruptly stepped away, pulled her shorts back up, her shirt back down, and turned on me, having covered almost everything that I was currently most interested in.

"See?" she asked. "I can do that even when I don't want to."

"You don't want to?" I asked, petulantly.

"No," she said, taking things—or rather 'thing'—in hand, "but it gets your attention, and makes you more willing to tell me things I want to know. Is that what this training is supposed to be about? If so tell me why you didn't want me to become an agent… when—over the past several nights while we were naked, coupled, in bed—you *absolutely* wanted me to become an agent?"

"I did?" I asked.

"Our very first night together," she replied, pouting, "you told me you dreamt of a home in Upper Westchester, with beautifully groomed lawns, beautifully groomed children… but that you couldn't find a woman who understood you, who could accept your past as a murderous, paid, highly-skilled assassin working for the betterment of The Free World, especially after you got blood on them. Which seemed oddly specific."

"Clearly," I said, "I talk too much when drunk."

"No, no, not at all," she said, coming closer, putting an arm around my waist, as her free hand continued to stroke my throbbing little agent gently—lovingly. "You were expressing your pain. A pain of loneliness that I understand all too well. It's why we decided—together—that I should become an agent alongside you. So someone *could* understand you. Accept you. *Love* you. Eventually marry you and give you three point two children. Or maybe four *whole* children."

"I…" I said. "What?"

"You wanted us to share this SADISTO life together, Trevor," she said, stroking me faster, making it focus to hard. No. Wait. Making it hard to focus. "Totally. Completely. And then when our careers were done—*if* we survived—we would transition into that other life you spoke so deliriously of… and even though I had always imagined a life alone on a tropical island where I could always be warm, safe, and serene, I began to share your dream of family, children, and a house filled with love until over the course of a few drunken nights it became a dream we *both* wanted," she leaned up, and kissed my lips as if they were the most delicious fruit she'd ever been offered, and lust-whispered, "the dream we both want so very badly."

"And…" I asked, more than a little surprised, "you *liked* the idea?"

"Of course," she said, nibbling my lower lip. "Didn't you?"

"I'm…" I said, "not sure."

"You *were* drunk. Really drunk. But I was there, and Gran captured it all on tape. You did… and you still do," she said, ardor filling the turquoise pools of her eyes, blood filling the fleshy pink of my cock.

I leaned down and kissed her passionately. Deeply. Surrenderingly.

Suddenly she pushed me away, and—disappointingly—let go of my stiffy. Hard-y. Rock solid-y.

"So teach me, Agent 8," she said, the sultry in her voice making me sweat rivers. "Bend me over this desk and school me in the ways of SADISTO love so that we can fulfill that dream."

"I…" I said.

She reached back and slowly slid her shorts down to her ankles and kicked them aside, turning that beautiful, bountiful bare backside toward me, rubbing its softness against my hardness.

"You didn't want The General to know that you loved me," she said, her voice a melodic purr, "even though you do."

"I…" I repeated.

"Slip inside me, Trevor, so you can remember how good it feels. Use the General's baby oil."

I took the bottle and popped it open expertly, squirted it along my length, spread it evenly, then gripped myself, aimed, and did as she had requested.

"Oooooh," she said, shuddering a bit with pleasure. "That's good, Trevor. Now, let's practice making those three point two children."

I began to move, very slowly, and thought how incredible it would be.

"Oooh," I said. "Yeees…"

"Now think about PTA meetings," she moaned, "barbecues with neighbors, beautiful spring nights on our patio under the stars and a full moon… just like this, with your dick inside me."

"Oh, my God, yes," I said, "I want it so bad…"

She gripped the desk drawer handles, as I leaned into her, our hips moving in heavenly rhythm, until one of the drawers popped open, spilling its contents onto the floor.

"Oops," she said, and as we stopped to examine the mess she accidentally pulled loose another drawer.

"Oh, oops, again!" she said, laughing, as its contents fluttered around the room.

Coming out of my fog, I realized what was happening, and how bad it could be. I yanked myself out of her, and stepped back.

"What are you doing?" she said, her voice almost pleading. "I was enjoying that. Weren't you? Why did you want me to strip, if not to do that?"

"No, that's..." I stammered, shaking my head to recover myself. "I mean, yes, but not for... I'm... I'm not finished teaching you other things, first."

"Ooh? Do tell."

"First we have to clean up this mess," I said, and bent to gather the spilled contents of the drawer. She knelt beside me, and grabbed my hands.

"You'll get baby oil on everything," she said, smiling that maddening smile. "Let me do it. I made the mess. I should clean it up."

She gathered the contents and began replacing them, but stopped when she saw a folder marked, "UTLRA COSMIC ALIEN AUTOPSY TOP SECRET." She opened it, and her eyes seemed to go blank. She stared at it silently for a surprisingly long while, until I began to think something was wrong.

I snatched the folder away, no longer worrying about baby oil, opened it, and looked at whatever she had seen. It was the photo of a dead Madame Phu on the bedroom floor where I'd left her, with a felt pen note scrawled across it by some unknown hand; "what we do, we do for the greater good."

I slapped the folder closed, and shoved it into the drawer, bending it a little in the process.

"That's too high a clearance for a cadet agent," I said.

She looked at me with that same, blank expression, and stared.

"Agent 8, Trevor Hawke," she said, almost mechanically.

"I..." I said, confused. "Yes...?"

"I want to suck your dick," she said, also mechanically, and fairly leapt at my crotch. Her mouth was around me so fast I nearly fainted.

"No!" I said, more harshly than I meant to, grabbing her arms and pulling her back upright. She stared at me, confused, then her eyes seemed to clear, and her sarcastic grin returned.

Abruptly her face scrunched up, and her lips smacked together like she was tasting evil.

"What the fuck?" she asked, and spit in the waste basket. "Is that baby oil? How did that get in my mouth?"

I grabbed a tissue from a box on the desk and handed her several. She wiped out her mouth and tossed the tissues, too. Then she turned and smiled at me, with the kind of lving warmth you only see on children, and women you've just made orgasm.

"You love me," she said. "Come on. Admit it. Don't you?"

"What?" I said, trying to gather thoughts. My thoughts. Her thoughts. Someone's thoughts. Any thoughts at all, really.

How was her mind bouncing around so much? And making mine bounce right along with it?

She leaned in and kissed me with such soft, warm, intense passion that it surprised me. I felt... Perfect. Loved. Whole.

And it had to stop.

I pushed her away from me, replaced the drawer, stood, and moved us both away from the desk.

"Is there more you want to teach me?" she asked, charmingly.

I looked her up and down, wondering what had just happened? Why it had happened? Was it just an accident, or was this something more?

At the same time, I felt a desperation to kiss her again, put my cock back inside her and talk about Westchester, children... love... *so much so that I suddenly **slapped** myself! It had to stop!*

Juliet was startled.

"Why did you do that?" She asked, sincere concern in her eyes.

"Just..." I said, not sure what to say to her, "I have to mentor. Not participate."

"But... you were teaching me *seduction*," she said, trying to be helpful. "Isn't this the logical conclusion to seduction?"

"What did you see in that folder?" I asked.

"What folder?"

"The... the one in the drawer," I said.

She looked around, and didn't see whatever she was searching for.

"What drawer?" she asked.

I just stared at her. Blankly. More blankly than a piece of paper a writer has to fill with the opening page of a novel he's already been paid for.

"You were teaching me seduction," she said, again, "and we were talking about how I wanted to be an agent by your side so we could make a life together, and he…" she pointed to my erection, "was inside of me. Why did you pull out?"

What had happened? Had something in the folder made her forget? Something she wasn't supposed to see? Some kind of protective device within the folder that had erased a few minutes of her memory?

"Trevor," she said. "Is something wrong? Teach me, so I don't fail. Even if… even if you don't love me, and it doesn't work between us…" she paused, and her eyes reddened, and dampened. "Whatever happens, I don't want to fail, and duh…"

She began to tear up. A woman's tears, a man's kryptonite.

"No, no," I said, profound empathy rising to the surface from somewhere very deep inside, surprising even me. "You won't fail. I'm here for you. We'll get through this."

She stopped crying, smiled through her tears, and gave me a quick kiss.

"Then teach me," she said, lightly touching my cock.

"Okay," I said, unsure where to go next, biting a lip, and mulling. "Sooo… em…let me think of how to explain this. I don't usually have a … um… relationship with my cadet-agents, so they just do what I say, but this is… well… you."

She smiled, and stroked me tenderly. "It is me."

"So, it's basically like this;" I said, "a male agent fights with—you know—guns, knives, hand grenades, feet, fists, and occasionally spoons, if they're all that's handy, a female agent's most dangerous weapon against a man is…" her tears, I thought, but instead I said… "her body, because men are basically stupid. They assume every woman in the world wants them sexually, even when no woman in the world would want them sexually, not in a million years. As I believed when you approached me that first time in my room."

"Oh," she said, apparently hearing the hurt in my voice, her inner eyebrows rising with empathy. "Sorry. I mean… I actually did think you were handsome, but… I surprised myself, honestly. I don't even know where that seductive side came from. I'd always been such a good girl, before Singapodia."

"Wait," I said, realizing this was another hint she had dropped about her past. "You were in Singapodia?"

"I don't want to talk about it," she said.

Her words had a deeply painful finality to them, and although I wanted to know—wanted to insist on knowing—I let it go.

"Okay," I said, the tone of my voice expressing my wish that she would talk, but that I understood. "You only have to share what's comfortable for you. We all have our history filled with secrets. I have a brother I don't like to talk about. So..."

"No you don't," she grinned. "You said that just to make me not feel guilty about keeping my secrets."

"No," I said. "I don't have that empathy gene. And it doesn't matter. Wherever you learned to seduce a man—and why—it's all right. You're just ahead in the agenting game."

She studied me a moment, and then smiled again, absently rubbing my erect tip, and nodding thanks.

"Because no matter how attractive the woman," I continued, "with but the slightest encouragement on your part, cadet agent Jones, the ugliest man in the world can—and will—believe that you would actually be thrilled to touch him naked. *That* is your power. And you must *use* that power. You must learn to think of your body as an array of weapons.

"Lips as bombs," I went on, "set to go off on a man's... well... everything lips can touch; fingers as venomous spider legs that can crawl over his most sensitive parts, and inject poison into them; breasts as deadly torpedoes pointed at the enemies of The Free World."

"Wow," said cadet agent Jones. "I was just using what I've got to get out of the gutter, and maybe earn some bigger tips. But I feel much more powerful, all of a sudden!"

I remembered back to the van, and the intense woman in its darkened back. Pieces falling together.

"Precisely because you are," I said, pleased that she felt she could share a bit more, thrilled that I had gotten us away from tears, and off the topic of 'love'. "And just as a real torpedo cannot explode until it makes actual contact with the ship it will sink, so a deadly female agent cannot explode into lethal action until her torpedoes—I mean breasts—I mean body—is pressed against the unsuspecting body of her victim."

"That is so cool!" cried cadet agent Jones.

"And," I continued, "just as a male agent may have to use *his* weapons many times before he reaches his terminal target, so must a female agent be ready to use her luscious body many times to reach hers. Like, for instance, suppose you were assigned the job of killing—oh, let's say completely randomly—a South American general who isn't gay."

"Yes sir," said cadet agent Jones, saluting, which made her bare breasts bounce sublimely.

"At ease. Now, how would you go about getting close to him—close enough to kill? To show me this, my dick cannot be in you."

"Oooooh," she said, disappointed. "That's why. Okay. Professional. Not personal. I'm getting it, now."

She stepped back from me, eyes never leaving mine, pulled the shirt bunched atop her breasts completely off, tossing it aside. Her bare breasts bounce-bobbled beatifically, giving off a holy glow, then flopped and swayed wildly as she abruptly bent to remove first one shoe, then the other, and fling them over her shoulder. Something broke on a shelf behind her.

"Oops," she said, giggling.

Cadet agent Jones, formerly On-Call-Girl Juliet Jones, now stood before me, fully nude and good lord, she had a body built for espionage. Magnificent was the only word for her. Especially her breasts. Neither perfect spheres, nor half domes, her breasts were a soaring symphony of compound curves, up-swirling, up-tilted arcs. They looked and acted as if they'd never heard of gravity, as if they were consciously defying the pull of the Earth.

Breathtaking.

Mouthwatering.

Breasts to make a man's palms itch, his fingers tingle, his teeth grind.

Magnificent.

Desirable.

Alluring.

And all belonging to me... I mean... all belonging to the forces of The Free World.

"Glunk glunk glunk glunk?" she asked, or perhaps replied. I'm not sure.

"What?" I asked.

"Eyes up here, Trevor," she said, pointing to her own turquoise gems, grinning that charming, sarcastic grin. "I said I get it. Fine. We're role-playing. I don't know you; you don't know me. Can I pretend I'm still dressed? I'm sort of done with the on/off 'strip' thing."

"Sure," I said. "You did the 'strip' bit quite well."

"Your dick certainly thinks so."

"But now I need to see how eloquently you can speak with your body to reach a potential target."

"Um… I'm *naked*," she said, clearly confused. "I'm hot. I have big tits. You're already hard. Your dick is so red it's glowing like Rudolph's nose, and Santa needs your help. But you're asking me to do—what? More foreplay?"

"Remember," I said, sighing. "Think of me as an ugly South American general. Who isn't gay, but who isn't interested in you… yet."

"I'm naked, and hot, but he isn't interested in me… yet?"

"Correct."

"But he's *not* gay?"

"Not gay. Or hard. Or knows what you feel like naked, in bed. And that's why he's hard. Why I'm hard. But he wouldn't be."

"Are you sure," she asked.

"I'm not sure of anything!" I snapped. "You keep confusing me! Just go with it! Or would you rather I brought a real, live, fat, hairy, ugly old General in here for you to actually seduce?"

"I'm pretty sure he'd already be seduced by now," she said, scrunching her nose and eyes. "Positive, actually."

"Want me to find one so you can prove it, or keep practicing on me?"

She lowered her eyes. "Keep practicing on you."

"Okay!" I said. "So, I'm a not hard, not gay, South American general who is suspicious of you because you just got naked in his office for no particular reason! Seduce me! God! This whole exercise works better when the cadet agent mentee doesn't know me."

"So, you've done this before…" she said, bristling a little, "with *other* cadet-agents? Cadet-agent women, I suppose?"

"I have," I said. "And when they're doing this, they have to pretend—or act—because they don't know me any more than they'd know the South American General, but because you do, things are getting weird."

"Well," she said, obviously still irritated, "seems my body has spoken eloquently enough. So, now he would proposition me, I'd undress him, lie him back on his office floor, take hold of his surprisingly large, and weighty cock," she took hold of mine, again, roughly, I 'eeped,' "and then I'd **kill him with a point-blank karate chop to his throat.**"

Still holding me, with her free hand she pretended to chop my throat, and cried, "HI-**YA!**"

I laughed, and shook my head. "It would never be as simple as *that*, cadet agent Jones."

"It wouldn't?"

"Oh, no," I said. "South American generals important enough to be worth killing just aren't that approachable. They're suspicious of everyone. No, you'd find your target hidden at the geometric center of a major military complex, protected by dozens of armed guards. To reach him you'd have to go through several layers of protection, starting with the main gate. And you know what you'd find there?"

She put her hands on her hips, and was clearly annoyed. "You keep changing the rules! You just said I was in his office, already!"

"Just go with it!" I said. "What would you find at the main gate?"

She groaned long, deep, and gravelly.

"So, now I'm not naked, and I'm back at the main gate?"

"Yes," I said.

"I feel like I just slid all the way back to square one in a bad game of *Sorry*."

"What do you find at the gate?" I asked, ignoring her petulance.

"A guard?" she said, knowing it was obvious.

"Correct," I said. "Armed and dangerous. And he'd tell you to halt and state your business. Instead of halting, though, you'd continue undulating slowly toward him."

"Fine!" She stepped back, and undulated slowly toward me, her full breasts also undulating. My penis began to leak.

"And," I continued, noting that my breathing had deepened, and words came with difficulty, "when he asked you your business, you'd wink at him and tell him you *were* the business—that you're a professional girl. But he's so handsome, and so virile, and you like him so much that he can be on your freebie list. So, what happens next?"

"He tears off my clothes, drags me into the sentry box, throws me over his control console, and shoves his *huge* cock *deep* inside me as I scream and beg for more?"

Was it just me, or had this hypothetical gone in an unexpected direction?

"Okay, that works," I said, noting the flush in her cheeks. "Sort of. But remember, cadet agent Jones, all this will be taking place in some humid, backwater, fever-ridden banana republic. The sentry on duty won't be a young, clean-cut type; he will be large, muscular..."

"Oh, God, so muscular..." she said in almost a whisper, as if visualizing a naked Clark Gable.

"... hulkingly muscular," I whispered back as her face drew close to mine.

"Pecs like mountains..."

"... an illiterate peon, unwashed, sweaty, smelly, barefoot, hairy and primitive."

She shivered. "Like Marlon Brando in *Viva Zapata*, only hairier," her voice fell to become very nearly inaudible. "God, I want him so bad."

"Don't romanticize," I snipped. "The sentry would only be the beginning of your... *ordeal*. Soon the corporal of the guard would stop by to check the sentry's box. He'd undoubtedly decide you were too good to be wasted on a mere sentry, and he'd take you off to his quarters, his *private* quarters..."

"A tall, dark-skinned corporal of the guard, ripped, and lean, and weighted down with an *enormous* cock," she said, her breath hot on my face.

"Well," I said, "let's not get carried away..."

"And after we got there, he'd spread my legs and plumb my depths two, three, four times, finally pulling out so he could titty-fuck me, and cum—hot and sticky, all over my huge, hungry tits. And after he was spent, he'd hand me over to his sweaty, short, slightly chubby, but kind of adorable, bearded sergeant who—surprisingly—also had a massively, thick dong. And after he was done letting me squat on that fat tree stump between his legs while playing with his beard, he'd pass me on to his albino lieutenant; a man with long, soft, white hair, piercing, violet eyes, and a thick, smooth, banana curved, snow-white cock that was sleek and long—"

"Yeah, yeah," I said, annoyed. "This isn't 'sex with the dwarves, and elves' from *Lord of The Rings*, this is government seduction training! No need to be quite so detailed. And there aren't that many large penises among our enemies. That's why they're evil. Small dicks make them irritable. The point is: you'd have to ravish your way up the entire chain of small-dick command."

"Oh, darn," she said, licking her lips. "What a struggle, being an agent."

"Right. But most times you won't be satisfied, or get *any* pleasure from it. Until at long last…"

"*Long* last…"

"I said, 'NO pleasure'… at long last you would get into a position to seduce and destroy your target, the general. Then you can hai-ya him. Now, cadet agent Jones, do you see why I want to know how well you can strip?"

"I can't imagine learning anything more important," she said. "I'll never question your orders again, Trev—I mean Agent 8—never!"

"Okay, then, enough training," I said, grabbing the baby oil. "Go ahead and bend over the General's desk."

"Yes, sir, Agent 8, sir!" She said with a smile and quick salute, throwing herself across the desk blotter, lifting that exquisite bare ass, and spreading her legs as I approached.

CHAPTER 9

I MADE A POINT of not getting drunk. I wanted to stare at my naked Juliet while she slept. Was it possible for a woman to feel so much love for a man after such a brief relationship?

Not according to my instincts.

She seemed so perfect for me.

Too perfect.

Her eyes, her face, her body, her *joie de vivre*, her lusty openness, her ass, her tits. She'd even agreed to a life in Westchester after not really wanting to. My dog loved her, and slept beside her even though I didn't want him to. She was flexible, and open to my needs and desires. No woman I've moved past the 'fun fucking' stage and into the 'actual relationship' stage has ever been open to my needs and desires. Not even the one I married. Something was clearly wrong, here.

Her explanations all seemed legitimate. And her affection for me seemed genuine. But when you've been an agent as long as I have, you have to question anyone this beautiful, sweet, and charming who says they love you for who you are—especially who I am—and wants to spend a life with you.

She'd spent time in Singapodia. Perhaps as a captive? Perhaps being brainwashed as a spy? Molded into a mole within SADISTO. Was she the great Madame Phu plot I had been sent to discover?

Besides inexplicably loving me, there was also the odd behavior earlier, 'accidentally' knocking open drawers, and then her strange reaction to that folder. I decided I had to bring this up to the old man, and find out for myself what was in that folder and what might have been revealed to cause Juliet's strange reaction.

I pushed Binkley aside, he growled at me, I growled back, and I bent down to my sleeping beauty so I could kiss the nipple closest to me goodbye. She 'purred' appreciatively, so I sucked it to plump life, circled its tip with my tongue, then did the same for the other as she 'mmmd' and squirmed slightly. Her legs opened again, and I bent down to kiss that, goodbye, as well.

"Ooooh, Trevor," she said, sleepily.

"I have to go speak to The General," I whispered, and I felt her hands on the back of my head, fingers gripping my hair.

"Not yet, you don't," she said smiling, eyes still closed. "You started this; you need to finish."

It occurred to me that at this late hour I really shouldn't disturb The General. He'd probably prefer I waited until tomorrow.

And Juliet definitely would.

8   8   8

Later—much later—waking up on the General's desk, slathered in baby oil, I looked around for my mentee, and said, "All right, cadet agent Jones—"

"Trevor," she urged, closing one of the General's cabinets. "Call me Juliet. We've been intimate for almost a week. Anyone with that kind of detailed knowledge of my pussy gets to call me Juliet."

"Yeah, all right... Juliet," I said, rubbing my eyes and wishing for coffee, wondering why she was going through The General's cabinets. "At least when we're alone." I cleared my throat. "What are you doing?"

"Looking for something to drink," she said. "Something caffeinated, and non-alcoholic, which doesn't seem to exist in this room." She turned and smiled that maddening, enticing, electrifying smile at me, her relatively light-skinned nakedness standing out starkly against the dark wood of The General's cabinetry. "I'm still on duty."

"Indeed," I said. "And the time has come for me to test you."

"Oh! Well, I'm ready, my darling! I mean 'my General!'" she cried, bounding over quickly, snuggling her naked, golden body close to mine, knocking various things off the desk. Important things, probably. Breakable things. "But what haven't you tested already?"

"I'm not talking about seduction, or more sex," I said, disentangling myself from her grasp and standing to don my clothes. "I'm talking about your capabilities as an agent of SADISTO."

"Oooooh," Juliet said, disappointed. "But we didn't get to finish playing seduce the muscular hairy guard in the guard shack."

"Another time."

She sat up, saluting. "Yes sir."

"Nix on the saluting," I ordered. "Agents can't salute in the field for obvious reasons, so don't get into the habit."

"No sir," she said, stopping short of saluting a second time, resting on her haunches and watching me dress. "Shall I put on my shorts and T-shirt?"

"No," I said. "Most of your work, your *close* work, will be performed while nude, so cadet agents are supposed to get comfortable living, socializing, and operating while unclad."

"Yes, sir," she said.

I stared at her for a moment. Waiting.

"No objections?" I asked.

"No," she said. "Why would I object?"

"Because we'll be going all over the SADISTO offices. Agents in the past often find that intimidating, and complain."

"I find it kind of sexy," she said, pushing out her chest, which made her breasts move in exciting ways. "I like to be naked, in case you hadn't noticed."

She placed her hands on her hips, and shook those magnificent tits, making them flop in multiple directions, and my mind flopped with them.

She giggled.

"Especially because you like my titties," she said, teasingly.

"I like all of you," I said, carefully zipping up my pants over an already returning erection.

"But you *particularly* like my titties," she laughed, rotating her torso to flop them around again. "Say it! Come on! Saaaaaay it!"

"Okay, yes, I especially like your titties."

She jumped up and ran over to throw her arms around my neck, beaming up into my face with a joy so radiant it nearly blinded me.

"I'm glad," she announced.

I stared into that lovely face, those entrancing eyes…

"And your eyes," I said. "I've never seen anything so beautiful as those transcendent, turquoise eyes."

I could see her melt a little. She rested her head against my chest.

"Let's get that house in Westchester. Let's get started making those three point two children as soon as possible, okay?"

I returned her embrace. "Okay."

"I knew you really loved me," she said, squeezing me tightly, a smile warming her voice. "Even when you weren't drunk."

I reluctantly stepped out of her embrace, and finished dressing, studying Juliet critically as I did. She would be a perfect wife—to someone. But something was off since the drawer incident, and if it all turned out to be completely innocent, even then, could she ever really be a wife to a dedicated agent of SADISTO? Survive being a dedicated agent of SADISTO, herself? She was great at seduction, but there was more to being an agent. So much more, and not all of it as fun as fucking strangers.

I sighed and shook my head.

"Why did you sigh and shake your head, my General?" She had started pronouncing General with a terrible Spanish accent as 'Hghen-er-al', as if she were coughing up a hairball in a Spanish-speaking adjacent country, mischief glinting instantly in her eyes.

"Because," I said, "I hate to think of losing you when you fail."

"*What?* **When** I fail?" she asked. "*You expect me to fail?*"

"Very few agents make it to the finish line, Juliet. I'll tell you one thing though; if I possibly can I'll see that you're sent straight to the rifle range."

She swallowed hard. "To be used as a—as a target?"

I nodded. "But I'll get you a quick death. Dum-dum bullets. Flame-throwers or poisoned darts or something highly explosive; whatever most violent is being practiced or tested at the time."

"You're so good to me," she said, sarcastically, but without her cute little grin. "You're going to make this body that you can't get enough of a target—*as a favor?* And you're fine with that?"

I nodded. "Agents die. Cadet agents die. And worse things could happen," I said, "even if you don't flunk."

"Like what, for instance?" she asked angrily.

"Well, you could get assigned to Advanced Interrogation as a victim. Subject, I mean. Interrogation subject. You know what goes on in that course?"

She shook her head.

"It's kind of like *What's My Secret*, but if you lose, you don't go home."

"But—why wouldn't the 'victim'—which sounds more accurate—tell their secret right away, just to avoid being tortured?"

"Because the victim doesn't *know* any secrets."

Juliet gasped, "So, in that case the victim would be—well, they'd just be tortured to death!"

I smiled sadly at her naiveté. "And then whoever is torturing you would make a bad pun about it. The organization *is* called SADISTO."

"And you just know I'm going to fail."

I said nothing. Only stared at her.

She stared back at me for a long time, challenging me silently to blink first, eyes like tiny turquoise blue egg yolks surrounded by lots of extra whites, nostrils flared, just breathing deeply, her naked breasts rising and falling slowly. I could have watched her do that for hours.

"Thanks for the confidence, Trevor. Is that the real reason you're distancing yourself form me all the time? Don't want to be too attached when I get questioned to death?"

"We call it maximal interrogation," I said, "but basically, you're right. The student torturer—I mean interrogator—isn't judged by whether or not he or she learns the secret, which is impossible anyhow, of course, but by the skill and technique with which he or she tortures—I mean interrogates—his or her assigned victim."

"And the victim learns…?"

"If you can think like a torturer, you can know what to expect as the torturee."

Juliet considered this.

"You'll learn them soon enough," I said. "When you're flunked, that is. And I'm pretty sure I'm going to have to flunk you, Juliet. You don't have the killer attitude."

"*I do!*" she pleaded. "*I'm really a killer at heart. Really! Grrrrr! GrrrRRRrrrRR!* James Bond and Matt Helm were my idols! Since I was a girl, I've always wanted to shoot and stab people for the betterment of The Free World. Always. But my mom wouldn't let me."

"Maybe so," I sneered, "but reading about killing an enemy, and *actually* killing an enemy, are two *very* different things. Sometimes, Juliet, an agent has to wade through blood to reach his or her objective."

Again, she swallowed hard, but tried to hide it.

"I'm ready, General, sir," said Juliet, hairballing the name, refraining from saluting only with obvious effort. "I'll shoew you. I have what it takes!"

I sighed. "All right, still cadet agent Juliet. Follow me."

"Yes sir. Where are we going, sir?"

"Obstacle Course. Floor Twelve."

8   8   8

I led the way down a busy corridor, my naked student pacing alongside me. Beautifully sculpted, jiggling firmly, alluringly, she drew a lot of attention. A couple other agents passed by with naked cadets of their own, and we acknowledged one another with curt nods that said; 'I feel your pain.'

"*Jones?*" A woman wearing a FUCK ME T-Shirt said to Juliet in astonishment. "You got out of Call-Girl Central, and into the *Agent Program? AND* they put you with Agent 8? Gaaawd. You lucky bitch!"

Juliet grinned a pleased grin, straightened up, shoulders back, firm breasts out, hardened nipples proudly pointing skyward. I also grinned at the young Call-Girl—SADISTO certainly recruited the most voluptuous ones—and gently patted Jones's lovely bare ass. Yes, she *was* a lucky bitch. I hoped she stayed lucky.

We reached the elevator, waited as the doors opened, and a female agent with a nude twenty-something boy in tow exited. He ogled Jones with each step, a sadistic grin spreading over his entire body as he studied her up and down from yellow-gold hair, to yellow-gold hair. Almost instantly his long is penis went from flaccid, to extremely full and erect.

"Oh," Said Juliet, "That's a nice one." She turned to me. "Do we have time to…"

"With another cadet?" I said, as if she'd asked to wear my dirty underpants. On her head. "No, we do not."

The boy's cadet agent-handler scowled, grabbed him by his cadet agent-handle, and jerked him down the corridor. And not in the good way.

"Control yourself," she snapped.

Elevator now empty we entered and Juliet stood silently beside me as we whizzed our way up to twelve. I led the way out. A withered, cruel-faced old man was sitting at a desk studying a racing sheet.

"Anybody using the Obstacle Course, Hans?" I asked him.

He shook his head, spat expertly into a nearby wastepaper basket, then let his eyes slither all over Juliet.

"Not a soul, 8," Hans grumbled. "You and your cadet-in-training kin go right on in. Heh, heh, heh! Nice titties. Kin I touch?"

He wiggled his fingers toward Juliet, and she stepped back.

"No," Juliet said, then looked nervously at me. "He can't, can he?"

"Not if you don't want him to," I said. "It wouldn't be considered part of your training."

"Then I *don't* want him to," she said, defiantly at him.

"Yer loss," he said, chuckled again, then went back to his racing sheet. "I'll get 'em later, though."

"What an obnoxious old man," Juliet whispered as we walked toward the door that led to the course. "What did he mean by that?"

"He means if you get killed," I explained, "he'll have access to your body. Or whatever parts are left intact. He's already decided which ones he wants, apparently."

"Don't let him! Please, Trevor! If all that's left of me is a nipple, I don't want that creepy old fuck anywhere near it!"

"All right," I said. "I promise. He won't."

"Who is he, anyway? Why doesn't someone fire him?"

"He's *Caretaker of the Obstacle Course*," I whispered back. "The General would prefer a better class of operator but, well, honestly, anyone with the job of *Caretaker of the Obstacle Course* would eventually go insane, anyway. Better to have someone who's already comfortably settled into his mental instability."

"You know," called out the withered old caretaker, looking up again, and staring at Jones' departing ass. "Yer a real looker from all sides, girlie! What state 're you from?"

Juliet stopped, and looked with fear from him to me.

"You can tell him," I said. "Believe it or not, he's cleared for Ultra Secret."

"Wes—" she stopped, and glanced at me, as if making sure it was all right to continue. I nodded, and she continued. "Wis... consin," she said.

"Wis-*con*-sin? Why dag-burnit that's wunnerful! I don't have a Wisconsin in my collection! If she don't complete the Obstacle Course, 8, I'll want her head, too. If there's anything left of it."

Juliet grasped my arm, and I patted her hand, gently, shaking my head. Then I gave a thumbs up to Hans, who gurgle-chuckled, and went back to his form. Juliet said nothing but her eyes widened, and she made a strange gurgling sound of her own as I led her toward a sliding door.

"Keep your head down, young lady!" called the caretaker, cackling evilly. "I sure wouldn't want nothin', to happen to it! Heh, heh, heh! Damn! It's so pretty. Heh, heh, heh. They make some lookers in Wis-CON-sin."

I slid the door shut behind us, shutting out the sound of his cackling voice.

"What a horrible human being," gasped Juliet. "He—he doesn't really have a collection of girls' heads, does he?"

I shrugged... "Some people collect bottle caps... some collect baseball cards. Heads are no sillier, as far as I'm concerned. The girls don't need them anymore."

"Not mine!"

"Don't worry, Juliet. Not yours. But you might ant to reconsider your first lesson, and think what you'd do if youhad to strip, and seduce someone like him.

She flinched as if she's been swatted on the nose with a rolled-up newspaper. Which she sort of had. Then seeing the gloat on my face, she quickly recovered, and became confident… even cocky.

"As long as I could murder him afterwards," she sneered.

"That's my girl," I said. "Now, cadet agent Jones," I went on, snapping up several light switches, "we—I mean you—are ready to face the challenge of… *the Obstacle Course*."

Juliet looked in front of her. "Wow," she gasped, "it looks exactly like a rocky Louisiana swamp."

"Precisely," I said. "It's one of the largest indoor artificial rocky swamps in the world. In a space half again as large as a football stadium, a complex winding path has been laid out, leading through pools, around rocks and shrubs, and so on. I think there's a couple alligators in there somewhere, too, if I'm not mistaken."

I turned to a table near the door, picked up a wrist compass with an illuminated dial and handed it to Juliet, along with a tiny flashlight and a map printed on oilcloth.

"All you have to do," I said, "is follow the circular winding path shown on this map. In the dark. It will take you halfway around the Obstacle Course. That is, you'll end up about fifty yards from here as the crow flies, but the trip is more like five hundred yards if you follow the winding, tortuous path outlined on the map."

"And if I don't follow the path exactly?" asked Juliet, eager as a girl scout.

"You'll get blown up by one of the hundreds of land mines scattered about," I said, settling myself down behind some sandbags. "Meanwhile," I continued, cocking the .30 Colt machine gun in front of me, "I'll be doing my best to shoot you."

"You'll be doing what?" she asked, looking like a blood vessel had burst in her brain.

"Don't worry, this gun is locked so that I can't aim it closer than a foot from the ground you'll be crawling over. So, if you wriggle on your stomach you won't get hit. It's a funny thing—men who fail to pass the obstacle course usually stick their heads up, and get them blown off. Girls usually have their rear ends shot off, which accounts for the fact that the caretaker has such a large collection of girls' heads."

"Good, God," said Juliet, under her breath. "This is unreal."

"One thing I should warn you about," I said. "This Obstacle Course is not only rigorous, it's intentionally designed to shock and nauseate you. Know anything about realistic combat obstacle courses, Juliet?"

"We learned about that in Basic Military Techniques," she said. "According to our instructor, most military-training obstacle courses were pretty simple until the early part of World War II, when the Army realized they were losing too many new men in action who weren't mentally prepared. That was when they started putting real land mines around the courses, and shooting real machine gun bullets over the trainees heads. Sometimes they draped the intestines of a horse or a cow over barbed wire the men had to crawl under, to get them used to seeing blood and body parts on the field."

"Excellent," I said, "you stayed awake in class. Better than I did. Now let's see you put that training to good use. On your mark, get set—"

"Wait!" Juliet cried. "You said this map only takes me halfway around the Obstacle Course. How do I get around the other half?"

"An excellent question," I said. "If you've followed your map accurately, you will find yourself in a deep foxhole. At the bottom of that foxhole there will be a package. Open that package, and a new map will be handed to you."

"Yes sir," said Juliet, snapping to attention, which did marvelous things to her nude breasts. "I'm ready, sir. And when I get back, you'd better be ready to pleasure the shit out of me."

"Roger that," I said, smiling.

I took two small bits of cotton out of a box beside me, wadded them in my ears, then waved her on, at the same time snapping out all the lights. I waited about ten seconds, listening to the slithering sound she made wriggling through the mud of the Obstacle Course.

I aimed the machine gun in the direction of the sound, depressed it as much as I could, let fly with a burst. The tracers lit her up beautifully.

"*Jesus!*" she cried.

She was crawling directly away from me, her bare rump about two inches below my tracers. Some girls, I reflected, had built-in handicaps; their buttocks naturally jutted further up and out. Well, that wasn't Juliet's problem. I fired another short burst, getting within an inch of her this time.

"AH, FUCK!" she said, possibly because she felt the wind of one or more of my slugs go past.

The Obstacle Course went over a slight rise, if I remembered correctly; maybe I could scrape a few bullets across her by then. I licked my lips in anticipation.

Now, you have no doubt already surmised that, although I had my doubts as to Juliet's capacity to make a good SADISTO agent, I nevertheless adored the woman, so much so that apparently while intoxicated I had asked her to be my wife (and being drunk, it was not legally binding). Mentally she was thrilling. Anatomically, she was a dream. I looked back with bliss to the time we'd spent fucking each other, and eagerly looked forward to fucking her in the future. Many times, in many different ways.

Nevertheless.

Nevertheless, once she got out onto the Obstacle Course, I ceased to think of her as a bed-friend-slash-potential wife-mate and mother of three point two or more of my children. She became instead: *A Target*; a target I was required as a Mentor Agent to riddle with expanding machine gun bullets if at all possible; a target it was my obligation to explode into red and white fragments of the *former* ex-cadet agent Juliet Jones as unacceptable for the ranks of SADISTO.

This doesn't mean I have a split personality—any more than most secret agents, I mean—it's simply testimony to the thorough, rigorous training we receive, training well calculated to make a killer out of us, and to make survivor killers out of my potential fellow agents. It was better to find out they couldn't cut it here—on these proving grounds—than out there amongst the real South American Jungle Swamps, and the 'not gay' Generals or Hans's who rule them where the Fate of The Free World was at stake.

I fired a few more bursts over Juliet. Damn. She was past the rise in the Obstacle Course now. I could see the tiny glow as she studied her oilcloth map. I knew the map by heart. Crawl ten yards south-south-east, she was now reading, then five yards east-north-east, then dive into pool and swim twenty yards due east.

I swiveled the machine gun, waited until I figured she was about where I was aiming, let fly. Hot damn! I'd come close to grazing her butt again that time! The tracers really lit it up. Such a pretty bottom, she had. I would miss that butt.

I heard a faint, dismal wail from out of the darkness. I chuckled to myself. Oh, yes, she felt the wind of them, again, all right. Any moment now she—

A ghastly scream reverberated through the indoor Obstacle Course. Again, and again the scream came, insane, demented, horror-filled.

I chuckled. Juliet had evidently just discovered that the pool she had to swim across was a pool of blood, filled with body parts, and six feet deep besides.

Although one of the most impressive features of the Obstacle Course, the pool—or pond, really—of blood was actually one of the easiest features of the course to construct and maintain. So long as you bring your own container, like a tanker truck, any slaughter house will sell you steer blood by the hundred-gallon lot at dirt-cheap prices. Then all you have to do is add an anti-coagulant, and you're in business. The body parts were fake, of course. I think. I'm pretty sure.

I fired a burst of machine gun bullets. The light of the tracers lit all of Juliet up, this time, doggedly swimming, pushing herself forward...

Well, the girl wasn't without guts, I'd give her that. Though perhaps my remark that sometimes a secret agent has to wade through blood to achieve his mission had tipped her off as to what to expect, at least subconsciously.

I kept on firing short, vicious bursts. Five minutes later another horrible scream was torn from Juliet's lips. I winced. Had I hit her? Almost hitting her was fun. But *actually* hitting her? I had drunkenly proposed to her, after all. I did have *some* feelings for her.

No, most likely she'd merely unwrapped the package at the bottom of the foxhole that marked the halfway point. Though my comment that the map for the remainder of her journey would be 'handed to her' should have tipped her off to the fact that inside the package holding part two of the map would be a severed human hand...

I chuckled. Ooooh, visual gags. Punnymany likely had a 'hand' in that one.

I kept on firing. Although I came pretty close a few times, I didn't manage to score any hits. Juliet obviously knew how to protect her pretty little ass.

She screamed again, and I heard a struggle, another scream, more struggle, as she wrestled something through splashy liquid and rustling foliage. It could have been anything or anyone, but was likely an animal of some kind that made its home on the course.

Finally, silence, until cadet agent Juliet Jones crawled back up to me, her lovely nakedness invisible beneath blood, muck, and alligator parts, to report that she was reporting.

"Good job, Juliet," I said, snapping on the lights.

"Good job?" she said, aghast. "That was only a 'good job'?"

I chuckled. "Well, as the cadet-agent course record holder, I have to consider your performance in that light."

"You hold the record because you cheated," a voice said behind me.

Pawnee Peterson walked up wearing moccasins and a loincloth. She ran Ordnance, was a good two inches taller than me, more muscular, and was carrying some armament boxes, probably to test on the range.

Pawnee was topless, as per usual, and her deep brown nipples stood up as she hefted her crates onto the table.

"Don't gawk," she said to me, smiling. "You like them so much, come by and suck on them later."

"I just may," I said, smiling in return.

"Hey!" said Juliet. "I'm right here!"

Pawnee looked down at her on all fours with barely contained disgust.

"Heard you had a jealous cadet shadowing you," she said. "How'd she do?"

"I did great," Juliet said to her. "Don't talk about me like I'm not here. What does she mean, you cheated?" Juliet asked me.

"I didn't cheat," I said. "I was 'lateral thinking'."

"He cheated," Pawnee said with a chuckle. "Ran around outside, in the surrounding corridor, and snuck in the back way through Kobayashi Maru's office."

"Ooooooh..." Juliet said. "So, you've never faced the no-win situation,"

"It's winnable," I said. "I won. So did you."

"Look at me!" she snarled. "This is not winning!"

"You can clean yourself off in that little shower room over there."

"Yes sir," she snipped, turning to crawl unsteadily on all fours toward the shower. "No sucking on her tits while I'm gone."

I watched her go, and even naked and covered in bloody guts and gore, she was still temptingly sexy. She stopped, and craned her neck back toward me, her gaze shifting between me and Pawnee, and back again.

"Why don't you come and watch me," she said, her voice a sultry mix of exhaustion, and jealousy. "Make sure I use the soap correctly."

Pawnee grinned at me devilishly. I felt myself starting to sweat.

"Everyone knows you can't resist soapy titties," Pawnee said under her breath.

"You said if I completed the course you would pleasure the shit out of me!" Juliet snarled over her shoulder, still crawling toward the shower.

I swallowed hard, nodded to Pawnee, and excused myself. Pawnee laughed.

8   8   8

Forty-five minutes later, clean (with a lot of help, and guidance, from me), dried, still naked, and looking almost human again, Juliet saluted me and said, "Cadet agent Jones, fully clean, thoroughly pleasured, and reporting for further training, sir!"

I pushed her salute down. I studied her. She looked, to say the least, kind of sick. Pale of face and dazed of eye. The Obstacle Course had shaken her. But it hadn't made a gibbering idiot, or a corpse, out of her, as I'd feared, and expected. Could it be that she really did have the makings of a crack SADISTO agent? And maybe even... a wife? Time and staying sober would tell.

On the way out of the Obstacle Course the caretaker took one look at Juliet—still whole, head attached—and groaned in disappointment.

"Poor old ghoul," Juliet said as I led the way into the elevator, "he really had his heart set on a head from Wes... consin. Sorry to disappoint you, you grisly fuck!"

"Don't," I reprimanded her, "speak ill to a fellow agent; one with many, many years of service."

"Experience doing what?" muttered Juliet. "Gathering severed heads for his trophy shelf. Using them to give himself 'blowjobs?'"

"Exactly," I said. "He was severing girls' heads, often from their living bodies long before you were even born."

"Wait. Is he a Nazi?" gasped Juliet incredulously. "Do you have former Nazi war criminals working for SADISTO?"

"Never!" I said. "I'm pretty sure! The Free World doesn't need Nazis working for them! Other than—of course—Operation Paperclip which was imperative to help The Free World gain technological superiority over the Nazis—I mean, we desperately needed the help of Nazi rocket men, Nazi physicists, Nazi businessmen, Nazi clericals, Nazi janitors, and, I don't know, maybe one or two Nazi killers got mixed up in the bunch, but not because we wanted them! Probably because they were double-threat killer/scientists, which..."

"It's just gross," said Juliet.

"Government sanctioned murder isn't pretty," I told her. "But it's what we do. Don't waste your time worrying about it. Clear your mind for the challenges that lie ahead. And speaking of heads," I said, chuckling and chucking her under the chin, "it may well be that the old caretaker will still get his wish; there are more ways than one for a cadet agent to lose his or her head."

I chuckled. Ominously.

Juliet glared at me, and growled like an angry cat that's about to be eaten by a wolf.

I almost felt sorry for her. She was, in a way, too young to die.

But she had wanted this.

CHAPTER 10

"IT'S NOT THAT I THINK I'm too young to die," Juliet explained. "It's that I don't *want* to die. Period. I have things I want to do. Like make babies... with you."

"Now, now," I scoffed, "that's no way for a nascent, dedicated killer to talk. Besides, the chances are almost fifty-fifty you'll survive this next test. And look at it this way. You're committed! You need to forge ahead and complete your second assignment, or I'll have to flunk you right now and assign you to Interrogation. As a subject."

"No, I—I'll do it," she said. And set about doing it.

"It" was really a quite simple thing. We were standing by a huge swimming pool on the seventh floor. Running lengthways over said pool, suspended from two poles, was a rope. All Juliet had to do was swing, hand over hand, from one pole to the other. Even completely nude, as she still was, it *seemed* simple.

"Really?" she'd said when I'd first outlined the assignment to her and led her into the huge room wherein was the swimming pool. "But that should be easy."

"It should," I said. "Except... the rope has been greased."

She frowned. "Well. That makes things a little tougher, but not impossible." She crooked her fingers. "By crooking my fingers," she said, "I can still make it across easy, swinging from hand to hand. The rope is taut, so there's no chance of my sliding to the middle and staying there. This one *is* easy because—"

There was a long pause.

"What?" I asked.

"Nothing," she said.

I chuckled. Evilly. "You were going to say '*Because, even if I fall, I'll only fall into the swimming pool*' weren't you?"

"Well, I was, yes," she admitted, already realizing there was more to it.

I smiled. Sadistically.

"Why are you smiling sadistically?" she asked. "I *would* fall into the pool, wouldn't I?"

"Oh, yes," I assured her. "You would indeed."

She frowned. "And I'd have no trouble swimming to the side and climbing out?"

"No trouble at all," I said, "provided you can swim several hundred miles an hour. Because if you swam any slower— Here, watch."

I picked up a chunk of raw beef, which sat in a box on a nearby table, hefted it, then hurled it into the middle of the enormous swimming pool.

Instantly the surface seemed to boil and swirl like the base of a waterspout, to splash as if a score of machinegun bullets were hitting the water; hundreds of tiny silver bodies glittering and flashing in and above the churning surface of the pool.

Then all was still.

"What," gasped Juliet, "was *that?*"

"Several hundred deadly piranhas devouring a chunk of raw beef," I said. "You have no doubt read about those tiny, but fantastically savage, and voracious Brazilian fish?"

"I've seen them in the movies," she said, still not getting it. "But that's a fiction. Piranhas have never actually killed a human. They're timid fish, and their teeth are more for self-defense, than eating."

"And what are you," I asked, surprised, "The Piranha Police?"

"I know some things," she said, simply, as if she were reconsidering the three-point-two children. With me, at least.

"Well," I said, "these are genetically manipulated by our SADISTO genetic manipulator-ers in Department X to be exactly like the kind of piranhas you see in the movies!"

Juliet's eyes widened, and she turned to stare at the greasy stain spreading out over the water's surface, above the sinking bone still popping to and fro with the remaining strikes and movements of the tiny, silver fish. She shuddered.

"Still think you know piranha?" I asked.

"Um," Juliet moaned, "maybe not."

"Always expect the unexpected," I told her. "Now start making your way to the other end of the pool, hanging by your hands."

Reluctantly, she did so.

"Actually," I said, "this exercise is a fine example of how a relatively simple task can be made difficult by an overactive imagination. If I hadn't told you that the pool was full of deadly piranha, you would be swinging blithely hand over hand without a worry in your head. But, because you *know* what would happen if you should slip, you are obviously in a state of enhanced fear and moving far too slowly. So... speed up."

Naked cadet Juliet Jones, who was now halfway across the pool, her feet waving scant inches above the surface of the deadly ripples, groaned and quickened her pace. Her nude body wiggled and jiggled in so many amazing ways it made me want to get naked myself, and slide across the rope to join her, and distract her in various fun and erotic ways.

Hmm. Maybe that should be a part of the test.

"There," I said a few moments later, after she'd safely reached the other end of the pool, unmolested either by me, or the piranhas. "That wasn't so bad, now, was it? So, rest for a few seconds, and then make your way back."

She groaned.

"By the way," I said, "do you know any poems?"

"Poems?"

"Poems? Sonnets? Light verse? Something you know by heart?"

"Well," she said, "I used to know all of Edgar Allan Poe's *The Raven*."

"Fine," I said. "Commence swinging your way back here, again hand over hand, reciting *The Raven* as you go."

"Trevor?" said Juliet.

"Yes?"

"I mean, sir. With all due respect, have you lost your mind, sir?"

"Not at all," I chuckled. "My request, and this carefully devised exercise, is both logical and reasonable. You see, cadet agent Jones, not only must a SADISTO agent be ever ready to take horrifying risks in order to accomplish his or her mission, he or she must also be able to think clearly and logically while doing so.

"For example, a couple years ago, in order to carry out my assignment to liquidate a potentially non-hostile Swiss neutral, I found that the only way I could gain entrance to his remote mountain chalet was to work my way hand over hand up a high-tension wire."

"Really?" said Juliet, hanging much as I had. Though naked.

I nodded. "Consider the difficulties I encountered. I had to swing my way uphill over half a mile of that wire. If I permitted myself to sway more than a few inches out of line, I would have touched the second high-tension wire, which would have barbecued me in mid-air."

"Whoa…" Juliet gasped.

"Quite. Below me was a four-thousand-foot drop, and I had no parachute. Also, I had no gloves on my hands, and the temperature was twenty below zero. Also, a fifty-mile-an-hour blizzard was raging. Also, two men were sniping at me. Also, a third was calling me names. Really unpleasant ones."

"Holy shit!" cried Juliet. "And despite all those distractions, you made your way successfully up the high-tension line?"

"I did," I said, "and at the same time I worked out my next tactical and strategic moves, and played two games of mental chess with myself, while also planning the following week's lunch menu. So, you see, Juliet, an agent *must* learn to use his—or in your case *her*—head while risking his—or in your case *her*—neck. Now, swing your naked way back across that greased rope, and recite *The Raven* as you do so."

She took a deep breath, and began doing so. I was almost regretting asking her to do it: I'd forgotten what an awful poem *The Raven* was.

"Once upon a midnight dreary, while I pondered, weak and weary," she said, pretty much by rote, with no real feeling, "over many a quaint and curious volume of forgotten lore—"

Inching her way slowly, Juliet finished reciting the poem while still only halfway across. "Do you want me to recite another poem, Agent 8?" she asked.

"Uh, no," I said. "That's enough. Your mind can obviously multi-task."

I got to my feet, and hurled another chunk of raw beef into the swimming pool. Inches below her bare feet the surface of the water boiled and seethed as the deadly piranhas tore the meat to shreds, then devoured the shreds.

"Just to remind you not to fall," I told her. "Try making your way hand over hand along the greased rope with your eyes closed," I suggested.

"Yes, sir," said Juliet, closing her eyes. She inched her way silently along the rope for a few moments. Then she screamed and almost fell, hanging now by only one hand, then by one finger.

"What's wrong?" I asked.

With a great effort she pulled herself up by the one finger, got her other hand over the greased rope. Below her four or five piranhas broke the surface in angry jumps, trying and almost succeeding in biting off one of her toes.

"You—you won't believe this, 8," she gasped, "but I was stung by a wasp, or something. On my left butt-cheek."

"You weren't stung by a wasp," I laughed. "You were struck by a steel ball bearing from this sling-shot I'm holding. The impact was carefully precalculated to cause pain exactly equivalent to that of a wasp sting. See?" I fired another ball bearing at her.

"*Aaaaaah!*" she screamed, almost falling. "You—are you *seriously* going to fire ball bearings at my naked ass while I'm trying to make my way hand over hand along a greased rope stretched over a swimming pool full of deadly piranhas?"

"Didn't I just say that?" I said, aiming for and hitting her right butt-cheek.

"*Why?*" she screamed.

"Well, because it's fun," I said, "but mostly I'm trying to create synthetically the kind of rigorous conditions you are likely to encounter in the field. Suppose, for example, you were making your way hand over hand toward your victim, and a swarm of real wasps...."

"Yeah, yeah, enough with the justifications. SADISTO for real, I—IIII!—" she gasped. "I thought you loved me!"

"If I said that, then I do!"

"So, you're doing this *because* you love me? So I'll be able to survive in the field, right?"

"Exactly," I said, firing another ball bearing at her unprotected stomach. "Now I suggest you move a little faster, keeping in mind the fact that the longer it takes you to reach safety, the more ball bearings I'll have time to fire. But also remembering that, the more you hurry, the more chance you have of slipping and falling into a swimming pool full of piranhas. Which neither of us wants."

Juliet said nothing. She merely glared at me, and screamed from time to time, whenever I hit her in a particularly sensitive spot with a ball bearing. I was reloading from a box of steel replacements when I heard her voice, suddenly cheery and kind of singsong.

"Oh *Treeeevooooor*," she said.

I looked up and saw her smiling the most charming, seductive smile I'd ever seen. Sober. Hanging from the rope, she looked like the world's sexiest mobile, toes pointed, her legs raising slowly on either side, spreading apart in invitation.

"*You could just slide down that rope, and riiiiight into me,*" she said in a husky, stage-whisper.

I dropped my steel ball bearing, and raised my flagpole.

It didn't help when she pulled herself upward, then—while maintaining her grip—dropped back down to intentionally make her tits jiggle. Afterward she turned herself slowly in semi-rotation to keep the movement going, and give a fuller view of all.

"Or you could just lasso me, and pull me toward you," she said, knowingly. "You don't want all this sexy getting eaten by some stupid piranhas, now, do you? Not when *you* could be eating me, instead."

"I—I—I—" A knocking at the door saved me having to form a coherent thought. The door opened and two young girls wearing only lipstick and identification anklets marched in. When they saw me, they saluted.

"Agent 8?" they asked, in unison.

I nodded.

"Cadet agent Ilsa reporting," said one, saluting again.

"Cadet agent Sayonara reporting," said the other, also saluting again.

"Ah, yes," I said, "I've been expecting you." I turned to Juliet. "I'm going to Big Brother these two girls as well as you, Juliet."

Juliet looked shocked, then turned to me. She rapidly hand-over-handed her way to the edge of the pool, her body parts flopping less seductively, but far more enthusiastically, and dropped beside me.

"Are you intending to teach them the techniques of seduction?" she asked.

"Of course," I said.

"And afterward, do you intend to fuck them?" She snarled.

"I do, indeed."

The girls looked at each other, surprised. Ilsa smiled.

Juliet growled at them, and then pouted.

"No pouting," I snapped. "From time-to-time we will each have to perform sexual acts with others for a mission, and to protect The Free World. Me probably more than you. So, you must learn to get along with all other agents, Juliet, and occasionally have sex with them as practice. It's essential in this line of work."

She stared at me, sadly, for a long moment, then eventually said, her voice a near-whisper, "Yes sir."

"Now shake hands with cadet agent Ilsa and cadet agent Sayonara."

She did so. Meanwhile I looked the new girls over. Interesting. Cadet agent Ilsa was tall, wide and handsome; a blonde-haired, fair-skinned Teutonic type with baby-blue eyes and a natural, low-hanging, fifty-inch at least, bosom. Cadet agent Sayonara was short but slender, a petite-breasted, long-legged Asian.

"Cadet agent Ilsa," I explained to Juliet, "is from West Germany. Cadet agent Sayonara, is from South Vietnam."

"But... isn't Sayonara... Japanese?"

I frowned. Hard.

"We frown hard on political correctness, agent Jones. We frown *very hard* on political correctness."

"So, Pawnee...?" she began.

"Don't..." I warned.

"But… Viet Nam… Sayonara… that's not—it's just… not logic—"

I shot her with a pellet. She shrieked.

"Right, sir," she said, saluting.

Everyone saluted.

"Your wish," they chorused, "is our command."

"And my command," I chuckled, "may be the death of you. Cadet agent Sayonara, your first assignment will be to trot down to the cafeteria and get a bunch of hamburgers for everyone, and two for me. I need a small snack."

"Yes sir," said cadet agent Sayonara, saluting and then trotting off, her cute, little bare butt wagging from side to side like a happy puppy's tail.

"With everything!" I shouted.

"Yes, sir!"

"Your first assignment, cadet agent Ilsa," I said, "will be to make your way hand over hand across that rope stretched above this swimming pool."

"Dot iss all?" asked Ilsa. "Dot I could do vit mine eyes close."

I smiled. Juliet smiled. "Tell her, Juliet," I said.

Juliet told her. Ilsa looked sick.

"You iss yoking, ya?" she gasped. "Piranha haf nefer actually kill human. Zey are timid fish…"

I held up a hand and signaled to Juliet. Juliet tossed a chunk of raw beef into the pool. Ilsa, her complexion already milk-white, didn't pale, but actually kind of greened.

"Also, the rope is greased," I added.

"Also, we're going to fire steel ball bearings at you," added Juliet, maliciously, taking the slingshot from me, thereby demonstrating the almost universal human trait I've observed in every man, woman, or college-aged child I've ever met, namely, that people take evil delight in watching other people undergo torments they themselves have had to suffer. It's the unifying core belief behind every fraternity and sorority.

"I may like to fire some ball bearings at Ilsa," I said. "You can't have all the fun. Actually, why don't you give me that back, and do some push-ups to fill the time?"

"Aw, but…" Juliet began, but cowed under my glare.

"Perhapsen," said Ilsa, "I could do der pushen-upsens and *she* could cross der svimmen pool?"

"Nein," I snapped. "Start crossing. And you, Juliet—push-ups."

As Ilsa started, Juliet glared at me.

"You," Juliet said, "just want to watch my tits moosh against the tile floor."

"No," I said. "I mean, yes. But I also believe in constant physical improvement."

I took a moment to observe her form, as—indeed—her hanging breasts flattened against the pool tile on the down, then distended again on the up. Admittedly, she didn't need much physical improvement. But it was doing wonders physically for me.

"*Yiii!*" screamed Ilsa, as the first ball-bearing I fired thudded into her more than ample right breast. She didn't fall, however, but continued doggedly making her way hand over hand along the greased rope.

"While doing your push-ups," I said to Juliet, letting fly another ball bearing at Ilsa's swaying, nude body, "please recite the multiplication tables. You also need to exercise your ability to think clearly while undergoing physical exertion."

"Yes, sir," groaned Juliet.

"Yiiii!" screamed Ilsa, as I landed another bullseye. "Two times one is two," gasped Juliet, "two times two is four—"

"*Yiii!*" screamed Ilsa, as I fired yet another ball bearing into her softly curved flesh.

"*YIIIIIEEE!* screamed Ilsa.

"Two times three is—*Eeeee!*" screamed Juliet.

I frowned. "I didn't shoot you, Juliet. Don't try to say I did. Why are you screaming?"

"No, look!" Juliet screamed. "The pole at this end is sagging! The greased rope is dropping closer and closer to the surface of the piranha-packed pool!"

I looked.

"*Help!*" screamed Ilsa.

"You're right," I said to Juliet. "The rope *is* sagging. Not only is it now impossible for Ilsa to climb to safety hand over hand, but in a few moments, she'll be dunked into the piranha-infested pool. Mm, mm, mm. Continue your push-ups and reciting the multiplication tables, Juliet."

"NO!" screamed Juliet. "The rope is sagging more—and more... Now she can only keep her legs out of the water by tucking her knees up under her chin... her milky-white ass is swaying less than an inch above the surface of the pool! You have to—"

"No," I said sternly, "*you* have to! Now is the time for you to start obeying orders. Namely, do your push-ups while reciting the multiplication tables."

"*Help!*" screamed Ilsa, whose milky-white ass was—indeed—now almost grazing the surface of the water.

"You see, Juliet," I said sternly, "many times in the field you will have to function clearly and alertly while a fellow agent dies horribly, as Ilsa is now about to die horribly. Oops—I mean, *is* dying horribly."

"*Help!*" screamed Ilsa. "*I am dying horribly! I am eaten alive being! Mine bottom is...*" She gave one last horrible scream and dropped into the pool. For several moments her legs and arms thrashed wildly, then all was still. All save for a widening red cloud, which diffused throughout the pool.

"*Good Lord—that's horrible!*" gasped Juliet.

"I'll say," I said. "That pool's filtration system is supposed to kick in by now and clear clouds of blood within seconds. I'll have to see about having that fixed. Ah, wait... there it is. The water's clearing. Bigger job than usual, I guess. Wow, what a thorough job those genetically altered piranhas would you look at that? Ilsa's skeleton has been picked clean."

Juliet swallowed hard, and looked ill. "Yes, I can see that."

I fixed her with a stern look. She grimaced, then resumed doing push-ups. "Two times three is six," she gasped, "two times four is nine, two times—*yipe!* Dammit, Trev—why did you shoot me in the ass?"

"Because two times four ain't *nine,*" I snapped. "An agent must be able to—not only think while undergoing physical exertion—but to think *clearly* and *correctly*. Try again."

Just then a knock sounded and Sayonara trotted in, hamburgers in hand.

"Oh, fantastic," I said, "lunch. You may desist from push-ups for a while, cadet agent Juliet."

"Here you are, sir," said Sayonara. "And here's your hamburger, cadet agent Juliet, and—wait... where's cadet agent Ilsa?"

Juliet pointed with a shaking finger. Sayonara looked, and paled. "No—not really?"

"Really," I said. "And since Ilsa won't be needing a hamburger, I'll take hers."

"You—you can actually eat?" gasped Juliet. "Seconds after a young, naked, vibrantly alive girl was eaten right in front of you?"

"Sure," I said. "You know, it's a funny thing. Whenever I see somebody else eating, even a shoal of piranha, I get hungry." I began chomping on my hamburger. "Weird, right?"

"Aren't you going to eat yours?" I asked Juliet a few moments later, licking my fingers.

She shook her head, and held it out to me. I shrugged, took the hamburger and ate it.

"You?" I asked Sayonara, who was staring glassy-eyed at the skeleton at the bottom of the pool. She also shook her head. I took her hamburger and started on that one as well.

"Mmmm," I said, sitting back and continuing to eat. "So, class, I think it's time you girls practiced a little close combat. You've both been taught judo, karate, sabot, Tango, commando tactics and the like, I presume?"

They both nodded. Both girls, I noticed, looked almost as green as Ilsa had before she was eaten.

"Excellent," I said. "Now, tell me girls, in a close combat duel, who would win—a judo/karate/commando-trained fighter, or a fighter with a knife?"

"The first," said both girls in unison.

"Right," I said. "But what if the fighter with a knife had also been trained in judo/karate/commando tactics?"

Juliet and Sayonara pondered this.

"The fighter with the knife," Sayonara said.

"But it would be a very close match," added Juliet. "As the one without the knife would be very motivated."

"Right," I said.

I picked up a long, wickedly sharp commando knife, hefted it, then tossed it handle first to Juliet. She caught it deftly.

"Prove," I said casually, "the correctness of your last response."

"I'm sorry, what?" said Juliet, staring blankly at the deadly two-edged knife she held in her right hand.

"Don't be shy," I said. "Prove that a knife fighter can kill a fighter without a knife, even if both know judo/karate and commando tactics.'

"You—you mean...?" gasped Juliet.

"Precisely," I said, with a bite of my burger.

"But—you can't mean you expect me to kill cadet agent Sayonara just to prove an abstract technical point, can you?"

"I can," I snarled, "and I do."

"But—but—but—" stammered Juliet.

While the fourth 'but' was only half-formed by Juliet's lips, Sayonara, seeing the deadly dual-edged blade pointed at her vitals, and Juliet's indecision—acted. She sprang forward, brought up her right foot in the sweeping kick that karate-trained women and men use to de-knife a knife-wielding opponent.

Juliet dodged just in time, then stepped deftly back to avoid the lethal swing of Sayonara's right hand, the edge of which came within inches of breaking Juliet's jaw.

Juliet countered with an upward defensive block, then a vicious low slash of the knife, which Sayonara met with a deadly stab of her left heel—and so it went.

I settled back in my canvas chair, ate and watched, fascinated. The two girls were closely matched. Sayonara, it soon became apparent, was much more skillful in judo, karate and the unarmed combat arts. But Juliet had a knife, a knife she knew how to use.

Which would win? I sat back, got comfortable and waited to find out.

Esthetically, the two nude girls fighting made a dramatic, erotic sight. Juliet was tanned a golden bronze, but Sayonara, being Vietnamese, had a natural golden tint to her flesh. The two, at times, resembled goddess statues of purest gold come to deadly life.

Around and around they circled, striking, counter-striking, feinting with hands, spinning arms and feet; practiced, deadly; Juliet, having more size in her huge breasts and full buttocks, was at a weight disadvantage compared to Sayonara, whose supple body could move with serpent-like swiftness.

Sayonara struck Juliet in the jaw, the nose, at one point swept a leg out from under her, and gut-punched her, but Juliet maintained her balance, recovered quickly, and struck back with superior strength. Efficiently. Effectively. Impressively.

And Juliet had the knife. A knife that was making more and more small marks on Sayonara's body.

There was, I decided objectively, no excuse for Juliet not to win within three more minutes.

Two minutes and forty-five seconds later Juliet got in a telling up-thrust, and Sayonara staggered back, hands clutched to her middle. Her middle which, I noted with interest, was now bisected by a thin red line from pelvis to rib cage.

"Got her!" Juliet snarled in triumph.

"Almost," I agreed. "At the moment I agree that Sayonara has been badly cut—only her own hands pressed to her belly are keeping her intestines and stomach from falling out. But it is quite incorrect to imply that she's as good as dead. At the moment she is suffering from nothing that a needle and thread couldn't repair."

*"She **IS** as good as dead!"* hissed Juliet, breathlessly.

"Again, I disagree," I said. "I refer you to Icelandic history. One of the Viking chiefs, I forget his name, once had his body cut open while storming a beach with his men. Not only was his stomach cut open, but his intestines spilled out onto the beach.

"Nevertheless, he continued fighting and killed his opponent, lopped the man's head off as I recall. Thereupon the Viking chief waded out into the sea, washed the sand off his own intestines, and stuffed them back inside. Then he boarded his ship, where his sister, who was handy with a needle and thread, sewed him back together. He lived, according to history, to a ripe old age."

"Maybe," hissed Juliet, "maybe not. But I guarantee nobody's going to sew this bitch back together!"

"Splendid," I said. "At last, you're getting the true brutal, callous, inhuman SADISTO spirit. Kill your helpless fellow agent, Juliet!"

"Mercy!" screamed Sayonara, still clutching her stomach and backing away.

Juliet hesitated.

"I don't blame you for hesitating," I said. "Finishing Sayonara at close range could prove to be messy; her insides might tumble out onto you. You may *throw* your knife, if you wish."

Juliet hesitated, then reversed the gleaming commando blade in her hand, drew back her arm, and threw the knife. The silver steel gleamed evilly as it spun through the air. Then, with a meaty thud, it buried itself in Sayonara's heart.

Sayonara quivered, her eyes rolled up, her hands dropped to her sides, her intestines slopped to the floor, and she herself toppled on top of those vital organs.

"Bravo, Juliet," I said, setting down my plate. "You have just passed another test, and you're that much closer to being accepted as a bona fide agent of—where are you? Oh, there you are!"

Juliet, the squeamish girl, had dropped to her knees and was retching into the swimming pool.

"A little retching," I told her, "is natural and normal after your first kill, but don't overdo it. Here, I'll hold your hair, and don't get your face too close to the pool. Piranhas, remember?"

Juliet jerked her face back just in time to avoid the savage bites of half a dozen piranhas that had frothed up at her. "I— I killed her!" she gasped.

"You certainly did," I said. "And quite skillfully, too. You may collect a souvenir, if you wish—scalp, ears, an eye, any little thing you feel like keeping. A lot of agents are sentimental about their first kill."

"Glug, glug," gasped Juliet, obviously on the verge of retching again.

"Come on, Juliet" I said. "Pull yourself together. Ilsa and Sayonara were sent here specifically to help train *you* as their final act. And you passed with flying colors! Be proud!"

Juliet rose to her feet and, with great effort, pulled herself together, and even attempted a smile, which was kinda gross because her mouth still had vomit in it. Her eyes, I noted with approval, looked dazed, almost insane. The turquoise had dimmed.

She was becoming an agent.

"Before we leave," I said, "you might want to tidy up a little, shove Sayonara's remains into the pool, and—oh, sorry; excuse me a moment, the phone's ringing."

I answered it. "Hans? Oh—oh yes. Right. Oh, uh... no, I'm afraid not. She was eaten alive by piranhas. Only her skull is left. You want that? No, huh? The girl from Wisconsin? No, she's still alive. Yes, I'm sorry. I know you were hoping."

I hung up, chuckling.

"Hans," said Juliet listlessly, "that dirty old man who looks after the Obstacle Course? He still wants my head?"

"Yeeeaaaaah," I said sympathetically. "He is pretty horrible, isn't he?"

"Yes!" gasped Juliet. "And so am I! You've made me into a—a monster! A killer! A ghoul! A—"

"A trained SADISTO agent," I corrected her. "Better to suffer your first kill in training than to be squeamish in the field, and be killed while vomiting."

She stared at me, her thoughts an obvious turmoil, and breathed in gasping breaths.

"Remember, Juliet," I said, "you were the one who wanted this work. You applied for the job, signed the proper release forms... I know I was drunk, but I must have warned you it would be tough, warned you that, before you could become a card-carrying SADISTO agent you would have to jettison all human feeling, all mercy, all compassion, all decency."

"You did, but..." she started, then didn't finish.

"You thought I was exaggerating. That this would all be cool, and hip, and sexy, and bloodless, like in the movies."

She avoided my eyes, turned away and reluctantly nodded her head, ashamed.

"Yeah," I said. "It's not."

"I see why women are reluctant to settle down with you."

Her comment shook me to my core.

"Yes," I said, pain fraying my voice. "I suppose so."

I watched her breath in deep, fearful gasps for a long while, as she stared at me, unblinking.

"Still want to become a SADISTO agent, cadet agent Juliet Jones?" I asked, hope fading.

Silence.

A very long silence, as her eyes turned inward and stopped seeing me. I knew she was mulling her options. Finish agent training? Accept death? Two difficult options once you see how truly dark keeping the Free World free can be.

Finally, reluctantly, faintly, slowly she reached out, took my hand, squeezing the fingers, lightly, and answered, "Yes."

There was more silence, and then "Was—was this all part of the *normal* SADISTO agent training?"

I nodded. "It was."

"But—surely cadets Ilsa and Sayonara—"

"I'll explain all that to you. But I think it would be a good idea for you to take a little break."

She sniffed, nodded, and began to cry.

I held out an arm, and sobbing quietly, Juliet came under it like a baby bird seeking protection from her mama bird. I guided her gently, at her own pace, toward the exit.

CHAPTER 11

FOR WHAT SEEMED HOURS, I held her while she sobbed.

Occasionally I would roll on top of her, kiss her luscious nipples, and enter her gently, but she would shake her head and ask me to pull out. Eventually I accepted that I had tried everything I could to comfort her, gave up, and just lay there quietly with her in the crook of my arm, feeling her tears get me all wet.

"You were right, Trevor," Juliet said, "I thought that this would be fun. If you see someone eaten by piranhas in a movie, it's a kind of scary thrill. You know it's all pretend, and shocking for entertainment value."

"Yes," I agreed, "seeing people pretend to die horribly *is* a lot of fun."

"But seeing it in this context," she said, sniffing back more tears, "knowing that she was a real, flesh and blood person..."

"*Real* flesh and blood," I agreed. "*So much* flesh and blood. Wow. You saw how long it took the filter to clean that out."

"She was a person that—in other circumstances—might have been a friend. Sayonara and I could have shared lipstick, traded silly notes taped to each other's doors... and I could die... just like her. And if I fail to perform, fail to learn, I *will* die... just as horribly. If not *more* horribly."

"But cadet agent Jones—I mean Juliet," I said. "Haven't you figured it out by now? Neither Sayonara nor—what was her name?—Elsa?"

"Ilsa."

"Right. Neither one had the slightest chance of becoming SADISTO agents."

"Yes, obviously, but...?" Juliet suddenly gasped. "Wait..."

"Exactly," I said. "You see it now. Sayonara was not Vietnamese, and Ilsa was not *West* German."

"Wait," said Juliet, a small light dawning. "Are you saying Ilsa was... actually... an *East* German *enemy* agent, and Sayonara some other Asian *enemy* agent?"

"Exactly," I said. "Sayonara was Chinese, with a Japanese name, knowing that we Americans don't even try to tell the difference. But thanks to our efficient polygraph tests and truth serums, we learned their true identities. In order to study their methods, though, we allowed them to think that they'd penetrated our intelligence network. Both Ilsa and Sayonara, until the instant they were utilized as targets, believed they'd infiltrated the organization as legitimate cadet agents of SADISTO."

"But...?" gasped Juliet.

"—how did they get this far?" I asked. "Simple. The enemy continually sends trained agents, disguised as refugees, or homeless people across our borders, where they try to infiltrate our intelligence networks."

For the shock of an instant, I flashed on the drawer spilling incident in the General's office and wondered if there were other ways to infiltrate SADISTO.

"Wow," said Juliet. "My gosh. Suddenly I feel so much better, knowing that I disemboweled an enemy agent instead of a failed cadet agent who could have done my hair on Friday nights after a difficult mission. And if I'd known that fat German girl who liked the idea of fucking you was really an enemy agent I wouldn't have gotten so upset when I saw and heard her being shredded alive by ravenous piranhas. I might even have laughed, a little."

"That's the SADISTO spirit," I said, "and really the whole point of this training. An agent *must* be prepared at any time to abandon or betray his or her fellow agents. A SADISTO agent's motto will always be: *The Mission Comes First.*"

"Yes sir," said Juliet, grinning, and almost—but not quite—saluting. Instead, she smiled, leaned up to kiss me quickly, and settled back down into the comfort of my armpit. Then she popped up again for another quick kiss. Then another. Then she reached down and took hold of Agent 8 and a quarter pretending to move it around like a doll.

"Wah, wah, wah," she said, and then in a male falsetto voice, "I'm Agent eight and a quarter, and I want to pop in to visit cadet agent Pussy Hole!"

I chuckled, and moved to lie on top of her, as she held on, intending to guide agent 8 and a quarter toward his mission. As we maneuvered, I saw her frown, and a tear begin to form, again.

"No more crying," I said, and lightly tapped her nose. Then I let my hand glide down her to her breast, and gently took hold, rubbing my thumb over its distending nipple.

"Yes sir," said Juliet, squeezing Agent eight and a quarter into the waiting cadet agent Pussy Hole. "No crying."

She gave me another quick kiss, and we both smiled. I noted Sayonara's blood still on her face, and melted a little inwardly. Maybe Juliet *was* becoming the perfect wife material for a SADISTO agent like me. Maybe I *was* right to drunkenly propose, and recommend her for full-agent training.

"Why didn't you apply to become an agent right away," I asked her, as I eased my way fully inside her. "Why become a Call-Girl, instead?"

"I didn't know becoming an agent was an option," she told me, wiggling her hips to help me get deeper. Then the frown returned.

"What?" I asked. "Why the sad look?"

She paused, bit a lip, turned away, and considered her next words carefully.

"I was just thinking that..." she said, slowly, "before we met... I would have welcomed dying. I wanted to die. Being eaten by piranha would have been a blessing. And now—when the odds are better that I actually *could* be eaten—I want so very much to live." She paused, and turned back to study my eyes. "With you."

"What happened to you that brought you down to such a place?" I asked, putting my arms around her, pulling her closer to me, and kissing her lips, lightly.

"You don't want to hear," she said. "It's not a very interesting story."

"I *do* want to hear," I said, gently. "Very much. It's *your* story."

She thought about it a moment, then kissed my chin.

"All right," she said, her smile returning. "But only if you move around inside me while I do."

I began to move, as requested, very subtly, and slowly.

"Mmmm," she said, closing her eyes, bending her head back, and smiling again. "Yes, that's nice."

Since it was offered, I kissed her neck, again, and again, and then her chin when she brought her head back down. Her transcendent eyes fixed on mine. Unblinking.

"I was…" she began, "visiting Singapodia. My family was in business with the former regime of President Chiau. We make ice cream. The cartons are produced there. Jonesys."

"*Jonesys Icey Creams?*" I said. "*Oh, my God, I love those!*"

"With the sprinkles already in. Yeah, that's us. Or, was."

"Then what the hell are you doing here?" I asked. "You have a business. A home! You must be rich!"

"I'll get to that," she said. "See, we had been in Singapodia only a few days when the coup happened—and in an instant everything changed; gunshots, explosions, fires, death, screaming, people getting shot or hung in the squares, restaurant service was just horrible. Madame Phu became empress, seized the banks, of course, so suddenly we had no money, or at least no access to it, and we were trapped.

"Phu heard we were in the capital, she wanted our company, and there was nowhere to hide. The hotels weren't safe, we knew people were coming for us—to ransom us, we thought—so we tried to run, but didn't get far. On a road out of town my father opened the car door ahead of a military roadblock and told me to run into the forest. Hide. 'Get to the airport,' he said. Though he didn't tell me how, or what to do when I got there. I had only gone about a hundred yards when I heard my mother screaming… and then shots. You stopped moving."

"I… what… oh," I said, and resumed. "Sorry I got caught up in your story. It's more interesting than you said it would be."

"If you say so," she said. "So, it turned out my father wasn't killed. Soldiers dragged him to Phu, and Phu forced him to sign our company over to her in a televised ceremony. I think he did it in exchange for my life, because people stopped looking for me. I was ignored, and left alive, though trapped, and broke. No way home. Worse, no one came looking for me. No family, no friends. I couldn't get out. It left me homeless and all alone in the world... trapped in Singapodia, a stranger in a strange land."

"They have churros."

"They have weirder things than that," she said. "And I ate a lot of them to survive."

"What happened to your father?"

She shrugged. "Dead, I guess. Or something a lot like it."

"How did you wind up here?"

"I was living in the streets, begging money off tourists... travelers in the airport... trying desperately to get help, find my father, find a way back to the United States, though to what, I don't know. Phu had our family business, so what had become of my life, here? My home? Why wasn't anyone looking for me? Trying to get me home?

"Cold, often wet, and hungry in a crowded, hostile city I didn't know if I even wanted to go back to West... to my home in the States. My family lived in a place with rich people who were emotionally disconnected, where it was also often crowded, cold, wet, snowy. I lie freezing in alleys in the overcrowded capital of Singapodia and instead of home, I dreamt of lying naked on a sunny beach eating tropical fruit with no one around.

"Last week I was begging in the international terminal when a weird man in a business suit approached me and offered to play me a children's game for money. I thought... is he serious? But he said he was, and showed me a wad of bills. Hundreds. So, I thought, 'what the hell,' right? Probably just an excuse to bed me, but I would have sucked him off in an alley for a ten, so, why not? Let's play football."

My eyes widened as I remembered.

"Paper football," I said.

"Yes," she said. "How did you know?"

"Never mind. Go on."

"Well... we sat at this table, and surprise, surprise, I was winning. He would hand me the cash, then ask for another game. After about half an hour, I had enough to go home." Her luminous eyes darkened, and she turned away. "But I got greedy. I lost the money going double-or-nothing—all of it. Even the few bucks I'd begged out of people that day. I started to cry. I didn't want to. I wanted to be strong, but... that's when he offered me a job as an in-house girl here at *The Place*. I was already considering doing it locally, in some whorehouse, anything to eat, but he offered me a lot more money than I could make on the streets of Singapodia. Plus a ticket home to the States, a bath, clothes, warmth, food ... my God, real food..."

"I was in that airport," I said, "I remember your..." glanced down at her magnificent breasts, "...your eyes. I couldn't stop thinking about them."

"*You're the man I flipped off,*" she gasped. "I remember you! You were fucking ogling my titties like a kid staring at a plate of cookies! *My* cookies!" She grinned, twisted her torso and shook the aforementioned titties, sweeping her hardened nipples across my chest. "You wanted them even then."

"I did," I admitted. "But it was really more..."

"I know," she said, smiling. "My eyes." She put fingertips to her lips, and the light returned to those eyes, as they suddenly saucered. "So *that's* why you asked for a woman with turquoise eyes. You were still thinking about me! How sweet! You know, your request got me out of sex-training with that poor Motor Pool guy. He was already hard, and getting naked."

"Scottie?"

"McCoy," she corrected. Again she touched her 'O' shaped lips, and her eyes widened with surprise. "You were the man in the van! I couldn't see you in the shadows, but I wondered what was so special about you that you got the front seat beside McCoy."

"Who's McCoy?" I asked.

"McCoy! The driver who picked you up at the airport."

"Oh, you mean Scottie?"

"I mean *McCoy*. His name is *McCoy*. When he pulled out his cock he called it 'The *Real* McCoy.' His name is McCoy. Are we doing an Abbott and Costello routine?"

"Um..." I said, scrunching up my face. "Who's on first, Scottie or McCoy?"

"What were *you* doing in Singapodia?" Juliet asked.

"Killing Madame Phu."

"You..." she looked at me with... what? Amazement? Awe? Fear? I couldn't read her expression.

Suddenly she smiled, and again kissed me. Deeply. As deeply and warmly and lovingly as I'd ever felt anyone kiss me before. I—gratefully—returned the passion in her lips, and when we'd finished, my gaze dove deeply into those turquoise passion pools of love.

"I could never forget those eyes," I said.

"And soon they'll be the only eyes you ever look into, mister soon-to-be former Agent 8. You don't get to sleep with no more cadet agents when we live in Westchester with our three point two children."

"Or more," I said.

We kissed again, deeply, passionately, longingly. My hands began to wander brazenly over her nude body, and hers over mine. I pulled back from the divinity of her embrace to gaze over every inch of her fabulous form, her magnificent mammaries, her admirable ass, her flawless flesh...

"I love your mind," I commented. "I see why I was so taken with you when we were drunk and sharing this bed together."

"*We* were taken with *each other*," she said, leaning up quickly to kiss me adoringly, "because we're so similar, and we like sex the same way."

The brightness in her eyes had fully returned. And for the rest of the night that brightness removed any suspicion of Manchurian plots from mine.

"Fuck me, my future husband," she said.

And I did.

CHAPTER 12

THE NEXT MORNING, AT SADISTO headquarters, we had fully resumed our mentor/mentee relationship.

Mostly.

As we walked through the building, me in my agent's business suit, her nude except for tennis shoes, we would briefly hold hands, then quickly let go, like high school kids afraid of being caught by the teachers.

In a break room, as she leaned on a counter, slathering a piece of toast with strawberry jam I walked up behind her and slid my middle finger into cadet agent Pussy Hole, making Juliet squeal, and laugh.

"Stop that," she said.

"No," I said, and did it again.

"Bastard," she said, and threatened me with a jam covered knife. "Don't start something you can't finish."

"I'm your Big Brother Mentor. I can start and not finish anything I want."

"Well, then, you can kiss my ass."

"Gladly" I got down on my knees, and kissed her ass.

"Woo!" she said. "That feels nice. I should have told you to do that days ago."

As I kissed, I slipped a few more fingers into cadet agent Pussy Hole, and massaged her little sidekick, Nubby.

"Ooooh!" She said, putting her hands on the counter to steady herself. "Whoah, God, you can *absolutely* keep doing that."

I did. Until she was on her tiptoes, eyes closed, gripping the counter so hard it threatened to shatter, her voice a loud, warbly vibrato calling out to various deities, in various dialects, and screaming for release. She came so hard, her knees got wobbly, and I had to put my arms around her, to hold her up. Which meant I was *required* to slide my hands up and down the soft, warm front of her lithe, nude body, stroke the suppleness of her belly, and fondle her generous, receptive breasts.

"You are insatiable," she said, reaching up and back to put her arms around my neck.

"Listen to miss Kettle, calling Mister Pott black."

"I wasn't this insatiable until I met you," she purred in my ear.

"You ever want to go back to The General's office and do it on his desk, again?" I asked, a suspicious tinge in my voice.

"Why wait," she asked, not hearing any tinge except lust, and bent over, squishing her tits onto the counter, into the bread crumbs and spilled jam. She lifted her pretty little ass, and leaned back against me. "Just do me here."

"But in The General's office..." I began.

"No," she insisted, as people came in and out for coffee and snacks. "Now! Here!" she rubbed herself frantically against me, and made it impossible to do anything but comply.

8   8   8

Later, when we stopped at the Security Office for her official "Cadet Agent badge," I was speaking to the guard behind the counter as she stood close, smiling up at me. Without anyone noticing, she nonchalantly shoved her hand down the front of my pants, and began playing with my surprised—and quite honestly delighted—cock.

'Woo!" I said.

"Woo?" asked the guard, his vision obscured by the counter. "Woo, what?"

"Yes, Agent 8," Juliet asked, grinning her sarcastic little half-grin, squeezing and pulling on Agent eight and a quarter, "what are you woo-wooing about?"

"I'm woo-wooing about... how great your badge is going to look on when I pin it on your bare chest."

"Oh, Trevor, you would never do that to me."

Still grinning, she gripped harder, and my voice rose an octave.

"Woo," I admitted.

"What happened to your voice?" The guard asked. "You sound like someone cut off your balls."

"Pulled them off, more like," said Juliet, grinning. "Or is about to."

8   8   8

Later, it was time to get back to murder practice, so we took the elevator down to The Stockyard.

"What's the Stockyard?" Juliet asked.

"You'll see," I said, grinning.

She scowled, never liking my non-answers followed by an evil grin.

When the elevator doors closed us in, without another word, I opened my fly and pulled myself out. Then I reached around, cupped her bare butt cheeks, and lifted her quickly up, toward my already pulsing shaft.

"Oh, my God, yes, but wait," she said, spitting in her hand, and smearing it over my throbbing head. Slickened, she gripped me with thumb and fingertips, guiding my tip inside her. Eyes closed, mouth opened with pleasure, she slipped down onto me. Fully, and deeply inside, I leaned her against the elevator wall, and began thrusting, pounding rhythmically into the tight warm wetness between her legs, the sumptuous bare flesh that formed the physicality of her joggled and jounced with each of my driving movements. It was a feast for the eyes, and a delight to my tightly gripped penile nerve-endings.

"Ooooh, I love your fucking cock," she said. "What took you so long?" she asked.

She inhaled me, our mouths clamping tightly to one another, her tongue diving into my mouth, wrestling passionately with mine.

"We do like sex the same way," I said, pulling back to take a breath.

"Constantly, and everywhere?" she asked, attacking my mouth, again. I laughed in her mouth.

Between kisses, licks, breaths, and slurps, I said, "Let's get off on The General's floor," gasp, "and do it in his office," lick, "again," deep tongue dive, "on his desk."

"Why?" she said, between gasps and full mouth assaults. "What's wrong..." tongue wrestle, "with right here?"

I gave up, and gave in. If she was secretly a mole, or counter-spy, she was too cunning for me.

We didn't notice when the elevator came to a stop, because we didn't. Come to a stop, I mean. The doors opened, and another agent in business attire, along with her naked mentee cadet agent stepped in, turning their backs to the opposite wall. They—of course—were fascinated by what we were doing. We stopped kissing, turned their way, and smiled without missing a thrust.

"Hello," Juliet and I said together.

The statuesque black female agent—42, she of the scuba tanks earlier onscreen in the General's office—smiled, and nodded her own 'hello.' The cadet agent could only stare, goggle-eyed, mouth open so wide I could see his tonsils. 42 slowly reached over and took her cadet agent's penis in hand, fondling it to life. It inflated almost instantly, though his expression and eye-direction never changed.

The doors closed, and as Juliet and I watched, 42— without taking her eyes from us—lifted her skirt until we could see her thick, tangled, black bush uncontained by underwear. Skirt bunched around her waist, she moved in front of her cadet agent, pressing her bare bottom to his front, still gripping his engorged length, apparently guiding it into her from behind. Her face showed it was a pleasant, uncomplicated entry.

"Oooooh..." Juliet and I said together.

The cadet agent's expression didn't change. He even leaned out to see around 42 so he could continue watching us.

Plainly getting no help from her mentee, 42 began moving her hips around in slow circles, her eyes never leaving ours. As her ass gently rotated on the cadet agent's stiffness, she unbuttoned her shirt, and pulled it open in front to reveal the luscious lovelies I'd observed floating freely in the water earlier. Unlike then, these were gently pulled from her blouse by the loving force of gravity, exposing them completely, as she began to massage, and squeeze them with adoring gusto. All while silently, unblinkingly, watching Juliet and I grind into one another.

"Oh, my," Juliet said.

"Well said," I agreed.

Juliet returned 42's favor by massaging her own golden globes, lifting, squeezing, pinching nipples, and I slowed my pace to ease all secondary in and out motion. I didn't want to disrupt our view.

The elevator also again eased its motion, and the doors reopened. Two agents—male and female—dressed in shorts, tennis shoes and T's similar to what Juliet had worn earlier, entered and took in the sights.

"If you're going to ride in *this* elevator," Juliet said, confidently, "you have to be naked, and she has to be sucking your dick."

I chuckled, as the new agents looked at one another, unsure, then shrugged, and had at it. She pulled up the front of her T shirt, popping loose a pert pair of choice chesticles then immediately yanked down the front of his shorts, setting free his quickly rising, rather average trouser snake. She dropped to her knees, gripped it firmly in her right hand and stimulated it to full size, then did as Juliet had ordered, first licking its length, and circumference, then kissing its tip, and finally sliding her lips slowly around it. She took it fully into her hungry mouth, lips sliding easily along its length before moving her head back and forth, using her hand to stimulate what dangled below. Her other hand reached down to simultaneously massage her own joyful jewels, and both of them quietly, and happily moaned.

"Now you," Juliet said to the happy recipient of the female agent's attentions, "lean down and suck on those lovely titties." She indicated agent 42.

42—still rotating her hips—grinned, let go of her own pleasure domes, and leaned back to give the newcomer free, and complete access. He smiled, obliged, and led with his tongue. He licked the tip of her nearest nipple, circling it, flicking it lightly, then moved to the other and repeated the dance. 42 delighted in the tease, even chuckling a bit, gripping her breasts underneath, and squeezing them out to delectable points.

The male agent bent further, lips enfolding, enveloping, surrounding... bud, areola, breast flesh, luxuriating in all of its dark brown, swelling fullness as he drew much of it into his mouth where he continued working it with his tongue— hard and slow. 42's head rolled back, eyes half-closed, lips parted, as potent sounds of pleasure drifted all around the tiny room.

I couldn't help it. The energy was too much, and I began thrusting harder and faster into Juliet, both of us watching with intensifying lust.

Again, the doors opened, and again Juliet took command, telling the newcomers if they wanted to stay, they had to get involved. They—of course—were more than willing.

"Okay," Juliet said, struggling to keep her voice strong while I bounced her with furious rhythm. "You... get-under-her-and-fuck-her-while-she-squats-on-you. (oh, God, yes, Trevor, that feels so good). You... spread-your-legs-so-he-can-lick-your-clit..." and on, and on, as my driving thrusts got harder and faster. The actions of the others all orchestrated, she reached down to massage her own bawdy button, breath deepening into lusty gasps.

On the next floor down, several scientists were standing outside the elevator doors when they opened, and I can only imagine what they thought as their silent waiting was broken apart by what was revealed behind those doors. The tiny room was now filled with naked, humping agents in all positions... moans, gasps, groans and shrieks of pleasure erupted out of the chamber, into and off the corridor walls all around them, until the doors finally, slowly closed, returning the narrow hall to its original quiet.

As the doors closed, I thought I heard one turn to another and ask, "You ever feel like we work in the wrong division?"

All at once, collectively, the room exploded in climax. I can only speak for myself, but as Juliet and I thrust together for one last grind and involuntary cum-spasm, my mind reached levels it had never imagined possible.

Then, all at once, the inside of the room went suddenly very quiet. I lifted Juliet off of me, and set her down, where she leaned against my chest, both of us—all of us, actually— gasping for breath. My hands wandered aimlessly across the luscious, naked smoothness of my cadet agent's skin as I tried to gather myself and focus.

Far too soon the elevator hissed to a stop at the bottom floor, the doors opened, I took Juliet's hand, and led the way out past the other agents, into the warehouse beyond.

As the doors closed behind us, I heard someone say, "Who wants to do it again on the ride up?"

"Oh, my God, not me," whispered Juliet, as the others cheered, still struggling for breath. "I'm spent."

She looked at me adoringly, kissed my lips lightly, then turned to take in her new surroundings. Her smile dropped off her face like a poorly hung painting, as the room she beheld plainly made her mind melt even more.

"What the—" Juliet gasped, taking in the enormous space, "what the hell is this place?"

Imagine an enormous, open warehouse, a hundred yards long, hundreds of yards wide, containing dozens and dozens of glass cells/rooms/cages, inside each of which a naked enemy agent was penned. Each glass 'room' was about eight feet by ten, and contained only minimal sleeping and sanitary facilities. Some of the agents were pacing back and forth in their cells, others were sitting or lying on the floor, sleeping or scowling at nothing. A few were having sex with other captured agents.

I smiled at Juliet, who stared in horror.

"This, my dear Juliet, is the Stockyard."

CHAPTER 13

AS JULIET STARED OPEN MOUTHED at the naked collection of prisoners, I explained.

"This is the floor where we keep captive enemy agents imprisoned until they are either needed up on the rifle range or sent out for scientific experiments."

Juliet was plainly shocked. I could well understand how she felt. The Stockyard was a little overwhelming the first time you encountered it.

"Is this—this is—am I—am I asleep?" gasped Juliet. "Am I having a nightmare?"

"Hardly," I said dryly.

"But—where did all these enemy agents come from?"

"Oh, all over. Russia, China, Albania, Czechoslovakia, Romania, Bulgaria, Poland, North Korea, Vietnam, Cuba, Zanzibar, Pennsylvania, Burbank—"

"No, no," said Juliet, "I mean, how did they find their way here, to the secret headquarters of the *Security and Administration Division of the Institute for Special Tactical Operations*, usually referred to as SADISTO?"

"Oh," I said, "through the normal channels."

"Normal… channels?"

"Yes. As you doubtless know from your training, when an enemy agent is captured, he or she is first interrogated in the field, then shipped to Washington for further questioning by various experts from various government departments."

"Right," Juliet said. "And how do they end up here? Naked? In these weird cells?"

"Well," I said, "imagine if a spy suspect was arrested in West Germany by the West German Secret Service, they would question him, then they would turn him—or her—over to our CIC for questioning, the CIC would then hand him—or her— over to the CIA who would question him—or her—in Germany and then, if he—or she—seemed like a big enough fish, the CIA in West Germany would ship the spy suspect to Washington so that the CIA higher-ups could question him— or her. After they got through, the spy would be made available to other interested security agencies. For example, the State Department's security men might want to ask a few questions, NSA might have more, ditto Army Intelligence, Navy Intelligence, Air Force Intelligence, AEC, FBI, Secret Service, Fish and Wildlife, and so on."

"You mean the spy suspect would get sent from agency to agency like... an inter-office memo?"

"Good analogy," I said. "Now, as you know, or should know, SADISTO, powerful and ruthless though it is, is one of the least known, perhaps *the* least known secret agency in the U.S. Hence, ours is always the last organization listed on the official Spy Routing slip. Hence, also, all enemy spies and spy suspects, with the exception, of course, of those given public trials, wind up here."

"And from here?" asked Juliet.

I smiled. Cynically.

Juliet swallowed. "You mean... from here they don't go anywhere?"

I cocked my head in the affirmative.

Just then an evil-looking old man came hobbling toward us, leering at Juliet's magnificent nudeness. Juliet shrank back against me for protection. "It—it's that horrible old man who's in charge of the Obstacle Course," she whined.

"Oh, no, it's all right," I said, patting her bare shoulder, and then, for good measure, stroking her bare breast. "That isn't Hans. It's his twin brother, Siegfried. How's tricks, Siggy?"

"Fine, just fine," he cackled. "You folks looking for anybody in particular, or just browsing?"

"Just browsing at the moment," I told him. To Juliet I said, "Want to look the place over?"

She swallowed hard, but nodded her head. I led the way over to the nearest glass cage, inside of which a young, thin, but full-breasted Asian girl was pacing restlessly up and down like an angry panther.

I read the small, white card fastened to the glass door. "Viet Cong guerrilla," I said. "Presumed age 20. Captured three days ago in a rice paddy armed with a machinegun, and several hand weapons. At first denied enemy activity, then confessed on promise of fair treatment and full pardon if she cooperated." I laughed. "Evidently she didn't know much of value, if she's been cleared for repatriation after only three days."

"You mean," said Juliet, "that the CIA thinks she's on her way back to Vietnam?"

"Sure," I said cynically. "But what the CIA doesn't know won't hurt them. Those boys are a bunch of softies, anyhow. Our way, here at SADISTO, is much better. Not only will the taxpayers be spared the freight of shipping this girl across the Pacific, she can, unwittingly, help The Free World by serving as a useful target on the rifle range, or as a useful subject for any of the many horrible—I mean important—experiments being conducted by our Research and Development People in Department X."

"Wow," said Juliet, pressing her nose against the glass. "She's an arrogant one, isn't she? She hasn't deigned to so much as glance at us through the window."

"That's because she can't see or hear us," I said. "The glass wall you have your nose pressed against is one-way. On her side, it's a mirror."

"Still," said Juliet. "A woman who doesn't look at herself in the mirror..."

"Come on," I said. "Let's see what other goodies are in the Stockyard today."

I led the way leisurely down the aisle. The Stockyard was really jammed; I'd seldom seen it so crowded; every glass cell was occupied by a nude, captive enemy agent. Or in a few cases, two.

"Oh!" Juliet stopped, and stared, surprised, and by the inflating state of her nipples, a little aroused. The girl was insatiable. "They're allowed to have sex?"

"They are," I said, turning to watch the young couple doing just that. "It keeps them calm, and entertains us."

"Although it doesn't seem to be making them very happy," Juliet noted, leaning against the glass for a closer look.

I had to agree. They were glaring our way, squinting, teeth-bared, apparently quite angry, even as the man continued thrusting hard, and deep, making the girl's soft breasts slam up and down in violent harmony. Her legs were wrapped tightly around him, but that, and his relentless movement was the only indication that either of them was remotely interested in the other. I had to remind myself they were not looking at us, but at their own reflections.

"Keep in mind," I said, "they're not looking at us, but at their own reflections. Probably opposing agents from antagonistic world organizations who aren't fully enjoying themselves."

"Like he's from Russia, and she's from the US?"

"Israeli, Palestinian, Iranian, French, German, Dallas, Philadeplphia—pretty much anywhere. You can always find agents who hate each other even from the same country, and yet are still quite willing to fuck."

"I'd fuck him," Juliet said, dreamily. "Or let him fuck me. Angrily."

I watched as the raven haired, darkly complected female agent focused, like she was staring right at me, and wished she *were* staring right at me, while I was on top of her, making her breasts flop around like that.

"Yes," I said, finally agreeing with Juliet, "a good anger fuck can be both pleasurable, and healthy."

"Are—are *all* these people destined to be—*used up*?" whispered Juliet.

"No need to whisper," I said, "they can't hear you through the soundproof glass. And yes, they'll all be, eh, 'used up', as you put it. Which reminds me. Let Siegfried here know if you see any targets that particularly appeal to you. He'll have them ready and waiting at the rifle range by the time we get there."

"How many will you be wanting?" cackled Siegfried.

I shrugged. "Oh, a dozen or so should do for today."

"Could you use two dozen? We're terribly overcrowded right now—it's why we put these two together—and I'm expecting a new shipment of subversive Albanians tomorrow."

"Why not?" I said. "Make it two dozen. We'll take the dark chocolate men over there, those guys who look like they're covered in sprinkles, and the glazed looking young women in the back. And throw in any plains you might have. I could use a little target practice myself, and like my runners, kind of basic. Not too much added flavor. See anybody you like, Juliet—or, eh, rather... *don't* like?"

"Gee," said Juliet, who looked rather pale, I noticed. "It's so hard to choose. I mean, there are so many of them."

She watched the angry couple for a moment, then looked at me out of the corner of her eye with a slight grin. A grin I returned.

"Yes," I said. "I think that's an excellent idea. Make sure we get these two, please, Siggy."

"Happy to make them available, sir," he said.

As we strolled through aisle after aisle we were met by a bewildering variety of human targets. Sloe-eyed Romanian girls, tawny as gypsies; arrogant East German men, flaxen-haired and well-muscled; enigmatic Red Chinese girls, high-breasted and haughty; sophisticated Russians; pagan-looking Arabs; savage looking Albanians; plump-looking Polish girls; ripe-bodied Cuban girls—dozens and dozens of boys and girls. Heavy on the girls.

"How does it happen," asked Juliet, "that eight out of ten of these nude captive enemy agents are females?"

"I was just wondering that very thing myself," I said. "Do you know, Siegfried?"

Siegfried cackled. "Teresa. She used up close to a hundred men, all on her own. Machine gun practice, hand grenade practice, choking practice, cutting up with a knife practice—you know Teresa! She likes to kill men!"

"She sure does," I said laughing.

"Who," said Juliet, "is Teresa?"

"Teresa the Terrible, also known as Agent 9, is one of our best female agents. A dainty, demure young girl in her early twenties, she has never failed to carry out an assigned mission. Her one minor fault is she's a bit kill-crazy. And she hates men. So... I guess that's two minor faults."

"And so," gasped Juliet, "she killed one hundred male enemy agents all by herself yesterday… just for fun—to satisfy her bloodlust?"

"For fun *and* training," I corrected. "Also, it's much better that enemy agents die by other agents than by some antisocial act like hanging, or the electric chair. If Teresa can't kill a certain number of enemy agents every week, she starts killing anybody who happens to be around. She's a little high-strung. But, basically, a sweet kid."

"Oh," said Juliet. "I—I wonder if I'll ever reach the point where I actually enjoy killing people."

"Oh, *sure* you will," I assured her with a comforting arm around her shoulder, and a gentle caress of her bare bottom. "Killing people is like smoking or drinking. When you first try it, it's disgusting. Kind of gross, even. Then you get used to it, and sort of enjoy it. Eventually it gets to be a habit that can lead to problems in your personal life, until before long everyone you ever knew or loved is dead at your hands. And then—you're a pro!"

"And killing people doesn't give you lung cancer or heart disease," piped in Siegfried. "It purges the emotions, releases pent up hostility and makes you more relaxed at home, provides plenty of healthy physical exercise, all while reducing the danger of over population."

"Right," I agreed. "Have you picked out any other special targets yet, Juliet?"

She shook her head.

I shrugged, turned to Siegfried.

"Just send up our choices, plus a couple dozen assorted targets," I said.

"Yes sir," said Siegfried.

"Come on," I said to my comfortably naked Juliet, and led the way back to the elevator, which would take us to the rifle range. It was still filled with naked, sexing agents—more than before. We did not partake, but watched with interest as we rode up to our destination.

When we reached our floor, the doors opened to a cacophony of angry noise, and violent activity. We approached the shooting area, stopping to let a cart go past.

Whereupon Juliet promptly fainted.

CHAPTER 14

"JULIET," I SAID, patting her face to bring her around. "Haven't you seen carts filled with blood-drenched human bodies and body fragments before? In basic training?"

She opened her eyes. "Noooo," she said. "Oooooh, God. Is this real?"

"Mostly," I said. "Pretty much. Well, yeah. It's all real."

"Well, the answer is 'no,' I haven't seen anything like this before," she said, watching another loaded cart being wheeled past us. "Holy shit, what happened to them? Never mind. I know what happened to them. Where are they going?"

"They'll be dumped down a disposal chute. The attendants here try to keep the rifle range tidy and uncluttered. We probably just walked in after the lunch rush."

"Ooooh," said Juliet, obviously still queasy.

"Mark!" shouted a demure looking girl in her early twenties.

I looked around for 'Mark' then realized, oh, no, wait. She's calling for a target to be released. Silly me.

At the other end of the target range a door opened suddenly and a worried-looking young enemy agent appeared. He glanced wildly around, then began to dash at top speed toward a door directly opposite, firing his gun blindly.

The demure looking girl flung her rifle to her shoulder, and sighted along its barrel. I ushered Juliet down behind a safety barrier, before turning to the gentle looking shooter.

"What's your point of aim, Teresa?" I whispered.

"I'm trying," said Teresa, her British accent appealingly evident, "to shoot off both his kneecaps with one shot."

"Ooooh," I said, with admiration. "That is a *very* tricky shot," I whispered to Juliet. "High degree of difficulty. The knees of a running man, viewed in profile, only come together for a fraction of a second and—"

Crack!

"Bullseye!" I crowed.

Teresa was nonchalant, but I could tell she was pleased.

The young male enemy agent at the other end of the rifle range rolled around on the ground screaming and groaning in agony, holding what used to be his knees.

"Excellent shot!" I exclaimed. "You not only shot off both his kneecaps with one bullet, you shot off his knees, entirely. Were you using exploding bullets?"

"Ra-ther!" said Teresa cheerfully. "Us exploding-bullet-users would rather fight than switch." She put her rifle down, picked up a razor-sharp dagger. "Now comes the part I like best," she crooned, and walked briskly toward her latest, writhing victim.

"So that's the Teresa you were telling me about?" whispered Juliet.

"That is she," I agreed.

"Why is she dressed from head to toe in that funny outfit?"

"What's funny about it?"

"Black leather boots, black leather gloves," whispered Juliet, "and a head to toe, form-fitting black leather jumpsuit with plunging neckline, that's entirely crotchless in front and back. I mean... it's kind of pointless, isn't it?"

"Oh, that," I said. "No. That's a typical English agent girl's killing suit, of course."

"An English agent girl's killing suit is crotchless?" asked Juliet, looking at me as if tapioca had begun oozing out of my ears.

"Well, hers is," I said, "you know the most popular television program in England is a show called *The Avengers*, and the heroine in that is dressed in a form-fitting black leather outfit she calls her '*fighting* suit.' Teresa calls hers a 'killing suit' and made it crotchless so she could have sex before, during, or after the fighting. Ease of access. Ease of cleaning. Quite convenient.'"

"I had no idea," said Juliet. "I don't have an English TV set."

At the other end of the rifle range the young male enemy agent continued to roll around groaning in agony as Teresa trotted toward him.

"She's going to finish him off with a dagger?" Juliet asked. I nodded.

"Wouldn't it have been simpler and quicker for her to just pump an exploding rifle bullet into his head?"

"Yes," I said.

We watched as Teresa squatted on her victim, and wiggled her hips, pressing down, taking in the screaming man. He made little noises of surprise, that were eventually replaced by hideous shrieks of agony. Shrieks that went on. And on. And on.

"Dear Lord—what's taking her so long?" asked Juliet.

I shrugged. "She's enjoying herself. Or cutting herself a souvenir while he's still alive. She collects souvenirs."

"You mean... like scalps?" gasped Juliet.

"Um... something like that," I said.

Meanwhile, at the other end of the rifle range, Teresa was still squatted atop her victim, bouncing up and down on what I had to presume was his autoerotic erection, and the ghastly screams went on. And on, and on, and on...

Eventually even I got annoyed. "Pick up the pace, will you Teresa?" I called. "It's our turn to use the rifle range."

"We're not called SADISTO for nothing, darling!" Teresa yelled back. "And he's still hard! Give me another half-minute!"

The horrible screams continued for about thirty more seconds, then died away in a bubbling groan. Teresa cum-shivered, and stood.

"How, cadet agent Jones," I asked, "did she finish him off?"

"*What?*" Juliet whispered. "*How would I know?*"

I frowned. "She cut his throat. That bubbling, groaning sound is unmistakable. Didn't they teach you *anything* in Basic Training?"

Juliet turned away. "There was a lecture on 'A Hundred and One Death Rattles You Should Know,' but you wanted to stay in bed, that day."

"Oh," I said. "Damn. You missed a good lecture."

Teresa trotted up brandishing the lock of hair she'd cut from her victim's… scalp.

"The range is all yours, chaps." She halted, and studied Juliet critically. "A Cadet agent?" she asked me. "Pretty. Nice rack. How is she at anything beyond Seduction? Likely to fail her soon?"

Juliet shrank back, and moved behind me a bit. I ignored Teresa.

"Hmmm," said Teresa. "Not exactly bursting with self-confidence. The General had me act as Big Sister to a couple of male cadet agents like her last week. Good looking. But nervous. Shy, even." She turned the blade of her little dagger over in her hands, the surrounding lights flared across its surface, making interesting rainbow reflections on Teresa's face as she smiled, darkly. "I flunked them both. Fucked them each as they died."

Suddenly she brightened, and sheathed her blade.

"Well, I must be off," she said, brightly. "My niece is having a birthday party, and I'm bringing the cake! Happy shooting!"

And—whistling cheerfully—she left.

Juliet stared at me. "Is she for real?"

"Oh, of course," I said. "One of our most deadly and efficient agents."

"Isn't she kind of conspicuous in that so-called killing suit? It's basically got no cloth down her entire middle. Just a belt holding the two halves together."

"She doesn't wear it all the time," I said. "Only when she's actually—you know—killing. Or doing something that requires her to be crotchless."

"Like peeing?"

"Peeing. Or killing *while* peeing, maybe. Or while fucking, as was discussed."

"Fucking her victim?" Juliet asked. "She was serious?"

"Sure," I said.

"Jesus," she said.

"Not for you?"

"I prefer my penises to be alive, and responsive," she said. "And yours."

I returned her sly grin.

"Fucking dead people is wrong, Trevor," she said, with a sudden flare of hostility. "That's necrophilia. Even SADISTO can't cross that line. Can it?"

"Well, they're not dead when she starts, and I believe she stops when they do die. And sometimes she could be fucking somebody else. Somebody alive and responsive while killing a different victim."

Juliet looked for a moment as if she were thinking, Charlton Heston-like; 'this place is a madhouse. A MADHOUSE!'

"Now," I said, deciding to ignore her obvious concerns, leading the way to a long, low, shooting table on which a variety of lethal weapons rested, "I'll explain how this shooting range operates. Note that the far end wall consists of stacked bales of straw. That's to absorb bullets or other projectiles and prevent dangerous ricochets. At the right of the backstop you can see a metal door. When you yell 'mark,' the door will open and a target will appear and sprint frantically in front of the bales of hay headed toward the door directly opposite. They will be armed, with live ammunition. When you yell 'pull,' a target will emerge from the door on the left, and sprint toward the door on the right, also armed, firing at anything they can. Very much like trap shooting. But in this case the clay-pigeons have guns. Clear?"

"No," said Juliet. "Why?"

"Why is one side called 'mark' and the other 'pull?' I don't know. Just a tradition, I guess."

"No, no," gasped Juliet. "I mean, why do the enemy agents cooperate by running the way they're supposed to?"

I laughed. "Because they've been tricked into cooperating," I said. I reached over toward a small intercom, flipped a switch. "Here, listen," I said.

"Pssst!" said a male voice through the speaker.

"That's Siegfried," I explained, "addressing a female enemy agent who is at this moment penned in a tiny cell patterned after those used to release bulls into a rodeo ring."

"Who is there please?" asked a lilting female voice.

"A friend," we heard Siegfried whisper. "Listen... the American imperialists plan to use you as a target on their rifle range. But I will help you escape!"

"May your ancestors be praised," gasped the gentle female voice.

"Evidently a Red Chinese agent," I said to Juliet.

"When I give the signal," Siegfried went on, "open the door of the tiny cell you are in—the door will be unlocked at that moment—then quickly sprint like hell across the rifle range toward a door marked *pull*. Behind that door you will find a helicopter waiting to take you to safety."

"Ah… so, I will do," said the female voice.

I snapped off the intercom. "Clever, eh?"

Juliet frowned. "Is there really a helicopter on the other side of the door marked *pull*?"

"Of course not," I chuckled. "Now grab a gun and yell 'mark.'"

Juliet gingerly picked up a Luger and called, "Mark?"

"Louder," I said. "Like this: **MARK!**"

The metal door on the right sprang open and a staggeringly voluptuous Chinese female enemy agent appeared, glanced around, fired in our direction, then began to sprint like hell toward the opposite door as she continued firing.

"Fire!" I yelled at Juliet. She raised the gun, yanked at the trigger.

Nothing.

"You forgot to release the safety catch!" I snapped, as the agent's bullets ripped through the bale of hay in front of us.

Juliet clicked the safety catch. Meanwhile the Chinese enemy agent, her buxom bosom billowing bouncily, was halfway across the range, still firing blindly, but bullets hitting too close for my comfort.

"Juliet!" I yelled as bullets whizzed between our heads.

Juliet closed both eyes and fired.

"Keep your eyes open!" I ordered.

She opened her eyes, fired again. A spout of straw and dust appeared just behind the frantically running girl. Juliet fired again, and again, the bullets striking in front of or behind the more than ample moving target.

Now the Chinese female agent had reached the door marked 'pull' and was tugging at it. Naturally, it didn't open.

"Now that you have a static target," I said sarcastically to Juliet, "do you think you can do a little better?"

"Yes, sir," said Juliet, clearly distressed. "I can. I will."

She aimed the Luger carefully, pulled the trigger. Nothing. She'd used the entire magazine.

"What now?" she gasped.

"Pick up another gun or reload; whatever works," I said with irritated indifference, but smelling failure.

Meanwhile the voluptuous Chinese enemy agent, realizing the peril she was in, was taking careful aim. She fired, and struck Juliet in the arm. Juliet screamed, and finally seemed to focus.

The enemy agent, still firing, had begun to stride with rising confidence directly for us. She fired my way this time, but her gun was also empty, and clicked on a spent casing. She threw the gun aside and ran toward the weapons table.

Juliet grabbed a Thompson submachine gun, leveled it, slipped off the safety catch.

"If you miss with that," I snarled, "I'll flunk you on the spot!"

Juliet eyed me intensely, angrily, then fired a long burst. She didn't miss. The voluptuous running Chinese girl suddenly dissolved into red and pink confetti.

"Did—did I get her?" gasped Juliet, still staring at me.

"Yes," I sighed. "Next time, look at the target, not at me."

"Yes, sir," said Juliet. "Uh, *pull!*"

The metal door on the left was flung open, and a wispy, nude girl with long blonde hair sprang into view. She glanced frantically around, then began to sprint across the rifle range. She had a machinegun but didn't get to use it. Juliet fragmented her with a short burst from her own weapon.

"Excellent," I said. *"Mark!"*

A slender white-skinned, bearded, dark-haired man— Russian or Albanian I guessed—darted out, began to run.

"Use a pistol this time," I ordered.

Juliet nodded, threw down the Tommy gun, picked up and aimed a .38 Colt revolver.

The gun cracked once, twice, three times. At the third report the dark-haired man clutched his hip and fell to his knees, turning to glare defiance at his tormentors.

"Fock you!" he said with a thick Russian accent.

"Now," I said to Juliet, "take your time and aim for the heart."

"Yes, sir," said Juliet, "a heart shot, yes, sir." She aimed carefully, fired.

A dark spot that suddenly welled crimson appeared on the dark-haired man's left breast. The man looked down at it stupidly, dazedly, then slowly pitched forward onto his face.

"Excellent shot," I said. "Now," I said, picking up a crossbow, "we'll let you try firing a few arrows at live targets."

Juliet was still staring at the dead man in the field. She was shaking a little.

"Juliet?"

She turned to me, as if surprised I was there. Her face was the color of children's paste.

"Crossbows," whispered Juliet, "and arrows?"

"Yeah, of course," I said. "Crossbows are awesome weapons. The British used them in Burma and Malaya during World War II, and our special forces have been experimenting with them for years. Their chief advantage is that they're silent. A sniper using a crossbow in the jungle can eliminate a dozen sentries without making any noise that might alarm the main camp. Here, try one."

I showed her how to wind up and then load the crossbow. Then I yelled, *"Mark!"*

A nude girl sprang into view. I chuckled. "Well, what do you know," I said. "It's that Viet Cong guerrilla we were looking at in the Stockyard."

The nineteen-year-old guerrilla began to run like mad.

"I'll slow her down for you," I said, "seeing as how you're not used to using a crossbow. It's trigger operated, just like a gun. Sight along the… that's it. Hey!" I yelled in Vietnamese, "not that way—*this* way!"

The girl skidded to a halt, turned and looked at us, shielding her eyes from the bright floodlights all around us.

The crossbow in Juliet's hands made a sound like a plucked then muted guitar string, and an instant later the Viet Cong girl was staring down in horror at the arrow buried almost to the hilt in her middle.

"Load, and fire," I said crisply. Juliet did so. The Viet Cong girl was swaying on her feet, clutching the shaft of the arrow buried in her, jumped as a second arrow thudded into her right breast. Juliet silently loaded, fired again. A heart shot this time.

The Viet Cong girl toppled slowly backward, the bright feathered ends of the arrows jutting up like flagpoles.

"Really excellent," I said, "especially for never having used the weapon. You're a natural, and getting over the buck fever you had at first. Now I think we'll try a few rifle shots under conditions of poor visibility. I'll switch off some of these floodlights and—hey. Juliet? What's the matter?"

Juliet had suddenly dropped the crossbow, and begun to shake all over.

"Cadet agent…" I began. "Juliet?"

"I—I don't believe it," she whispered. "I don't believe any of it. This isn't happening. I'm not really shooting at live human people. None of this is real; it can't be. It's all just a horrible dream fantasy nightmare. Isn't it? My family makes ice cream. I'm still in Singapodia. Asleep in a gutter, somewhere, having the worst dream of my life."

"And that would be…" I said, unsure, "… preferable?"

I put a gentle hand on her shoulder, attempting to comfort. A less experienced agent than I might have flunked Juliet right then and there. But I knew she could come back. Plus… it was Juliet. The woman I saw now that I loved totally and completely without question. I'm pretty sure.

"I want to be on a quiet beach…" she closed her eyes, "lying in the sun…"

She was slipping into denial; going into shock. Being intelligent and experienced, I knew that her attack of the jitters wasn't serious, and wouldn't last. If I could keep anyone else from finding out, she wouldn't be flunked. But she had to snap out of it. In the end, I knew. I could see it now. Juliet had The Right Stuff. Both for SADISTO, and for Westchester.

I also felt responsible. In order to mold her into a trained, efficient SADISTO agent I had been systematically brutalizing away her more gentle, delicate sensibilities as a way to stamp out all mercy and compassion. Soon, very soon, I'd make her into an inhumanly efficient killer. She was almost there. Her disbelieving reaction now simply represented a last, desperate attempt of those empathic, sensitive—supposedly 'higher' feelings to reassert themselves. With careful handling, I could easily finish off this last, drowning spark of humanity.

"What do you mean," I said gently, "when you say this can't be happening?"

"This—*everything!*" gasped Juliet, her eyes desperate, frantic. "People don't really use other people as clay pigeons— *not in real life*. This—this whole underground headquarters…" She looked around, the light dimming in her beautiful, turquoise eyes. "It can't… it can't really exist—can it?"

"It can and it does," I said soothingly. "And as far as believing that places like this can't exist; I don't think you've *really* considered the depths to which human depravity can go. Especially when it thinks it's right, and threatens The Free World."

"But..." she said, losing touch with me, with reality, "...you mean our enemies, right? Or do you mean... us?"

"Our enemies," I said with certainty. "I think. I mean, this isn't depraved, it's reasoned. Intelligent. Fighting fire with fire, and all that. But you know we're the good guys, right?"

"Do I?"

Now I was worried. She had to come back from this, or The General would make her a target, and probably in one of my training exercises as punishment for us both.

"Juliet," I said, struggling to keep the flow of concern off my face in case the General was watching on that ten-foot TV of his, "Juliet, you haven't considered what our enemies would do if only *they* used these methods, and we refused to."

"I..." said Juliet, "no, I guess I haven't."

"No, obviously not," I said, grasping at a straw of hope. "And we need to meet... and beat them. We're practically a *humane* organization here, really. I mean, compared to camps that have existed in the recent past. We don't burn children alive here, except in rare cases where it's scientifically essential to determine the effectiveness of portable flame-throwers, and the children are annoying. And as for using human beings as clay pigeons... well.... what *should* we use to train for life-or-death situations we might encounter out in the real world where we need to kill people... like clay pigeons?"

"I guess," said Juliet. "you'd have to—"

"Yes, you'd *have* to. Exactly! Right now, for example, test teams are operating in Vietnam, trying out various weapons under various test conditions. The AR-15 rifle, for example, has been extensively field-tested. Which means it's been fired at enemy soldiers or sympathizers, or just really stupid ugly people, and the damage it does is carefully noted and photographed. So, if the Army can try out various weapons on human targets *in the field*, why can't we try them out here, under controlled conditions? The targets we use are spies, aren't they? Bad spies. Bad spies who did bad things. And bad spies are traditionally executed, anyway, aren't they? Why shouldn't we combine executions with…" I gestured vaguely to the course, "training?"

Juliet looked around, slowly, then coming back to eventually stare at me, the joy in her marvelous eyes darkening… fading away. It hurt to see.

She hung her head.

"Juliet," I said, "What we do, we do for the greater good."

Suddenly she raised her head, and the light had returned. Sort of. In a different way.

"You're right, Agent 8. You're absolutely right. I'm so— *so* ashamed. I see now that I was doing this just to get closer to you. But how could I have doubted the rightness and importance of this training program—the essential grandeur of learning how to protect *The Free World* of all things, as a glorious agent of SADISTO?"

"Yes. Yes, Juliet, exactly! I'm so glad to hear you say that, cadet agent Juliet Jones. Now," I said, placing both hands gently on her shoulders, and speaking like the loving, caring mentor of violence that I was, "No more pointless sentimentality?"

"No," she promised bravely, eyes boring into mine. She bent over and snatched up the crossbow. "No more. In fact… *watch this! Mark!*"

A terrified-looking enemy agent—Bulgarian, I guessed— ran frantically across the rifle range. Juliet carefully aimed and fired the crossbow, and the arrow skewered the man's calves together. Two legs, one shot. My God. She really did have the right stuff.

The enemy agent collapsed, screaming. Juliet picked up a small dagger, and caressed it lovingly.

"I'll go," she muttered, almost to herself, "and finish him off. Slooooowly."

She sauntered toward the helpless enemy agent she'd winged, her bare buttocks swaying with magnificent confidence.

"*Siegfried,*" she yelled! "*Send out the dark man we requested who was having sex in the Stockyard!*"

The 'Pull' door opened, and the dark-skinned young man from earlier was shoved out, trying to cover his nakedness.

Juliet veered towards him, slapped his hands away, grabbed hold of his manhood, and stroked it furiously to life, taking it in her mouth a couple times to really urge it into stiffness, then pulled him by his hardened dick over to her victim. She knelt down to finish the girl off, raising her own smooth, tanned, young ass—that lovely ass I knew so well, and so intimately—high into the air, wiggling it.

"FUCK ME!" She commanded, pointing her gun at the erect captive agent. He immediately complied, dropping to his knees behind her and entering her as if his life depended on it. Which it did.

"Oh, God, yes—" Juliet moaned, *"FUCK ME HARD! ANGER FUCK ME! SLAP MY ASS!"*

He moved his hips faster, one hand lightly slapping her rump.

"SLAP HARDER!" she screamed, and he complied.

"YES," Juliet screamed. *"YES! YES! YES!"*

And as he leaned in to his work, so did she.

Horrible scream after horrible scream of the Bulgarian agent filled the air, and I found myself almost choking up with pride. Juliet Jones had made the grade. She was not, I realized, a cadet agent any more. She was a full-fledged SADISTO killer. A killer for The Free World.

I wiped at my eyes and—I'm not ashamed to say—my eyes were not entirely dry.

A SADISTO agent had been born...

But then it hit me.

"All right, all right, all right," I said, walking toward the dark-skinned man boning her from behind. "That's enough of that!"

Juliet pointed her gun at me.

"I'll decide when it's enough," she said, and to the man up her ass, "Keep going."

Hands raised, I backed away slowly, and for the first time began to question the wisdom of what I'd done.

CHAPTER 15

"YOU BROKE HER," THE GENERAL said a couple days later, smiling.

"Broke her *in*, you mean. Yes sir," I said, proudly. "She has the makings of a real homicidal maniac who will gladly kill on behalf of The Free World."

"I agree," said the General gruffly. "You did a fine job brutalizing her, 8. I've been watching you over my closed-circuit TV from time to time. Especially when you're alone together at night. And in that elevator. You have some real stamina there, you two. And she showed some fine command skills in organizing that impromptu orgy."

I smiled, and nodded a 'thank you,' overall, feeling very pleased with myself. Overall, but not entirely.

"I thought she did especially well in Interrogation yesterday," the General said, admiration adding a seldom heard warmth to his voice. "I've been in this business more years than I care to think, but some of the diabolical tortures she thought up to inflict on her screaming victims were entirely new to me. Cruel, and inventive."

"Yes, sir," I said, thinking of our future together in Upper Westchester, raising our children. "She does seem to have a natural flair for torture."

"Yes," continued the General, "agent Jones seems to have only one handicap at the moment."

"She… what?" I said, scratching my head. Mentally. I had to stop scratching my head *physically* around the General. He might think I had dandruff, which he hates. Or lice. Which he also hates.

"She has a handicap," growled the General. "She now looks and acts like a homicidal maniac. Those glassy eyes of hers, her habit of continually muttering 'die, enemies of the Free World,' under her breath. Mannerisms like that would easily arouse the suspicions of any intended victims. South American Generals in particular."

"She's doing that?" I asked.

"Hadn't you noticed?"

"Well, since her breakthrough our mouths have been otherwise occupied. She's become much more intense and focused in the bedroom."

A slow grin spread across the General's face, and he grew glassy-eyed, himself.

"Yeah," the General said, eyes rolling up in appreciative memory of some video, no doubt. "Quite hot. Although more violent, and less loving than it used to be," he shook his head to clear the thoughts. "I'm going to have to fail her."

"I'm sorry, you're going to have to what?" I asked.

He put a comforting hand on my shoulder.

"Don't worry, 8. She'll be decommissioned. We may still find a use for her in certain high-body count situations that don't require her to be clandestine."

"But… no. Sir, I have to protest. She's perfect."

Ignoring me, he pressed a button, said into the intercom: "Have agent Juliet Jones sent to Decommissioning. Full mind-wipe. Give her back her homeless clothes, and dump her back in Singapodia."

"But… General, *please…*"

He turned to me, shocked.

"Agent 8. Are you… pleading? You know I hate pleading. Almost as much as I hate dandruff and lice."

"I am not pleading, sir," I lied. "But Jones, and I… it's just that…"

"The boys down in Decommissioning will teach her how to *simulate* youthful innocence again, once she's on the outside." He chuckled. "Hard to believe that only a short while ago she actually *was* youthful innocence."

"Yes, sir," I said, swallowing hard with remembrance of her charm, her joy, her lusty and affectionate way of fucking me. A lot. The General was right. Our lovemaking had changed, and become less loving... more... angry.

Thoughts of retirement, a happy future filled with love, and turquoise-eyed children began to evaporate from my dreams, once again. A gut-eating sensation of *All Hope Lost* began to spread out like a nasty oil slick from the general vicinity of my heart. I had cost myself the perfect companion. Tormented the things that had drawn me to her—empathy, sensitivity, passion, and compassion—love—savaged them right out of her. On purpose.

This job had made me do it. Made me do it to myself. And I had reveled in it. Why?

"May I see her before..." I started to say.

"*God, no!*" The General snapped. "Buck up, there, boy. There must be hundreds of other sexy, stunning, large-breasted blondes with turquoise eyes out there!"

"Oh, sure," I said, my voice barely audible. "They grow on trees."

"Besides, she won't remember you after all this, anyway, so what's the point of saying goodbye?"

I sighed, and looked away. I considered arguing, but then realized it was pointless, and would just anger the General.

"So," I said, fighting the urge to fight, "can I at least take a short vacation?"

"Vacation?" snapped the General. "You had all that time off in bed with Jones! Now you want to loll around on vacation while all over the world the forces of good are locked in mortal combat with the forces of evil?"

"Sooo...?" I said sadly, "that's a 'no', then?"

"Yes. That's a no. You have to look into that business on Jícama with the agents who disappeared; Strangeways, and Trueblue. Hunt them down. Kill them. Only now you need have to do it alone, as I've declared Jones unfit for standard duty. Get down there in the morning. I need you back on your game."

I nodded my head like a dead-eyed bobblehead doll, then dropped chin to chest as the beautiful dream I'd been allowing myself to have, the dream to replace *The Dream*, suddenly crashed down around my ankles, and shattered on the floor. I headed for the door of the General's office, dejected, and left the dream pieces where they lay.

Before exiting, something wormed its way out of my brain—something I hadn't been able to stop thinking about.

"Sir," I said, "When I was in here with cadet agent Jones on her first day of mentoring, something... fell... out of one of your drawers."

"I don't wear drawers," he said, confused.

"I meant your desk drawers," I corrected, patiently. "A folder. Top desk drawer, left side."

The General looked down at it, then pulled it open.

"This one?" He asked.

"Yes," I said. "I remember the color-coded tab and UTLRA COSMIC ALIEN AUTOPSY WAY ABOVE TOP SECRET marking. May I ask... what's in that, sir?"

He opened it, and showed me that it was empty.

"Nothing," he said, unnecessarily. "It's just a folder."

I took it and looked it over from all angles. There had been a photo of Madame Phu in here. As I remembered her, dead on the floor. Where had it gone? Then I noticed the words under the plastic color-coding.

Manchurian Plot/Phu

"Was there something in here, before?" I asked.

The General glowered. "No. You failed to get the information from Phu, remember?"

I nodded, unable to forget, and without another word I returned the folder, and walked through the door into the outer office.

"Punny for your thoughts?" Punnymany said, reading my mood.

I was too low to spar with her, too distracted by whether the General had just lied to me, or someone else had removed the contents of that folder. Without a look in her direction, I walked out with no puns left to give.

8   8   8

It was late, and although Gran offered me one or more replacement girls—all with turquoise eyes if that's what I wanted—I waved her off. I wasn't in the mood. Instead, I got

Scottie to take me into town where I wandered the streets for a few hours, hoping someone would try to mug me so I could kill them.

Ironically, I found myself in front of a *Jonesy's Icey Creams Shoppe*.

I looked through the paned glass at a happy family ordering cones of varying flavors and sizes. I wondered if they'd come down from Westchester. Then my heart sank when I saw my own reflection in the window, tired, worn, pale. Beside my face there was another, on a printed poster taped inside the window, facing the street. Facing me.

I choked on my own despair. It was a photograph of Juliet.

Younger. Happier. Her turquoise eyes bright, and lively, filled with youthful innocence, looking right at me. The poster made my heart hurt even more.

JONSEY'S HEIRESS MISSING
$3 MILLION DOLLARS REWARD
$ $ $ $ $ $
For any and all information
leading to her safe return

There was a number you could call at the bottom.

I entered the brightly lit little shop—or *shoppe*, which sounds the same, even though it has the extra letters—as the cheer-filled family walked out past me. I told myself I was just curious, just wanted to look around, but I really wanted to punish myself. I stood there in the clean, happy little world, wishing I'd been able to enjoy it with Juliet, and our various children, instead of drunkenly recommending that she become an agent – slash – partner – slash – uncontrollable psychopathic killer. Why hadn't I—instead—drunkenly made her go home? Drunkenly driven her myself, back to her friends? Her family? Her life? She would be rich. Alive. Free. With all the ice cream she could ever want.

But no. I had to bend her to my world. Make her everything she wasn't so I could remain who I was, and have what I wanted. When I didn't even want to be who I was.

What was wrong with me? Why had I been so selfish? Why did I want ice cream?

Spooning the place in through agonized, desperate eyes, my gaze drifted pointlessly across the promotional images of happy kids, happy lovers, happy dogs, even happy cartoon insects all eating delicious-looking ice cream *(with the sprinkles already inside!)* in bright, cheery places. I shuffled to the counter where a teenage boy stood behind a seemingly endless number of refrigerated tubs of kaleidoscopically colored confection.

"Can I help you?" he asked, pleasantly.

"Yeah," I said, looking at the vibrant cakes in the side fridge, another REWARD poster taped to its front. "Do you know anything about the heiress? Juliet?"

"No," he said. "Heiress of what?"

I turned and fixed him in place with scathing anger. It made him flinch.

"The heiress of *Jonesey's*," I said, pointing to the window, and the refrigerator, and the counters, as surprised as him by how angry I was. "*Her face is all over the place.*"

"I didn't put those up," he said, as if that excused his stupidity.

I stared at him, and considered killing him. I could do it. I had a license.

Instead, I ordered a *Jumbled Jumbo*.

To go.

8   8   8

I stood on the sidewalk slowly spooning down my ice cream, staring at the picture of Juliet, and my own reflection beside her. Shoulda, coulda, woulda played an angry game of tag in my head. At one point I made a pucker motion so my reflection could kiss her cheek, and was caught by the kid inside watching me. I tried to pretend I was just—I don't know—yawning, or about to eat another scoop, or something, sort of wishing I could go back in time, and...

Then it hit me. Hard enough to loosen teeth.

I raced inside, ripped the poster off the window, tossed my ice cream in the trash, and ran.

8   8   8

After being pulled off by the night guard, a rather large and far too-interested black man, and confirmed as the actual, circumcised Trevor Hawke, Agent 8—and no, you can't have my phone number—I was riding down one of the main elevators inside SADISTO headquarters heading toward **CENSORED** on Floor 8, where they were supposed to be Decommissioning Juliet. I checked my Smith to make sure I'd loaded it, flipped the cylinder back into place, cupped my gun hand, aimed at the doors and waited impatiently for them to open.

When they finally rattled apart, I was glad to see the waiting room on the other side completely empty, mostly because I hated the thought of killing someone I knew. And maybe liked.

Holding the gun out before me, I moved past the empty waiting area with a sign above the desk that read:

MIND CONTROL

I strode quickly down the main hall. Doors on all sides were closed, and there was no sound. Not even from the rapid movement of my feet. It felt like a deserted hospital. Without medical equipment. Or chairs. Maybe what it really felt like was an empty office building. Which is more-or-less what it was.

Without incident, I rounded the first corner, a pair of double-doors at the end, above them, another sign.

DECOMMISSIONING

I walked the length of the corridor, and—again—was pleased not to have to kill any friends, while at the same time wishing I could kill *someone* to ease the tension. At the double-doors I carefully peered through the porthole windows, into the corridor beyond.

Glass walls on either side of the next hallway disappeared into the darkness of what could have been the entire depth of the building. The clear walls provided visibility into observation rooms so guests and distinguished visitors could stand outside and watch spies, captured officials, foreign dignitaries, or swimsuit models undergoing whatever mind control technique was being used inside. In this case— assuming Juliet to be in one of them—The Decommissioning mind control technique meant going through an agent's entire SADISTO history to date in order to record, and suppress it for various purposes; retirement, mission failure, secret locations, and sometimes just to locate lost keys.

Juliet was here because of me.

Behind each glass wall darkness sat heavily in most of the rooms. Only one, about three rooms down, was lit up. I couldn't see anything other than shifting shadows, and the disgusting 'medical green' color of the enclosure walls. I crossed my fingers (mentally, of course, actually doing that would make it difficult to pull the trigger, and shoot anyone, obviously) that Juliet was inside. I silently pushed open one of the double-doors, and crept through.

To make sure I wasn't seen, I checked each darkened space as I passed. All had the same basic setup; instruments hanging from the ceiling above a reclining chair bolted to the floor in the center of the room. Medical tables and equipment scattered about, near the chairs. All rooms were empty of people.

Still making no sound, gun at the ready, I reached the lighted room, peering around the wall separating it from the darkened room beside me. Inwardly I prayed that the other side of the glass was mirrored so I couldn't be seen. I was pretty sure it was, but I had skipped the mandatory *Agent's Tour of Decommissioning*, so I wasn't positive.

As I moved forward, more of the room became visible, including a man wearing a full body smock, surgical hat, and mask. He was adjusting some science-fictiony looking thing that jutted down from the ceiling, a metallic cone-device that reminded me of the *Inner Space* ride at *Disneyland*—but without the pretend miniaturized tourists. My heart missed one or more beats when I saw a pool of blood on the floor, puddled around his booted feet. Afraid of what else I might see, I cleared the room's edge, and nearly choked on my own tongue.

The man manipulating the device wasn't manipulating anything. He was just hanging there. Hands impaled with scalpels, sticking him to the machine. Blood and entrails hung out the front of him, spilled onto the floor. Across the room, a second man, dressed similarly, but without any pants on, sat in a corner of the room with a metal tray embedded in his ruined face.

Curled into a fetal position not far from him was Juliet. Naked. Her body and hair red with crusted blood, and gore.

She held a couple nasty looking probes defensively in each hand, also covered in crimson muck. Wires were attached to her forehead and scalp under her disheveled hair, wires that trailed from her head, up to a large monitor screen on a shelf above that displayed an image of Madame Phu leering into camera, and laughing on a short loop.

I shot the transparent wall. It shattered, and Juliet jumped, terrified. She looked at me and tried to make herself smaller in her corner. As I approached, crunching over the mess of blood and broken glass, she moaned—a heart-piercing wail that shattered my soul. She looked at me with no recognition, tensed, fearful, raising the probes with legitimate threat.

"Juliet," I said, calmly. "It's me. Trevor."

Her eyes were pan-sized with terror, her mouth ready to scream, breathing wet, ragged gasps, and chuffs.

"I'm not going to hurt you," I said. "I'm here to get you out."

In response, she continued to push herself into her corner, her frightened breathing so sharp, and explosive that spit, and blood sprayed from between her lips.

I pulled the crumpled poster from my pocket, and showed it to her.

"I'm going to take you home, Juliet," I said, attempting a smile. "Home."

She studied the poster, and her breathing increased. Not the response I was expecting. Her eyes bounced to me, to the poster, back to me. Suddenly she swung one of the probes at my face, and I blocked it before it could plunge into my eye. We struggled for far longer than I want to admit, probe inching toward my dilating pupil. And she nearly beat me.

Instead, she collapsed into my arms. I clutched her before she hit the dangerous, glass strewn floor.

In the silence I heard Madame Phu laugh, rewind, and laugh again. I looked around trying to sort out what the fuck had happened in here. I could only guess that once Juliet was strapped in, one of the Decommissioning guys got randy, and Juliet's training kicked in.

Good girl.

I lifted her into my arms and as quickly as I could and lay her on the 'interrogation chair.' I bent and grabbed the probes she'd been using to protect herself, and jammed them into the monitor harassing the room with images of Madame Phu, shorting it out, halting the insane cackling. Then I did the same to whatever recording equipment was attached to it, and finished by throwing it all against a wall, and stomping on it. Whatever was on there was something Juliet had never told me about, and was certainly something she hadn't wanted anyone else to know.

I hefted her back into my arms, moved toward the exit, kicked through the double-doors, and stopped before someone I didn't recognize—a guard reaching for a gun.

"Hey, what the hell?" he said, as I pumped a slug into his open mouth.

Carrying Juliet, I stepped over the fresh body, and made it to the elevator without any further interference. Inside, I hit the button for floor 8.

New level reached, the doors opened, and the letters on the reception wall told me I was where I wanted to be:

THE TIME FUNNEL

But the way in was blocked by barricades, yellow warning tape, and a big sign:

CLOSED TO RESET TIME
Our hands are full. Watch this space.
We will clock back in in a timely fashion.

Punnymany, and her signs!

I swore—a lot—then hit the button to Department X. The elevator stopped on a different floor, and opened on another surprised guard carrying a Detex Guardsmen's clock and key. He quickly realized his hands were too full to defend himself and only had time to slump and groan before I plugged him. He died sighing, rolling his eyes up into is head as if feeling he deserved it. Which he kinda did.

Body having fallen safely backwards, the doors again closed until they reopened on a room full of people in colorful spandex milling around the Department X lobby, including Professor Ex. All hours of the day and night, those X people were working on something crazy—often wearing the most outlandish outfits.

The Professor was sitting in a corner as if watching her X Men—who were mostly women—perform some kinky Mardi

Gras fashion show. Why? I don't know. And Ex wasn't telling. Her thoughts were her own, as she, and everyone turned to me with understandable concern, froze, and went silent. Juliet was still nude, still dripping blood on everything, especially me, and I was holding a gun. That kind of thing grabs and holds your attention.

I didn't have enough bullets to shoot them all, so instead I focused on Professor Ex, vaguely threatening her with my pistol.

"Take me to Deadly Vehicles," I said. "I need to get her out of here—*now!*"

Ex looked at me, then at Juliet, and finally waved at the gun.

"Put that stupid thing away," she said, standing, and motioning for me to follow.

The gun I didn't, but follow I did. She moved briskly through the parting crowd of colorful X-Men, into a hallway, turned, hurried down another hallway, rounded another corner, and sped down a third hallway. At its end she entered a smaller, back elevator, held the single door open, and motioned me in. I looked at the tiny room, and considered my options.

"Trust me, or don't," she said. "But figure it out, quick. You don't have a lot of time."

Behind me, I heard doors slamming, boots racing across tile.

I got in the elevator.

Ex pressed a button, and the doors closed just as several guards rounded the corner, skidded to a stop, lifted their weapons and aimed. Too close to my head bullets whistled, metal pinged, and the inside of the doors closed and indented toward my face.

I stumbled a bit as we moved… sideways.

"They can't follow us in this," Ex said.

"Wow," I whispered.

"Yeah," Ex said, proudly "I got the idea from the 'Wonkavator' in Charlie and the Chocolate Factory…"

"Will there be Oompa Loompas where we're going?" I asked. "I could really use some chocolate."

Ex laughed.

Juliet stirred.

She raised an arm, putting it around my neck, and looked at my eyes as if seeing them for the first time. She startled a bit, then settled when she remembered.

"Do I know you?" she asked.

My heart ached. "Apparently not."

She rested her head against my shoulder, and I felt her relax.

"Well, thank you for helping me," she said.

"You're quite welcome."

"You rescued someone?" Ex asked.

"Sort of. Depends from which side of the equation you're viewing it," I said.

"Mmm." Ex said, considering this.

"Mmm," I mimicked.

"Not very 'SADISTO', of you," Professor Ex said, continuing down the tracks of whatever train of thought she was on. "You actually have quite the humane streak in you, Agent 8."

"No need to be insulting," I said, surprised. "I am not humane. I've just been feeling a little... off, lately."

"You've always been nice to me," Ex said without turning around. "Always took the time to talk to me. Compliment my work, ask about it, and my life. Respect my intelligence. Treat me like a peer," she said. "So, for that, I thank you, as well."

"I'm telling you," I told her, "I'm really not nice. I am full-on SADISTO's top agent! Ruthless, and... and ... ruthless! And I don't see you as a peer!"

"Oh?" Ex stiffened. "No?"

"No," I said, snarling. "You're *way* smarter than me, and you know it. So irritating."

Ex softened, then grinned, appreciatively.

"That certainly seems true at the moment," she chuckled.

I laughed as well, and I felt more than saw Juliet puff a small giggle.

The 'elevator' finally opened onto a hangar filled with strange vehicles of violence. Trucks tricked out with weapons, tanks, sports cars sporting weapons, go-karts gone crazy with weapons, ultralights ultralighted up with weapons, jetpacks jetting out with one small, but pretty nasty looking weapon, planes planed out with weapons, hot dog and hot pretzel carts cooking with weapons.

"Back along the far wall," Ex said, pointing. "There's a series of ATVs—All Terrain Vehicles—in small, individual chutes. Pick one, press the red 'Launch' button in the center of the dashboard, and hold on. When it lands, it drives like a car."

"Thanks, Ex," I said. "I owe you."

"Oh, yeah, you do."

We smiled at each other until I turned and ran, as quickly as I could carrying Juliet.

"We could run faster if you put me down," Juliet said.

"Yeah, but..."

"Or are you carrying me because you *enjoy* cradling my bare-ass?"

"Well," I said, smiling, "I don't *not* enjoy it."

She laughed as I set her down, and together we did run much faster. Though how she managed it with those gazongas wrecking balling around on her chest is beyond me. Practice, I guess.

Behind me, to the far right of Ex, a wall exploded.

Without slowing—actually I speeded up—I craned my neck around to see a side wall crumbling open and a wave of heavily armed SADISTO security men racing through the dust, flames, more dust and collapsing rubble. I guess they didn't need no sideways elevators, neither.

Machinegun fire ripped into the vehicles beside me with heavy, metallic punching sounds. We ducked down to use them as cover intentionally instead of by accident, and scuttled toward the promised ATVs.

I kept my body between the guards and Juliet as she ran around the vehicle to jump into the passenger seat, then I leapt into the driver's side next to her.

I searched the dashboard for the button Professor X had told me about. I swore she'd said a red button. But there was no such thing. I looked in the ATV next to me. It had a red button! So did the next one! And the one beside that! *How did we jump into the only one without a red button?*

That's when the bullet ripped through my shoulder. It drove me forward enough that my face nearly touched the dashboard. 'New design?' I thought to myself fighting the lance of pain. Old design? *Bad* design? I was just gonna have to guess. I had my hand hovering above an orange button, when feminine fingers settled on mine, and gently enfolded them.

I looked over at the beautiful turquoise eyes and her lips parted ever so slightly with that ironic grin.

"That's my ejector seat," she said, "You can read, right?"

I looked, and saw that it was—indeed—labeled 'Passenger ejector seat.'

"I used to be able to," I said.

I looked down and saw that all the buttons were actually labeled. She moved my hand over to a smaller red switch that said, "POWER" and used my fingers to flip it to "ON."

We were instantly on a rocket sled down a tunnel into hell. The little ATV shot forward pressing us both against our seats as bullets exploded around us. We shot into a tube barely larger than the vehicle we were in, and raced along at speeds that made my cheeks flap around like a dog's face stuck out a car window doing a hundred. Lights passed us fast in rhythm, kaleidoscopically, hallucinogenically.

I turned my eyes toward Juliet, and saw her face flapping, brightening, and darkening with the passing lights the same as mine. Weirdly, it was having a similar effect on her tits, and I was momentarily mesmerized by the rippling, water-like flap-flap, glow on, glow off and flow of her titanic two.

Finally we launched out of the tube, and into the air, to sail high above the fake country club buildings, over the neatly trimmed golf course, rocketing our way to… God only knew where.

Far ahead was a thicket of trees, and we were sailing straight for one or more of their black trunks. Juliet screamed, and I'm not ashamed to say that I screamed along in harmony, chorusing beautifully with her until the wheels made a harsh squeaking sound like the landing gear of an airplane striking asphalt. The little ATV bounced once, twice, scootered down a ramp built between the evergreens, onto a little path, careening neatly out of the copse and onto a tiny, paved roadway. Almost as if someone had planned it that way.

Oh, Ex, you crafty devil.

The gears started to grind, and the engine sounded like it was going to explode. Realizing it needed to be out of first gear, I kicked the clutch, and the grinding sound immediately stopped. I jammed the stick with one hand, took hold of the wheel with the other, started the engine, released the clutch, and gave it gas. We surged forward, racing down the little path, deeper and faster into the darkness of the woods.

I had pretty good control of it, and before long had figured out the steering well enough to mostly keep us from running into things. I nearly lost control with the explosive sounds far behind me. The same sounds our ATV made being shot down the tube.

Not surprisingly, we were being followed.

I jerked the wheel one way, then the other to stay on the little path, and realized I probably shouldn't be doing that. At the next curve of road, I let the little ATV all-terrain itself off the road, through the tree trunks, and over the matted pine-needles, leaves, and earth that formed a carpet between them.

Presently I heard the distant jet-airplane squeal of tires on asphalt once—twice—three times. Then no more.

Three vehicles, hunting us. How easy would we be to find?

Unfortunately for us, the ATV was not a quiet machine. Designed for all kinds of rugged terrains but not for stealth, its engine sounded like an irritating neighbor's riding lawn mower—one I would have words with.

Deciding that hiding and cowering might be the better part of valor, I brought the speed down, slowing us to an easy stop alongside a good-sized river. I flipped the power switch to 'off.' The neighbor's lawnmower went silent.

"Juliet," I began to say.

"You know my name?" She interrupted.

"Uh... I do, yes," I said. "But you don't know mine."

"Oh," she said, seeming sad about that. "So, what is it?"

"Trevor," I said.

"Trevor," she said, as if remembering... something. "I like that name. Why was I in there? What was that place? Why am I naked?"

"I'm not really sure I could explain it," I said. "It's really complicated. What's the last thing you remember?"

"Oh, I uh... I don't really know," she said. "It's all kind of a jumbled jumbo."

"Like the ice cream. 'Five crazy flavors'..."

"... and at least one toy," she said, as if embarrassed. She pointedly said no more.

"Do you know where we are?" I finally asked.

"Well, we were in our hotel—my parents and I—and we…" she stared ahead, her eyes bouncing around in thought, "I guess I remember trying to escape to the airport…"

"But right now," I asked. "Do you know where you are, right now?"

"Singapodia?" she said, or rather questioned.

I shook my head. Her expression dropped and she looked around. After a few minutes of searching the area, and her thoughts, she turned and showed me she was a deer in the headlights, clearly distressed. A deep sadness filled her eyes with a pain I couldn't fully understand.

"My parents were killed," she said. "And I was kidnapped."

Or maybe I could understand. That's right. She had told me about that. But not the kidnapped part.

"Did you already know?" she asked, then shook her head. "Of course you knew. You just rescued me."

I smiled, attempting to be reassuring. I took her hand, and held it, quietly stroking its back fingers with mine.

"So, you know *who* you are, right?"

"My name is Juliet Jones," she said, a little unsure. "My family actually makes *Jumbled Jumbo's*. We're *Jonsey's Icey Creams,* and I…" she paused, bit a lip, squinting her eyes as if struggling with some horrible honesty, "I'm rich."

I nodded, still attempting to be reassuring.

"Really rich," she emphasized. "Really, really super fucking rich."

I continued smiling, and nodding.

"I can tell by the way you're smiling and nodding that you knew, and that you did this for the money," she said.

"What? No," I said, panicked. "No, I did it… I did it for other reasons."

"Oh," she said, looking shy, kind of glancing around, then staring down at my hand caressing hers. "Well, um, okay. God knows you're cuter than anyone else I've ever been with, and this is a nice place for it. Could we do it down by the river? I'd enjoy that. But I don't have condoms, and I'd prefer it if you used one…"

"What," I said, stunned. "No. That's not… no. Not that I wouldn't love to—really, *really* love to—" I glanced at the tiny, picturesque river. "It would be nice, actually…" I shook my head. Seriously. Someday my dick was going to get me into real trouble. *More* real trouble. Again. "I don't want anything. I just want to get you home. Safely. Back to where you belong. Where do you live?"

She stared at me a long time, and I began to wonder if she'd fallen asleep with her eyes open. I opened my mouth to ask if she was okay, when she stunned me.

"I live in Upper Westchester."

CHAPTER 16

This time it was my turn to stare blankly. For a long time. Her eyebrows knitted into a worried frown.

"Trevor?" she asked, finally. "Are you all right?"

"I..." I said, then stared more. "Yes," I finally blurted. "I'm fine. Sorry."

"It's okay," she said. "I was just worried about you for a second, and I wanted to make sure you're okay." She smiled. "You're my hero, after all."

She turned away to look again at the moonlight flickering diamonds across the swirling flow of the river, then she climbed out of the vehicle, walked a few paces toward the glistening ripples, her bare backside the gore covered marvel of sensuality I so well remembered. She stopped walking and slowly, shyly, turned back to me.

"I want to clean all this... gunk... off of me," she said. "Then... afterward..." she licked a lip, and smiled, with invitation, "maybe it wasn't the reward you were thinking of, but it could be a fun way for me to say 'thank you.' If you want to, I mean. Down by the river? Or... in it?"

She flashed a brighter smile, then turned and walked quickly away, still glancing back over her shoulder, bare bottom jiggling rhythmically with each nervous step. She crossed the river's silted bank, and turned to face me as she backed the rest of the way in. Her front bobbled and bounced as enticingly as her rear had.

"Do you enjoy touching as much as you enjoy looking?" she said, voice soaked with sultry, sexual meaning. And in case I missed the meaning, she hefted one of her enormous breasts, and licked her own nipple.

Men's pants are not designed for sudden erections. It's just a fact. I shifted in my seat, adjusted fabric to avoid pinching, and painful binding.

When she had backed up to thigh deep in the liquid darkness she released her tit, turned away once more, wiggled her ass playfully, laughed, and dove beneath the lazy swirls of moonlight.

I stared at the spot where she'd disappeared a while longer, wondering about the bizarre ethics of this. I try not to think about ethics—most days it gets in the way of my job—but this was a new one for me. We had already been intimate. A lot. Yet, I would be keeping a secret of our past few weeks together while partaking intimately of a body I already knew so well— and still wanted so badly. Was it a right thing? A wrong thing? Good? Evil? Sometimes it's easier having sex with bad women. You never worry about things like truth, honesty, feelings, emotions, right or wrong. You just plunge in, and come what you did for. I mean, did what you come for. Came for. Do.

I leaped up and stripped as quickly as fabric, and personal hooking devices will allow, tossing all into the back of the ATV. Then I broke all land speed records down to the riverbank, wading hornily into the spot where she'd just been, hoping my divining rod would locate her first.

Sadly, no contact came.

A little scared—she'd been under quite a while—I began to search the area, frantically splashing and groping under the surface, and calling her name.

Nothing!

For a moment I was terrified. What if she'd gotten tangled in something? What if some enormous fish—some rare, fresh water, Great White shark had swallowed her whole under the surface, and…?

Then it hit me.

She'd escaped.

She hadn't wanted me. She had wanted to get away from me.

But… why? I was her hero.

Feeling a little rejected, a little heartbroken, I called her a few more times, and waited for a response that would never come. Finally, I dragged my sorry ass back to the ATV, intending to get dressed and head back to SADISTO to face whatever music the General felt like playing.

That's when I heard my irritating neighbor start up his lawnmower. Then a second neighbor. And a third.

She hadn't escaped. They'd found her.

I raced back to my own ATV, flipping the power on before even fully sitting down. It responded instantly, which was good, but the engine noise cost me my ability to hear them, which was obviously *not* good.

I floored it in the direction I'd remembered, six wheels spinning shit into the air—dirt, needles, rocks, some unlucky insects and maybe an unfortunate animal or two.

If they'd taken her underwater right in front of me, they had to be close. I felt myself stop blinking as I searched every dark shadow of the woods around me. Rumbling along I realized the sound of their motors would prevent them from hearing me, as well, and that might prove an advantage.

Before long I saw movement between the trees, and I angled toward it. As I drew closer, I searched the ATV for any kind of weapon—gun, knife, wrench—even a used, inkless pen would do at this point. But nothing. Only my clothes.

Slowly it occurred to me, and I smiled to myself.

The first ATV came through the woods in a clear hurry to get back to SADISTO HQ, and that was my second advantage—I knew where he was going. I simply had to get ahead of him on the path he was taking. The driver was so focused on maneuvering the thick trees and shrubs, he didn't bother to look up. The crotch of my pants looped easily around his neck from my perch in the trees above, I pulled on each leg and twisted, easily yanking him out of his seat, and tangling him in a makeshift noose. As his vehicle bounded off into the darkness all on its own—no Juliet inside—he swung below me, kicking and trying to scream, until he obligingly passed out. Or died. I didn't care which.

I dropped him to one side, leapt down, dragged his body under a bush, and took his sidearm. I was belting it around my naked body when I realized, took the pants from around his neck and put them on, hopping my way as I did back to my own ATV. I listened, and heard lawnmowers off to my right.

The second ATV was much easier, given that I was now armed. I simply pulled alongside the driver and shot him in the face when he turned his stunned eyes my way. Unfortunately for me, he also didn't have Juliet in his vehicle.

I gunned the engine, once again searching the darkness with unblinking eyes.

After what seemed like miles and hours... nothing.

I pulled over and stopped.

Listened.

Even more nothing.

Then I saw the path. The asphalt path I'd veered off of.

The one that led back to SADISTO HQ.

8   8   8

The third ATV ambled along, apparently in no hurry, driving easily atop the tiny, asphalt escape road carved through the forest. In the distance, the section of HQ that was above ground, the faux country club, was lit up in the darkness. It would have been a simple matter to gun the vehicle, and be there in minutes. But instead, the guard pulled over and slowed to a stop.

Slumped in the seat beside him, Juliet—still nude, and now damp from her river cleansing—breathed quietly, her lovely large breasts slowly rising and descending. Movement which had apparently become too much for the guard to resist.

He removed a glove, reached out and touched one of her breasts, gently at first, softly, then more firmly, and finally squeezing as if he were catching a hacky-sack.

"Mmm..." Juliet moaned, a slight grimace on her features. "Not so hard, Trevor..." she whispered, lustily.

The horny sound of her voice apparently ignited his own lust, and the guard shed his pants like the snake he was. Already hard, he yanked Juliet's legs apart, and climbed between them.

Juliet struggled for consciousness, pushing feebly at his arms, and hands, but he persisted.

"You're not Trevor," she said, her eyelids fighting to separate, her voice a slur of fog and frightened darkness. "No, I don't know you... *stop it...*"

But there was no reasoning. No requesting. No listening. He took hold of his pink violator and aimed.

As I took hold of his ears, and slammed his head into the passenger door of the ATV. He shrieked and fumbled for his gun, but I took that from him easily, punching him in the face with it. Blood spurted from his nose and lips, and he went down like a sack full of wet soap.

"My hero..." Juliet said, warmly, still lost in the hazy murk of whatever drug they'd apparently given her.

I dragged the guard off her completely, and tossed him to the ground, kicking him in the gut for good measure.

But I wasn't done. I was still angry.

I took a knife from a sheath on his belt, knelt beside him, and exposed his neck. I set the blade to his throat and was about to shove, when Juliet sort of screamed.

"Noooo," she said. "You save' me. Tha's enuff. Tha's enuff, my hero."

I held the knife at the snake's neck for a long while, my eyes locked onto his horror-filled eyes, the eyes of a dead man standing before Satan. I wanted to shove the blade. I wanted to feel his blood on my hands. And he knew it.

"Find a new line of work," I said.

He nodded his head like it was on springs.

"And a new place to live," I noted the ring on his finger, "and tell your wife what you did here, tonight, unless you want me to drop by your house and tell her myself, after which I can finish this."

He continued nodding, realized his mistake, and shook his head, then nodded again, confused but desperate to communicate compliance, making his eyes as sincere and puppy-like as humanly possible.

"Leave your pants," I said.

He stood, stepped out of them and ran, looking back occasionally to see if I was following.

I turned to Juliet, and felt the glow of a love so wonderful, so pure, the kind that can only be felt by a man who knows he's already lost it. She was no longer cadet agent Jones. She was the woman I had actually fallen in love with before I ruined her.

I was an ass. And a killer. Something so far removed from Westchester and family and children that I had no business even dreaming of them, especially not with someone as glorious as Juliet. I had thought I needed someone to be more like me. But for the happiness I craved, I would have to learn to be more like her, and it was far, *far* too late for that. I had immersed myself in the SADISTO world, and reveled in it. There was no going back.

So, the least I could do was give Juliet back the life she'd lost. I couldn't go back in time to change things like I'd wanted, but at least I could take her home.

She reached a hand out to me, and smiled.

"My hero..." she said, her mouth a slurry of words and saliva, "come live with me on my island... make love with me on the beach... in the sun..."

Spit dribbled from between her lips, waterfalled down her chin, and onto her chest. She was never more beautiful to me. Her hand slowly fell from mine, and she dropped into a happy sleep.

8   8   8

Juliet snored gently in the passenger seat of the ATV wearing my suit jacket as I drove, and barely stirred when I stopped at a payphone to call the number on the reward flyer. Her body had fully succumbed to whatever drugs they'd given her, and I watched her slumber for a while before stepping into the booth. She was the most beautiful woman I'd ever seen, and my heart ached to stay with her.

But I couldn't. I would only further destroy her.

After a seemingly endless number of rings a sleepy male voice on the other end of the line answered, and—weirdly—didn't seem all that interested. He didn't even ask who I was.

"She's alive?" the man asked, no concern in his voice. Just... curiosity? Annoyance?

"Yes," I said, feeling something was off, but not fully getting it. "She's fine. Healthy, and unharmed. Where would you like me to bring her?"

"Oh," the voice sounded surprised. "Why don't you tell us where you are, and we'll come get her."

"Why don't you want me bringing her to you?"

"We'll bring cash," the voice said, ignoring my question.

I said nothing. I pursed my lips, and fidgeted while my mind raced.

"Where are you?" the voice asked with more authority.

I hung up.

Something wasn't right.

I called a friend familiar with Westchester. He knew the Jones place, and gave me directions.

An hour later I was standing at the door of an elegant mansion, ringing a bell. It took a while, but lights came on—first deep in the house, then in the corridor beyond, visible through the dimpled glass panes and sidelights. A recently sleeping butler with a nervous housemaid close behind opened the door cautiously, and only a few inches. He looked me up and down, lingering his attention on my shirt and tie covered in dried blood.

"Yes?" he asked.

"I have Juliet Jones," I said simply.

The maid gasped, hands flying to her mouth, and the butler's eyes widened. Four simple words, and I'd gotten more emotion from these two than from the man on the phone.

"Is she hurt?" the maid asked.

"No," I said, stepping aside to give them full view of her in the driveway.

Guided by the butler, I carried my sleeping princess in through the front door, down the lighted hall, and into some kind of sitting room/reading room and lay her on the sofa. It was the kind of room I always wanted to have where I could hide away from my children, and pretend to be annoyed when they bothered me. The maid—instantly, and caringly—began tending to her.

"You'll be wanting money," the butler said.

"No," I said. "I won't."

Off their surprised looks, I turned to leave. The maid called to me, sharply.

"Why is she naked underneath this coat?" she demanded.

"I don't know," I lied. "Maybe she can explain that to you, when the drugs wear off."

"Drugs…" she said, paling a bit with fear and concern.

"Who are you," the butler wanted to know, more commanding and insistent, this time.

I paused. Unsure how to answer.

"Her hero," I said, sadly.

I turned away again, and he grabbed my shoulder, gently.

"How can we reach you," he asked, more kindly this time. "In case she wants to find you? And you must have some kind of reward."

I looked at her sleeping on the sofa. Her face angelic in the warm lamplight.

"Knowing her has been reward enough," I said. "And she should never try to find me. None of you should. Please take care of her."

Without another word exchanged, I walked back outside, got into the ATV, and drove out of Juliet's life.

CHAPTER 17

The General sat across from me, tapping the remote control for his immense, ultra-high-definition television on his desk. If his eyes could leap from their sockets and grow hands, I'd have been strangled to death the instant I'd been escorted into the room.

"Where is she?" The General asked. Tap, tap, tap.

"I'm sorry, who?" I asked, like a kid who's never had his hand in any cookie jar, ever.

"You know who," he said, his voice chilling the room a good ten degrees, tap, tap, tap.

"I'm sorry, General, I really don't."

"We spent a lot of money training that girl," he said, "filling her brain with SADISTO secrets. Then carefully walling them off again. Don't think for one second that we're just going to let her walk away with all that expensive, classified knowledge in her head."

"I thought you erased all the knowledge in her head?"

"Technically, nothing is ever erased," the General said flatly, "only blocked. But she had other…"

He stopped short of revealing something he suddenly realized he didn't want me to know. I said nothing. Tap, tap, tap, tap, tap, tap… After what seemed an eternity of tapping, staring, staring and tapping, followed by a little more staring and tapping—he held up the remote, showing it to me as if I'd never seen one before.

"It's a paperweight, now," he said. "Useless."

He stared silently, a while longer, until he tilted his head toward the television itself. The thing had a chair sticking out of its shattered screen.

"Did you do this?" he asked.

"Why would I smash your television set, and all the other and television sets, and the security cameras, and recording devices throughout the entire complex?" I asked, so innocently even I almost believed me.

"*To cover your escape with Juliet Jones!*" He snarled.

"Is that who you keep asking me about?" I said, turning my eyes upward, and searching his ceiling. "Juliet Jones, Juliet Jones... that's the cadet agent who flunked out yesterday? The one I warned you wouldn't be able to make the cut?"

"*You know damn well it is!*" He growled. "You were having sex with her! Lots of sex! Don't think I believe that you forgot her like most of the women you bang! In fact, I think that's why you broke her out! I think you developed feelings for the girl!"

"Oh, General," I said, dismissing the notion with a wave as patently absurd. "I had feelings for her *boobs*. Lots of feelings for those boobs. God, they were nice. And her ass. Great ass. But let me tell you, her best attribute was that soft, tight..."

"Yes, yes," he said, adjusting the front of his robe for comfort. "Enough of that, you lying sack of..." He stared a minute more, and finally waved me away. "Get out of here and prepare for your mission to execute Strangeways, and Trueblue. Your flight leaves at 0500 tomorrow. And you need to get treatment for that bullet wound in your shoulder before you go."

He glared at me as I stood, his anger seeming to expand into something larger, and more intense, developing a life and will of its own.

"If you weren't my best agent..." he growled.

"But I am," I said, grinning.

8   8   8

The twenty-two tons of deadweight of the C-140 Jetstar descended to the tarmac of one of the most beautiful, and fertile islands in the world: Jícama.

Beautiful, and fertile. Just like Juliet.

I had dreamed of her during most of the flight down, which was a bit of a relief from *The Dream* of the wife that I'd killed. But only just a bit. My sleep was haunted by three children, and Juliet joyously holding the happy, severed head of another child, with turquoise eyes. The head kept saying in a Ralphie from the Simpson's kind of voice, *'I'm point two.'*

I checked through customs, my natural suspicions aroused by anything and everyone.

"Business or pleasure," the agent asked.

"Pleasure," I said. "I hope."

The uniformed man looked at me, and I realized I had made a rookie agent mistake. Never draw attention to yourself with uniqueness or charm. The uniformed man grinned darkly at my comment.

"There's definitely pleasure to be had in Jícama if you know where to look."

"Half the fun is in the looking," I said, glad I wouldn't have to kill him. I wasn't in the mood. Well, I was. But I wasn't.

You know what I mean.

Outside a woman in a mini-skirted chauffer's outfit, hat and heels was waiting with a car. I hadn't ordered a car.

"Mister Hawke," she said, taking my heavy bag, and tossing it easily into the open trunk. "I was sent by representatives of our agency to accompany you to your hotel, where I will help you check in, and then have passionate if meaningless sex with you."

"Ah," I said. As always, the General provides. "Fine. But first, take me to the field office where Strangeways, and Trueblue worked."

"But… don't you want to check in after your long flight?" she asked. "And have sex?"

"The flight wasn't that long," I said, immediately suspicious that she didn't want to change her plans. "The mission is the important thing."

And solving it quickly meant I might get a day or two to relax. And have sex. With her. Maybe.

"Of course, it is," the chauffer said. "No problem. It's not far out of our way."

We drove through the deepening purple shadows cast by the mountains, as lights twinkled and sparkled to life throughout the city. She pulled into the parking lot of a small bungalow surrounded by a tropical floral outburst, frog sounds, shady palms, and stopped the engine.

A sign on the door read: *Universal Exports, we export... universally!*

"Through that door," the chauffer said. "You have a key?"

"A key *code*," I said. "Yes."

We eyed each other in the rearview mirror. She said nothing. I said nothing.

I exited the car, stepped to the bungalow door, found the keypad behind a palm frond, entered the correct series of numbers, and letters. The lock clicked, and the door opened easily.

I was barely inside when I heard it close behind me. I pulled my Smith, and whipped around to find the chauffer, back against the door, smiling with lusty interest. She was naked, except for the hat, gloves, and heels.

"I thought to myself," she said in a purr. "Self? Why wait until we get to the hotel to have sex when can have sex right here?"

I ran my thumb over the safety of my weapon, and mulled things over. Her body was magnificent. Long neck, soft, full breasts, a gentle curve of hip that smoothly sloped down into legs that didn't need heels to look magnificent. Lean and muscular, she clearly worked out.

"True," I admitted. "But the mission comes first."

"And you cum second," she said.

We both grinned. I holstered my Smith, and reluctantly returned my attention to the room. The place was quite clean. Too clean.

There was no sign of anyone ever having worked here. No stray pencils, no family photos, no coffee cups, no coffee pot, no coffee, no coffee filters—I really needed coffee—no anything to make it feel personal, or lived in. Even fakely lived in, like fake photos, fake awards, fake decaf coffee. Was the entire building a front? Or had the agency come through and stripped out everything personal?

"Did the agency come through and strip out everything personal?" I asked.

"No," said the chauffer, looking around with me. She pulled absently at her pubic hairs. A nervous tic no doubt. I wondered how she managed while wearing clothes. "Nothing has been removed pending your investigation. The files have all been inspected. Nothing out of the ordinary."

"But there are no personal letters?" I asked, going through the drawers. "No love notes between the two suggesting they might run off together?"

"None that I'm aware of."

"Hunh."

"You find that odd?" she asked.

"Only because the agency *assumes* they ran away together. But there's no sign of anything to indicate that?"

"No. Nothing I've heard about. Maybe the agency knows more than it's saying? What did they tell you?"

I looked at her. Studied her to see if she was fishing for information. As I scowled into her lovely, smiling face, she walked over to me, and began unbuttoning my fly.

"Oh," she said, looking at her work. "Goodness. I was beginning to wonder if there was anything in there, you showed such little interest in my being naked. But there it is."

She pulled my stiffness free of its confines, and stroked it gently.

"And this isn't a *little* interest at all."

She dropped to her knees, and inhaled me—which made me gasp rather unmasculinely. She was already stroking with her right hand as her mouth slid along the entire length of my shaft. The fingertips of her left danced over my dangling balls while her tongue and lips worked magic just above.

"Wooooaaaah..." I said.

"Mmmmm..." she said.

Her hands suddenly grabbed the waist of my trousers, and yanked them down to my thighs, cupping my ass and gripping it with desperate intensity to pull me deeper into her mouth. Then—just as abruptly—she popped her lips and dancing tongue off of me in a way that nearly made me faint. She stood, pushing me back onto what had likely been Trueblue's desk. Or was intended to appear to be.

The chauffeur walked her legs to either side of me, guiding my spit-soaked head into her soft folds while pressing her own hips forward. The heels brought her high enough for easy entry, so as I lay back, she hip-thrust and quickly swallowed me fully inside her.

She smiled, and moaned with pleasure.

"Nice cock," she said.

"So I hear," I said.

She abruptly shifted her hips, and nearly made me cum with that single movement.

"You like that?" she asked.

"Can't you tell?"

She abruptly shifted again. I abruptly moaned again.

"Yeah," she said. "You like that. Tell me what more you know about Strangeways, and Trublue?"

"I can't..." I began.

She pumped her hips again, and I nearly exploded.

"Nothing," I said, trying to fight it. "The assumption is that they ran away together. That's all I know. I'm supposed to find them."

"And do what?" the chauffer asked, grinding her hips rapidly in multiple directions until I thought my dick would come off inside her so it could live there happily, forever, and ever. "And do what?" she repeated with more ferocity.

I pressed the muzzle of my Smith under her chin.

"What do *you* think," I said.

"No," she said, softly. "I had you in my power."

"Yeah, mostly," I said. "But we SADISTO agents are trained to resist amazing sex. Whom do you work for?"

She just grinned. I clicked back the Colt's hammer. Her smile vanished, but she remained silent. I moved myself around inside her, rapidly, and she gasped.

Two can play at that game.

"Doctor Sin," she said, flushing red.

"Medicine woman?"

"That's Doctor *Quinn*."

"Of Romney Marsh?"

"No, that's Syn," she said. "Spelled with a 'y'. The other one. This Sin is spelled with an 'I'. Of Krabs Key. Krabs with a 'K'."

"Like Mister Krabs?"

"What? No," she said, confused, "like the island. Krabs Key. What are you talking about?"

"What does this 'Sin' have to do with the Strangeways, Trueblue disappearance?"

Again she returned to silence. Once more I stirred my straw inside her drink. She gasped, biting a lip.

"I don't know," she said. I stirred again, harder. She groaned, but stayed silent.

I reached my free hand down and tapped her fun button.

"AH! Please!" she begged. "Believe me!"

Another fast in-and-out. Another several taps, and a gentle rubbing massage. Another gasp, her eyes closing briefly.

"Oh, oh, oh, God! No more!" she gasped. "I know nothing. I was just supposed to find out what *you* knew."

I pressed my free fingers around her hard, pink, hot bob. She grabbed my arms, and leaned into it.

"Ah, my God, I'm telling you the truth!" She said, eyes closed tight, hips still grinding. I pumped and tickled, drove and rubbed. *"Please! Ah, ah, ah, I don't know any more! I swear to you! Stop!"*

She began to shiver, tremble, shake, and I knew I had her. She grabbed one of her hardened nipples between thumb and forefinger, and squeezed, her hips grinding hard, grinding fast.

"They went to the island of Dragons to investigate some mysterious bird poop, and that's all I know, I—ah, ah, AH, AH, AH-AH-AH-AAAAAAAAH..."

She shook violently, thighs clamping around me, head down, shivering, gasping.

Time stretched out into infinity as she periodically twitched, and spasmed, which shook her softly swinging orbs deliciously. Finally, after a long breath, she slumped, and panted.

Slowly she lifted her head and stared at me, her chest heaving, her beautiful, bountiful breasts rising and falling and jiggling with each, nipple-hard-earned breath.

"You bastard," she whispered, then lunged on me, kissing me as if she intended to suck the skin off my entire head. Her mouth worked on mine with the apparent goal of removing lips *and* tongue; her own tongue licking around inside my mouth, over my teeth, until—slipping outside the confines of my mouth it slurped my lips, chin, cheeks, and eyes. When she was done, I was quite wet.

She stepped back, pulling herself off my still stiffened stiffness, grabbing it to give a quick tug, and slow, slick, sliding pull.

"Mmmm," she said. "You have given me what no man has ever given me."

"An orgasm?" I asked.

"That, too," she said. "I have to go. But perhaps when you've finished your business, before you leave, you'll stop by my place and come inside for another visit?"

"I would like that," I said.

"And by 'come inside,' I meant, 'come inside my pussy.'"

"I got that. The agency has a class in double entendre. I earned a special commendation."

"Stay away from Krabs Key," she warned me, unexpectedly, suddenly deeply serious. "If you go there, you will die. No one goes there, and returns... alive."

She reluctantly let go of me, and as I reached down to pull up my pants her eyes suddenly widened, blood leaking from a hole in the center of her chest that hadn't been there before. Then another. Then another.

She collapsed into my arms and smiled.

"I die, happy," she said.

I kissed her gently, sweetly, as she did.

Tossing her body aside, I searched the room, and spotted a silenced gun disappearing out a back window. After yanking up my trousers I smashed my way through the patio doors and saw a man scrambling over a garden wall. I ran to him, grabbed his pant waist and began to drag him back to my side. But the pants tore away in my hands. I looked up in time to see a naked, hairy ass disappear over the wall.

"Eeeew..." I said, tossing the pants aside, leaping up after the killer.

I scrambled after the man, falling to the other side myself after my own pants got hung—maybe on a nail, or the rough corner of a brick—I don't know. Now equally naked from the waist down but still armed I searched the street for the killer, spotted, and set off after the man. The two of us—both bare bottomed—raced along the pretty little Jícaman street, flowering bougainvillea, Jamaican, sun dappled ramoon, rustic walls on all sides, him screaming, me firing, civilians trying to escape.

Lovely. Just lovely.

"STOP!" I yelled.

"NO!" He yelled.

I fired again, and unfortunately missed. Clearly I needed more 'shooting and running' practice on the training field. I stopped to take careful aim, as ahead of my prey, a bus stopped, opened its folding doors, and the bare-assed man leapt inside.

I stopped sighting and resumed the chase, leaping in just ahead of the closing doors, slamming into my quarry.

He fell over onto the driver.

"No!" he screamed. "Leave me! Please! She will feed me to the dragon!"

I grabbed him around the neck, slamming his head into the driver-side window.

"*Who?*" I demanded. "*Who sent you?*"

"*Ung,*" he replied. I slammed his head again.

"*Who will feed you to **what** dragon?*" I further demanded.

"*Uckle,*" he replied. Once more, I slammed his head. Harder, this time, until his head cracked the glass.

"*Who do you work for?*" I further, *further* demanded.

"*Siiiiiin,*" he replied, before slumping into unconsciousness.

I put my hands on the small of his back, lifted myself up, and saw a distinctive octopus tattoo on his upper left butt-cheek. I bent closer to study it, noting it's precision, and clean lines. Almost as if it was made using a template.

Murmurs arose from the body of the bus, and I looked toward the crowd, noting that the gunman and I were, rather understandably, the center of their attention. I smiled and waved, reassuringly.

"This isn't what it looks like," I said, only now sort of realizing that they were seeing two bottomless men fight, one apparently mounting the other from behind. "Well, it is. But not in the way that you think. I don't know this man."

The crowd gasped.

"I had to do this."

More gasps.

"It's not sexual, or anything," I said, waving my hands. "No, no. I just needed to make him to squeal."

Even more gasps, and now a couple men were standing, and talking amongst themselves, stepping my way.

"Okay, that sounded bad. I meant confess. See, this was… okay. I was having sex with someone else, right?" muttering and more gasps, "Then this guy comes along …" I sighed, and put my hand over my face. "You know what? Never mind."

I pointed my Colt at the standing men.

"Sit back down."

They did.

I stood up, and for reasons I don't fully understand I was erect, which elicited more gasps from my captive audience. Ignoring them, I exited the bus. I considered tossing a pocket-grenade back on board, but I didn't have my pockets with me, so I let it go. As I was walking away, I heard the gunman moan behind me, and remembered.

"Oh," I said to myself. "Right."

I turned back and shot him in the head, and he stopped moaning, but everyone else on the bus started screaming, so I decided it was time to be somewhere else. I returned for my pants, and headed down to the harbor, so enchantingly lit up with the night, and looked into hiring a boat.

I intended to make my way immediately to the island the chauffeur had told me about. Krabs Key.

The one with the mysterious bird poop and maybe a dragon.

Sure. Why not?

CHAPTER 18

THE LITTLE RENTED BOAT took many hours to reach the Key.

We'd left an hour before midnight, and it should have been a pleasant, star-spangled trip, but the Jícaman SADISTO agent paddling us out was so combative, so argumentative that it ruined what should have been an experience of immersive peace. After enough of his contrarian attitude, I started calling him 'Bicker' and the entire trip he just kept proving why the name fit.

"You're the kind of guy that obviously gets coddled," he said, his every movement, every gesture designed to irritate and annoy. "Good food, hot women... I bet the agency hands out babes to you pretty boys like candy."

"They do," I agreed, no longer interested in arguing. "My dick is rarely dry."

"Pssh," he fairly spit. "And for what? Because you're *pretty*." He said 'pretty' the way other people say 'what's this brown stuff on my shoe?' "Pretty boys get all the best shit. Right? They give you all the best shit because you're so *pretty*?"

"Of course," I said. "Good looks get a man everything he could ever want, and more. Which you'd know if you weren't so goddam ugly."

"Pretty," he said as if it hurt, "tall, built. I bet you don't even have to work out. You just use one of those mail-order electrical things that exercises for you."

"While I sleep. I wake up, every morning, more jacked. Usually being blown by a hot, naked girl with huge tits."

"Pssh. I believe it. I bet your daddy's rich, too, isn't he?"

"Seventh on the list of Richest People Alive. Mom's third."

"Pssh. Bet it's a shallow bunch, your family. Can't trust the rich. But then…" he grinned, darkly, "the rich can't trust no one either. 'Cause people only want you for your money. Bet no one has ever *really* loved you."

I flashed on an image of Juliet. Her turquoise eyes, her radiant smile, her huge tits. Her reluctance to return home.

"Who needs love?" I asked, knowing exactly who. "Now shut up before I shoot you in the eye and piss in your screaming mouth."

"Pssh," he psshed, then chuckled, knowing he'd finally gotten to me.

In blessed silence the boat gently rose and fell on tiny swells as the island gradually increased in size with every up and down movement. In the distance you could hear the rumble of the breakers, followed by the calming sssshhh of those breakers rolling across the sand.

Once we'd floated over the coral reef that formed a barrier and surge suppressor around the little lagoon, the waves flattened out into gentle, glassy, crystalline shallows. We leapt out into the warm, clear water intending to pull the boat ashore. I grabbed the little canoe's edge, but "Bicker" shooed me away.

"Get off. I'll do it. You don't know how."

"I prefer to be waited on, anyway, so have at it."

He grumbled, and I made out the words, "entitled," "lazy," and "bumfoogle," though I can't be sure about 'lazy.'

Ignoring his noise, I strolled up quietly onto the soft, sandy shore as the sienna sun surfaced behind me. I breathed deeply of the serene, sea scented air, and calming tranquil beauty that was Krabs Key. As my gaze wandered about the pristine cove, I kept wondering what the chauffeur could have meant by 'mysterious bird poop.' But there was nothing to explain it; only lush, green, tropical forest as far as the eye could see, and a single, treeless white mountain in the near distance, at the Island's center.

Hmmm… treeless, white…

Nah. That would be ridiculous.

"Rub out your tracks, you moron," snapped 'Bicker.'

I did, continuing to brush them away as I backed up toward the tree line, all the while mumbling to myself.

"Longest six hours of my life…" I said under my breath.

"Speak up!" Bicker yelled. "You got something to say, say it!"

"I was just saying I wish there were two of you," I chirped, cheerfully, finger-gunning him. "Double my pleasure, double my fun."

Bicker groaned.

"Commercial jingles," he said. "TV makes people stupid. Though clearly, they had a head start with you."

Bicker dragged the boat up the sand until, at last, it was over the back tideline and among the rocks and turtle grass and low sea-grape bushes. Complaining all the way, he pushed it another twenty yards inland to hide it under some mangrove. There he covered it with seaweed and bits of dried driftwood. Finally, he broke off a few lengths of palm frond and went back over our tracks—even the ones I'd already swept—sweeping and tidying, and whistling a little.

I listened carefully. Yes, he was actually whistling. Happily.

Whatever.

It was getting light, the sun stretching in from the east, brightening from the orange of dawn, blossoming into the full white of day. I was dead tired. I exchanged a few testy words with Bicker, and he went off to sulk and sleep among the rocks along the promontory. I removed my soaked clothes, hung them over a palm trunk that had grown sideways out of the embankment, and dug a hole for myself out of the fine dry sand beneath a bush covered by fronds thick enough to shield me from the already scorching rays. Really not giving a shit about what animals or bugs might come out to nosh on my bare flesh, I lay down in the cool divot, and closed my eyes for a few minutes rest while my clothes dried.

8   8   8

I dreamt of Juliet. Better than *The Dream*, but not by much. She was naked, shaking and shivering, gooseflesh all over her lovely body as she demanded of me how I could be so heartless as to murder our babies. Then she showed me four dead children lying in the sand, once much smaller than the others. Their heads were squawking parrots, except the fourth, which was a frog. They screeched, and croaked, louder, and louder until I wanted to scream.

Hours later I woke up to the sound of screeching parrots, and frogs. The feel of the sand in my joints, around my balls, and in the crack of my ass reminded me of where I was. I groaned and glanced at my watch. Ten o'clock. I closed my eyes as the sun scorched through the round, thick leaves of the palm-thingies hanging over me. It was already hotter than shit. Sweat trickled down my skin to mix with the dirt and grit that covered me.

A shadow moved across my eyelids. Bicker?

I turned my head and peered through the leaves and grass that surrounded me. I stiffened at what I saw. My dick stiffened at what I saw. My heart missed a beat and began pounding like it would charge out of my chest. My engorged penis throbbed and bobbed like it wanted to jump off me and run out to beg pets from what I was seeing. Or rather, 'whom' I was seeing.

Through the blades of grass there was a girl. A naked girl. Her back and bare behind were to me. Well, not quite naked. She wore a broad, white, military style belt around her waist with a matching sheath and hunting knife on her hip. And that was all. That lone belt made her nakedness so unexpectedly erotic, so thrilling that I felt faint. She stood not more than five yards away at the tideline studying something in her hand. I lie not five yards away in the bushes studying her. We both seemed to be enjoying ourselves.

She had a gorgeous back. A fantastic backside. Sunkissed an even, uniform, aureate brown by a constant and adoring sun. No pale buns; skin color unbroken by white panty or bra string lines. The gentle sweep of her spine, smooth, lovingly indented, a full, ripe breast peeking out under one slightly raised arm, and that soft, smooth behind; so round, so full, so womanly—curving gently down into legs that flowed all the way to the ground, straight and beautiful and strong. All of it begging the blood to burst from my body through the pounding peak of my penis.

Her hair was sun-lightened blonde. Darker at the roots, raggedly cut below the shoulder blades, hanging long and thick in wet, curly strands. A pale-blue diving mask sat high on her forehead, it's matching rubber snorkel dangling alongside her nearest cheek.

The whole scene, the empty beach, the turquoise sea, the arresting, naked girl with twisting strands of fair hair, reminded me of something—something meaningful. I searched my mind, but couldn't come up with it. Instead, my brain cells were flooded only with memories and images of Juliet. I forced those dream images away, and focused on the joyous reality of the girl before me.

Who was she? How had she gotten here? What was she doing? I looked up and down the beach. Empty other than a scattering of shells, small, and large. They looked lovely, as if placed intentionally to decorate this supremely picturesque, tropical, Playboy Centerfold scene.

To the girl's left a canoe had been drawn up behind her under the shelter of the rocks. Was it light enough to be drawn up by her alone? *Was* she alone? I couldn't imagine she would be. A girl as beautiful as this would have a companion of some kind. Protection. Lover. Friend. Mate. A man who was made as horny by her as I had been, who wanted her to put down the seashells, and take firm and loving hold of his engorged cock. But I saw only a single set of footprints leading down to the sea, and another single set coming out of the waves from up the beach to where she now stood at the tideline.

I considered the island. Were there homes here? My research hadn't told me of any. But maybe? Did she live in one, or perhaps just survived in the wilds? Or had she, too, sailed over from Jícama during night? If so, she only impressed me all the more.

What the hell was she doing here?

She tossed the large shells into the sand beside the others. Pink and white and orange and marbled, I wondered what they were and why she was gathering them. Nothing about this moment made any sense. A nude white girl on a deserted South American beach that was home to a mysterious Dr. Sin?

The girl slipped the mask down over her face, preparing to return to the calm waters of the lagoon. Settling it securely into place, she slowly danced herself toward the turquoise-blue sea, arms up, hips bopping hard one way, then the other, moving to some unique rhythm only she could hear.

But then I realized I *could* hear—could *barely* hear—her singing softly to herself. The song sounded familiar, but it took a while to place it with that mask covering her nose and making the song oddly, nasally, muted. She had modified the tempo to something more of a Calypso beat, but it was an old Gershwin tune she was making faster, and far, *far* dirtier than the original.

> *"You really shouldn't have done it*
> *(Boom, Boom)*
> *"You hadn't any right*
> *(Boom, Boom)*
> *"I really shouldn't have let you*
> *"Fuuuuck meeeee."*
> *(BOOM)*

On that last beat, she stopped, arms above her head, and thrust both hips forward, that magnificent ass clenching tightly to press her unseen pussy out toward the fortunate sea in a move so sexy it nearly caused me squirt onto the sand. Her voice grew louder, and her motions more languorous the further into the water she got.

> *"And though it may be wrong*
> *(Boom, Boom)*
> *"I never was that strong.*
> *(Boom, Boom)*
> *"So now since you've done it*
> *(Boom, Boom)*
> *And you know I want it.*
> *(Boom, Boom)*
> *Oh. (BOOM) Oh! (BOOM) OH! (BOOM)*
> *Do. (BOOM) Do! (BOOM) DO! (BOOM)*
> *Do it again!*
> *(BA-BA-BOOM, BA-BA-BOOM-BOOM-*
> *BOOM)*

She was now shin deep in the soft waves, the speed and intensity of her dancing increasing with her singing volume. I stepped from the bushes and leaned, smiling, against a tree, continuing to be a peeping Tom, but less secretively. Part of me wanted her to turn and catch me. To dance with me. To want me. To fuck me right here, in the sand, as she continued singing to me.

> *"I won't say no.*
> *(BOOM)*
> *No-no-no-no.*
> *(BOOM)*
> *So do it...*
> *(BOOM)*
> *Do it ...*
> *(BOOM)*
> *DO IT AGAIN!*
> *(BOOM)*
> *My pussy aches!*
> *(Boom)*
> *To have you take!*
> *(Boom)*
> *this body (BOOM)*
> *That's waiting (BOOM) for yooouuuu*
> *(BA-BOOM-BOOM, BOOM, BOOM)*

She was mesmerizing. Enchanting. As sexy as Juliet had ever been at her most seductive. This girl would put the most experienced stripper to shame. Her movements became more rapid, and tribal, and her body responded accordingly. Flesh swayed, bounced, shook in amazing and thrilling ways. Her full behind, and large breasts jiggled and jounced with intensity and rhythm, passion and joy. She didn't know I was here, but she had to be speaking to me.

> *"You know if you do it*
> *(BOOM)*
> *You won't regret it*
> *(BOOM)*
> *So come on and get it.*
> *(BOOM)*
> *Oh!*
> *(BOOM)*
> *Yes!*
> *(BOOM)*

Oh!
(BOOMBOOMBOOM)
"Are you thinkin' what I'm thinkin'?"

RECORD SCRATCH!

Out of nowhere Bicker was at my side—whispering—an oily lust lubricating his voice.

"I seriously doubt it," I said.

"You hold her down," he said, giddily, "and I'll take her first."

She spun so quickly I almost didn't see it happen. Her hand blurred to her waist and the knife came at me in a flash. Fortunately, it came at my head, so I only had to move a few inches to avoid death. But it was close. I'd moved instinctively, so by the time I was fully aware I was staring at a blade already stuck mere inches away from my nose, embedded in Bicker's cheek, going right through the other side, and pinning him to the tree.

"Ah..." he said, afraid to touch it for fear it would only hurt more. "Aaah..."

I returned my attention to the girl, and saw she was breathing deeply through the pinching mask. Whether from fear or anger, or all the singing and dancing, I'm not sure. But her breasts rose and fell and bobbled with deep gasps, and I couldn't help stare at the glory of them as they moved and swayed from all the rapid action.

Her hands rose up across that heaving chest, rotating upward, middle fingers extended.

"I think you've had enough of the free show," she said, her nose-pinched voice hauntingly familiar.

I raised my eyes to hers. Or where hers would be if they hadn't been hidden inside the breath-fogged mask.

"I think you've staked him the cover charge," I said.

"Ah..." said Bicker.

She didn't seem amused. But my *Post Murder Punning Instructor* would have been quite pleased, I'm sure.

"Sorry," I said. "I... *we*... didn't mean to take in the entire show. I just didn't know when would be a good time to announce we were here."

She dropped her hands to her side, and I couldn't help it. My eyes flitted back down to those tremendous trembling tits, then right back up again.

"Sorry," I said, "again. It's difficult to control. You really are quite stunning."

"At least my tits are," she said.

She stood there, legs slightly apart, feet buried in the tide and sand in a strong, confident stance, staring at us silently through the misted glass.

"Ah..." said Bicker.

"Do you live on the island?" I asked the girl, ignoring him.

"No," she said simply. "Do you?"

"No. I didn't think anyone did."

"People live here. And a dragon."

"A... dragon?" I said. "Is that a metaphor for the island's owner?"

"No," she said matter-of-factly. "It's an actual dragon. Breathes fire. Kills people. Eats them."

I stifled a chuckle.

"Stick around," she sneered. "You'll see." Her head moved down, slightly, and I saw she was taking me in, as I had her. When her gaze stayed down, apparently fixed on the area between navel and thigh, it reminded me that I was as naked as she. And erect.

"That's... uh..." she said, her head still down, gaze still lingering on my upthrust cock. "That' really hard."

"You have no idea," I said.

"Ah," said Bicker.

The girl seemed to have lost her train of thought. She kept her head down, then eventually shook it, stared some more, shook it again, and finally moved her attention back up in the general direction of my face, regaining some of her intensity and focus.

Some of.

"Who are you?" she demanded. "What are you doing here?" There was the slight lilt of Jícaman accent in her voice. Her tone sharp and confident. And weirdly familiar.

"Just a guy looking for bird poop," I said.

Her head tilted to one side.

"You came all the way out here to find bird poop?" she asked, expecting no answer. Simply declaring me an idiot. "I could get you all you wanted back on the main island."

"There's supposed to be something special… something *mysterious* about the bird poop over here."

"It's the world's best fertilizer," she said, apparently astounded by my stupidity. "Anyone back on Jícama could tell you that. No boat ride required. You can even buy some there if it interests you that much."

"Okay," I said, grinning, "You plainly think I was stupid to come here. I could have found everything I wanted back on the main island. So, what's a *good* reason for being here? Why are *you* here? And who *are* you?"

"I'm no one. Just a girl from Jícama. I collect shells."

"You came in that canoe?" I asked.

"Yes."

"All that way. Seven hours. By yourself?"

"Five hours. Yes." She looked around, then back at me. "Where's *your* boat?"

"Ah," said Bicker.

"We've hidden it in the mangroves," I said.

"There are no marks in the sand of a landing," she said, in clear disbelief. Or was it distrust? "I always check."

"We covered them up," I said. "I guess that's why you thought you were alone."

She just stared, hands still on her hips. I pulled her knife out of Bicker, and the tree, wiped its blade on my pants still hanging over said tree, then walked it back to her, holding it out by the handle. Bicker fell to his knees, holding his face as blood flowed all across the front of him, around and between his fingers.

He basically just moaned and bled, as the girl stood there silently, staring at me, uncertain of my approach. I took the moment to study the front of her as I had the rear. Same seamless, golden color, same sun loved flesh. Heavy, proud, firm, upthrust breasts that reminded me so much of Juliet's it almost hurt to ogle them. Same long legs that came up to the inviting female 'W' of her front, almost obscured beneath a tangled scrub of brown-blonde hair, as lightened by the sun as the curls drying atop her head. She obviously spent a good deal of time in the sun. With nothing on.

"You're quite good with that," I said, offering her the knife.

She took it from me carefully, and expertly returned it to its sheath, like a samurai, without looking.

"Hiding the boat didn't help you," she said. "They'll know you're here. They've got stuff that can see you."

I looked around, scanning the bushes, listening for sounds, then returned my gaze to her, with a smile.

"Not yet, apparently," I said, and scowled, slightly. "Who are you? You're quite cautious and aware for a shell collector."

"You have to be to avoid the dragon," she answered.

"Ah, yes. The dragon."

"You'll see."

"What's your name?"

She debated a moment, whether or not she should, then sighed, and gave in.

"Sunny," she said. "Sunny Bunz. What's yours?"

"Sunny…" I stifled a laugh. With some difficulty. I'm sure I pulled a muscle. "That's a lovely, joyful name. I'm Trevor Hawke."

She smiled, which looked weird with her mask scrunching down on her upper lip.

"Trevor Hawke," she said, smiling. "I like that name."

"I'm glad. Tell me about these people that can see you, and about this supposed dragon."

"There's nothing 'supposed' about it," she said, annoyed.

"I'm sure there's some logical explanation for it, other than an actual, living dragon. A marsh buggy, perhaps. The kind of vehicle used for oil prospecting, that can cover any kind of terrain, but has been decorated to look like a dragon, adapted that way to frighten and burn in order to scare people away."

She stared a moment, her smile completely gone.

"I know the difference between a 'marsh buggy' and a fucking dragon, asshole," she snapped, ripping off the fogged mask to—I presume—glare at me more forcefully, and I nearly fell over.

It was Juliet.

It had to be. But it couldn't be. But it was.

Those eyes…

Those eyes widened as she stopped talking and studied me with concern, worry, apparently deeply affected by the shock on my face.

"What?" she asked, gently. "What's the matter?"

Her features were a little more chiseled, as if she'd lost weight, or firmed slightly with constant exercise. Her hair was longer, less coiffed, both above and below. But it was her. Or more correctly for the benefit of the General, it was *she*. My cadet agent love. Juliet Jones, of the turquoise eyes.

But it couldn't be. The brown tan of her skin, the lean muscularity of her body would have taken weeks, or months to acquire. I had just seen Juliet the other night.

The world tilted on its axis in more ways than one as a sudden hackle-raising, tree-rattling roar shook the forest. I turned toward the sound and searched the thick foliage.

"What was that?" I asked in a very, *very* frightened whisper.

Sunny/Juliet said nothing. She simply looked around, as frightened as me.

And then it was there! An enormous tyrannosaur-like beast exploding through the trees, its massive, open maw filled with twisted, ripping, glistening teeth! It bent forward, leaning down directly toward me. Or us. All three of us. *But mostly me!*

"*What the actual fuck?*" I said.

"Told you," said Sunny.

CHAPTER 19

BICKER, STILL HOLDING HIS face, stood, screamed, and began to run—right in front of the dragon—and in response the thing exploded fire all over him, cooking him instantly where he stood. His eyes darted back and forth a couple times, until his crisping corpse dropped over in the sand, continuing to scream, horribly, until the inevitable instant life fled his body.

"Yeah," I said, "I'm not gonna miss him."

'Sunny' picked up one of the larger shells, hooking it to her belt, then grabbed my hand and began to run. I followed, peering back over my shoulder as the creature took chase. There was no way we could outpace it. Its single stride was twenty of ours. But Sunny seemed confident.

Then I saw her plan. She was running *toward* the water.

We sploshed in as deep and as fast as we could, leaping up and down to avoid resistance. Ten or so yards beyond the tideline Sunny dove under the surface, and I followed.

As we swam into the deeper part of the lagoon, everything around us lit up; orange, red, white, as the dragon raged fire in the air above us. I looked up and saw bubbles form as the ocean's surface boiled, steamed, evaporated, the heat of the dragon's breath bleeding down to me through the clear waters.

I turned back to Sunny, or Juliet, or whomever she was, as she arced downward, her nude body twisting, and flexing to pull her as fast as possible through the intense blue of the sea. I did my best to follow, but I was working against my own, personal rudder and the significant drag it created between my legs. Sunny's naked magnificence was only making things worse. (I was—at this point—honestly astonished at my ability to get and maintain an erection at any time, under seemingly any circumstance.)

She was swimming straight for the coral reef that had formed across the mouth of the lagoon. I didn't know her plan beyond that, and I wasn't sure I was going to make it. My lungs were already bursting, and my body screamed for air.

Hers too, apparently, as she turned and kicked hard for the surface. I became immediately concerned, glanced back toward the shore, and saw that the dragon had stepped into the shallows, legs visible under the water, moving side-to-side, as above it was apparently searching for one or both of us.

Sunny had nearly breached the waves, but stopped short, adjusting her snorkel, waving me over.

Smart girl.

Without poking her head out, only the snorkel, she took a deep breath, then pushed the mouthpiece to my lips. I took it gratefully and inhaled, just as the air above us exploded again with heat and light. I coughed as the air I was breathing suddenly became scalding and toxic.

We pulled ourselves down, away from danger, and saw that the plastic snorkel had melted, bubbled, and blackened. Dropping it as useless, Sunny turned and dove in the direction she'd originally been heading, confident I would follow.

Confident in her, I did.

She reached the coral, twisted and tucked and tortured herself nakedly through a narrow, bending passage that led completely through the reef, opening out on the broader ocean side. I followed, less agilely, and at a slower pace. Once free of the hard, sharp branches, we swam further out to sea, then rose up—we both hoped—a safe distance from the dragon. I surfaced alongside her, and turned back to check on our pursuer.

The dragon stood there, lagoon water at crotch-level, blowing pillars of flame in our direction. The flow of fire rose up ineffectually long before it reached either of us. For whatever reason the dragon was unable to cross the coral reef, and didn't seem happy about it.

"Why can't it just break through?" I asked.

"I don't know," Sunny said. "But it can't. Or won't. Come on."

She dipped again under the waves, and I followed as she swam more easily through the now tranquil waters toward, and around the rocky headland, coming up on the other side, close enough to the promontory to avoid being seen. I stayed near while she pulled her nude self from the water, and crept along the rocks toward shore.

Once on the beach, she walk-ran quietly and quickly up to the tree line, and beyond, ducking under thick, tangles of mangrove, saltgrass, Devil's ivy, snake, and Ti plants. In a small clearing beneath some thick, spreading fronds, she crouched in the cool sand, and caught her breath. I knelt beside her, looking around to see if anything was approaching.

"The dragon burned my boat," Sunny said.

"I saw."

"How will I get home?" She sounded desperate.

"Home?"

"To Jícama. My sister, my mother, my dog."

"You..." I struggled, "You have those things?

"Why would I lie about that?"

"You wouldn't," I said, softening. "How long have you lived on Jícama?"

"My whole life. Everything I am... all I know... is that island."

I studied her, her tan, the slight differences in her look, and realized as much as it couldn't be, it *had* to be true.

"Don't worry, Sunny," I assured her. "I'll get you back there."

"Trevor," she said, as if speaking to a small child. An especially stupid small child. "You're as naked, unarmed, and trapped as I am."

"Yeah, but..." I absorbed her beauty, and unique charm. How could she not be my Juliet?

"I can take care of myself, Trevor," she said. "I don't need a man to rescue me."

"Okay," I said. "Fine."

"So..." she asked, shifting uncomfortably, "why is your dick still hard?

"Oh. Uh… why is my—right. Uh… I don't know. It happens sometimes when I'm…" I didn't have any idea why it happens sometimes, and just stopped talking.

"Aroused?" she said, helpfully, smiling, and I swear she had the same sarcastic curve to her lips as my beloved cadet agent. "I know why dicks get hard. You haven't been able to stop looking at my tits, even when it could literally get you killed."

"True. But this is mostly… well… your song," I said. "It stuck in my head, and that combined with your… well…"

"My big ole titties?" she laughed quietly.

"With your *dance*," I said, honestly," *and* your—you know…"

"*Bouncing* big ole titties," she said, laughing again.

I laughed with her.

"I get it," she said. "I know men love big tits. And, well… your fault for peeping at me. But don't you think you should do something about it?" she waved a hand toward my stiffy. "Seems like it could be a problem while you're running."

"Oh, it is," I admitted. "While running. While swimming. Pretty much doing anything other than what it's intended to be used for."

"Well, we can't do that," she said, still staring at it. "So maybe something else. You could pull yourself off. I'd be happy to wait."

"And watch?"

"Sure. You watched me, I get to watch you…" she said, laughing. "What's good for the goose, and all that. Got a problem with that, mister?"

"No. But I wasn't watching you masturbate."

"Mmm. Tomato, ta-mah-toe," she said. "That dance was kinda getting *me* off, too."

"Well, I'm glad we both enjoyed it," I said. "But hence why it's a part of my problem. Still. I think I'm just going to have to suffer with it."

"Suit yourself," she said, shrugging lightly, and leaning back on one arm. "In the meantime, I'm open to any thoughts and ideas about how we get out of this."

"We find another boat," I said.

"Where's yours?"

"I'm not sure," I said. "The man I was with hid it. Probably somewhere behind the dragon."

She grinned with snarky eyes. "I told you it was real."

I almost laughed, but remembered we were hiding. "You sure did. So… do you know where we might find *another* boat?"

She looked around, not at anything, just thinking. As she did, I again studied her perfect form. Which didn't help my erection problem. But I had to know. She looked too much like Juliet. And after weeks of sleepless nights rolling around on her, there was no woman's body I was more familiar with. Sober, or drunk. Sunny's breasts, nipples, arms, neck, chin, lips, face, pubic hair, pubic region, moles, legs, toes… they had to be Juliet's. There might be differences, the deeper tan, the leaner body, the shorter length of hair, the painted nails, but nothing that said, "Oh, no, this is someone completely different."

As I looked her over, I wondered if SADISTO had found her. Taken her back to finish Decommissioning, and if they could have done more than erase our escape, and her recent 'fall into instability?' Could they have given her an entirely new history? New memories? A new home? New family? Mother? Sister? Dog? Was it like some high-end witness protection program? One that actually made over the 'witness' into the fictional character they were creating?

I didn't know. Decommissioning was a division I had no experience with other than shooting my way out of it. I'm pretty sure. Suddenly I began to wonder about my own memories. Were they real? Was I who I thought I was? I felt a profound urge to call my mom.

"Juliet?" I said, hopeful.

But 'Sunny' didn't respond. She was looking around, thinking deeply, biting a lip in a way that made me want to kiss her. Kiss my way down her chin, her neck, across her shoulders, the front of her chest, letting my mouth trace circles all over those amazing breasts of hers. I longed to taste her nipples, take them into my mouth and massage them with my tongue, first one, then the other, then back again as my fingers sought out the delicate tangle of hair between her…

"Did you hear me?" Sunny asked.

"Uh, no," I said. "I was just—"

"I know what you were 'just'. Your eyes were practically sucking on my tits, *and* you were drooling. I *said*… the only boats that I know of would be the ones that bring over food and supplies to the workers. Those would be in the main harbor on the other side of the island."

"Sneaking around is going to be difficult without clothes," I said. "Speaking of which... why are *you* naked?"

"I like to be naked," she said, simply. Very Juliet. "Especially when I'm swimming, or diving for shells. And there's usually no one around when I come here. *Never* anyone around, actually."

"So, you just canoe over here with nothing on..."

"I have clothes, Trevor," she said with irritation. "*Had* clothes. In my canoe. Which are now ash. I don't come here naked. I take my clothes off to swim *after* I get here. It feels nice, and, I don't get hung up in the coral."

"And you feel safe? The dragon has never come after you before?"

"Oh, it has," she said. "That's why I know how to get away from it. But it doesn't care if I'm naked. And I never see any people. No guards, even. They know I'm not a threat."

"They know... how do they know that?"

She looked at me like I was stupid. "I walk around *naked*. I collect *seashells*."

I guess that was answer enough. And suddenly something occurred to me.

"Wait." I said. "*Who* knows you're not a threat?"

"The security men."

"What security men?"

She shrugged. "The men with masks, and guns."

"Armed security? Guarding bird shit?"

She nodded again. Then shrugged. "It's high-quality bird shit," she said, as if that were reason enough.

Now it was my turn to look around and bite my lip. I couldn't make this place out. Dragons. Mysterious poo. Masked armed guards. Strangeways and Trueblue. What was I missing?

I turned back to Juliet and caught her staring at my cock. Wide eyed and drooling.

"Hey," I joked. "Eyes up here."

"Sorry," she said, her turquoise-blues popping back to normal. "I was just..."

"I know what you were just."

"*Well, it's so hard!*" she said, almost too loudly. "And throbbing, and... kinda big. *But so hard!* Why is it so hard?"

"Because you're a fucking sex goddess, Sunny, and you remind me of—"

I paused. She waited. I waited. She waited some more. And scowled.

"Juliet?" she asked.

"Oh," I said. "You heard that?"

"Yes. I thought you were scared, and thinking out loud about someone."

"Yes," I said, almost breathlessly. "I was. Not scared, but..."

"Your wife?"

"No, but..." I thought about how deeply I felt for Juliet. *Really* felt. It didn't matter that she had no interest in Westchester. "I was going to ask her to be."

"You were?" Sunny asked, with a tinge of—I don't know—empathy? "Then... what? Did she die?"

"No. Just..." I looked her in those intensely blue eyes that matched the sea we'd just swum in, "no."

"Oh. She left you? Sorry. And she looked like me?"

I nodded.

"Was she... pretty?"

"Radiant," I said. "So beautiful."

"And she ..." she asked, brightening a little, "she looked like... me?"

I nodded.

"You think... *I'm* beautiful?" she asked, seeming a bit surprised. And hopeful.

I gave her a look of *Duh!* And gestured to the thing that would not die.

"Well, men get those even when a woman *isn't* beautiful. Men are like dogs. They smell heat, and woop! Hard. Then they try to mount you. Lifting your skirt, rubbing their dick on you in a crowded bar, thinking no one will notice, but come on! Who's not going to notice a guy rubbing his dick under your dress in a crowded bar?"

I stared at her, my mind melting a little.

"Yes, Trevor," she said. "It actually happens. Men."

Suddenly something occurred to me. Something she'd said...

"Sunny... you said the boats 'bring food and supplies to the workers.' What workers?"

"The ones in the arena," she said.

I was stunned. "What arena?"

"The one in the volcano."

"Show me," I said.

She thought about it. She nibbled her lip again for a while, glanced down again at my flagpole, then suddenly decided.

"Okay," she said, turning her gorgeous, sand dusted rear end toward me as she moved cautiously, and quietly out of our hiding place. "But we have to be careful about the other dinosaurs."

I was so intent on the loveliness of her behind that it took a moment for her words to register.

"I'm sorry," I said. "Be careful of the what, now?"

CHAPTER 20

It had taken us hours to get here, both of us still nude except for Sunny's tactical belt, knife, and seashell, but we'd finally made it up the 'white mountain' near the middle of the island, and were about to trek over its outer rim. It wasn't actually a mountain at all. It was more an extinct volcano with a fairly level central basin a few hundred feet below sea level; a deep, flat, natural crater; a low bowl formed thousands or millions of years ago, that someone had recently spent a great deal of time and money building out with an enormous entertainment complex.

Sunny had been right. There was an arena. Big enough to hold a couple baseball games, and maybe an extra football game on the side.

The journey to the central volcano had been tricky. We had indeed passed a few dinosaurs, one herd of stegosaurs in particular grazing on a patch of high, marshy grass. Fortunately, most of the animals we saw were of the vegetarian variety, and the ones that weren't were too far away to bother with us. Other than the mind-bending aspect of... 'holy shit; actual dinosaurs!' The trip was no more eventful than avoiding muggers and bad neighborhoods in New York.

The journey up the outer surface to the summit was actually more difficult, to be honest. There was very little natural brush to hide us during our climb so we'd waited until dark, and the terrain was rough, rugged, and the crumbly, white ground gave off a weird, acidic stench that curdled the very air around us, it was so intense. Breathing was extremely difficult. According to Sunny the land on the outer slope of the volcano was made up mostly of that famous, mysterious, bird shit in its purest, most potent, undiluted form—so raw, and toxic it had all but decimated the plant life.

But beyond the summit, the inside of the crater had been mined free of the concentrated fertilizer. Once cleared, the flora had returned in abundance, fed by the remainder of the bird shit at lower, life-enhancing levels, and reliable, daily tropical rains. Thanks to good ole Mother Nature we now had an abundance of lovely, flowering, hiding places behind which to hide.

We had crept our way down far enough to get a good view, squatting to take refuge behind some ivy-covered boulders surrounded by grasses, tall palms, and purple flowers of some kind.

Far below us the arena was lit-up, operations in full swing. We could hear cheering, moans, boos, corresponding to whatever events played out inside. All around the main building sat the maintenance and security offices, vehicles, and support structures. Various people walked to and fro carrying packages, clipboards, wearing lab coats; security guards with gun belts, hefting shotguns and machine guns, guard shacks, and towers everywhere, each guard garbed in distinctive, purple uniforms and black masks emblazoned with concentric circles like bullseyes on their faces.

"Something very weird is going on here," I said. "We need to find a boat and get off this island so I can report it."

"Report it?" she said, surprised. "You act like it's nefarious. Maybe it's just a local sporting event. A Cricket match, or soccer game, or whatever."

"With heavily armed guards wearing masks?" I asked, focusing on the arena itself. "Yeah, I don't think so. You don't know what's going on inside?"

Sunny shrugged. "I never needed to know."

"What about now? Curious?"

She bit a lip, thinking it over, glancing at the arena, then at me. Juliet's curious mind, and inquisitive eyes, I thought.

She sneered. "I'm not exactly dressed for it."

"Me neither," I said. "But I have to know what this is all about."

"Why?" she asked, insistently. "Who are you, Trevor Hawke? Why are you here? And don't tell me bird poop!"

"Yeah," I admitted. "I'm looking for more than that."

"Didn't take a genius to figure that out," she said. "Is it about the dragon and the other dinosaurs?"

"No. Some friends of mine disappeared," I said. "I think they learned about this island, the dinosaurs, maybe, or this arena, and it could have gotten them killed."

She studied my eyes, her own, turquoise blues unblinking.

"Was one of them Juliet?" she asked.

"I..." I said, averting my gaze. "Yes. Also, a man named Strangeways, and a woman named Trueblue."

"Never heard of them," Sunny said, and I couldn't detect any falsity. "So, you're going down there? Naked?" She glanced at my crotch. "And hard."

I looked down at it too. Jesus.

She took a moment to examine it, tilting her head from side to side, visually taking it in from all angles.

"It's been hours," she said. "Aren't you concerned?"

"A little. I guess. But following your amazing ass up and over that ridge didn't help."

"You think my ass is amazing?"

"I don't think. I know."

She melted a little, then quickly recovered.

"I mean, really. That can't still be because of me," she said, dismissive. Then she raised a hopeful eyebrow. "Can it?"

"If it were, would you be willing to help me with it?"

"Help you, how? I don't even know you."

"You need to know me to have sex with me? It's the sixties."

She considered that.

"Yeah, not happening," she said, flatly, surprising me. Hmm. Maybe she wasn't Juliet. "I'm saving myself for true love, and marriage."

Okay, *definitely not* Juliet.

"You're..." I almost gasped, less out of surprise, more out of disbelief. "You're saying you've *never*..."

"Don't sound so shocked! You said it yourself; it's the sixties! Not the far flung 2000's where people fly around naked with jetpacks and do it in the sky! I'm a good girl! I just happen to like to swim in the nude. And walk around outside in the nude. And inside in the nude... but nudity and looseness are *not* the same thing."

"Okay, okay," I said, "you're a good girl. So, you won't even help me with a little hand job..."

"I will not."

"And I can't touch your..."

"You cannot."

"Can I at least look at you while I..."

She thought about that. For quite a while.

"Yeah, okay. I guess so," she said. "But I get to watch you, too."

"Sure. Goose. Gander. All that," I said, got up on my knees, and took things in hand.

"I'll still be a virgin," she said.

"I—yes," I said. "I'm quite certain that you will remain a virgin with this method."

"Just like those guys who rubbed their dicks on me in bars never actually had sex *with* me."

"Uh... no. They did not."

She watched me as I stroked my length, staring at it with focused intent. Up, down, up, down, up, down ...

"Why do you keep looking at me?" She asked.

"Because it helps," I said.

"Aaaah," she said almost imperceptibly, her voice catching.

She didn't say more. Just kept staring.

"Aaaah what?" I asked, still stroking.

"Aaaah..." she said, quietly. "Oh. Sorry. I didn't realize I said something. I was mostly just curious to see how a man does that, but now it's sort of... you know..." she licked her lips, and glanced at my eyes, shyly, "turning me on."

"That's okay," I said. "There's nothing wrong with that."

"Maybe," she said, her eyes returning to my sliding hand and its diligent work.

"I could finish faster, you know," I said, "with a little help. Would you mind...?"

She didn't seem to hear, and I was about to repeat myself when she looked up into my eyes. "What?"

"Would you mind?" I asked, and she just kept her eyes locked to mine, silent. "Play with yourself," I added. "You'd still be maintaining your virginity, of course."

She continued to stare, silently. Then she glanced down at my stroking hand, my fondled cock.

"I guess…" she said. "I suppose I could."

"Sure, you could."

"I do it when I'm alone, sometimes," she admitted, with a little embarrassment, leaning slowly back against an ivy-covered boulder, surrounded on all sides by hundreds of tiny, purple-blue flowers reflecting the moonlight. "There's nothing wrong with it."

"I certainly don't think so."

"Me neither," she said, far too defensively, eyes on my stroking hand, and pulsing shaft, as she nervously spread her legs, resting her own hand atop her chest, just below her neck.

Watching me work, slowly gaining confidence and desire, she gradually, tentatively, pressed her hand downward, sliding her fingertips across those full, heavy, rounded breasts. Her nipples popped forth, areolas rounding, swelling, and I heard slight moans of pleasure drift involuntarily out of her.

My pace quickened as I pulled and pushed the thin flesh surrounding my pole a little roughly, my own desire increasing, breath deepening, Sunny's magnificent body making it difficult to hold back the coming tide.

Growing more comfortable, Sunny began kneading, and cuddling her breasts with both hands, never taking her eyes from my manhandled cock. Then, maintaining her intense focus, she slid her right hand down, firmly, along her ribs, over her belly, past the tactical belt and attached seashell, through her sun-lightened nether hair, to slip her fingers into the gap between her legs. Two of those fingers plunged deep, she gasped, her eyes narrowed, her other hand still squeezing one soaring, searing, sumptuous breast.

"Oh, my God," she whispered. "this is so fucking hot."

After a moment of watching, and diddling, unblinking fiddling, she leaned forward abruptly, letting her breast fall and bounce loosely, reaching with the now empty hand. "Come here," she said, wiggling her fingers at my reddened, robust ramrod.

I shuffled toward her grasp on my knees, until she could wrap her fingers around me, helping me massage myself for a moment before gently pushing me aside.

"Let me," she said, and I released myself to her loving care.

And loving was the right word.

She continued to finger herself, and look at me from about a foot away as her hand slid slowly up and down over the soft-hard flesh of my pulsing penis, twisting gently as if she had always imagined touching one, and was simply marveling at the reality of it.

"I'm still a virgin," she whispered, then to my surprise, leaned down, and sweetly kissed my head.

She pulled back, still looking at it, her face flush, then glanced up at me.

"That's okay, isn't it?" she asked.

"That's very okay," I said.

She smiled a little, bent forward and kissed it again. Then again. Then once more, this time keeping her lips pressed to the tip. She held her mouth there for an erotic eternity, until I began to feel her tongue rubbing the end of it, tentatively deciding how far she wanted to go. Slowly, very slowly, she pushed her lips down, around and over my glans, enveloping and enclosing the whole of my cock's head, her tongue slipping over it like a lollipop, with pressure and warmth and wet.

After several stimulating seconds she reversed the procedure, sliding slowly off of me and smiling at the object of her amorous attentions.

"That's nice," she said, resuming her gentle massage.

"I'll say," I said.

She smiled up at me, and I nearly dissolved from the salaciousness of her expression. Encouraged by my appreciation she grasped me firmly, pulled with a tight grip from base to tip, and back down again, then followed her fastened fist with her mouth, slipping her lips again over my end, down the length of me, her tongue dancing lustily on the underside as she went.

"Oooooh," I moaned, and suddenly she pulled me out of her mouth with a popping sound.

"No!" she said, rising. "Not yet. Stand up."

"What?" I asked, as she used my handle like a joystick to move me around, lifting me to my feet, manipulating me toward her as she leaned back on the boulder and spread her legs further.

"I changed my mind," she said. "I want you inside me."

"You do?" I asked.

"Don't tell my future husband," she said.

"I would never."

"I won't tell Juliet," she said, and my heart skipped.

She pulled my slick, throbbing cock toward her with one hand, spreading her lower lips with two fingertips, finding the space between with my engorged head. Once it had been enfolded, she moved her fingers to her own, pulsing button, rubbing with gentle, swirling pressure. I put my hands on the boulder to either side of her, and slowly pressed myself up, and in—my full length slowly, gently filling her warm, wet, tightness. She closed her eyes, and moaned very softly.

"Oh, my fucking God..." she whispered, her fingers moving faster over her joyful jewel. "You feel so damn good."

"You feel perfect," I said, sliding out, then back in, out, then in. "Absolutely amazing."

She smiled, a maddeningly adorable smile, almost, but not quite, turning up sarcastically at the corner.

"Cum for me," she said. "Cum inside me."

"Oooooh, with pleasure," I said, wanting nothing else in the world. "Oh, God, so much pleasure."

Attempting to follow orders, I began to move faster—in, out, around, as her voice—ragged with lust and strained breathing—sang quietly to me.

> "You know if you do it...
>   (THRUST)
> "You won't regret it.
>   (THRUST)
> "So come and get it.
>   (THRUST)
> "Oh!
>   (THRUST)
> "*YES!*
>   (THRUST)
> **"OOOOOH!**
>   (THRUST-THRUST-THRUST)
> "*No one is near...*

(THRUST)
I may cry out, Oh!
(THRUST)
Oh!
(THRUST)
OOOOH!
(THRUST-THRUST-THRUST)
BUT NO ONE CAN HEAR! GOD!
(THRUST-THRUST-THRUST)
FUCK ME MY DEAR!
OHGOD (THRUST) ***OHGOD*** (THRUST)
OHGOD! (THRUST)
(THRUST -THRUST-THRUST)

She stopped singing, but not thrusting, and kissed me. Lovingly. Lustily. Libidinously. Our mouths welding one to the other, tongues loving inside each other's mouths, with peaking passion and purified pleasure.

And that was it.

We soared, we flew, we landed, leaning into each other, pressing deeply, embracing tightly, tensing, twitching, trembling with release.

Trying desperately to breathe without stopping our kissing, we held each other desperately, gasped, kissed, nibbled necks, ears, chins, gasped then kissed some more, eventually falling against one another, holding tightly, breathing passionately.

"You must have done that before," I said.

"In my mind," she said. "Many times. And I wanted to, but..."

"I know," I said. "You're a good girl." I bent down and kissed a heaving breast, sucking hard on a nipple, and puffy areola, then releasing. "So damn good."

She laughed, and her voice was music for my soul.

"I live in a small community with Spanish customs" she said. "This—what we're doing—is not allowed." She kissed me again, then backed away and smiled. "But it should be."

She kissed me repeatedly, and I returned her passion until we both jumped at a loud banging sound from far below.

We turned and saw immense, double metal doors slamming open on the main building. Several men were coming through pushing wheelbarrows and handcarts piled high with dead bodies, and body parts.

CHAPTER 21

THEY TOSSED THE BODIES and pieces of bodies into industrial sized trash dumpsters atop piles of other bodies and pieces of bodies I hadn't noticed before.

"Oh, dear God," Sunny whispered. "Are those people?"

"Yeah," I said. "And something nefarious definitely killed them."

"We have to get out of here," she said, fear eating at the softness of her voice.

"Yes, you do," I agreed.

She looked at me with terror overtaking her face.

"Trevor, no," she said, her voice trembling. "You have to come too."

"I can't, Sunny," I said. "I have to go down and find out what the hell this is all about. It's clearly evil, and stopping evil from assaulting The Free World by any means necessary is pretty much what I get paid for."

I kissed her sweetly, pulled my at-long-last deflating erection out of her, and moved around the boulder, heading down the hill. She grabbed my arm to stop me.

"I'll come with you," she said.

"No," I said. "There's no reason for you to. You'll only get hurt."

"Would Juliet come?" she asked, then shook her head, and grimaced. "I mean… would she come *with* you, not like I just did on your… you know, though I bet she did. Often. But I mean would she come *help* you? I bet she did that, too. And so can I."

"She was highly trained," I said.

"I can still help," she said. "And maybe it's post coital need, or something, but I don't want to be climbing down the other side of this mountain, alone and afraid, and… and worried about you. I'd rather be *with* you. And… you know… worried about you."

She kissed me, with lovingly deeper meaning this time; Westchester and kids, kind of meaning. I thought about it for a minute, not wanting her to be hurt, or killed, starkly realizing that such sentiments were oddly unselfish of me. And I kind of liked it.

"All right," I said. "But stay behind me."

"Promise," she said.

"The first thing we have to do is get weapons," I told her.

"Not clothes?"

"I can protect us better with weapons."

"Makes sense," she admitted.

We moved quietly down the slope, trying to keep tall bushes, boulders and plants between us and all lines-of-sight of the guards. But it was difficult. The complex was enormous, and security was stationed at every angle and all elevations. I quickly realized that in our favor they didn't seem to expect a threat from outside the complex grounds, and rarely looked up the hill, out of the caldera. Their attention was focused on the arena and its environs.

As we neared the crater floor the spectator sounds grew louder and more intense. We reached the base, the cheering surged, and we moved out of the foliage to creep up behind one of the oversized dumpsters into which the bodies had been had thrown. Sunny and I scaled up its side to look in.

Yep. We had seen correctly. Bodies, and parts, all sizes, genders, and races. Some violently torn apart. Some bullet riddled. One or two had spears, shurikens, or other hand weapons embedded in them. Blood soaked everything, everywhere, all at once. The stench was like a physical thing pushing against us.

I looked at Sunny, and she returned my horrified grimace.

"They're all wearing the same kind of track suit," Sunny said, "different colors, but all the same."

"It's clear we don't want to steal *their* clothes," I said. "Someone is killing people dressed like this."

"A guard's uniform seems best," she said, looking around. "They also have those masks which would hide our faces."

"Yeah," I agreed. "The trick is getting some."

"Maybe not such a trick," Sunny said, confidently.

8   8   8

One of the guards was relieving himself on a wall between buildings.

"I can think of better uses for that dick," Sunny said, and the guard spun to her, tried to get control of both his guns, and failed.

Even I had to admit she looked sexy as hell in that tracksuit. It was—as she'd insisted—too small for her, and fit too tightly in all the right places. The original occupant had been stabbed in the back, so there was no blood or damage on the front that the guard could see. If his face had been visible I'm sure it would have been wide eyed, and open-mouthed with brain-boggled interest.

"You're not supposed to be out here," the guard said, his voice awash with *'I'm SO glad you're out here.'*

Sunny sauntered slowly his way, and even more slowly pulled down the zipper that enclosed the luscious front of her, neck to crotch. As the zipper fell, the manhood in his fingertips rose, lifting its sleepy head to look around.

"What's your business, here?" he asked.

"Oh, sweetie. *I am* the business," she said, sultry dripping off her sensuous lips as she pulled the track suit open far enough to fully reveal the pink edge of her nipples; groomed hair also peeking out a mere hands width below her navel. It had the desired effect as his penis jumped up and barked for treats. "I'm a professional girl. Though I still like to do it just for fun, and my goodness," she eyed his panting dog, "you do look fun. So virile, so handsome and I like you so much that *you* can be on my freebie list."

Hmm. Why did all that sound so familiar?

"I'm not supposed to fraternize with the contestants," the security man said, clearly sweating under his mask, and wanting oh-so-badly to fraternize with *this* contestant.

"Oooooh," Sunny said, sounding legitimately disappointed. "Are you sure?" her voice was desperate, needy, pulling open the front of her tracksuit to let her glorious orbs fall free. "But don't *want* to fuck me?"

He stood. Motionless. For what felt like an eternity. So did I. His finger twitched on the trigger.

And then—amazingly—he bought it. Men really were idiots.

In a blink he put down his machine gun, leaning it against the wall, opening his own outfit, yanking it wide and quickly pushing it down to reveal a pale, less than athletic body. Suit now around his shins, he shuffled toward Sunny with arms open and penis erect to embrace her, and—he honestly believed—have willing sex with her. I—of course—immediately stepped out of the shadows behind him, picked up his gun, and leveled it at his back. And that's when I noticed his exposed butt was marked with the same octopus tattoo as the guy I'd shot on the bus.

I chambered a round in the machine gun with a click and a klatch. Sunny immediately closed the velour around her treasure chest. The guard flinched at the sound, and slowly turned to me.

"Oooooh, shiiiiiiiit," he said, putting his hands up, sounding younger every second. "Don't kill me. It's just a job. Pays better than fast food."

"What job?" I asked. "What is this place? What's with the octopus tattoo?"

He stood silently for a moment, and because I couldn't see his face, it was impossible to read why.

"You don't know?" he asked, jerking a thumb toward Sunny. "She's wearing one of the suits."

"Explain it to me, anyway." I said, curtly.

"It's a show," the guard said. "The Octopus Game. You compete to win three million dollars, tax free, in front of an audience. So, why is she out here? And why are you naked?"

I unconsciously glanced down, but bounced my eyes quickly back up to glare at him.

"I'll ask the questions," I said. "What are all those bodies in the dumpster?"

"Those?" He asked, glancing that way. "Those are the losers."

"They..." I said, stunned. "... the losers? They were killed... for losing? Losing what?"

"The game. That's how it works. Who are you? Don't you know anything? They died trying to win. It's a game to the death." He turned and looked at Sunny. "You knew that, didn't you? I thought that's why you wanted to—you know. Because you might die."

Sunny just stared at him.

"Quite a few of the women want to," he said, and his voice seemed to indicate a smile under the mask. "To feel alive... and to maybe learn some secret or cheat for winning. Which we kind of encourage by pretending to know things. Banging desperate chicks is..." he chuckled, "one of the perks of working here."

Sunny's face shriveled in on itself as if I were watching several days of a discarded, time-lapse apple decomposing.

"Eeeew," she said. "That is gross."

"Show me this 'Octopus Game'," I snarled.

8   8   8

Wearing the teenage guard's outfit and mask, I 'escorted' him and Sunny at gunpoint—now both in tracksuits—through the double-doors, and into the packed arena. The crowd, facing away from us, would cheer or moan as one, rising and sitting in response to whatever attention-seizing event was transpiring down on the field. Dying of curiosity, we braved the fact that we looked out of place, moved from the tunnel shadows closer to the action for a clearer view.

We stepped slowly forward into the arena lighting behind the crowd, and even through the full facemask I could see the field as clearly as if I wore no mask at all.

The floor of the stadium was filled, wall-to-wall, with an obstacle course, like a children's playground—or rather two identical playgrounds, running side-by-side. The only difference between these playgrounds and actual children's play structures was that adults were running across them, not kids. The two sides were in obvious competition, trying to knock people on the other structure off with spears, clubs, throwing knives, bows and arrows, along with a host of other weapons left scattered about the 'play area.'

The courses themselves ran the length of the field, stretching across pits of molten lava, raging fire, boiling water, spike pits, snake pits, alligator pits, and some kind of bubbling green liquid that must have been acid. To confirm my suspicions, partially dissolved body parts bobbed about in it, smoldering, and liquefying.

The dead lay scattered; missing pieces, impaled, boiling, swollen with bites, the dead dispersed across the crazy jungle gym in various ways, murdered with various weapons, or no weapons at all.

The structures themselves were a marvel of Rube Goldbergian insanity. Wheels spun, platforms rotated, axes pendulumed, giant rocks rolled down crazy stairs, cages rose and fell along ratcheted risers, ropes swung from one end to another. It was like a giant version of that crazy Ideal Toys *The Rat Trap Game*. With humans as the rats. Kinda makes sense

At the end nearest us a couple was swinging together on a rope, trying to cross over a series of buzzsaws sliding back and forth on tracks, when someone from the other side threw a spear and impaled the man. He understandably let go, nearly dragging the woman down with him into the spinning blades, where he was instantly sliced and diced into multiple, convenient, blood-spewing, fireplace-sized pieces.

The audience both roared and groaned, depending on which side they were rooting for, I guess.

Meanwhile, the surviving woman managed to drop safely onto the opposite side, but made the mistake of celebrating—jumping up and down, raising her arms in the air—making herself the perfect target for someone on the opposing team with a crossbow.

Once she had followed her partner bloodily into the buzzing blades, an alarm went off, and the crowd leapt to its feet, clapping, cheering, screaming louder and longer than they had since we'd entered the extinct volcano.

Apparently, the game was over. Someone had won.

On the field, three remaining members of the opposing team made their way out of hiding, and stood at the finish line of their jungle gym. Two rugged-looking men, and one statuesque blonde woman. One of the men—the one with dark hair—threw his hands up in victory, went off-balance, slipped and fell onto some nasty looking spikes, dying almost instantly. The crowd laughed, and cheered even louder.

Sunny turned to me, pale, sick, shaking, indescribable horror ruining the beauty of her face, clearly regretting her decision to follow me down here. She'd probably rather face the dragon, again.

I felt the same when a phalanx of guards instantly surrounded us, too many machineguns aimed directly at us. At their urging, I lowered my own gun, and removed my mask.

"Trevor Hawke," a woman's voice said over the loudspeaker.

I froze, stunned. At the center of the arena was an immense screen, the size and clarity of which would easily put The General's high-definition office monitor to shame. My surprised face appeared on it, an equally startled Sunny by my side, some nearby camera apparently trained on us from amidst the crowd of purple uniforms and target masks.

I handed my weapon to an insistent guard, and we were corralled forward to the fence encircling the arena.

"Trevor Hawke," The female voice repeated, "Although most of you know him as Agent 8 of the ultra-secret US organization SADISTO! We were wondering when you would get here!"

CHAPTER 22

I STOOD AT THE edge of the arena, dumbfounded.

I looked slowly around at the madding crowd. All eyes had turned to me with intense curiosity. A few people smiled darkly.

Finally, my shocked gaze settled on Sunny. Her expression was hard to read, but I was pretty sure it wasn't trust I saw in those eyes.

"They were expecting you?" she asked.

"I'm as confused as you are," I said, trying to reassure her. Reassured she wasn't.

"Well," the booming female voice said, "I guess I can't blame you for being late."

Suddenly a movie of Sunny and I, nude, having sex against the rock, surrounded by purple flowers filled the immense screen.

Sunny gasped.

"No," she whispered, horrified that her loss of virginity was being exposed to anyone and everyone in pristine, Technicolor maximum definition, thirty feet high.

"You feel perfect," my big-screen self said, sliding in and out of her. "Absolutely amazing."

"Cum for me," her giant self said, a maddeningly adorable smile, almost, but not quite, turning up sarcastically at the corner. "Cum inside me."

"You never could keep it in your pants, Trevor," the booming female voice said drawing cackles of laughter from the crowd. "And I see to make things easier you've just altogether given up wearing them." More laughs, and cackles. "I suppose it makes it quicker and easier to rack up those notches on your bedpost."

The crowd 'ooohhed,' and chuckles bubbled up in various spots throughout the arena, as Giant Sunny was beginning to sing to Giant me.

> *I may cry out, Oh!*
>   (THRUST)
> *Oh!*
>   (THRUST)
> *OOOOH!*
>   (THRUST-THRUST-THRUST)
> *BUT NO ONE IS NEAR! GOD!*
>   (THRUST-THRUST-THRUST)
> *NO ONE CAN HEAR!*
>   *FUCK ME MY DEAR!*

"Mmm," said our torturer. "Quite the singing voice you have there, Sunny."

The crowd was laughing riotously now, as the Sunny beside me was hiding her face, whimpering, sobbing, refusing to allow me to comfort her, though I tried.

Sunny slapped my hand away as if it were a disgusting spider that had crawled onto her shoulder. She shot me a look of horror, anger, fear, humiliation—a swirling blend of poorly digested emotions, all of them backing up in her system. Behind her, the two of us were passionately pounding one another to the cheers and appreciative whoops of a stadium full of strangers.

"Deflowering some poor, young, native, Jícama girl that no decent man will never want for a wife, now, poor thing. Not that *you* care about things like that, Agent 8. But then, the woman can never truly be divorced from blame."

"You're a good girl," Giant me said, as he bent down and kissed one of Giant Sunny's ten-foot-high heaving breasts, sucking hard on a nipple, and puffy areola, then releasing. "So damn good."

Giant Sunny laughed, and her voice was—still—music for my soul.

Tears formed in Sunny's eyes beside me, but she rubbed them angrily away, denying the sadness with seething savagery, turning away from me. I tried again to put a hand on her shoulder, but she jerked that shoulder away.

"There are hours of footage just like this, ladies and gentlemen! With an endless stream of innocent, young girls! Agent 8 uses his dick like a weapon against all womankind. And woe be it to the poor female whose heart is impaled upon his spear."

Sunny arched her back forward, curving it protectively inward like an armadillo-shell, and moved away from me. I felt a stab of my own pain, and desperately wanted to reach her, make her understand that I...

That I what? That I wasn't anything that this evil, female voice was portraying me to be? That I hadn't bedded dozens, maybe hundreds of beautiful, sexy women over the years both in and out of the line of duty?

In reality... I had. And reveled in it.

"So, my friends," the acid-tongued woman on the loudspeaker continued, "let us retire for the evening, and prepare to place our bets. Who will survive tomorrow's grand finale? One of today's champions, Gunter, or Gudrun? Or will it be one of our newly arrived surprise contestants, the arch-villain, Trevor Hawke—Agent 8—or his lovely, loose, little Lolita, the *naïve, naturist, the shell-collecting beachcomber Sunny Bunz?*"

Sunny raised her head as the reality crashed into her skull, turning to me in wet-eyed horror. We were going to compete in this horrible Octopus Game, and only one of us was intended to survive? Before either she or I could speak, question, despair to one another, the guards were shoving us roughly back through the double-doors, down the stadium corridor, and toward... what?

8   8   8

We passed through a metal door off the corridor and entered an office area with desks, chairs, phones, a water cooler, a coffee pot, coffee cups—man, I could use some coffee—photos, some personal items, and were forced through a set of more elegant doors—wood instead of metal—that opened into a central office filled with rich furniture, and fine décor. Photos postered the walls of this 'bosses' office, with mostly disturbing images of tattered, frightened people, many covered in blood, one holding a severed head.

Past games? Past winners?

A guard walked over to Sunny, grabbed her collar, and yanked. Apparently familiar enough with the tracksuits to know exactly how to tear the specially designed clothes from her body with easy, specific movements. She was already half-nude before either of us had time to react, and when I moved to her defense, I took a vicious rifle butt to the head for the attempt. The impact drove me to my knees, and I saw suns, not stars, entire galaxies filled with bright, fiery suns.

"Take off that uniform," my assailant demanded, as the other guard finished rendering Sunny entirely nude.

She—for her part—glared at his faceless mask with a sun-fueled intensity of her own.

I struggled free of the purple guard's getup and handed it over. The two men then exited. Finally, we were left alone.

"Sunny," I began.

"Don't talk to me," she snipped, turning away to study the photos on the wall. Or pretend to.

"She wasn't clear," Sunny said, apparently deciding that *she* could talk to *me*, "the woman on the loudspeaker. But it sounded as though there's supposed to be a single winner of this game."

She turned to me with—I don't know—anger? Warning?

"Only one," she said.

I didn't speak.

"You can talk," she said. "Just don't do any of your stupid reassuring. It's patronizing, and annoying."

"Or confident," I said.

"Don't," she warned. "They knew we were coming. Wanted us to come. And for one of us to kill the other. How? Why?"

I shrugged.

"Did you recognize her voice?" she asked.

"It sounded familiar," I said. "But I couldn't place it. And I honestly can't imagine who it would be."

"She knows you," Sunny said. "Knows you're a slut."

"Women are sluts," I corrected. "Not men."

"How many women have you slept with?" she snarled.

"Well, by 'sleep' do you mean actually 'sleep,' or do you mean…" I guess I wasn't as charming as I was trying to be. Sunny didn't respond, and started blowing holes through my skull, mentally.

I sighed.

"I don't know," I said. "I have sex with women, not numbers."

"That many, hunh?" She looked my naked body up and down. "Men can absolutely be sluts. Trust me."

"You make me sound like the kind of guy who would rub his dick on a woman in a bar."

"Are you?" she asked, sounding quite serious.

"No!" I snapped. "Believe me when I say, the women I've been with have always wanted me as much as I wanted them. Or more. *Usually* more."

Sunny crossed her arms defiantly over the bounty of her bare breasts.

"Well," she said, after some lengthy thought. "I guess you didn't force *me*. And I'd be stupid to hold a grudge about our lovemaking being exposed out there when you'll probably have to kill me tomorrow, anyway."

Tears suddenly soaked her eyes, and her lip quivered uncontrollably as the events of the day overwhelmed her. I moved toward her, opening my arms, and though she was initially reluctant, she quickly opened her own to me and fell sobbing against my chest.

"This has been—like—the best and the worst day of my entire life," she said through gasps and whimpers. "All at the same time."

I held her more tightly.

"I'm glad we made love on those flowers," she said, squeezing me in return. "It was actually kind of beautiful to watch. Our bodies together… you kissing me, loving me, moving inside me surrounded by all that lovely violet. I'm glad it was you I was with before I die."

"You're not going to die," I said.

"No, she probably is," a female voice said, entering the room.

Sunny and I turned as one to watch a woman in a strange, metal mask stalk through the door followed by a man wearing a cat mask and suit. At least I think it was a mask and suit.

For some weird reason it didn't cover his penis, a rather lengthy affair that swung freely as he walked. He also had a tail that he actually seemed able to move.

The woman wore knee-length sandals, and a long, flowing, silken, pinkish-purple hooded cape, a gun belt, and… nothing else. Her smallish breasts bounced freely with her confident stride as she strutted behind the office desk, to stand, hands on hips, her back to the huge, wall-window looking out across the caldera and lagoon, her face and mask to Sunny and me.

"That's the whole point of this," the masked woman continued. "One winner takes all."

"Takes all, what?" Sunny and I asked simultaneously.

The mask cocked a bit, sideways.

"You don't know?" the woman asked. "Interesting. But SADISTO isn't actually a detective organization, is it? You pretty much just murder people."

"Pretty much," I admitted.

Sunny glanced up at me, and I didn't meet her eyes to read her thoughts. I didn't want to know them.

"Which is why you're here," the masked woman said. "The endgame surprise. The second act twist that drives us forward into the third, and final act." She held up her hands as if picturing a movie theater coming attraction. "A professional killer set loose among amateur killers. *And who will win?*"

She said the last part like a television announcer, throwing her arms wide for emphasis, and continued speaking in a 'you have to see it to believe it!' tone.

"Will it be Gunter, the Norwegian pike fisherman? Or Gudrun, his best friend since childhood, schoolmate from his old fishing village, kind and loving daughter of the local seamstress, and young apprentice to the trade who used to darn Gunter's socks, bring him sweetness and chocolates for lunch, while waiting patiently for his proposal of marriage until the day he left her and moved to the big city without even a goodbye?"

She really sold the 'without even a goodbye.' For a moment I thought she might cry.

Sunny and I looked at one another, horrified, yet at the same time curious about our perceived roles in all this.

"Or will it be the professionally trained hitman," the masked woman continued, apparently to answer our curiosity, "or could the newest fan favorite, the long-shot, charming, young nudist shell collector who looks almost exactly like his dead girlfriend."

"*Dead...* girlfriend," I said. Or asked. I'm not sure which. My mind had gone kind of mushy.

"Oh," the masked woman said, putting her arms down. "You didn't know? Yes, Juliet is dead. We hoped to get her here, actually, to go against you in our finale. The stakes are always so much more interesting when the finalists know—or better yet—*love* one another. But apparently someone helped her attempt an escape the other night, and she nearly made it until SADISTO agents caught up with her at her family home, and... well... she *had* killed a pair of their best Decommissioners..."

"How do you know all this?" I asked.

The Masked Woman shrugged, casually. "I have my sources," she said, simply.

"Are you Doctor Sin?" I asked.

"I am!" the voice behind the mask said like a perky teenager, straightening up proudly in a way that made her nakedness jiggle and jounce. "Sin with an 'I', not the one with a 'y', obviously."

"Is this what you did with Strangeways, and Trublue?" I asked. "You forced them to play your weird little Octopus Game?"

It was hard to tell through the mask—and with my attention distracted by her nude body—but there seemed to be a slight flinch, a momentary pause before Doctor Sin gathered herself and spoke again.

"They were finalists in our last show," she admitted. "Sadly, both of them were losers."

I absorbed that. Glenn had been a friend for many years. I'd done threesomes with him, and with Trueblue, together and separately, and enjoyed them immensely. We had eaten together, drunk together, and shared a lot, including his wife. And now he was dead.

"And you wanted me..." I said, as it all bored its angry way deeper into my mush-mind, "and Juliet... to go against one another in the same way? Compete to the death?"

"Oh, yes," the masked woman admitted. "Absolutely. We had made arrangements to capture her after she'd finished her SADISTO training, and everything. Figured you'd both come here to investigate Strangeway's disappearance. But sadly, cadet agent Jones scratched out, went mad, murdered a bunch of people she wasn't supposed to, and got herself killed. So, we were shit out of luck on that one. Although—even nuts—I still would have wanted her to compete. You were so obviously smitten with her, and that kind of emotional connection really connects with an audience.

Sunny shot me a look, and I ignored her, which I shouldn't have.

"Then I thought… wait," Sin said, putting a finger to her immobile metal lip, miming a light-bulb moment. "Maybe if we could find someone who *looked* a lot like her, someone who—as we hoped against all hope—you might quickly develop a very strong affection for—or at least fuck a little. Which you did. It was so cute." She moved her hands over her bare breasts so she could rub fingertips across her nipples. "And pretty hot, I must say. Mm-mm-good, that's what Sunny's cunt is…"

I felt Sunny tense in my arms, and lean, as if she wanted to go for Sin, herself.

Sin seemed to notice the movement, and waited until Sunny backed down. Sin then nodded to the nearby cat-man, apparently summoning him over. He moved quickly her way, as she flipped aside her robe, and bent over her desk. He stepped behind her exposed bottom, holding his hardening member, and guided it into her.

"Mmm," she said, as he apparently achieved his goal, grasped her hips and began thrusting mechanically.

Sunny and I stared briefly at them, again turning surprised eyes to one another. I gently pulled my nude, shell collector to me. I was moved, and so very glad when she didn't resist. I was even more pleased when she put her arms around my waist and held me tightly, resting her damp cheek against my chest.

"Miss Bunz," the masked woman said as her cat-suited henchman continued driving in and out of her from behind, "had already been coming here, to the island, for months. Braving the dinosaurs to search for seashells, of all things. Proving herself to be quite intelligent, actually… cunning, and formidable, staying safe from guards, and beasts alike."

"Beasts," I said "like dinosaurs? How and why did you make dinosaurs? How exactly did your Octopus Game get started, here? *What is this place?*"

"Oh, it's just a place," said Dr. Sin, rolling her hips, and lowering her head for a moment to just enjoy the feel of her feline lover. "And I didn't make the dinosaurs… Lots of… um… ooooh… previous businessmen started projects here, which all quickly failed. Yeah, you can go faster." The cat-man complied, and she moved with him, moaning loudly for a few strokes.

"Private islands are great places to do insane things for fun and profit," Sin continued. "Aaaah, the first guy—mmmm, yes, that's good—Raphael Hythlodaeus, I think his name was, tried to build a Utopia but based around some monastic, narcissistic, celibate bullshit, where only high-minded, perfected men were allowed to live, along with a standing army of foreign mercenaries, of course, to protect those non-violent high-minds. The Greek ideal of Elysium, home of heroes and Demi-Gods, regular mortals excluded; or Plato's Republic where food is either 'medicine,' or 'penance'—your choice—everyone fasts all the time, anyway, people are treated as equal, except for women, minorities, lawyers, deformed offspring and, of course, bad poets.

"Ooh, ooh, yeah, baby, but move it around, a little. Don't just go in and out.

"Well, you know people," she continued, turning back to me as she rocked along with her lover's movements. "Before long in any restrictive environment everyone's lying about compliance, witch-hunting those who aren't austere enough, fighting for resources, dying from malnutrition, too tired to accomplish anything, secretly fucking like rabbits, and basically killing each other with their tiered spirituality."

She dropped her head again, rocked, and thrust for a while in rhythm with her partner.

"Oh, God, yes. I've been dying for this since I saw you and Sunny doing it on that big screen. So fucking hot. Anyway… after that, other than some stranded survivors who went native, the island was mostly empty. For quite a while, really. Not much useable land, mostly covered in bird shit, so no one wanted it. Ah, ah, ah, mmm. So you could get it pretty cheap. You can go harder. Huh. Huh. Yeah, baby, yeah. Like that. Eventually some other doctor came here and got those natives to help him do terrible things to animals in an effort to make them human... and it didn't go well.

"This guy here..." she cocked a head toward the cat-man up her ass, he smiled and waved, pleasantly.

"Hello," he said.

"He's a straggler from those hybridization experiments, Sin said, her voice in lusty rhythm with her partner's movements. "Half human, half house cat—all dick. Got little spikes on it for her pleasure. Oh, my God. You should try it, Sunny. Feels like nothing you've ever had up your pussy. HA! Pussy up your pussy! I didn't mean to do that."

"I'll pass," Sunny said. "But thanks." Then to the Cat-Man, she said, "no offense."

"None taken," he said, cheerily, never missing a beat.

"Anyway, that was a bust," Sin continued. "These guys went nuts, killed the island's owner, Maroni..."

"Mor*eau*," the Cat-Man corrected.

"Whatever. Killed him, killed everyone, then wandered into the jungle and tried to survive along with the locals. Not exactly a success story. So, the place got even cheaper, and then the last guy came in and bred dinosaurs all over the place—ah—ah—ah—fuck, that's good—thinking he could turn it into a zoo, or some shit. Mmm... mmm..., pinch my nipples, honey, pinch my nipples."

The cat-man quickly responded.

"Fucking dumbass," she said, with a little laugh, and I wasn't sure if she was talking about the cat-man, or the previous owner. "The dinosaurs ate him while he was having ice cream." Ah. The owner. "The things people do on these islands. His heirs couldn't wait to unload this crap-covered, man-beast infested, dinosaur strewn hunk of rock. Yeah, manhandle 'em, baby. Squeeze 'em like you mean it, and fuck me like the animal you are! AH GOD! SOOOO GOOOOOOD..."

Their rhythm and movement increased in tempo and intensity, and her history lesson got louder.

"So I bought this entire place for a song, uh-uh-uh changed the zoning laws to make murder legal as long as it's consensual, ah-yeah-ah-yeah-ah-yeah and now we put on closed circuit shows a few seasons a year. Mmmmm-mmm good. Kinda taking things back to the original idea of a Utopia but skipping right to the part where it's all gone wrong, I took the name Doctor Sin. Massage my clit. Yeah. Yeah, yeah, yeah. Just like that, fur fingers, feels nice. Rich people fly in from all over the world to watch poor people kill each other, and bet on favorites. Got a closed-circuit TV deal. Makes bank."

"And now you think," I said over her moaning, and increasingly active love-making, "that Sunny and I are just going to 'consensually' walk out onto that obstacle course, and fight to the death against Gudrun, and Gunter…"

"We won't do it!" Sunny said, bravely.

Doctor Sin's response was predictable.

"Sure, you will. Or I'll just fucking shoot you right here," the masked woman said, panting, her voice rising and falling with pumping, penetration, and passion. She tried several times to push a button on her desk, but found it difficult with all the hump and grind. I finally reached forward and did it for her. It was driving me crazy.

"Thank you," she said, as two armed guards came instantly in. "Take them to the bedroom complex. Ah, ah, Oh, God, I'm cumming… And the audience always prefers Unh, unh, unh, an underdog to win. MM! MM! MM! So we're going to separate you… in—oh—tomorrow's… MM… competition. It'll be boys… huh, huhh… against girls. AAAHYES!! YES!! YES!!"

The guards moved forward, jabbing guns into my and Sunny's ribs, forcing us through the door as our captor shrieked in ecstasy, leaned forward on her desk, shaking uncontrollably. As the door closed, we heard her breathless voice, and though I couldn't see her face, I knew the bitch was smiling under her mask, and not just from sexual gratification.

"Enjoy your final night together."

CHAPTER 23

TIRED, COLD, NAKED, SUNNY returned from a trip to the bathroom, and huddled with me on a single bed in the middle of an immense room filled with single beds, some of which were stained with dried blood. More blood was smeared across the floor. It all told a story of false safety, violence, and poor housekeeping.

Apparently, the games didn't end on the 'field of play.'

From the far side of the room Gudrun and Gunter watched us with fierce, unblinking eyes, also huddling naked on a bed of their own, Gunter atop Gudrun, thrusting absently.

"Don't look at them," Sunny said, sliding under me, wrapping her legs around me, turning my face toward hers. "Look at me."

"I was thinking maybe I could go talk to them," I said, "perhaps..."

"Ssh, sh, sssshhh," she said, smiling sadly up at me. "Don't even think about them. Just be with me."

"But..."

She pressed a fingertip to my lips.

"Tomorrow, I will be dead," she said, still smiling, and not meaning it. "So tonight, I want you to be with me. No guilt. No shame."

"Sunny. We can get out of this…" I began.

"We," she said, pointedly, interrupting me, "*can't. You* can. You know weapons, and fighting, and all that stuff. Maybe Juliet knew it, too." A tear budded at the corner of her eye, and slowly streamed its way back along her cheek toward her ear, but her eyes never left mine. "I… don't.

"I'm glad you know those things," she continued. "I want you to live. But I… I am going to die."

"Sunny," I said, desperate to comfort her, but she would have none of it.

"Suddenly it all seems so stupid," she said with a tiny laugh. "Worrying about being a 'good girl.' Saving myself for marriage. Worrying that it's wrong to be naked on a beach. Worrying that it's wrong to play with myself. Worrying that I wanted to be naked with a man. Worrying that I would enjoy it, worrying that I would never find love, but…" she stared deeply into my eyes, and smiled, so sweetly, "just… worrying. About everything. People always say 'life is short' but you never imagine…"

She pulled me down to her, and held me tightly. I slid my arms under her back, and returned the embrace.

"I never imagined…" she continued, faintly, barely audible, "So tonight, you are mine. In all ways. I want you to please me, to give to me, to be everything I ever wanted. Make me happy this last night. Be my love slave."

She reached down and took hold of my flaccidity, pulling gently to encourage firmness, then guided it home, wiggling its tip inside of her, shifting her hips, and scooching herself down to envelop, enfold.

"Sunny," I said. "They'll be filming all this…"

"Sshh," she said. "I don't care. You belong to me, not them. It's slave time, Trevor. You must do what I say, and please me. Now, move slowly at first while you stare into my eyes. Then kiss me… gently, and tell me you that love me— even if you don't."

I began to move, as slowly, and gently as I could, never letting my eyes wander from hers.

"I love you," I said, surprising myself with my sincerity. She didn't have to ask.

"Mmm..." she said, shivering a little. "That's perfect. Now kiss me."

I did. Softly. Sensuously. Sublimely. I gently licked her lips, then returned smoothly across them with my own lips.

"Yes," she said. Now..."

"I love you, Sunny," I said, again.

I kissed her lips more firmly, more lovingly.

"I worried I would never find love..." she said, softly.

"But you did," I said, pausing my kissing only long enough to speak the emotion, continuing to move gently in and out of her, around in circles, her throat filling with an appreciative moan.

"I love you, Trevor," she said, closing her eyes, and feeling me, rolling her hips with, and against mine. "I love you, and I want you. Always."

I kissed her harder, with increasing passion, deepening desire, shoving myself into her to both our limits. Her nails began to rake along my spine, her legs rising up to wrap around my waist.

I pulled back from the intense hunger of her mouth.

"I love you," I said, meaning it.

"Oh, God, I love you so much, and want you so badly," she said, kissing me again, quickly, over and over again, "I want to make love to you like this every day. I want to be your wife, to have you cum inside me so I can give you children... three—four—all the children you want, as long as we can make them like this."

She ground her hips into mine, as I drove mine into hers.

"I love you, Sunny, and I want those things, too. I want to fill you every day with love, and passion, and... and love, and... I know you don't want to hear it, but we will get out of this. I will stop this madwoman."

She stopped kissing me, and stared, uncomfortable.

"You mean kill her?" she asked.

"Yes."

"But... that would be murder."

"Yes."

"Trevor," she said, a little horrified. "You could actually murder her?"

"Easily."

"So, she was serious when she said you basically just murder people."

"It's my job. It's what I'm trained for, and it's training that's going to get us out of this alive. I know it seems harsh, but killing is sometimes essential. My organization exists for it, it's important and vital. What we do, we do for the greater good."

She smiled up at me, and the last thing I remember is joy and hope in those precious, beautiful turquoise eyes before she stopped smiling, growled, pulled back a fist and knocked me unconscious.

8   8   8

My vision returned from black, to gray, to fuzzy-white, and I thought someone was leaning over me. Someone blonde, someone tan.

"Sunny," I said, quietly.

When my eyes slowly cleared, I saw that that there was, indeed, someone blonde and tan leaning over me.

Gunter.

"Good morning," he said, with a strange cheer in his voice. "You slept for long time. I consider killing you vhile you sleep. But then I think better of zis."

I looked around at guards posted in the corners of the room, and knew they were more than likely the real reason he hadn't killed me. Sin wanted her big ratings finale.

"You seem special," Gunter said, continuing his lie. "Zhey vant us to battle. So ve vill battle"

"Yeah, I don't think so," I said, leaning up on one arm, and immediately regretting it as my head painfully expanded to ten times its normal size. At least it felt that way. "I'm not a trained monkey."

"Vhat means?" Gunter asked. "Trained monkey? Do Americans train monkeys to kill?"

"No," I snarled, irritable for so many reasons, not the least of which was Sunny punching me. "They train monkeys to entertain. To put on a show. And I won't be putting on any shows."

"Make no sense," Gunter said, and as we stood, I saw that he was a good six inches taller than me, maybe two feet wider at the shoulders. "Ve are here to kill. Not entertain. No monkeys. Oh! Or do you mean Monkees? Vis two letters 'e'? *Here ve come... vokking down ze street... get ze funniest looks from...* still make no sense."

"NO!" I snapped. My head really, really hurt, but now because Gunter was an idiot. "Dear, God, no. Don't sing. I didn't mean that kind of monkey. I meant actual monkeys, which are trained to... you know what? Never mind. Just stop talking."

"No," Gunter said. "Please explain. I must learn language for vhen I am rich because of vinning Octopus Game contest so I move to LA and become movie star."

"When you... what?" I asked. "What do you mean when you become rich?"

"To vin Octopus Game means to become rich. Is right vord? Rich? Is vhen you haf millions dollars?"

"Yes," I said. "That's the right word, but... how will you become rich?"

"Vhen I kill you. All uv you. Prize for vinning is millions of dollars. Three. Three of millions."

"When you kill all of us?"

"Yes," He said as if he were discussing clipping his toenails. "Kill you. Kill Gudrun. Kill blond gorl who has huge pupper."

He cupped his hands before him as if he were joyously carrying two enormous imaginary watermelons home from the market.

"Gudrun doesn't mean anything to you?" I asked. "You were making love to her in bed... when was it? Last night?"

"Oh, yes. Always like to fuck on her, but she is not for me to marry. I vill haf many vomen. Movie star. Me. More important... vant to live. And be rich. So Gudrun, pupper gorl, you."

He made a 'chrrrk' sound, and slashed his thumb across his neck.

"And what makes you think you'll be able to kill me? Kill all of us?"

He looked at me for a long while as if I was stupid, then laughed.

"You are so small," he said, again discussing toenails. "Veak. You can not hurt me. I kill many to be here for millions. Is vhy I not kill you in sleep. Vill kill you in front of many peoples during show. AH! Like trained monkey! *Now* make sense!"

He made motions like an organ box grinder, and gurgled a darkly twisted tinkling circus sound as he paraded around the new, smaller room we occupied. For the first time I noticed the armed guards surrounding us, and felt fairly certain they were the more likely reason he hadn't killed me yet.

"Trained monkey, dancing before peoples," he said, nodding his head. "Yes. Is how you vill die."

CHAPTER 24

NAKED, AND UNARMED, GUNTER and I were 'escorted' at gunpoint along a corridor toward the now familiar double-doors that would let us out onto the 'playing field.'

"Do not be semitimental," Gunter said. He hadn't stopped talking since I woke up. If I didn't think it would get me shot, I'd have killed him already. Violently. With glee. "You morder pupper gorl. I morder Gudrun. We vin. Then tomorrow ve—you—me—real fight and I vin. Is certain, and then…"

"Yeah, yeah, yeah," I said. "You move to Los Angeles and 'mack luf vith' many movie stars. Shut the fuck up already before I cut off your huge dick and feed it to you."

Out of the corner of my eye I saw that he was actually hurt by my anger.

"Is not needed to be mean," he said, an odd kind of petulance in his voice. "I sought ve be friends."

"I have no friends," I said. "And if I did have friends, one of them wouldn't be you."

"Why we not be friends? Even little bit, for short vhile?"

"First of all, you're an idiot," I said as if it had been clearly printed on the package he came in. "Second of all, I'm going to kill you, and I don't want anything making me feel bad about that."

"Ha!" Gunter laughed. "You... kill *me*? Such funny you are."

"Yeah. Something you should know about me, Gunter? I'm a professional assassin. I know a hundred and fifty-seven ways to kill you right now, and that's naked, without a weapon."

"You..." Gunter said, his voice catching. "You are professional? Paid for to kill?"

"Yep," I said grinning at him like a mischievous child. "But you I'm going to kill for free."

He shut up. Finally. And turned white.

We reached the doors, and waited. I heard footsteps behind us, and turned to see Sunny and Gudrun, also being escorted by armed guards, also both still naked, though Sunny had apparently convinced someone to give her back her belt, and seashell. I noted that Gudrun had two black eyes, and a bandaged, swollen nose. I guess she had considered killing Sunny at some point, too, and Sunny had knocked her out, as well?

I tried to get Sunny to look at me long enough to ask the silent question: why? But she refused to make eye-contact.

Their little troop stopped moving about ten feet away— guards grabbing each of the women's shoulders to stop them in place. Sunny was being brave, but was clearly afraid. She wasn't Juliet. I could see that, now. But my feelings for her might well have been deeper, more protective. Juliet had always seemed able to take care of herself. Sunny seemed as though she needed me, and what man doesn't want to be needed, even just a little?

So why had she punched me? Knocked me out?

I continued to try to make eye-contact, and did briefly, and she abruptly calmed, as if someone had thrown a switch, and Sunny's expression... changed. Her brows fell, her turquoise eyes half-lidded, shining like beacons, as a charming, sarcastic flicker turned up the corner of her lips to form a dark, and knowing smile...

Wait. It couldn't be. Could it?

"Juliet?" I whispered.

She didn't respond. Not with words. But her eyes bore into mine, darkened further, and her smile turned up just a fraction more.

And I knew.

I don't know how it had happened, how Sunny had lived a life here, visited this island for months—the same months that she had been in Singapodia, and later as I was living a life somewhere else with cadet agent Jones, but I knew.

Sunny was my Juliet.

"*Juliet?*" I shouted.

But she only continued her maddening, half-smile, and unblinking stare, until finally, she flipped me off.

What the hell was going on here?

I started to say more, but the doors behind us opened to cheers from the crowd, the guards forced us through, and into the arena.

The teeming masses of uber-wealthy gamblers was even more enthusiastic than they had been the day before; cheering, stomping, waving their arms, and applauding. They were in various stages of dress, and undress, some wore masks, some groped each other, or made love while they cheered.

High above, the giant screen had pictures of the four contestants, myself included. Numbers beneath each photo showed odds, or votes, or some such nonsense. Gunter and I were apparently evenly matched. The women had numbers in the single-digits, with odds through the roof.

On a platform before the screen Doctor Sin strode out, wearing a similar outfit to the one she'd worn the day before, only today's color scheme was deep purple instead of pinkish. Still naked from neck to knees other than jewelry, she strode to the railing, arms up to excite the crowd.

"Today," she began, her confidence echoing along the walls, "we bring you what promises to be our greatest finale! Two amateurs, and by now you know their story well. Like all our contestants they were in dire financial straits and happy to kill others in order to erase their debt and become rich, or die themselves rather than return to a life of poverty, and shame. Ladies and gentlemen, give a warm welcome to your two finalists... *Gunter and Gudrun!*"

The crowd erupted. Cheers, whistles, applause. The masked so-called doctor dropped her arms, holding them out, looking down on us. There was no way to know, but I don't think she was looking at the Norwegians, or Sunny. She seemed to be looking directly at me.

Beside me Gunter raised his arms triumphantly, confidently, playing for the adoring crowd. But his confidence faltered when he glanced over and saw my face, staring calmly into his. Trying to hide his fear, he returned to his place beside me, and tried to focus on the adoring crowd, with a trembling smile.

"And competing against them," Sin continued, "please welcome our charming little 'good girl' local with the all-over tan, Sunny Bunz, and her lover, the highly trained, world-class SADISTO agent, and killer, *Trevor Hawke!*"

More cheers, and a smattering of boos from the crowd. 'Sunny' and I stood still, gave no reaction, not even a look around at the crowd.

We were both staring out at the arena, planning our first moves.

Today's twin 'playgrounds' were bigger, more elaborate versions of yesterdays, and bore an odd similarity to the SADISTO training center I had run Juliet through during cadet agent training. This was more a 'jungle' and less a 'swamp', but I could smell the pools of blood, hear alligators, and other wild animals, saw tripwires along paths, combined with the various monkey bars, cages, and *Rat Trap* craziness of yesterday.

I also took in the hay bales piled high along the sides of the course, to—I supposed—protect the audience from stray weapons fire. Fire to be provided by a table full of weapons just a hundred feet beyond the starting gate. It was piled high with everything from grenades to machineguns to knives to spears to melon ballers.

"Is lot off veapon," Gunter said as if imagining all of them shoved up his ass. By me. "You know how to use?"

"Yes," I said.

"How many vays you kill me now...?"

"Seven hundred and fifty-two."

I heard him gulp.

"All bets are placed!" Doctor Sin called out over the crowd. The numbers shifted slightly a few more times, then froze. "Ah! Wait! I see we have a new betting category!"

A picture of Sunny and I making love against the rock among the wildflowers popped onto the screen.

"Apparently we have a few of you who think that Hawke, and Sunny will fight together, and escape!" Sin said, as if the idea just delighted the pants off her. Or would have, if she wore pants. "Well, given what a selfish prick Agent Hawke is so well known to be, that's a bet I'm willing to take! Any other gamblers?"

Since when was I a selfish prick? That she knew of?

The numbers shifted minimally under our photo, and froze.

"A few, I see! Excellent! Always happy to take your money! And now," the masked woman said, "are you ready?" Cheers. "I said: *are you ready?*" Louder cheers, hoots, and applause. She flipped aside her robe to expose her ass, leaned against the platform's railing, and gestured to a new naked animal man, this one more wolf-oriented. He walked up quickly behind her, took hold of her hips, and shoved. "Aaaaah, FUCK YES! The starting gates open in ten, nine, eight..."

I glanced over at 'Sunny' and saw her staring at me with that beautiful, charming, sarcastic, Juliet grin. But for the first time, it worried me. She was Juliet, and that meant she was a trained, effective, and as I'd seen personally, talented SADISTO agent. And she had punched me. Knocked me out. Was she intending to win this game, or...

I had no idea.

I thought of that time in the General's office when she'd spilled the contents of his drawers. The blank look on her face after she saw that folder reminded me of the moment just before she'd punched me. I remembered the change in her when she went from demure to killing machine with just a head nod.

What did it all mean? In short: Gunter wasn't the one I had to worry about. It was Juliet. While Gunter was distracting me.

And he was already cheating. He had leapt over the gate and was racing toward the weapons table, heading straight for a machinegun. Guards ran forward and began shooting in his direction, but I guess they were also a bunch of kids who really should have been working in fast food, not playing with pistols. Kinda like most of the soldiers in Viet Nam. They wound up hitting everything but Gunter.

The table before him splintered, bushes erupted in blasts of leaves and twigs, dirt clouds flew up and obscured views. But Gunter reached the machine gun, and one or two other items, then disappeared quickly into the fake jungle with a quick grin and a spurt of his own machinegun fire back in my direction.

I was expecting it, and had already shielded myself behind one of the guards, who fell over, dead. Gunter was a better shot than I gave him credit for.

"... two, **ONE!**" Doctor Sin finished.

A buzzer sounded, the gates flipped up, and the remaining three of us raced to our tables, one dick, and four tits flopping insanely. The crowd loved it.

"*Run to Kobayashi Maru's office!*" Juliet yelled.

"*What?*" I yelled back.

"*Don't try to save me, do the Kobayashi Maru end run around!*"

I stared at her, lost, and Juliet laughed as she descended on the table, shocking me by tossing Gudrun a pistol. The two immediately chambered rounds, turned and fired in my direction. I ducked, as bullets ripped through the air where I had been standing, killing two of the guards nearest me—one shot each—center head—as I barely managed to make it under the table for cover.

"Oh, my God," Juliet shrieked with delight. "*I just realized they've got fucking TARGETS on their faces!*"

So... she *meant* to hit him? She turned and aimed at another one, dropping him instantly.

She *was* shooting at them!

"This is easier than the practice range!" she cheered, and giggled. "And so fun!" She shot two more guards in their 'targets,' and laughed even harder.

Without slowing down, I scooped up an armload of weapons, ignoring the path Gunter had taken. Instead, I skittered along the edge of the jungle, toward the track separating it the from the arena seating.

"Kobayashi Maru's office!" I called to Juliet, with a grin of my own.

"You'll always be a fucking cheater!" she said, a giggle rising in her voice.

"You said I'd never faced a no-win situation!" I laughed. Then I stopped and faced her. "But that was before I had to give you up."

Even from fifty yards away, I saw her face melt, and her heart sing. She touched her chest. Then she scowled, and flipped me off, her face flooded with anger, as she raised her gun.

"Fuck you!" She snapped, firing a shot at me.

I ducked, and the guard behind me with a gun to my back fell, Juliet's bullet dead center of his bullseye.

So... she was aiming at *him?*

"I now see the wisdom of lateral thinking!" She called over her shoulder as she raced toward the opposite side of the arena, Gudrun in tow.

Another guard stepped up to block me, and I drilled him dead center of his targeted face. He fell backward, and I hurdled over him, onto the hay bales leading up into the crowd, and opened fire upon the glittering masses.

Expensive clothes, flashy jewelry, personalized coffee mugs, elegant hats, hot dogs, pretzels, and bare skin ripped, shattered, tore, and reddened with blood. People screamed and ran for cover, begging for mercy. But the only real cover was other people screaming and running for cover, begging for mercy.

"Oh, shit," I heard Doctor Sin say into the loudspeaker. "They're not supposed to do that!"

"Lateral thinking!" Juliet and I shouted simultaneously.

As I ran, continuing to fire, I could see that Juliet/Sunny and Gudrun were creating the same kind of carnage and chaos as I on their side of the arena. It was like watching one of those tricks grade-school teachers use to wow the kids by sprinkling pepper onto the surface of water, then putting a drop of soap in its center, making all the pepper race immediately away from the drop to the edge of the bowl. The crowd was pepper, and Sunny/Juliet was the drop of soap.

The people Juliet was unloading machinegun fire on were leaping over seats, other shrieking fans, and hot dog vendors, alive, injured, and dead. One man threw money in the air in Juliet's general direction, I guess he hoped she might stop to shooting and grab the cash.

She didn't.

She ran over his corpse like a naked soldier with huge tits storming the beach at Normandy. She trod over several other downed spectators, with Gudrun trailing along behind. They reached the doors that would lead out of the arena to an escape, and Sunny—Juliet—my beautiful, turquoise-eyed angel of vengeance, stopped to smile at me. I smiled back.

"You're a dead man, Trevor Hawke!" she yelled.

My smile fell. She noted my response, laughed, and ducked out the double-doors along with her new sidekick.

I felt a surge of fear and shock, wondering why she'd turned on me. What had I done? Or was everything we seemed to have had just a lie? A pretense?

Or was all this just a pretense? Was Juliet-slash-Sunny a multiple personality?

I forced myself to focus. I really didn't have time to be distracted by questions I couldn't answer, especially once a grenade rolled between my legs. At first, I thought I was the one who'd dropped it. But the pin had been pulled, and I knew I'd never be that careless.

I dove over the railing, stumbling end over end across the hay bales just as the thing exploded where I had been standing. Metal bars, concrete, and hay whistled in all directions, and I was thrown into the fake jungle where I landed hard on loose dirt.

After recovering my senses, I sat up to see if I'd lost anything important. Once I'd made sure it was still there, I checked the rest of my body.

Scrapes and contusions, but nothing broken, nothing blown off.

Other than all my weapons.

I stood and searched quickly around, not seeing so much as a knife anywhere near me, wondering where the hell everything had gone, and hoping Gunter was somewhere far from me. But he had to be the one who'd thrown that damned grenade. And I'd bet money he'd stood around to watch how it went boom.

I crouched low, and listened. If he'd seen me fly down here, he'd want to make sure I was dead, and sneak up on me to finish things. If he hadn't, he might assume I was blown up, and start moving freely. Either way, he'd be shuffling around nearby.

Sure enough, there were some bushes rustling off to my left, I turned, and saw tanned skin-colored movement. I crept in that direction as silently as I could, but he was moving fast. It forced me to pick up my speed, and make a little more noise than I would have preferred, when…

Dammit.

I stopped. Listened.

...
Nothing. I'd lost him.

Then I stepped on something buried in the dirt, and heard a loud ratcheting sound. I looked up just as a brightly colored rat trap cage fell on top of me.

CHAPTER 25

THE WALLS OF THE CAGE slammed to the dirt on all sides of me.

Rat.

Trapped.

I ran to the bars, and shook, but it only *looked* fun, and easy to lift. It deftly defied my meager rat-muscles.

A machinegun clacked, and I turned to see it aiming at my gut. Gunter smiled like The Joker about to deliver the best punch line ever to Batman. Or—in my sad case—Robin. And not one of the good Robins.

"You are not so much killer man," he said. "Pff! I sink you know zero vays to morder Gunter."

"I know quite a few," I said. "I just... can't use any of them at the moment."

"Oh," Gunter said, feigning disappointed, "you cannot because of my veapon? I should put it down, maybe?"

"Lift this cage, and fight me man-to-man," I said. "Yes."

"Of course!" he said, bending to put the gun down on the dirt between us. "I must prove my manhood to you because..." He abruptly pulled it back up, and aimed it again at my navel. "No, you idiot, I am no idiot. You are idiot! I did not be vinner of Octopus Game by being man vis no brains. I will just shoot you dead, zhen kill Gudrun, zhen Pupper gorl, after I fock on her much times. Squeeze her giant pupper. And suck on zhem! Much times!"

He made weird, calf-suckling sounds with his pursed lips. His eyes were wide and crazy.

"Are you… trying to piss me off?" I asked. "By telling me you're going to murder your girlfriend, and then rape mine?"

"See? You are idiot. *Yes! Is what I am saying!* Kill Gudrun. Fock gorl vis giant Pupper much! Laugh about you, who will be *dead!*"

"Pupper. Is that how you say 'tits' in your language?"

"Yes! Pupper!" he snapped. "Stop the ruin of my joy! Pupper! Tits! Tittsies! Titty, titty, bang bang! I suck on your gorlfriend tittsies! Over your dead body! *Laughing!* You are not reacting in vay zat make me enjoy taunting!"

"Um… sorry?"

He raised the gun to shoot, but his finger relaxed on the trigger as his head caved in.

His body fell forward into the dirt before me, revealing Sunny—Juliet—standing behind him, holding her machine gun like a club.

"I was out of bullets," she said.

"And yet, still quite effective with the weapon," I said. "Someone trained you well."

She dropped her club, and picked up Gunter's guns.

"Damn," she said, looking down at the fresh corpse. "I was hoping to make him anger fuck me while I killed Doctor Sin. Just goes to show how a day never ends like you think it will when it starts off. He was hot, too."

"He wasn't that hot," I said as if someone had kicked my puppy.

"Ooooh," Juliet said, coming toward me with sympathetic eyes to caress my cheek through the bars. "Is someone jeawous? Is my widdle Trevow jeawous?"

"Eeew, don't talk baby talk," I said. "It's creepy when grown, naked women talk baby talk."

She stepped back and twisted her torso side-to-side, shaking her 'pupper' and making them sway hypnotically.

" Because I'm not a baby, am I? Look how grown up I am," she said, giving her breasts a quick bounce. "I bet if these talked baby talk you'd still want them. In fact, I think you'd *love* my giant baby tawking tittsies."

"Titty, titty, bang bang," I admitted.

"Mmm..." she cooed, stepping forward to fondle my for a change flaccid self through the bars. "I like the bang bang part."

I grabbed her and pulled her to me.

"God, how I missed you," I said, leaning down, pressing my lips to hers.

Her arms went around my neck, her tongue flowed over mine, and I felt my erection solidify. So did she.

"Is that for me," she asked, flowing away from my lips, "or for Sunny?"

I pulled back a step and studied her.

"But..." I said, confused, "you *are* Sunny."

"No," Juliet said. "I'm actually not."

"What?" I asked. "But ... you have to be. Even though you were here at the same time you were with me at SADISTO, I..." I rubbed my temples, more lost than I realized. "I don't understand... ooooh, time travel? Is that it? They repaired the Time Funnel, and..."

"That's not the point!" Juliet snapped. "You like Sunny more than you like me! You told her you loved her, you weren't even drunk, and I think you meant it!"

It slowly began to dawn on me that I was in trouble. But in typical male fashion, I really and truly didn't understand why.

"Is that why you punched me?"

Sunny—I mean Juliet—vibrated with fury, then turned and stomped off, into the fake jungle. After losing myself in the magnificence of her softly jiggling ass, I realized I should stop ogling, and sort this out.

"Sunny," I said, "I mean Juliet..."

"See?" She snapped, stopping and turning on me. *"SEE? You can't even call me by my real name!"*

"But it *is* your real name..." I said, as she spun once more on her heel, moving quickly further and further into the jungle. "At least it's the one I'm most used to *today*..."

"Stop talking Trevor!"

"But Sunny... I MEAN JULIET!"

She froze, and held up a hand to freeze me. I thought she was just angry and shutting me up, but then I heard the low rumbling sound coming from somewhere close by. Several somewheres close by. She began to back toward me, very carefully.

I looked where Sunny—JULIET!—was staring, and saw it.

A tiger, low in the bushes, its unblinking eyes laser pointed right at her. She took a few more steps backward as it glided out of the jungle shadows, and into the light. The other growls continued rising from all sides, including behind us. Juliet reached the cage, and I put a hand on her bare backside to stop her from tripping. At least I think that's why I did it.

She swatted my hand away, but still stopped and listened. A quick glance around to the source of the sounds revealed more animal eyes focused on us from four or five different directions.

Slowly, silently they all began to move into the clearing— and stand up.

With mounting fear, we watched as they rose on their hind legs to our eye-level, and in some cases, beyond. Two of them were well over six feet, even with backward bending legs. By the time they moved clear of the surrounding foliage, we could see they were animal-human hybrids like the ones that had been fucking Doctor Sin; athletic and muscular with bestial features, fur, and tails.

"Hi," the lead Tiger Man said, rubbing his hands together, nervously. "Are you guys with Doctor Sin, or… what?"

"Uh… no, not really," I said. "We were brought here against our will."

"Well, *you* were," Juliet said.

"What?"

"Later," she said. "And you? Are you with Doctor Sin?"

"Depends on what you mean by 'with'," Tiger Man said. "She abuses us and takes advantage of us."

"She makes me have sex with her!" One of them yelled. I looked his way, and saw he was the friendly fucker from last night, also sort of tiger-like, but cuter. More like a stuffed animal gone slightly wrong, than an actual animal. He wore a loud Hawaiian shirt. **Very** loud. The kind that looked like it needed to be recharged every night.

"Oh, right, yeah, hi," I said, reaching through the cage bars to shake his… er… paw. "I'm Trevor. We sort of met yesterday."

"Yeah, I remember," he said, taking my hand. "Talky Tony. How are you?"

"Been better," I said. I nodded, grinning, toward my predicament.

He looked the cage up and down with disdain.

"Yeah, that wasn't very smart of you," he said, scrunching up his nose like he smelled shit. My shit.

"No… it was not," I said, surprised by the criticism. "Thanks for pointing that out."

"That trigger mechanism wasn't even fully buried," Tony said, clearly aghast at my poor observational skills.

"Wasn't it?" I asked, not really wanting an answer.

"No! And then you mostly just stood there while the cage came down! You could have dived out of the way, or even just stepped aside nonchalantly! I mean, I would have, and I'm not even… aren't you supposed to be a professional, highly trained assassin?"

I stared at him, so glad to have gotten rid of Gunter, and instead was now be allowed to play Calvin to this chatty Mister Hobbes.

"Why don't you introduce us to your friends?" I said, hoping to distract him, and wishing his shirt would burst into flames.

Tony put hands on hips, and snarled, "Don't think you can distract me from getting an answer to my question." He pointed to his head. "I am an intelligent creature."

I had my doubts.

Because distracted he was, as he pointed to the more threatening looking Tiger fellow.

"This is Kzinti," he said, then motioned around to a wolf-looking fellow, "Lon," then an elephant sort of woman, "Gaja," and a kind of porcupine man, kid, thing, called "Pete."

"Hi, hi, hi, hello," Juliet and I said, waving to each.

"So, you're not with Doctor Sin?" Juliet asked Talky Tony. "You don't enjoy having sex with her?"

"Would you enjoy having sex with a creature of a different species?" he asked as if he'd just eaten peanut butter by mistake and gotten it stuck on the roof of his mouth.

Juliet's eyes elevatored up and down Kzinti's impressive, nude body.

"That may not be the best question to ask her," I said.

"It really isn't," Juliet said, ogling Kzinti as I often ogled her. "But if it doesn't work for *you*…"

"*It doesn't!*" Tony snapped. "Sex isn't actually pleasurable *at all* for cats!"

"I kind of enjoy it," Kzinti said, now looking at Juliet in the same lip-smackingly lusty way she'd looked at him.

"Liar!" Tony said. "And anyway, we just wanted someone to help us, you know? Guide us so we could live in peace. Build homes, communities, have families, develop friendships, enjoy neighborhood pool parties, and barbecues, share gardening tools, and play Wednesday night canasta..."

"Oh, I love canasta," Juliet said.

"So do I," I lied. "Maybe when we..."

She held up a warning finger, and I stopped talking.

"Sin put us to work, instead," Tony groused. "Made us into her personal sex slaves."

"Mmm, Personal Sex Slaves," Juliet said, her mouth forming the words as if she were making candy with her tongue, she and Kzinti studying each other lustily, mentally licking on the same candy.

"But you're a skilled fighter," Tony said to me. "Or are *alleged* to be. Told you we'd get back to that question." He grinned, darkly, and pointed again to his brain. Or where one was supposed to be.

"We heard it on the loudspeaker," Kzinti agreed, not looking at me, and was he standing a little more... erect? "You're a killer. Though *she* seems to be the competent one."

"Oh, I'm more than competent," Juliet said, licking the lips of that sarcastic grin, squinting her sex-hungry eyes, though not at me.

"And we were thinking that... maybe..." the elephant person whose name I'd already forgotten ventured, cautiously, "we could work... together? Help each other out?"

I smiled.

"How strong are you?" I asked.

8   8   8

After helping me out of the rat trap cage, we returned to the weapons table, Juliet, myself, our five new animal-beast-hybrid friends, and loaded up, carrying as many weapons as we could carry into the relative safety of the fake jungle.

"I've never used a gun before," Tony said.

"None of us have," Kzinti admitted.

"How do you protect yourselves?" I asked.

In answer he just held up a paw, which looked furry and soft, until four-inches of multiple claws popped out.

Juliet gasped with delight, and shuddered a little.

"Yeah, those would work," I said. "Up close, anyway."

"Yes," Juliet agreed, her voice a husky whisper. "Up close."

"Can you show us how to use these human weapons?" Tony asked.

"It's easy," I said. "Just point and pull the trigger. Most of the people we'll be chasing will be unarmed and running scared—faster if they're being shot at. Accuracy won't matter."

"Trevor and I will handle the people who can defend themselves," Juliet said, chambering a round, "guards, or anyone who might have a personal weapon, especially that Doctor Sin bitch."

Tony tried to fit his finger into the trigger guard. It wouldn't go. I tried to help him, but after a few minutes of pointless squishing, bending, painful, and awkward maneuvering, I took the gun away and handed him a knife.

"Where's Gudrun?" I asked Sunny. I mean JULIET! "You two seemed to be pretty chummy."

"We bonded," Juliet said, cryptically, and said no more.

"Let's get out of this crazy maze, and back up into the stands," I said.

We made our way around in much the same way I had earlier, only to find the path blocked by Target Faces. They formed a ring around the back half of the arena, apparently intending to limit our escape routes, and give them high ground advantage.

"Shit," I said.

"No Kobayashi Maru's office for you," Juliet said. "I guess you have to face the no-win situation."

"I keep telling you," I said with more edge in my voice than I intended, "It IS winnable! I *won!*"

"Cheating isn't winning!"

"So, you're saying this is a no-win scenario?" I asked, furious.

Juliet stared a moment, and a sadness welled up in her eyes that surprised me. What was she thinking?

"It's winnable," Kzinti said.

We all looked at him, and hoped he wasn't being optimistic.

"This way," the Tiger Man said, turning on his furry heel and disappearing quickly and silently into the shadows.

Together with our newly armed companions we followed him into *The Rat Trap Game* filled fake jungle.

But before we could safely reach, and hide among the foliage, I heard a distinctive sound.

A machinegun safety being released.

CHAPTER 26

"EVERYONE GET DOWN," I said.

"Why?" Talky Tony said, looking at me with more certainty that I was an idiot.

Bullets whipped past him, and saved me having to explain. He, and everyone, ducked down.

"How did you know?" Tony whispered.

"I have the hearing of a tiger," I whispered back.

I noticed Juliet smiling at me, and winked at her. The happy expression exploded off her face like she'd been punched. She scowled as if I'd done the punching, then turned away.

"Move on all fours," she whispered to the others.

Tony got up on his knees, jamming angry fists into his hips.

"Just because I *look* like an animal doesn't mean…"

Another series of bullets whipped past his ears, ripping up jungle foliage on all sides of him.

"All fours," he said, quietly, dropping to his hands and knees. "I see the value of all fours."

Juliet chuckled.

"I bet Hans doesn't have a Talky Tony head in his collection," she said, giggling, and I was pleased that even though she was furious with me, she still wanted to share private jokes.

"What does that mean," Tony said. "Is that some kind of anti-animal joke? Animal bigotry?"

"Oh, my God, will you shut the fuck up?" Juliet and I snapped at him in unison. We laughed together, and Kzinti and the elephant girl joined in.

"Is profanity *really* necessary?" Talky Tony muttered to himself. "I—think—*not*."

"Sunny," I stage whispered to her crawling, bare behind. She spun angrily on me, flipping me off. "I MEAN JULIET!"

Before she could turn away, I jerked a thumb to our right, and smart girl that she is, she pushed down her resentment, hunkered low, and squinted through the bushes.

I saw her see what I had seen. Two men in target masks, moving our way through the bushes, carrying machineguns. Searching.

Juliet turned to me, gestured with pointed forefingers and curving hand motions that we should circle in opposite directions to surround them. Naked and unprotected as we both were, we had to be careful, and sneaky, so I got her meaning. We began to crawl carefully away from one another in opposite directions.

"Where are you going?" Tony asked, too loudly.

Juliet and I spun on him, furiously slamming index fingers to our silently puckered lips.

"It was just a question," he said, perturbed.

We both looked at him in frustration, spun back, and moved away faster, just as the two Target Faces burst through the foliage, aiming their weapons directly at Tony's Talky mouth.

"Oh," he said softly, raising his hands in surrender. "I see."

The men jerked their weapons back and forth from Tony, to Kzinti, to Elephant girl, to Wolf Man Lon, and back again, their body language clearly distressed.

"We're not supposed to shoot them, right?" One of them asked the other. "The animal people?"

"No, you're supposed to shoot us," Juliet said, standing from behind a clump of cover and opening up with her own machinegun. I got more than a little aroused by how it made every naked part of her jiggle fleshily like sexy Jello riding over a bumpy road.

One of the Target Faces stood still, his body jerking and twitching with each, well-aimed shot—as the other ducked, avoiding most of the incoming while returning fire blindly. The ducker grabbed his stomach where Juliet had caught him a good one, and using his buddy as a shield ran quickly away from the chaos—which brought him instantly to me—facemask to barrel with my leveled gun aimed directly at the center of his concentric circles.

"Really poor mask design," I said, firing.

His body flopped backward, and when it hit the dirt, there was a loud click.

"Uh, oh," I said.

Overhead there was another loud click, and a crashing sound as a large round ball fell into a bathtub, rumbled to a hole at the other end, and fell through onto a wooden plank. Suddenly Tony, and Pete, the porcupine boy, flew into the air, and sailed off to God knew where. I swore I heard Tony 'Wilhelm scream.'

There was a distant splashing, a thumping, more screaming—this last sound quite blood curdling and painful to even hear.

Leaving the Target Face bodies where they lay, we took their weapons, and raced in the direction of those screams with Kzinti in the lead. We started to pass through a small clearing, and were immediately fired upon by the Target Faces up in the stands. Ducking under cover, we circled back so they wouldn't know exactly where we were, and avoided any open areas as we returned along a new path toward the screaming— whoever it was.

A guard burst through the bushes, with Pete and his quills embedded in his target face. He was the one screaming— understandably—as Pete kept yelling, *"I'm sorry, I'm so sorry!"*

Juliet pumped a slug into the screaming man's ear, and silenced him. Then we all worked together to pull Pete out of the guy's skull. It took some doing. Pete lost some quills— and a little dignity—in the process.

Settling Pete, and assuring him it wasn't his fault, and anyway the guy he quilled was evil, we set off in the direction he had come from in search of Tony. It didn't take long to find him.

He was standing up to his neck in a pool of blood, surrounded by floating body parts, and crying.

"Come on, Tony," I whisper-shouted. "We have to get out of here!"

"I caaaaaan't," he whined. "I'm stuuuuuuck. And I have a heightened sense of smeeeeeeell."

I sighed with frustration, and turned to Juliet.

"Let's leave him," I said.

"Because that's what you do," she said. "You leave."

"I... what?"

"So, if that was one of our children sinking in the bloody muck, screaming and whining, and inconvenient to you, would you leave?"

"What?" I said. "No! Of course not, I..."

"We go through all that training," Juliet continued, her voice sounding like it was coming from the bottom of a grave—probably my grave, "ignoring Ilsa's screams as she dies, crawling through pools of blood and body parts to anesthetize us to any sense of humanity those parts might have once had, not because we have to, but because you like it that way."

"What are you talking about?" I asked. "I don't enjoy that! Or this!"

"It is called *SADISTO*," she said in a mocking voice. Mocking whom I'm not sure, but I got the feeling it was me. "They didn't come up with the acronym *WARM AND FUZZY*, now did they?"

"Juliet, no, I'm simply pointing out the most expedient way of finishing our mission..."

"What mission?" she demanded. "We have no mission. At least *you* don't."

"What does *that* mean?"

"Rescue..." she said, her eyes like turquoise torches. "... *Tony.*"

"But... no. We have to..."

"These are tests, Trevor, and you're failing."

My mouth hung open so far flies circled in and out of it. I looked around for hidden cameras. I don't know why, but I did.

Juliet growled, turned from me, placed her guns down on the fake earth, and waded into the pond of muck and blood exactly as a mother would enter the 'baby pool' to 'rescue' a toddler with a hurt toe, heading straight for the pathetic little stuffed-toy tiger man, murmuring soft, pleasant, reassuring sounds.

"Guards are going to come," I shout/whispered to her. "You're going to get killed!"

"So, watch my back!" Juliet hissed.

'I already am' I thought, my mind awash in the *ha-ha-ha* of petulant fifteen-year-old hormonal energy. 'I love watching your back. Especially when it's **naked. So there.**'

As expected, Tony grabbed onto Juliet as one grabs a lifeboat in turbulent seas, mewling like a frightened kitten, wrapping his arms around her face, her shoulders, her neck. She struggled in his grasp, jerked and hefted, getting him unstuck from whatever held him under the surface, then carried him back toward the shore.

She was nearly out of the pond, reaching for her weapon when a couple Target Faces broke into the clearing, all guns trained directly on her and Tony.

I moved to leap between her and the Target Faces, when she held up a warning finger, clearly telling me 'No.'

Why?

As they pulled their triggers, Tony cat-screeched, back arching, hair standing up—or trying to under the mat of blood and guck. His rapid weight shift made Juliet stumble ahead of the bullets tearing through the air they had occupied instants earlier. Seeing no other options, she dove beneath the surface, and the last I saw of them was Tony's terrified eyes, and screaming maw as it submerged in the pool of red.

The gunmen dragged their machineguns across the surface of the blood and entrails, the surface exploding with bullets and shells. That much firepower didn't need to be carefully aimed.

I raced over to the pond, firing my own weapon, the guards turning to unload on me, and the air between was filled with so much lead Superman wouldn't have been able to see through it.

After what seemed like hours of machine guns clacking, bullets whizzing, ricocheting, ripping up grasses, leaves, branches, and tree trunks, all chambers clicked on empty.

I checked myself. Rechecked. Not a scratch. The guards checked themselves. Rechecked. Looked at one another in surprise. Nary a fabric tear among the lot.

We all tossed aside our machine guns, and they pulled pistols. I pulled nothing, being naked and otherwise unarmed. I raised my hands, knowing it was pointless.

I was toast.

That's when the Hybrids attacked.

Led by Kzinti, the group—which had added a few members in the few minutes since I'd last seen them—dove on the Target Faces, ripping with claws, teeth, bigger teeth and more claws. One newcomer was an alligator man, another a wolf woman, and the third appeared to be a very tall, white, red-headed rooster. He did very little fighting, apparently seeing himself as more of a cheerleader.

"You—I say—*you're doin' FINE, there, son!* But *bite them in their **delicates***! *The **softer** places! Don't waste energy on the* **BONY** *parts!*"

I ran to the pond, searching for signs of my beloved Juliet. I MEAN SUNNY!

Oh, no, wait. I did mean Juliet.

The surface was placid, and appeared almost solid.

"Juliet?" I said to the viscous muck.

Nothing.

My heart stopped beating.

My mind raced with all the things I should have said but didn't, with leaving when I should have stayed, with…

Juliet burst up out of the pond, gasping for air, Tony bubbling up beside her under his own power. Even covered in a thick layer of blood and muck Juliet was more beautiful than anything I'd ever seen.

"*Once again I had to go into the bloody pool that you've never gone into yourself!*" she snapped at me. "*You ran around the outside corridor and you cheated! You say you did what it took to become an agent, but you really didn't! Just like you said you wanted a wife who understood you, who could handle it when you got blood on her, but then left me on a doorstep as soon as I became that woman!*"

And now we had finally gotten to it. The reason for the anger, the slaps, the knockout punch.

"You had a woman who understood you," she said, dragging herself from the muck and walking right up into my face. "I fought by your side, did everything you asked of her no matter how stupid, or dangerous, or insane, and you could have left the agency for me *at any time,*" her voice began to catch with emotion—sadness, fury, loss, "but instead you left *me*."

I didn't know how to respond. Didn't know if I wanted to respond. I felt angry. Hurt. How could I be expected to respond when I didn't know what the hell was even happening? She was Sunny. She was Juliet. She was decommissioned. She's here on a mission.

Not only didn't I understand, she herself didn't understand. Couldn't understand. She couldn't know what I knew. That I'd put myself in jeopardy with The General, and SADISTO—for her! To get her safely out of there before it was discovered that she...

"Why does this place have such a similar layout to the SADISTO Obstacle Course?" I asked no one. Perhaps myself. Perhaps Juliet. Maybe Sunny. Definitely not Tony.

Juliet scowled.

"What?" she asked, as if I'd wanted to know why the sun was yellow and the sky was blue. But slowly her expression changed, softened, filled with surprise, and a bit of fear.

"Good question," she said.

"I think I know who Dr. Sin is," I said.

"Who?" Juliet demanded, her anger bubbling up once more like an overheated pot that's been put back on the burner.

"You wouldn't know her," I said.

"But you would, Trevor," the now very familiar voice said from behind me.

We turned to see a platform crane lowering Doctor Sin from somewhere above down to our level. Once the platform touched the arena's ground, she opened the safety gate and stepped sensuously, nakedly toward us, open robe flowing, sandaled feet striding confidently into the arena, flanked by a group of guards who moved with far more efficiency and precision than the high school kids we'd been killing.

She was still as nude as before, other than a gun belt slung around her hips.

She moved seductively to within five feet of me, and stopped, reaching up to unfasten something on the side of her mask.

After a couple tense moments of struggling with the catch, she pulled the mask free, and smiled at me.

"Hello, Trevor," she said, warmly. "Long time no fuck."

CHAPTER 27

"WHO'S THIS BITCH?" Juliet snarled.

"Margaret Trueblood," I said. "The woman I was sent to kill."

"Well," Trueblood said, "You missed your chance with that. I already killed Margaret. I'm Doctor Sin, now."

"And Glenn?" I asked. "Strangeways?"

"Oh, he and his wife were the first losers in the first Octopus Game two years ago. They've been dead quite a while, but I had people impersonating them go have sex in that office now and again, just to keep up appearances. See… he wanted to dump me and go back to her, and… well…"

"You went crazy," I said.

"Uh, no," she said, scowling as if I were a child who had just told her two plus two was eleventy-seven. "I got smart."

She stepped back as several hybrid-animal people trotted in carrying an elegant table, shiny food trays, silverware, embroidered tablecloths, and velvety seats. They arranged everything just so, then held back the chairs for us to sit in. Stacks of warm, moist towels arrived and attendants used them to wipe Juliet and I clean of muck and dirt.

"Please," Sin said after we'd been made 'presentable,' "Sit. The villain explaining their convoluted plan is always so much better over a delicious meal."

Toweled, blood-and-dirt-free and dried, feeling a little more human, Juliet and I sat. Without waiting Juliet began piling food onto her plate, and into her mouth.

"Wait for us to say 'grace', dear," Formerly Margaret/Doctor Sin said.

Mouth already full of bread, Juliet stopped chewing, stunned, and began to spit it back out into her palm.

"I'm kidding," Sin said with a smile. "I kid. Just my quirky sense of humor. No need to wait. Dig in."

Juliet began to chew again, slowly, side-eyeing me with an uncertain expression. I just shrugged in reply.

"So, you really are Juliet?" Sin asked.

"Yes," Juliet said, her voice muted by partially masticated dough.

"And also, Sunny?" Sin asked.

Juliet glanced at me, nervously, then quickly away again.

"Yes," she admitted.

"Fascinating," Sin said. "The Time Funnel?"

Juliet chewed on that a while, then slowly nodded.

"Among other things," Juliet/Sunny said. "And you were an agent of SADISTO?"

"Oh, no, not an agent," Doctor Sin said. "I was a glorified receptionist—slash—kept woman for the real agents. I flunked out of the training, but they kept me around for the things I excelled at. Like sucking dick. Isn't that right, Trevor? You used to like how I sucked *your* dick."

I said nothing, and avoided Juliet's glance across at me.

"It's funny, isn't it?" Sin asked Juliet with a smile, about to say something I doubted would be in any way funny. "We change ourselves for the men we love, do any crazy thing they ask thinking 'oh, my life will be a fun-filled adventure with this guy' and then one day, suddenly, you're just the girl they talk about around the water cooler like you were nothing more than an inflatable plastic doll they stuck their dicks into every now and then. And you've been discarded just as easily."

This time Juliet's gaze wouldn't be denied, as she stared at me with her unblinking, turquoise interrogators. I cringed, inwardly, as they gradually shifted; from hot fury, to bloodshot horror and finally to profound sadness as Sin continued speaking.

"You crawl through bloody pools of severed body parts, murder naked people in human shooting galleries, do things you'd never imagined doing in bed. You shut down your horror, your fear, and on some level, you learn to enjoy it all because you think to yourself 'he's the one. We're sharing something special, something unique, and we'll always be together to remember and laugh about these crazy times.'"

Sin turned her attention directly to me, her smile faltering.

"And then one day he's just gone," she said. "Done. And you've become the mistress to his best friend. Not even a wife. Nor a mother. Just the guy the second-place guy fucks while he's pretending to be at work. Until one day even that guy decides he wants something more. Life. Love. Children. But not with you. No, never with you."

She stared at me. Juliet stared at me. I said nothing. Ate nothing. I was too busy swallowing it all.

"So, I found some investors," Sin went on, "bought this island, and everything on it—all based on one thought, one idea. Did these men really love their prim, and sexless women, their conservative virgins? Or were they just making different, selfish choices for appearances sake that ultimately meant nothing if their own lives were on the line?"

"So, you put them to the test?" Juliet asked.

"I did," Sin said, eyes misted and melancholy. "And Strangeways killed his first choice, in the end. Then begged me to protect him and take him back as another contestant beheaded him."

The table fell under a dark silence. Sin smiled.

"God, that was so satisfying," she said, lost in the memory. "And not just for me. People flocked here, not only to watch poor people fight it out to the death. That was mostly a scam to get money from the rich thrill seekers looking for a way to feel naughty while being validated that they were better than everyone else. It was always more about the discarded people seeing those who wronged them getting theirs."

"So, this *was* about Trevor," Juliet said. "You brought him here for more of your own, personal revenge."

"Oh, no," Sin said, genuinely surprised. "Not me. Although I admit to getting some real satisfaction out of watching Agent 8 squirm. No, I let go of Trevor long go. And watching Glenn get beheaded kind of took all that anger out of me. It was quite freeing. On that day I really did stop being Margaret, and became Doctor Sin. I do what I want, when I want, and people pay me for the privilege. No... Trevor is here because of you. You're the one we really wanted."

My mind rolled out onto the floor. I think Juliet's was doing the same. We both sat there, speechless, brain-dead, immobile, gawking at Sin for what seemed like the length of all existence.

"Me?" Juliet finally managed to whisper. "Wh... "

"What?" I said, completing her thought.

"But you made such a big deal out of Trevor when we first arrived..." Juliet stammered.

"That's because I knew him," Sin said. "You, I'd never met before, and know shit about—other than what your uncle told us."

"Wait. My..." Juliet said, "*my* uncle?"

Sin shrugged.

"You pissed him off, apparently" Sin said, "The entitled heiress of an ice cream fortune. Not interested in the family values. Wasting a fortune on alcohol, drugs, fast men, faster cars."

"That's bullshit," Juliet said, her anger rising so fast I thought her head might burst like a cartoon thermometer.

Sin shrugged again.

"Whatever. Not like I really care," No-Longer-Margaret said. "After your parents were murdered, he inherited the company, and offered you up. At first, I honestly wasn't all that interested. He wanted a couple million for you, and I figured you wouldn't make it past the first round. Hardly a worthwhile expense. So, uncle dumped you in Singapodia. Faked a kidnapping, sold you off to Madame Phu for the continuing rights to some ice-cream company carton factory Phu had nationalized. Crazy, but true. Then I got a call from the good Madame with a rather delicious offer."

"My uncle sold me..." Juliet said, Sin's words pinging around in her brain so loudly and painfully that I could hear them from where I sat, "for a *carton factory?*"

"And that's not even the best part," Sin said, chuckling. "He told Phu she could do whatever she wanted with you; sell you into slavery for all he cared. Wild, hunh? Phu wasn't interested. But then—as I started to say—she had this genius idea…"

Juliet looked over at our animal-hybrid companions listening intently to every word of our conversation.

"There are plenty of chairs," Juliet said.

"We're good," said Tony, oddly brief, still covered in bloody scum, with a nervous glance in Sin's direction.

"Oh, come on," Juliet continued. "Grab a—"

"What genius idea?" I asked Sin.

Juliet looked suddenly nervous, shook her head at Sin, and Sin grinned, very, very darkly.

"Can I offer you something to drink?" Sin asked Juliet and I, obviously teasing Juliet with the possibility of still answering me. She ignored Tony, and the other hybrids.

"I'll take a Coke, please," Juliet said, calmly.

"Coca-Cola?" Sin asked. Juliet said nothing. "Certainly. El Capitan Sam, put the shaker beside the man and a bottle of Coca-Cola beside the girl."

As Sam—an unusual character with a mostly fur face and a cowboy hat that was bigger than he was put the shaker beside me alongside a bottle, and a bowl of lemon rinds—I felt oddly stalked and creeped out.

"You remember that I like a medium dry vodka martini preferably with Russian or Polish vodka—and a slice of lemon peel—shaken not stirred."

"Mmmm," Sin said, "No, I don't remember any of that shit. It's in your dossier. I made Sam read it. I mean really… shaken, not stirred? What difference does it make?"

"It tastes better."

"It tastes the same," she dismissed me as if I were discussing varying shades of white for a very boring bedroom wall in our grandparent's home, and looked at Sam, nodding happily in agreement with… someone. Maybe everyone. "It's about eight-ten. We'll have dinner at nine o'clock precisely."

"Why precisely?" I asked.

"Things to do," Sin said with a smile, "places to be."

I felt a moment of relief. Sin/Trueblue was enjoying her teasing performance, which meant at least another hour or so of life.

"Please," Sin said, gesturing to the bowl of cooked shrimp that had been placed between us. She gave her own bright smile an extra, winking dimple crease. "Eat up, you two. You probably haven't had any food since before last night, and you've both been *very* physically active. Don't worry. You have nothing to fear. For the next hour your desires will be satisfied."

"My desires are usually satisfied," I said.

"Don't I know it," Sin said, squirming her hips in her seat. "Mmm, baby."

Juliet scowled as Sin popped a shrimp heavily laden with cocktail sauce—Coctel de Camarones estilo Mexicano by the scent of chilies and cilantro—into her mouth. The good 'doctor' chuckled at me as she chewed, a dollop of bright red plum tomato puree plopping onto her chin.

"That's what it means to be a man in this world of ours," she said between chews. "You are allowed to satisfy your desires, enjoy your life to its fullest, while women wait at home. Which is why I decided to behave more like a man."

"And you think behaving more like a man will... what?" Juliet asked. "Make you happy?"

"It *does* make me happy," Sin said around another shrimp. "Deliriously so."

"You think a woman..." Juliet asked, "being a man... is a goal worth pursuing?"

"I'm not a closet transsexual, if that's where you're going with this," Sin grumbled.

"It's not," Juliet said, as if speaking to a child.

"You think you have a point to make," Sin said. "Make it."

"I have no interest in provoking you further."

"This is not provocation," Sin said. "It is depth. I prefer depth in conversation over the shallowness of small talk.

"Since when?" I asked.

Sin's eyes flicked my way.

"This from a man who thinks a '*deep* conversation' is, 'oh, baby, can your pussy take all of me?'"

Seeing she'd scored her point, Sin grinned ever so slightly, and her eyes returned to Juliet.

"Does knowing that your man's cock has pleasured me upset you?" Sin asked.

Juliet stared for a long, long moment.

"Yes," she finally admitted. "It does."

"It shouldn't," Doctor Sin told her. "It doesn't bother him. Nor would it upset him if you were being pleasured by some other man's cock."

"Yes, it would," Juliet said, confidently, surprising me.

"You respond emotionally," Sin dismissed, "and assume he does as well. Don't confuse the competitive male ego with connection or feeling."

"I'm not," Juliet said calmly. "I've seen his jealousy, and found it endearing."

"You misinterpreted some other selfish reaction."

"The world is a dark place for you," Juliet said, and Sin smiled. "Black and white. Simple. A man desires, and therefore *cannot* feel. A woman desires, and therefore *should* not feel. And yet we are complex, unique, individual beings. We can be many things—loving *and* desirous, feeling *and* unfeeling, and many combinations of a blended spectrum of emotions."

Sin seemed unconvinced, and continued chewing shrimp.

"You then leap to the conclusion that freedom and power for women will be found in acting like men," Juliet continued, "without understanding that men are as unhappy as we are, desperately pursuing short term physical pleasure in a vain attempt to alleviate deeper pain, and loneliness."

Sin wiped her mouth, and leaned back in her chair, studying Juliet, sucking for a long while on an errant piece of shrimp. She then spoke to me without taking her eyes off Juliet.

"Are you unhappy, Trevor? Hiding a deeper pain? Answer honestly."

I turned to Juliet, who continued her stare-down with Sin. I thought of our nights together, our days, our laughs, our joys, our many pleasures, the thrill of touching her, the joy of discussing children, and how I longed for that in my future.

"No," I lied, turning back to Sin so I wouldn't have to see Juliet's reaction. "I have no pain to hide."

"You think because he talks about Westchester, and children," Sin goaded Juliet, "that he actually *wants* those things?"

Juliet sat silent.

"He talks about them because it makes the women he's with more willing, more responsive. They don't complain about his shortcomings, they believe his promises, and choose to ride along with his corruptions, his darkness, his SADISTO life—perhaps even join in with it all—because of the sincere belief that he'll change. That he **wants** to change."

I couldn't look at Juliet's face, but I knew she was hiding her hurt. She made no witty reply.

"No," Sin continued. "No. Instead you wind up going down that dark path of black and white, good and evil that might even have seemed fun for a while," she paused for effect, "until suddenly... quite shockingly and suddenly... it wasn't fun any longer. But by then you've gone too far. It's too late to turn back. **You**... have changed."

I finally turned to look at Juliet. She sat rigid, still, silently staring at Sin, like a wax candle in a fireplace, willing itself not to melt.

Her eyes shifted abruptly to mine, but she remained quiet.

My mind staggered like a drunken sailor on a sinking ship. Did Trueblue/Sin have a point? Was I basically a complainer who—by giving voice to my dreams of a more fulfilling life— led women to believe that I wanted those changes with them? And had that history now cost me the one woman I sincerely did want those things with? At least the one woman since the other one woman I'd had to murder on our wedding night?

"All we want is to believe we're normal," Doctor Sin said as Juliet continued to stare at me. "That being horny is normal. That wanting to touch a man's naked body, to fuck, to be fucked, suck, or be sucked, is normal. And that afterward we are still worthy of love. Of being held. Caressed. Cared for. Adored. Cherished.

"So, we take the next step," Sin drove on, "and the next, and the next, incrementally moving forward with his desires, *his* needs, *his* wants, *his* perversions until the inevitable moment when he leaves and never looks back..."

Juliet's eyes seemed to pale.

"Because he no longer respects what we were willing to do," Sin trudged on, stomping over our hearts, "how far we were willing to go. He would rather have someone new. Someone pure. Someone unspoiled. Someone he is not ashamed to introduce to mom and dad."

As Juliet and I stared at one another, unblinking, I knew she was thinking of 'Sunny;' her 'virginity,' her being a 'good girl,' and how I had told 'her' I'd loved her—willingly, adoringly… soberly. Worse, I was thinking of it myself, and feeling ashamed. An emotion I wasn't used to.

And then slowly Juliet smiled—that disarming, beautiful, crooked, sarcastic smirk, that puckered into a quick air-kiss.

For me.

My heart grew wings, deployed rocket engines, soared into the highest clouds.

Then I crashed back down as a tear leaked from one of her eyes, and trickled down her cheek.

"I am so stupid," she said, almost too quietly to hear.

"What?" I said, momentarily lost.

"And that's the *real* reason you wanted Trevor to come here," Juliet said to Sin. "It was never about me, or Strangeways, or anything else you were jealous of—or angry at. You didn't want SADISTO's top agent as a… as a 'get' for your bizarre television show because you were over him, or never really had feelings for him in the first place as you've tried to imply. It was because you absolutely wanted him to pay. By dying, physically—or emotionally—because he was forced to kill me… certain that he would respond exactly as Strangeways had done."

"Juliet is not what you think she is, Trevor," Sin said.

"And before that end point," Juliet pressed on, "you meant to hurt us both as much as possible. Devastate me, take my life, my family, my whole world from me…"

"Madame Phu, and I *trained* your darling Juliet…" Sin interrupted again, her demeanor turning almost fearful.

"… make me question and doubt Trevor's feelings;" Juliet continued, her voice rising, "even learn to hate him by orchestrating everything with 'Sunny.' Making me think that he loved the sweet, sexy virginal shell-collector… but not me. *Never me.*"

"We trained her to be the perfect bedmate for Trevor Hawke," Sin snapped.

"Because you *had* done all those things, Margaret," Juliet said, nearly shouting to drown out Sin, "and they *had* to be why he wasn't interested in you."

"Then Phu got her a free ride into *The Place* …"

"There couldn't be any other reason," Juliet yelled. "You couldn't feel so deeply for him, and just not be right for each other! *And there definitely couldn't be anything wrong with* **you!**"

"*... The Place, where Juliet had perfect sex with the one man who could get her into the cadet-agent program...*"

"*So, you brought me here,*" Juliet interrupted, standing and leaning toward Sin over the table. "*Because you knew, Doctor 'Sin'—somehow you had discovered through your SADISTO connections—that I did all those things for Trevor, as you had, but it had gone differently because he was actually—really and truly—in love with **me**;*"

Sin stopped talking, and just stared. Stared at Juliet, looking for the life of me like a lost, little girl.

"Horny, foul-mouthed, passionate, far from virginal Juliet," Juliet said, more quietly, but far more intense, "and that meant he *would* never—*could* never—*had* never—***ever***—loved you. And for that sin—and that sin alone—I had to die."

Sin/Trueblue stared at Juliet with glassy, unblinking eyes for a very long, very silent moment as the world seemed to sit frighteningly still on the point of a pin.

"Yes," Sin whispered, in the heart of that horrible stillness. Then she pulled her gun from its holster and shot my Juliet between the eyes.

CHAPTER 28

"WAIT, WAIT, WAIT," Jelena said. "Juliet *DIES?*" She studied my unblinking stare, and then seemed to genuinely want to cry. *"NO!"*

"But…" Pyotr said, horrified. "I thought *Gran* was Juliet."

"Did anyone ever say that?" my wife asked.

"Well, no, but…"

The room sat in silence for a long, stunned moment.

"Should I finish my story?" I asked.

Every head nodded.

"Okay, then," I said, and continued on.

CHAPTER 29

I CRADLED MY DEAD love in my arms, and wept. I didn't care about the blood. I didn't care about anything. There was no resuscitating her. No fixing the tunnel through her skull. No way to bring back the mischievous turquoise light in those loving, still-open eyes. The only thing I could do was cry.

After God only knows how long I lay her gently in the dirt and grass of the arena and stood, barely aware of the twisted expressions of shock and horror carved into the faces of the hybrids around me; Tony, Kzinti, Wolf Man Lon, Porcupine boy, Elephant Girl, and the Giant Rooster.

My singular focus was on Doctor Sin.

She still held out the gun she'd used to kill my beloved Juliet.

"You lied," Tony said to me. "You said you didn't love her."

"Because I knew Sin would kill her if I didn't say that," I said, my voice tight and controlled.

"Well, that worked out well, now, didn't it?" Tony said, his snark further assaulting my broken heart. My glare must have been pretty intense, because he actually flinched and moved behind Kzinti for protection.

Uncaring for my own welfare, I stalked toward Sin until an alarm raked its nails across a blackboard somewhere high above us.

It was nine o'clock.

With a jerk, and a sound like the mouth of hell releasing all the desperate cries of the damned—the ground beneath my feet began to move.

Without so much as shifting her weight, Sin was drifting away from me. Or was I drifting away from her? Were we both drifting away from one another? For a moment I thought I'd eaten a hallucinogen, or drunk a drugged martini, but no. I had ingested nothing.

I looked down and saw the earth and sod separating between us. Rather quickly the dining table was off-balance, falling through the forming gap. Food, silverware, plates, serving trays, glasses, chairs… all spilled into a widening maw of darkness.

Steadying myself against the motion, I searched the expanding gloom below to see what was being revealed. Metal girders, reinforced struts, cables, and supports. Lights, more metal, the carved-out rock of the island beneath us. Gangways, guards, weapons, and far below on a cavern floor, a flat-topped vehicle and track of some kind.

Finally, very finally, there was a missile. A big one. Its nose close to me, nearly poking through the growing space between Sin and I, its base nestled securely a hundred feet below on a launching pad at the end of the track. Flames erupted urgently beneath it, the heat scorching the front of my still naked body.

"*Where's it going?*" I demanded of Sin on the other side of the hatch.

"*SADISTO headquarters!*" She yelled, with manic delight. "*No point pretending any longer! The explosion will reach all the way to The Fucking White House, and you can't do a damn thing about it!*"

"*This set up was all to finance a **revenge** scheme?*" I asked, more than a little stunned.

"*And a damned good one!*" Sin said, replacing her mask over the insanity her amusement. "*You, Juliet, The General, and all of SADISTO all in one go!*"

I sneered at her on the other side of the still widening gap, and she laughed at my impotence, turning her bare ass toward me so she could walk away, disappearing with some of her guards into the fake jungle.

A Target Face on my side of the growing chasm struggled to stay upright beside me on the still moving hatchway. I kicked him in the balls, and stole his machinegun, shoving him backward into the widening hole. He fell away, screaming, bounced off the rocket, and impacted somewhere in the darkness below, creating a minor flash of some kind.

The rocket wobbled.

I turned to another staggering Target Face, shot him, took his gun, and tossed it to Kzinti. Immediately I spun back to the spreading hole in the ground, and unloaded my machinegun on a third guard on the gantry attached to the top of the rocket. He shook with the impact of my bullets, until he fell backward over the railing.

At which point I leapt into the abyss.

I floated across the darkness, and landed gracelessly on the service platform. I moved toward the edge of the rocket and placed a hand on its surface, shoving with all my strength. To my shock, the thing actually tilted very slightly backwards.

"Are you *crazy?*" Kzinti yelled down at me.

"Yes!" I called back. "But if I can knock this thing even partially off its launch trajectory, I can save Washington DC!"

"But... *then* where will it go?" The Tiger Man asked, confused.

"I don't know," I admitted. "But maybe I can destabilize it enough that it will land somewhere harmlessly!"

"*Maybe* land somewhere harmlessly?" Kzinti said. "*MAYBE?*"

I shrugged and grinned up at him.

"Maybe is all I've got right now," I said. "Unless you have a better idea?"

Kzinti stared back wide-eyed.

"Yeah, didn't think so," I said, still smiling, putting the machinegun strap around my neck and leaning my shoulder into the rocket. "So, I'd run, if I were you. Just in case I really fuck this up."

"*But you'll die!*" He said, the horror raising the deep tenor of his voice an octave or more.

"Looks that way," I said.

He, Tony, and the others took a long, last look at me. Finally, Tony pulled Kzinti by the shoulder, and they all ran.

The rocket was too heavy for me to make much progress, but by shoving, then letting gravity rock it back toward me, and shoving again in unison with its momentum, I got a nice wobble going. Hopefully enough that it would fly a little crooked, then impact somewhere far out to sea, and not simply relocate all the destruction to Baltimore, or Delaware, or Richmond, or wherever.

The wobble was increasing enough with each swing that the rocket was starting to bend the gantry I stood on, steel screeching, struts twisting with pressure, and release. I realized it was bending back and forth on both the to and fro action, and saw that it hadn't yet been detached from the service platform. Which might mean...

Abruptly the rocket began to rise, lifting off its pad, struggling to free itself from the confines of the gantry—failing—and dragging the walkway, and me up with it. The bridge bent, screamed, tore, the rocket already tilting in my direction, now being pulled completely off-balance by the weight of the service tower. We rose slowly, almost elegantly into the air, and the part of my idiot brain that thought I'd get out of this against all odds jumped up, danced crazily and laughed at me.

'You,' it said to me, 'are a stupid, *stupid* dead man.'

In answer, I smiled, closed my eyes, and thought of Juliet.

"OPEN YOUR DAMNED EYES!" I heard someone shriek.

I did, looked over and saw Kzinti reaching toward me from Sin's mechanical lift, as Tony operated it. Kzinti leaned out from the platform across the space between us as the rocket rose away from him, paw grasping for me. I was hanging from the gantry as it twisted up with the rocket, and grasped back at him.

We were too far apart, the distance only widening.

"I can't..." he said, leaning, stretching.

"MOVE ASIDE!" I said, and let go, pushing off with my feet before he could even react.

I hit the railing encircling the platform and it felt like I broke a rib. But I held on. Kzinti was there in an instant, helping me over and onto his side, and the relative stability of the cherry-picker's floor.

Seeing we were safely inside, Tony slammed the control lever, and we backed quickly away from the rocket as it rose, and rose, and rose. We all recoiled from the scorching heat of the rocket's thrusters. The gantry whined, and squirmed and tried to free itself of the rocket's grip, but the rocket held tight, pulling itself off balance, pointing—I was beginning to see where.

"We have to get the hell out of here," I told Kzinti.

"I think we're safe," he said. The rocket will go where it's going to go."

"I think it's going to go right back here."

"What?" He said, horrified.

"I think the weight of the service tower is going to spin it around, and point it bright back down onto the island."

"Oh, shit," Kzinti whispered.

"Yeah," I agreed. "Oh, shit."

We got the cherry-picker over land, jumped through the safety gate, and ran. We looked back over our shoulders to watch as the missile lifted more or less into the air. In confirmation of my fears, we saw that it was slowly being pulled horizontal by the weight of the tangled metal of its former support structure.

We burst out of the fake jungle, and saw the Elephant Man waving us toward an open double-door in the far wall of the arena.

"RUN!" Kzinti and I shouted.

Looking up to see the missile dragging itself out of the hole in the ground, toward the sky, Elephant Man didn't need any further encouragement. He turned and bolted. Kzinti, Tony and I ran after him as the thrusters cleared the chamber's threshold behind us and began roasting the world.

Trees, plants, rocks, water, and by the screams and howls over the roar, Target Faces and hybrids alike all blasted away from the rocket thrust and mostly toward or past us. A screaming, burning Target Face slammed into the wall beside the double-doors as we raced through.

Inside the corridor beyond we raced past a kitchen, restrooms, a locker room, around a corner, and down a hall—flames and searing heat chasing us up that tunnel and down its branch. We managed to stay ahead of everything except the heat until we reached an 'Exit' door where the giant rooster stood holding Juliet's dead body.

"I felt," he said, "I say, I felt it only right that we should bring her with us…"

"RUN!" we all shouted desperately outrunning the superheated liquid propellant on our asses.

"Excellent idea, son," Giant Rooster said, "indeed that is an *excellent idea!*"

He turned and kicked the exit door, and burst through, the three of us right behind. Once clear, he used his clawed foot to slam the door closed between us and searing death.

The door warped, bubbled, the paint on our side peeling, smoldering, catching fire. Behind us, yells and screams pulled our attention away from our gratitude, and we turned toward madness.

From chaos, we had stepped out into greater chaos.

Between us and the upward slope of the caldera was a small cove. The wealthy spectators pushed and shoved down arena stairways toward various waiting vehicles—helicopters, VTOLs, boats, and several expensive limousines—apparently there to drive them to different helicopters, VTOLs, and boats at some other place on the island. One older, balding fat man and his supermodel date were strapping on jetpacks.

He looked at us in horror, or at least he looked at Giant Rooster in horror, then pressed a button, and flew off with his girlfriend.

"Look!" A topless woman on board a speedboat shouted. She was pointing skyward.

We all turned and did as requested. A few hundred feet above the arena we saw the missile, of course, spinning wildly in the air, pinwheeling overhead like a deflating kid's balloon.

As we watched, the tangled support structure's weight dragged it around, and straightened it into a new course that would bring it directly down on us.

CHAPTER 30

THERE WAS NOWHERE to go. We were, quite simply, seconds from death.

"Agent 8!" I heard from above, and turned to see Professor Ex dropping with a parachute attached to a jungle camouflaged ATV. She smiled down at me. "Can I offer you a ride?"

"It's more appealing than dying here with my thumb up my ass," I said.

The vehicle bounced off the ground not ten feet from us, bobbled on its overinflated tires, and once it had settled, Ex began waving us over.

"Then come on!" she yelled.

"Shotgun!" Tony yelled.

We all ran and leapt into the vehicle, crawling over one another for the remaining seats. I noticed the giant rooster was standing aside, still holding Juliet's body.

"There isn't," he said, "I say, there isn't enough room for the both of us."

"You can pile on top of..." I said, then realized. "Oh, you mean for both you and Juliet."

I studied the forlorn birdman and understood his pain. I walked over to him, staring down into the face of my beloved Juliet. Her expression was beautiful, almost calm, serene. The wound in her forehead seemed smaller, less tragic with much of the blood wiped away, as if it were now just a puncture, or bump she'd gotten in some silly way. I found myself wishing she would open her eyes and say, 'Oops. *What did I walk into?*'

"We can't," Rooster Man said, "I say, we *can't* leave Miss Juliet behind. She loved you … I say, she loved you so much."

He was right, at least as far as I was concerned. I touched her cheek, then kissed her lips with love and sweetness, immediately regretting it.

"Ew," I said, "that was gross. She's cold, and already getting rigor. Not as romantic as it looks in the movies."

Gunfire exploded dirt, branches and leaves all around us. I dove backward, toward the ATV, and the giant rooster fell over atop Juliet's naked body. He lifted his head weakly and smiled at me.

"They got me, boy," he moaned. "They got ole Rooster Glaghorn. Run, son. Save yo'self. I'll protect… I say, I'll protect Miss Juliet. She died… protectin' you. She sure wouldn't… want… you… to… get… killed…"

And with that he collapsed across her, as dead as she was.

"Your thumb is still up your ass!" Ex screamed.

I stood, took one, final look at my beloved's still, and silent face peeking out from under a giant rooster, ran back to the ATV and dove into the only remaining vacant seat. Ex gunned it.

The vehicle lurched forward, careening toward the tunnel that would take us out of the caldera, hopefully to the safety on the other side of its rim, and into the surrounding jungle.

Behind us a vehicle full of Target Faces raced after us in pursuit. Weapons fire erupted all around us, and Tony jerked forward, screaming from the impact of a slug in his back.

"Teaming up with you and the girl seemed like SUCH a good idea," he whined. *"They're professionals! They can save us! Now I'm shot, Rooster Claghorn is dead, God knows where Porcupine Pete, and Gaja are, and there's no way we're going to escape that…"*

"Will you shut up!" Kzinti, Ex and I interrupted simultaneously.

He reacted as if he'd been slapped, which—verbally—he had. I looked back and the missile was still a good half mile up. Tony was wrong. We were going to make it—safely and with time to spare. We all turned our attention back to the road ahead, specifically the entrance to the tunnel through the volcano wall that would take us to safety.

"Shit," Ex said.

It was jammed with traffic. A line of limousines clogged the entrance to the tunnel, and disappeared into its depths beyond.

"Is there another way out?" Ex asked.

I looked up the wall of the crater.

"How 'all terrain' is this All-Terrain Vehicle?" I asked.

"Too steep," Ex said. "Beyond thirty degrees and we'll just roll back down! Too much distance to even try."

"How about over those?" I asked, pointing at the limos.

Ex laughed, then abruptly stopped, and cocked her head, seeing my wisdom.

"You know… worth a try," she said, and gunned the engines. *"Everyone lean when I say lean!"*

The ATV impacted the rear of the closest vehicle, slamming it a few feet forward, its knobby tires gripping the bumper.

"Lean back!" Ex commanded.

We all did, the front wheels of the All-Terrain latched onto the limo's bumper, its trunk, and finally yanked us onto its back, and across its roof, which we crushed down onto the people inside. It then rolled easily over onto the limo's hood and across onto the trunk of the next limo in line. It wasn't fast, but it was effective.

And that's when the Target Faces pulled up alongside, guns aimed directly at us, and I saw in the jeep's passenger seat—holding a rocket launcher—one bloody, very angry, and still naked Gunter.

Shit.

"Vell, vell, vell," he called to me, still cocky and arrogant. *"How many vays you know to morder me now, Agent Stupid man who not understands taunting?"*

That's when a dinosaur ate him.

Seriously.

A massive Tyrannosaurus Rex stepped from the foliage alongside the road, bent down and scooped him up in its mouth. It chewed him almost in half, tossed his nearly severed pieces into the air, and pretty much gulped them down in two quick swallows.

A naked Gudrun was in a saddle on the dinosaur's back, petting him—or her—it—affectionately.

"Goot tyrannosaur," she said, sweetly. "Vell dun."

She smiled down at us.

"What the hell?" I asked.

"I vork for man who start Ddinosaur Island zoo many year back vhen as trainer," Gudrun explained, she and her pet dino pacing us as we continued rolling over limos, and crushing passengers, "When zoo fail, I am broke, so Doctor Sin offer me to vin money, and maybe get revenge on Gunter."

"I'd say that last part worked out for you," I said.

"Yes!" She said, delighted. "It does! He punch my face so he can fock Juliet and her pupper," Ah, I thought, understanding her facial wounds, now, "Guards take you and him away, and zen Juliet offer me money to bring dinosaurs to rescue her and everyone. So I do! Vhere is she? Vhere is Juliet, my friend?"

No one said anything, but my expression told the whole story. It slowly sunk in, and I could see Gudrun was sincerely saddened, though said nothing. She looked back at the approaching missile.

"Ve shoult horry," she said, turned the T-Rex, spurred it like an obedient horse, and galloped off toward the tunnel. At first, she and her dinosaur ran ahead in the space alongside the vehicles, but when she reached the entrance, she spurred again, they clambered atop the limos before us, and led the way through.

Professor Ex—ever observant and efficient—said nothing, and gunned the ATV right along behind her.

We passengers turned to watch the missile arc its way downward, straight toward the arena. That's when I saw, in the floor-to-ceiling window of Sin's office, the good Doctor herself, still wearing her mask, still nude other than sandals and robe, staring up at her imminent doom. Just before the missile struck, and we disappeared into the mouth of the tunnel, I swear I saw her mask turn my way, her nearest hand raising, her middle finger extended.

Then all was fire, and light… fire, and darkness.

CHAPTER 31

I SAT UP IN THE DIRT road on the other side of the tunnel, smoke and debris still billowing out of its mouth from the explosion on the other side. All around me lie the hybrids, Gudrun, her T-Rex, Professor Ex, the ruins of several limousines, and the mangled ATV. Everyone seemed fine, simply reeling from our narrow escape.

I stood and stared up at the rim of the caldera, the fire, and sparks, as they drifted lazily into the sky from the opposite side. I couldn't imagine anyone inside the natural bowl of that mountain had survived.

Good.

I turned back to the others, waving away the fumes, and drifting ash.

"God, I hope this isn't radioactive," Tony said, holding his injured shoulder. "That would be the perfect end to my perfect day."

Beyond him a shadow was moving toward us through the fog of destruction. I looked around and studied our group. Everyone was accounted for.

A limousine passenger?

At first, I couldn't even make out if it was male or female, but then a familiar gait, a sensuous sway of hips, and heavy breasts became apparent.

"Juliet?" I asked the air, hopefully.

Tony and the others turned toward the shadow. The smoke drifted, revealed, then obscured again.

"Juliet," I said louder, and moved in that direction.

The smoke cleared, and a familiar smile cheered me.

"Juliet!" I cried.

Now I was running to her, but her smile was falling away.

"No, it's me," she said as I threw my arms around her. "It's Sunny."

"I know, but..." I laughed, holding her bare skin tightly against mine, "you're also Juliet."

"No," Sunny said, her voice very dark and far away. "She told me she'd tell everyone that. To save you. To save you from Sin, and trying to protect me, and because you'd die, and Washington DC would be destroyed. But she was Juliet. And she knew that she would die, instead. But she wanted you to live, and be happy."

I pulled back, and stared at her as my brain cells slowly coagulated into a solid, worthless mass.

"What?" I asked, more out of self-defense, to slow the damage to my thinking thing in skull, than in expectation of any answer that would make sense to me.

"I don't know," Sunny said. "I don't really understand it. She traded places with me when we were separated last night, while I was in the bathroom. She told me you loved *me*, not her, and that she had come back to save you from the biggest mistake of your life. But she was wrong, wasn't she? She was the one you loved all along."

I heard Juliet's voice again in my head, echoing distantly.

Saw the tear on her cheek glisten.

"I am such an idiot," she'd whispered.

I replayed every moment I could remember in my mind's eye, trying to see how it all fit together. But the jigsaw bits couldn't be pieced in place as a cohesive whole. It was like trying to understand Marvel Comics continuity. After a while, it doesn't matter. It just is what it is.

I looked around for Ex, and found her near the wrecked ATV. Her eyes were sad, devastated actually, head slightly down as she stared at me through half-lids.

"What's this all about, Ex?" I asked her.

"I don't know," Ex said, quietly. "Juliet came back to my office the night after you two had escaped. She seemed... different. More focused. More aware. The bloody girl you came through with was more like this," she nodded in Sunny's direction. "Juliet told me you were in danger, someone wanted to kill you, and gave me instructions for when and where on this island to arrive with the ATV. And that was pretty much it. She asked... I came."

I looked at the others. Tony and Kzinti avoided eye-contact. Gudrun, also clearly sad, held the reigns of her T-Rex, a similar expression on her face as the one Ex wore.

"Sunny is right," Gudrun said, quietly. "When Juliet arrive in sleeping room last night, and punch on your face, she tell me her plan. At start of this day game, Juliet ask me to find Sunny in bathroom, and bring her with me. I see Gunter is still such asshole, will fuck on me, but will also kill me. So, I agree. Juliet says you will do Japanese thing, and run outside of arena. So, we plan same. I find Sunny, we leave arena. Sneak away."

"I got to ride my own dinosaur," Sunny said, proudly, and turned to a second shadow following her out of the smoke wearing a saddle. And ankylosaur that nuzzled her, affectionately.

"I named him Trevor. Because he likes kissing me."

Tears streamed down her cheeks.

I did like kissing her. I took her in my arms and showed her how much. She responded. Nervously at first, tentatively, then ardently, with as much passion as I showed her. Perhaps more.

Arms still around my neck, we separated, and smiled at one another. But her sadness was still a wall between us.

"I know you loved Juliet," she said. "But if you can at least love me half as much as you loved her, it would still be ten times more than any man has ever loved me."

My lips fell onto hers again, and we melted into one another, kissed, deeply, wetly, passionately, her moans, and heat rising as our hands found every inch of the other's smooth nakedness, wanting to hold it all at once.

"Oh, my God," Sunny said, breathlessly, "you're hard again. How is your dick always so hard?"

"Because it loves you as much as I do," I said, "and I love you so very much."

"Mmmm. Is it slave time, Trevor?" she asked, and giggled.

I kissed her again, pulled her down with me to our knees, then lay her back gently on the road, and immediately pushed myself deep inside her. Her mouth left mine to gasp, and call my name, again, and tell me how much she loved having me inside her.

"Um…" Ex said. "You think maybe you two could wait *at least* until after people have stopped screaming and burning on the other side of that caldera wall?"

I looked up at the good professor, but didn't bother to stop moving in and out of Sunny's warm, soft embrace.

"I'm really glad she's alive," I said.

"I can see that," Ex said, grinning.

Sunny laughed, and looked a little embarrassed.

But only a little.

8   8   8

My days and nights on the weird little island of *Krabs Key*—which we had unofficially renamed *Isla Julietta*—were some of the happiest I can remember. We had gone to the village of the hybrids, which was little more than an encampment on the beach, and settled into a kind of familial bliss. They all had family there, the different breeds coexisting in an unusual sort of suburban domesticity. Tony had a wife and kids, though none of them seemed at all happy to see him.

"Did you bring us something to eat?" his wife asked.

"I got shot!" he said, angrily.

"But you didn't die!" she responded. "And we're hungry!"

Sunny and I spent our time sunning, swimming, and sleeping on the beach, perpetually nude and making love as much as possible whenever and wherever the urge arose. And urges—as we have established—arose quite often.

During one particularly lovely encounter, as I lay atop her, comfortably situated snugly inside her loving folds while she ate mango and bananas rather sloppily under me, she lamented having to go home to Jícama and leave our state of non-connubial bliss.

"Why do you have to go home?" I wondered, sincerely.

"You need to go back to your headquarters," she said, slurping mango, "and your job, and Sunny needs to sell some seashells by the seashore to pay her bills. We have lives to live. As much as I've enjoyed slave time, Trevor, I can't keep you as my personal fuck-friend forever."

"You could try," I said.

"I'm just a poor, island girl, and you have places to go, people to kill. It could never last."

Something occurred to me. Or rather… some things.

"That bothered you before," I said, trying to stoke the thoughts in my head from dying embers into full-blown flames of memory. "When I said I would kill someone, it bothered you. And you punched me."

"No, I didn't," Sunny said. "That was Juliet."

I stared at her.

For a long while.

"No, Sunny. I know who I was lying on top of. And it was you. Not Juliet."

"No," she said, shaking her head. "Juliet switched places with me when I was in the bathroom. And she was pretty mad because you loved me, and knocked you unconscious. Not me."

"But …" I said.

"She said you wouldn't be able to tell the difference between us."

I thought about that for a few minutes, and stopped moving inside her.

"Hey," she said. "I liked that. Don't stop."

"If *I* couldn't tell the difference," I said, "Nobody else could."

"What?" Sunny asked, thoroughly confused.

I smiled.

"You're never going to have to sell another seashell," I said.

CHAPTER 32

THE BUTLER AND MAID LET us in again, staring at Sunny, aghast.

I was right. No one else could tell the difference, either.

The maid hugged her, warmly, and cried.

"Your uncle said you had died," she whispered. "How could he be so wrong?"

Over Sunny's shoulder the old woman smiled up at me.

"You really are her hero," she said.

"What happened after I dropped her off with you the last time?" I asked.

"We don't know," the butler whispered, obviously afraid someone would hear. The mysterious uncle, no doubt. "Mister Jones arrived shortly after you left. He was quite agitated, and somehow knew—or suspected—that miss Juliet had been returned to us."

"He got a call that alerted him," I said, remembering the odd conversation I'd had on the phone with the mysterious voice.

"He and Miss Juliet argued, it became quite heated, then suddenly became very quiet, and Miss Juliet—very calmly, and almost as if no longer able to see us—walked out the front door, climbed into her sports car, and drove off."

"She was still nude," the maid said, obviously distressed by everything.

"What did he say to her?"

The butler looked perplexed, turned to the maid, who looked equally lost and confused, then turned back to me, and shrugged.

"Where is he?" I asked.

8   8   8

I kicked in the bedroom door. Which hurt my ankle. It was made of some pretty solid wood. But it had the effect I wanted. The two people in bed stopped fucking, and stared at me with the appropriate amount of fear.

I recognized them instantly. The fat man and the supermodel with the jetpacks.

They stared at the gun in my hand, and sweated profusely, but not from the sex. I'm pretty sure. Then, weirdly, they both got even more frightened when Sunny walked in behind me. It was all starting to make sense. Kind of. Sort of.

Actually, no, it still made no sense, but I was a little less confused.

"You're alive," the fat uncle whispered to Sunny.

"Start explaining," I said, gesturing with my gun. "Singapodia, Madame Phu, Juliet's parents, and how you got Juliet into the Octopus Games. Everything."

It all shot out of him like spew from a horny teenager's dick on prom night. He didn't know it all, but he provided enough that I could fill in the blanks.

"I sold out Jack, my brother," Pasty Fat Uncle said. "And his wife, I guess, as well, to Madame Phu. They'd gone to renegotiate the ice cream carton manufacturing with the new regime, and I made a deal with Phu before they touched down. Somehow Juliet escaped."

I was sitting opposite him with my gun on my knee, trigger-finger twitching as a reminder that I was eager to shoot Juliet's uncle if I felt he was lying. He and naked supermodel lie back with the sheets bunched over them. Sunny stood nearby, listening quietly.

"When Phu found her," Uncle continued, "she decided not to… um… well…" he glanced at Sunny/Juliet, nervously, "kill her…"

"She was supposed to kill Juliet," I clarified.

"Yes," Uncle owned. "Kill…. Juliet. She had some other plan for her, a way to make more money, and maybe get revenge on someone. I didn't care, so long as Juliet never came back here to make a claim for the company."

"Because she's the inheritor, not you," I again clarified.

He paused, not wanting to own that part, but I cocked the gun, and he reconsidered.

"Correct," he said. "I didn't actually help start the company. I just worked there, but with Juliet gone…"

"Good to know," I said. 'What are these code words for Juliet?"

"Well, one is…"

"Don't say them out loud," I snarled. 'Write them down."

He took a pen and paper from the bedside drawer and did so.

"So the *'Have You Seen This Girl'* flyers were a sham," I said, as he wrote.

"Yeah," Uncle admitted, handing me the code-words, which I immediately folded and pocketed. "Just corporate P. R. No one was ever going to find her, according to Phu."

"But I screwed up Phu's—and Sin's—plans by killing the good Madame."

"And by falling in love with me," Sunny said with a smile.

A smile I returned.

I turned to the butler who had guided us upstairs.

"Is there a good place near here to murder people?" I asked. "I have a license."

"Wait," Uncle said. "What?"

"There's a hunting shed at the back of the property," the butler said, seeming quite happy to help. "Secluded, and the mess won't matter."

"NO, WAIT!" Fat uncle said. *"I told you everything I know!"*

"I believe you," I said. "Really helpful. Thanks. But you wouldn't have if you'd known I was going to kill you, anyway."

"By 'murder people' you just mean him, right?" The supermodel asked. "Not me."

"Oh, no, you're a matched set," I said.

"But..." she said, sputtering, "I'm a *model!*"

"She'll sleep with you!" Uncle said, "And I have money!"

"Yes!" Supermodel said. "I'll sleep with you!"

"He's already sleeping with me," Sunny said. "Exclusively. And you *don't* have money," she said to her 'uncle.' "*I* do."

Uncle's mouth moved open and closed like a fish on the bottom of the boat that's too tired to fight anymore.

"You don't mind that I'm going to murder them?" I asked Sunny-pretending-to-be-Juliet.

"No, I really don't," she said, sincerely, though she was obviously still getting used to the idea. "Who doesn't love some therapeutic revenge porn, now and then, especially on such truly awful people?"

"I'm not as bad as him," Supermodel said, rather huffily. "I don't even really *like* him."

"You flew down to an island to watch me be murdered in a game show."

"Oh, my Gawwwwd," Supermodel said. "You make it sound so much worse than it was."

"And how—exactly—could it *not* have been as bad as I just made it sound?"

"You could have won!"

"Did you bet *on* me, or *against* me?"

Supermodel's mouth began the fish movement, as Sunny/the New Juliet stared at her a long, *long* while, then finally said to me; "Can I be the one to kill her?"

"Sure," I said.

And without another word being said—though there was lots of crying by some—we made our way to the hunting shed.

CHAPTER 33

WE BOUGHT THE ISLAND for a song.

Literally.

Apparently Sunny/the New Juliet had a music library as part of her extensive financial portfolio and one rather modest hit song paid for the entire island, dinosaurs and all. Who knew music was so lucrative?

Sunny/the New Juliet began investing her millions into new construction right away, and built up a beautiful little recreation of her Manchester neighborhood. But this one was near the shore on *Isla Julietta*. So we both got our dream; me Manchester, her living naked on a mostly empty beach.

The new neighborhood had a home for Tony, another for his ex-wife, one each for Kzinti, Porcupine Pete, Elephant Girl, Wolf Man Lon, and Gudrun, as well as the other surviving hybrids on the island. We even set up a little vacation spot for Professor Ex. Sunny provided a small grocery store and people to run it, a radio station, television access, and—of course—a *Jonsey's Icey Creams*.

"I feel a little guilty about taking Juliet's money," Sunny said one day as we sat staring out at the sun dipping languidly into an amber ocean, "her name, her neighborhood, and most importantly," she wiggled her bare ass in my naked lap, swirling me around inside her in a way that made us both feel wonderful, "her man."

"*Your* man," I said.

She 'Mmmed' and butt wiggled some more.

"And on top of that, her maid and butler," I said, reaching around to cup her breasts, and gently twiddle her nipples.

Walter, was his name, and he brought out two dishes of *Jumbled Jumbos*, handing one to each of us with a warm smile. He then went over to sit with Eleanor, the maid, in their conjoined beach chairs. The two held hands.

Sunny lay back against my chest, cooed, and luxuriated in the evening glow. And my dick.

"The moon is out," she said, staring up at it. "You always wanted to sit on the porch with your cock inside me, looking up at the moon and stars.

I stopped eating my ice cream. I set it down on the side table.

"How do you know about that?" I asked.

"I just remember you saying it," she said. "A few times, actually. Why?"

"Because I never told you that," I said.

"You must have," she said. "How else could I have known?"

It was a good question. I had no idea.

8   8   8

I lie awake that night holding my naked Sunny while she slept, just thinking. Not my usual M. O. when it came to insomnia with a naked woman, but my agent's paranoia was in high gear, and my libidio in low.

Rooster Glaghorn had called Juliet 'Miss Juliet' as if he had known her. But how had he known her?

Sunny remembered things I was pretty sure I had only told Juliet.

Sunny had punched me the night before the Octopus games. I was sure it was Sunny. Why had she told me it was Juliet?

Juliet was the Manchurian plot of Madame Phu's that I had been sent to uncover. That was clear. But what *was* the plot? Sin's word couldn't be trusted. She had a personal agenda. So why had Madame Phu sent Juliet to SADISTO? And what had Decommissioning uncovered in her subconscious?

I felt certain there were more code-phrases than the few Uncle had given me. One of which was the same phrase that had been inside that folder, scribbled on the photo of the dead Madame Phu, and what had caused Juliet's sudden personality shift in the General's office.

I could test that code-phrase on Sunny, but what would result? I was too afraid I would ruin all this; my beautiful dream life, my beautiful dream girl. But my mind wouldn't let it go.

Trying the phrase, or continuing to search might be the worst form of self-sabotage; exactly the kind of thing my paranoid spy-self would normally do—and shouldn't. Let sleeping Sunny's lie. Have your life, your three-point-two children. Be happy.

But I couldn't. I couldn't stop thinking about it. Fears of it unraveling anyway wouldn't stop nagging at me. I knew I had to go back to SADISTO and face The General. Turn in my notice. Leave the agency, and let go of my last chance to know, and return here, to my joy.

My brain, and my fears wouldn't stop. I had to know.

I looked down at my lovely, sweet, delightful Sunny, and knew she was being honest with me. She was everything she claimed to be. But was she more? If I went digging around and uncovered some truth about her that I didn't want to know, how would this end—this perfect happiness that was continuing to grow between us?

I looked at the face I loved and thought about how devastated I would be if I messed this up. After a while I stopped thinking, and decided.

I had to know.

8   8   8

Dusk was softly spreading when I landed the JetStar at SADISTO's small private airport near Washington. I slogged, wearily toward the parking lot where, a few weeks before, I'd left my pearl-gray, completely restored twin-carburetor-equipped, supercharger-fitted Lagonda drophead coupe. One of the shallow perks of the spy game.

The parking attendant touched his hand to his cap. "Nice evening," he said conversationally.

I nodded, not happy to be there. My hands had begun to shake, and my eye to twitch at the thought of arguing with The General for my release from the agency.

"What happened to that gorgeous blonde who followed you to Hickama few months back?" the attendant asked. "You know, the cadet agent with the…" he cupped his hands before his chest with the universal sign-language that indicated 'enormous breasts.'

I said nothing. Just stared at him. Coldly.

"She came here…" the attendant continued, trying to explain his curiosity as normal and unworthy of my intense reaction, "… the night you left. I thought… maybe… you were meeting… on Hickama. You know. For business, of course. Important business."

"You," I rasped, "pay too much attention."

"I know. I do," he said, nervous lips twitching in rhythm with the one eye. "Sorry. Really sorry."

He stood stock still and stared, then panicked, and closed his eyes as if waiting to die. When he didn't, he turned and ran quickly away.

I got in my car, and was heading directly for *The Office* and my 'exit interview' with The General. The temptation to stop at *The Place* and check in with Gran was intense, but I resisted it. She might know something about Juliet, but this time I wasn't going to let myself get distracted. And I shouldn't anyway, I had a girlfriend/sort of fiancée; so this time I was going to confront The General while I was still relatively fresh—and angry. This time he was going to give me some answers about this crazy Manchurian plot, followed immediately by my instant release from SADISTO so I could be with Sunny-slash-Juliet *or else…*

The ex-country club that now housed SADISTO's secret headquarters hove into view and I slammed on the brakes, skidded a hundred yards or so, and halted by the main entrance. The parking lot was unusually empty.

After showing my forgery-proof ID card five times and giving eight different passwords, I finally reached Central Visitor Control. Again, oddly deserted.

Suzi—the cold-eyed blonde with the expert hand job skills usually on duty there—was gone. No Ruth, either, thank God. A warm-eyed redhead was in their place.

Curious.

Curious, too, was the fact that all of the guards I'd passed on my way in were *new* guards. Even more curious was the fact that the redhead told me to go right down to the General's office. I had already unfastened my slacks.

"You don't want me to drop my trousers?" I asked. "You know...so you can inspect things?"

She looked at me with unbridled disgust, and some fury.

"I do *not*," she said. "You're expected in The General's office," she repeated, curtly, "now."

Only when I was in the elevator did I realize that, always before, I'd been told to report to The General—not to his *office*.

Most curious.

I entered Punnymany's office. No Punnymany. No puns.

Even more most curious.

And suspicious.

I loosened my silencer-fitted gun, stepped into The General's comfortable, rather untidy office.

The General was gone. His bottles of baby oil were gone. In their place were two lean, wiry young men, one white, one black, in trench coats watching a football game on the giant, high-definition screen.

My hand streaked for my left armpit.

Their hands streaked for their left armpits.

They had a head start; their hands reached their armpits first.

I bared my teeth in a snarl of frustration, withdrew my hand, empty. They withdrew their hands.

"Trevor Hawke?" one asked.

I nodded. "Where's the General?" I snapped.

They exchanged glances.

"You tell him," said one.

"Might as well," agreed the other.

"I'm Smith, CIA. This is Jones, FBI." said the second young man, as the first went back to watching the game, "The man you call the General is in a top-secret loony bin."

I said nothing; my mind had begun to whirl.

"Hawke," said the CIA agent sadly, "you've killed a lot of people for the General, haven't you?"

"More than my share," I said.

"How many men, women and children do you think you've slaughtered following his orders?"

I shrugged. "Who keeps score? Hundreds. Thousands, maybe, if you count innocent bystanders. But it's all on the up-and-up. I have a license to kill."

The white FBI guy stopped watching the game, and turned to his CIA friend, obviously horrified. Then they turned to stare at me for a moment, and finally turned back to look at one another to stare some more. Then the white one laughed. Very hard.

"It's not funny," said the CIA guy.

"It's funny in a 'if I don't laugh, I'll lose my fucking mind' kind of way."

The CIA man snorted, and returned his angry eyes to me.

"License to kill, huh?" he asked.

"All SADISTO agents are," I said.

"And how does that work, exactly?" he asked, folding his arms, eyes going from angry, to darkly smiling. "Say, you're sent to France to kill someone, do you just drop by the Triple AAA for a 'travel license to kill'?"

FBI Jones chuckled to himself, and without taking his eye off the game held up a hand, that CIA Smith low-fived.

"I don't know... '*Smith*'," I said. "How did it work with MK Ultra?"

The CIA man's eyes stopped smiling. So did his mouth.

The FBI agent kept watching the game. "There is no such thing as a license to kill."

"Not in the FBI, maybe" I said.

Jones sighed again, and side-eyed me.

"We looked through the General's records," he said, turning his eyes back to the game. "He sent you out to use your 'license' quite a lot. He was mad, you know; fucking nutballs. That last assignment he sent you on—liquidating two fellow agents who had defected from his ranks—"

"A mission," I said, "which I successfully resolved."

"A mission," groaned the CIA agent, "which didn't need resolving." He picked up a scrap of paper, read aloud: "Have Strangeways, and Trueblue liquidated—they are Lizard people in disguise." He dropped the paper on the General's desk. "That's the General's whole file on the—uh—well, the 'job' you just completed."

"Await," I scratched my head. "You mean Trueblue was a Reptilian? How do the Octopus Games figure into the plans of the Reptilians?"

"*They don't,*" snarled the FBI agent, completely dragged from his game. "There are no reptilians, Hawke! *Wake up!* Can't you get it through your thick skull? The General was insane! Totally off his fucking rocker. Loony goddam Tunes."

"SADISTO was nothing but a massive boondoggle," Jones threw in, trying to calm Smith, "a complete creation of your General's sick mind."

"That can't be," I said, almost whispering.

"It can," said the FBI agent. "And it is!"

"Come on," Smith said. "Think about it. How realistic is any of this? Hand jobs from the receptionists to prove you're a real agent?"

"I kinda liked that idea," Jones joked. "Oh, baby."

"Yeah," Smith agreed, chuckling. "From that Suzi in particular. But really. Hardly realistic in a truly professional organization."

"But—" I gasped. "It can't—How—?"

"I think it's finally sinkin' in," The FBI man said to Smith, and sighed even more heavily and spoke to me. "It's kind of incredible, isn't it?"

"Not really," Smith said, "once you consider how many separate top-secret agencies we have in Washington, most of them—" he shot a baleful glance at his FBI colleague "—most of them supplied by funds carefully concealed in other black-budget appropriations; funds checked up on by nobody. The fact is, Hawke, the man you knew as the General was really just an ex-corporal who escaped a sanitarium in Arlington and started SADISTO from a closet in the basement of this building. Filled out some forms, got approval, and when someone tried to check on him, they were told "Need to Know" and "Black Ops" and everyone just rubber stamped his requests."

"That's... No, I—I don't believe it!" I gasped. The wheels in my head spun rapidly. "On the other hand," I said slowly, "I can see how such a thing *might* be possible. Like, how they run the Secret Space Programs, the Alien Technology Back-Engineering Programs, the pocket phone technology from the

Emerald Tablets of Atlantis Programs, unless… I mean, who would be in a position to even check, right?"

"Nobody," agreed the FBI man, happy I was getting it so he could return to his game. "In the FBI we were told that SADISTO was involved in overseas operations—which puts it out of our jurisdictions."

"And the CIA," said the CIA man, "was led to believe that SADISTO was an internal security outfit—out of *our* jurisdiction. The Budget Department wasn't told *anything*. They just kept getting Ultra Secret requisitions for tens of millions of dollars, which they discreetly honored, and pretended had never happened. It's a governmental rounding error, really."

"Fantastic," I mused.

"Deplorable," snarled the CIA man. "We of the CIA may pull some pretty sneaky deals, but we don't run around slaughtering crowds of people wholesale."

"Why not?—you should!" I protested. "Don't you understand? The Free World must use any and all means to defeat those who believe that the end justifies the means. Only by becoming more brutal, more inhuman, more bestial than our enemies can we prove the superiority of our civilization!"

The CIA man and the FBI man did another look at each other, look at me thing, and then simply stared at me, wide-eyed.

"You… are sick," said one.

"Sicker than the General," said the other.

"I thought you were just a dupe following orders, but… how can you believe you gain moral superiority by being more immoral than your opponents?" Jones asked.

I glared at him. "You lousy defeatist pacifist presumed left-winger," I snarled. But I snarled it to myself. In my head. They *were* faster on the draw than me.

"Fuck you, Hawke," said the FBI man, getting up from his game, possibly reading my mind. "You and all your fellow SADISTO agents, are out of jobs. We're here to dismantle SADISTO headquarters and—"

"*Dismantle SADISTO headquarters?*" I gasped. "But—but you can't! The techniques, the training programs we've pioneered, they're all too valuable to lose!"

"Why do you care?!" Jones said, touching a folder on the desk. Presumably mine. "Your dossier says this was all too much for you! That you wanted out of this madhouse to get married— raise children. Live up in Manchester!"

It began to hit me. Hard. No more victims to torture, stab, shoot, eviscerate, burn alive or mutilate. No more world travel, first class. No more unlimited expense accounts. No more gourmet meals at the world's best restaurants. No more vintage wines sipped at taxpayer expense. No more fast cars and faster women... no more seducing women I didn't like, or murdering people I did.

It was all over. And I didn't have to quit.

I took a deep breath. I calmed.

I was free.

Someone else had forced the issue, and I didn't even have to convince The General.

I had Sunny—slash—Juliet, and life was just handing me to her.

But...

But I still needed to know the truth about Sunny—slash—Juliet. And they were going to destroy it with everything else.

"Can I grab a few things before I leave?"

"What?" FBI asked, irritated. "No! You're not leaving!"

"Whatever happened here—stays here," CIA interrupted, again playing the calm cop. "No records, no files, nothing that can come back to haunt any administration. And there are some people out front who will decide if you're suitable for either FBI, or CIA transfer, or..."

"Yeah, and in case it's 'or'..." FBI said, holding out a hand to me, "hand over your gun."

"You want my gun?" I said gently, "well—here it is!" And in a flash the little silencer-fitted Beretta was in my fist. The girl-sized gun sneezed twice, and both the CIA man and the FBI man sprouted crimson holes in their foreheads.

I went around the desk to the General's drawer, and pulled it onto the floor the same way Juliet had. Within the spilled mess I found the folder the General had shown me. Still empty. But on the back I saw something I hadn't seen before.

Time Funnel Report

Then I noticed in the back of the desk cabinet, jammed in so that they had been crumpled and smashed between drawer and interior desk wall, I found what had likely been inside.

Five or six papers, all labeled "Above Alien Autopsy Cosmic Level Top Secret. Eyes Only."

And on those papers? Information about Juliet's role as Madame Phu's spy, her activation code words, and phrases.

And at the top:

"What we do, we do for the greater good."

I had said those words to her. Both here, on this spot, and the night before the Octopus Games.

The code phrase was labeled: "RESET: JULIET JONES, PRE-CADET AGENT, Seduce and gain love of Agent Trevor Hawke. Seduce him to gain entrance to cadet-agent program."

Juliet had reset and immediately tried to suck me off. On Krabs Key Sunny had reset to Juliet—who then punched me.

Sunny and Juliet were the same person. And they—she—didn't know.

'Trevor Hawke,' they'd both said, 'I like that name.'

My worst, paranoid fears seemed to be grounded. Sunny-slash-Juliet... they probably didn't even love me.

Had the General known about this? Used this information? As part of some greater plan?

Had he been working with Phu on something that used Juliet as one of the pieces on his global chessboard, Jícama edition? I remembered the dinosaur on that board, with its little, naked doll rider, thinking it had been a mistake, or a moment of whimsy, or childishness. It hadn't been. It had been Gudrun. I looked at the papers for more answers.

The next phrase was labeled; "RESET: JULIET JONES, PRE-SINGAPODIA/SUNNY"

Below that, "RESET: AGENT JULIET JONES, POST-SADISTO TORTURE TRAINING, PRE-DECOMISSION"

And in red beneath that:

To be used only with extreme caution

But... not all these phrases could be from Madame Phu. These supposed answers led only to more questions.

I heard footsteps approaching in the hallway. Now wasn't the time to sit around figuring things out. I jammed the papers into their folder, shoved the folder into my suit jacket, and opened the door, peering into what had been Punnymany's office.

Empty.

Behind me, the knob on the direct outer door to the elevator clicked against its lock. Then rattled.

I stepped into Puynnymany's office, and out the other door into the waiting corridor. No one there. I stepped carefully to the end of the hall, and peeked around to the elevator. A man in a trench coat was pulling his silenced gun to shoot the knob he'd been rattling. The gun popped, and so did the door. He stepped carefully inside.

Seconds later, moving quietly, I was in the elevator. The doors closed as the gun toting trench coat returned to the corridor, and took aim, but I was the only one who fired. As the doors closed I saw his body fall backward into the General's old office, blood spurting from a hole in his forehead.

A few moments after that I was back at Central Visitor Control, walking past the redhead with a grin, and a wave as if nothing was wrong, I hadn't just killed three men.

The redhead was clearly startled to see me: her mouth opened wide in surprise, her right hand reaching behind a desk for a small weapon. The gun was back in my hand and sneezed, she closed her mouth, toppled slowly backward as blood shot in a thin stream from between her lips.

None of the other guards tried to stop me, fortunately for them. Moments later my Lagonda was roaring down the highway followed by several unmarked cars. And then—then I began evasive tactics.

After gaining some time between me and my pursuers, I stopped at *The Place* and other than some losers in trenchcoats hanging around out front, found it—like headquarters—oddly empty. Everyone had obviously left in a hurry. I made my way to room 42, passing mostly open doors to empty rooms that looked like they'd been vacated hastily. One contained a man in a trench coat driving hard into a girl on the bed.

"Tell me how much you love my CIA cock," he cried.

"I love your CIA cock, so much," the woman yelled, sounding sincere.

I shot him, not because he was CIA, but because he was so irritatingly insecure about his dick size.

"Thank you," the woman said as she struggled out from under him. "I didn't really love his CIA cock."

"I figured," I said, and told her the safest way out.

I made it to 42 with no difficulty, and stepped inside. Binkley lay faithfully beside the bed, waiting. He leapt up and ran excitedly to me, I gave him quiet pets and cuddles, and led him silently back to my car.

This isn't the time and place to detail all the tricky tricks I pulled, tricks I'd been trained in pulling. Suffice to say that I outdistanced and eluded all my pursuers in action packed adventures that could fill a book. A different book. This one's pretty full, already.

Once the FBI almost caught me in Seattle, and twice the CIA nearly cornered me in Costa Rica, but when I slipped into Hong Kong a week later, I knew I'd finally shaken off all pursuit. It gave me time to devour the still maddeningly incomplete contents of Juliet's folder. The papers told me nothing of how much The General had known, or when, or if he was using Sunny-slash-Juliet-slash-cadet agent Jones for his own ends.

Or most importantly, if Sunny really loved me.

The only new thing I discovered was a line that mentioned FUTURE AGENT JONES, and 'nanotech'—whatever that was.

I made my decision, closed the folder, and considered burning it, but knowing my memory retention skills I decided to hide it, instead. With luck I would never need it ever again. But if I did...

And now I would simply head home.

Home.

Home to my beloved Sunny—slash—Juliet, so I could love her for the rest of my life—the rest of *our* lives, because in my fantasy we died together, at the same moment. While fucking. And whether or not she had been programmed to love me didn't matter. Sunny *did* love me, and always would.

In the darkness of my Hong Kong hideaway, I scratched Binkley's head, and smiled. My perfect life was finally about to begin.

CHAPTER 34

ABOUT AN HOUR AFTER the missile detonation, Agent Juliet Jones, post-SADISTO torture training, pre-decomissioning, woke up. She was under something heavy, and very confused. How did she get here? She had just been in Interrogation getting royally anger fucked from behind by that darkly handsome Saudi agent while she tortured some poor Singapodian to death.

Hadn't she?

Her body was stiff and her head hurt.

Really hurt.

She rubbed the spot between her eyes, felt a dent, there, and some dried blood.

She tried to sit up, but struggled under the weight of whatever was on top of her.

Or *whomever*.

She pushed against the whatever—or whomever—and felt that it was fleshy, and kind of dry. Crispy, even.

Suddenly the fleshy-crispy whatever gave, greasily, and shoved off its bone.

Weird.

She brought the chunk of flesh close to her nose, and smelled.

Chicken?

She gave a huge shove, and the meat really came away in clumps. As she struggled out from under it, she realized she had grease, flesh, and skin all over her own flesh and skin.

Hmm. She was naked. And a mess.

Not that she minded, but how? Was this another SADISTO training course? Had she blacked out? Been knocked unconscious? Where was Trevor?

She stood and tried to wipe the grease off her body, but only succeeded in smearing it around. Which felt kind of good. Just for fun she squished her breasts up smoothly, as far as she could, until they slipped through her grip, and flopped back down again.

"Boi-oi-oi-oiiing. HA!"

As she looked around, she continued fondling herself absently, enjoying the slippery, greasy feel of her hands on her body. It felt especially good on those tits, which she kneaded and squished with slippery delight, taking time to focus attention on her hardening nipples.

"Mmmmm," she said to herself. "Where *IS* Trevor. He should be doing this *for* me."

She reached down and grabbed a hunk of chicken, biting off a mouthful.

"Damn," she said, chewing. "So hungry. Wonder when I last ate?"

She looked down at what looked like a body that had been lying on top of her, hidden beneath the shadows of the evening.

"Hope that wasn't anyone I knew."

She bit off another piece of 'chicken.'

"Whoever you were, you needed salt."

She began walking in no particular direction.

"Treeeeevooooor?" She called to the night air. *"Ooh, Treeeeevooooor? You better not be off somewhere fucking someone else!"*

8   8   8

Near as Juliet could tell, she was on an island.

She'd walked past burned bodies everywhere inside what appeared to be a volcano, or a crater. Burned wrecked cars, burned boats, burned helicopters, and burned destroyed buildings seemed to indicate a bomb of some kind had gone off.

Wow.

She'd found a road that led into a tunnel clogged with burned and wrecked limousines and burned dead bodies, and crawled over everything, groping her way through the darkness, out of the volcano, toward the island proper. On the other side of the tunnel, she stopped for a moment to gather herself, and fondle her greasy erogenous zones. The road here was clearer, and a direction more obvious.

With nothing specific in mind, except perhaps to masturbate, Juliet continued down that road munching on roasted chicken flesh, deeper into the jungle. Between bites, she sang.

> *"You really shouldn't have done it*
> > *(Boom, Boom)*
> *"You hadn't any right*
> > *(Boom, Boom)*
> *"I really shouldn't have let you*
> *"Fuuuuck meeeee."*
> > *(BOOM BOOM)*

8   8   8

After a few hours of walking, Juliet came to a small lagoon, and a landing pad with a motionless helicopter resting quietly on its surface. Between her and it a limo had stopped in the middle of the road. A man in a suit was standing beside it holding something that looked like a World War Two walkie talkie to his ear.

"Can..." he said, "can anybody hear me? Please?"

After a few minutes of futile listening, he cursed, and jerked the thing away from his ear, shrieking.

Juliet strolled toward him, covered in grease and flecks of chicken meat, still absently fondling her pussy.

"I won't say no.

(BOOM)
No-*no-no-no.*
  (BOOM)
So do it...
  (BOOM)
Do it ...
  (BOOM)
DO IT AGAIN!
  (BOOM)
My pussy aches!
  (Boom)
To have you take!
  (Boom)
this body (BOOM)
That's waiting (BOOM) for yooouuuu
  (BA-BOOM-BOOM, BOOM, BOOM)

"Oh," he said, hearing, and finally seeing her, grimacing at the mess of a woman, her dirty hair sticking out in all directions, her entire body covered in muck, meat, and mucilage. "Gross. You... uh... you must be a local." He spoke louder, and with bigger gestures. "Can... you... *help*... me?" He pointed to himself as if he were the most important thing in the area... maybe on the whole island.

"Help you, *what?*" Juliet asked equally loudly, chewing, and really squishing one over-large breast especially hard.

"I need to get off this island," he said, still louder than he needed to, absorbed in watching her grope herself. "My driver and helicopter pilot were eaten by dinosaurs, and they left me in kind of a bind."

"Dinosaurs?" Juliet asked absently, as if they were quite common in her life—in anyone's life—still more interested in her own breast than potential death by 'Terrible Lizard.'

"I know," the man said, "sounds too bizarre to be believed, but they were actual dinosaurs. Snatched up my men, and ran off into the jungle with them."

"Cool."

"No," the man said, taken aback. "Not cool. They've left me all alone—stuck here—and I don't want to be around if they come back."

"Especially if they're hungry," Juliet said. "The dinosaurs, I mean. Not your men. I doubt your men are hungry. Or alive."

"I suppose this is the stupidest question, ever," the man said, looking Juliet's naked, greasy, dirty body up and down, "but you wouldn't happen to know someone who can… um… fly a helicopter, would you?"

"Yes," she said, absently.

"Really? Can you take me to them?"

"I am them. I'm fully rated on a Bell Helicopter 47 G-2, which is what that is."

He again looked her up and down. Her hands had moved to absently scratch around in the tangle of hair between navel and lower lips.

"You're kidding," he said.

"Yes, I'm kidding," Juliet said, her face scrunched up as if she were smelling something other than roast chicken. Something unpleasant. Like him. "Because I have nothing better to do than joke around with some dumbass who has his own helicopter, but doesn't know how to fly it."

"Well," the man said, unsure, "if you can fly me out of here, I can make it worth your while."

"Would you help me find my boyfriend?" Juliet asked, hopefully.

"Of course," the man said. "Happy to! I'm a rich man, and have vast resources. Finding your boyfriend will be no problem. Once we're out of here."

"Cool. But I don't need money. I'm rich, too. Why are you rich? What do you do?"

"I'm a music producer. I heard you singing. Do you like music?"

"I do," Juliet said, happily. "I love to sing. Dirty stuff to myself in the shower, mostly, but… you know."

"I do know. Well, we'll get you a shower as soon as we're off this island, and you can sing all you want."

"I have a boyfriend," Juliet repeated, a heavy dose of threat sprinkled into her voice.

He held his hands up as if he were being robbed. "Not even interested in touching you. Promise."

Juliet looked him up and down. She kind of liked what she saw. She smiled.

"He lets me fuck other people, though," she said, her tone more inviting. "And sometimes he watches."

"Interesting," the man said, not really interested. "Why don't you tell me all about this boyfriend of yours and your open attitude toward sex while we fly out of here."

"Okay," Juliet said. "But keep in mind… he's a spy, and he could kill you if you mistreat me. So could I, for that matter. We're both basically trained killers for a super-secret organization called SADISTO. That's where we met. Don't tell anybody."

"Not a word," the producer said. "Fly, please."

CHAPTER 35

SUNNY STOOD IN A lovely garden she'd had constructed at the center of our private little Manchester. She was nude except for the tactical belt, with the seashells adorning it, singing to herself, trimming flowers, as perfectly lovely as I remembered.

"Binkley!" I called, as he ran away from me, and directly for her.

She turned, her bare breasts swaying deliciously, turquoise eyes twinkling with excitement, her smile lighting up my soul.

Yes. She would always love me. And I would never give her reason not to.

She laughed when Binkley leapt up on her, demanding love and attention.

"Well, hello there," she said, happily scratching his neck and ruff. "So, you're Binkley? I've heard a lot about you."

"He acts like he already knows you," I said, "and loves you, as much as I do."

She turned to me, her eyes welling with tears, and joy.

"You've been gone for over a month," she said, her voice trembling. "I was so worried."

I stepped up to her, took out my handkerchief and daubed gently under her eyes. I swear, I heard the gentle sounds of 'Somewhere Over the Rainbow' in the distance.

"I heard the plane arriving," she said, putting her hands on my chest, her weepy eyes locked to mine. "I wanted it to be you. I wanted it to be you, so badly."

"Don't cry, shell girl," I said, drying her tears. "Don't cry. You know nothing could ever keep me from always returning to you, my darling, *darling* Sunny."

We leaned together, and kissed. Warmly. Passionately. Enduringly. And spent the night together... sleeplessly.

CHAPTER 36

SOMEWHERE IN A MONITOR room, a woman in a white robe sat in a wheelchair petting a silky, white cat, watching me kiss my beloved Sunny from multiple angles, on multiple screens. The woman was alone, so she spoke to no one. Maybe the cat.

"You win this round, Agent 8," she said, with a slight laugh. "As Doctor Sin has failed me. But Juliet won't be there to help you next time."

The mystery woman laughed, and continued to laugh as she activated the motor on her chair, backing away from the glow of screens, to move out of the room. Or try to.

She bumped into a closed door, tried to reach around for the handle, the cat hissed, and yowled, and leaped from her lap, clawing her thighs in the process.

"Ow! Dammit!"

Finally, she gave up.

"Wong!" She called. "Wong! I've wedged the chair against the door, again! Can you get this damn thing out, please? I mean, really! My own lair really should be wheelchair accessible..."

No response.

"Wong? This isn't funny. I need your help!"

She waited.

"DAMMIT WONG!"

EPILOGUE

"YOU MADE ALL THAT UP," my oldest said.

"If you say so," I said with a shrug.

"There were too many references to contemporary times and stuff that isn't real. Aliens, and all that."

"Says you," said my wife.

"I'm telling a story about the past, and using contemporary references so you'll understand," I said. "Monty Python instead of Uncle Milty. Doesn't mean I'm making anything up."

"Who's Monty Python?" Jelena said.

I sighed.

"So which one was Gran?" Pyotr asked.

"You'll have to wait and find out."

"Whattya mean, wait?"

"The story's not finished," I said.

"I think it was Sunny," Sasha said.

"Maybe," my wife said with a sarcastic half-grin. "Now you have to tell them about the girl from Mephisto,"

"Is there more sex in it?" Pyotr asked, hopefully.

"Probably," my wife said. "We had a *lot* of sex, even back then. We just didn't own up to it in public."

"Then I'm in," Pyotr said, rubbing his hands together. "Get started."

ABOUT THE AUTHOR

Chuck Austen is a real person living somewhere in the United States. He is writing more books, for good, and evil. He is already finishing the next four books in this insane series. You can see pictures of the covers on the next page, and they're more interesting than anything on this page, that's for sure, so go check them out.

Clyde Allison was one of the pseudonyms used by William Henley Knoles when he wrote the original SADISTO books, among many others. He was a genius who deserved greater recognition. Chuck hopes he would have enjoyed what was done with his original characters, and stories.

Look for other SADISTO books
SOON
wherever you found this one!

OUR GIRL FROM MEPHISTO

NAUTILUST

GNATMAN and BITING MIDGE

THE LOVE BOMB

SADISTO ROYALE

FOR THE LOVE OF RAPTURE

MERCILESS MERMAIDS

PLATYPUSSY

THE TIME FUNNEL

And many more!

HAWKE FACES "THE HORNY HORROR OF TEENAGE GROUPIES IN THE ARMS OF
A WIMZI LIBRARY BOOK 103 $14.99
OUR GIRL FROM
MEPHISTO
#2 IN THE AGENT 8 SEXY COMEDY ADVENTURE SERIES!
CLYDE ALLISON JR.
Agent 8 Battles The Temptress of The Deep Captain Nympho!
Nautilust
#3 in The Agent 8 Sexy Adventure Series!
Clyde Allison, Jr.
GNATMAN
AN EMBER LIBRARY BOOK EL 309 75¢
#4 IN THE AGENT 8 SEXY ADVENTURE SERIES!
CLYDE ALLISON JR.
AGENT 8 TEAMS UP WITH HIS CHILDHOOD HEROES!
Agent 8 battles the lusty peril of the Busty Bombers in
Clyde Allison jr.
#5 in The Agent 8 Sexy Adventure Comedy Series
THE LOVE BOMB
EMBER LIBRARY BOOK EL 302 75¢